Praise for T

"The magic is believa
the twists, turns and
You will never forget these characters or their world.
—*Jacqueline Lichtenberg, Hugo-nominated author of the* Sime~Gen *series and* Star Trek Lives!

"Alastair Stone is like Harry Potter meets Harry Dresden with a bit of Indiana Jones!"
—*Randler, Amazon reviewer*

"Somewhat reminiscent of the Dresden Files but with its own distinct style."
—*John W. Ranken, Amazon reviewer*

"I am reminded of Jim Butcher here...Darker than most Urban Fantasy, not quite horror, but with a touch of Lovecraftian."
—*Wulfstan, Amazon Top 500 reviewer*

"If you like Harry Dresden and The Dresden files, or Nate Garrett in the Hellequin series than this series is for you."
—*Amazon reviewer*

"Once you enter the world of Alastair Stone, you won't want to leave."
—*Awesome Indies*

"I've been hooked since book 1."
—*Penny B. McKay, Amazon reviewer*

"It's getting hard to come up with something better than great to describe how good this book was."
—*Ted Camer, Amazon reviewer*

"You cannot go wrong with this series!"
—*Jim, Amazon reviewer*

ALSO BY R. L. KING

The Alastair Stone Chronicles
Stone and a Hard Place
The Forgotten
The Threshold
The Source
Core of Stone
Blood and Stone
Heart of Stone
Flesh and Stone
The Infernal Heart
The Other Side
Path of Stone
Necessary Sacrifices
Game of Stone
Steel and Stone
Stone and Claw
The Seventh Stone
Gathering Storm
Shadows and Stone (novella)
Turn to Stone (novella)
Devil's Bargain (standalone novel)
Stone for the Holidays (short stories)

Shadowrun
Shadowrun: Borrowed Time
Shadowrun: Wolf and Buffalo (novella)
Shadowrun: Big Dreams (novella)
Shadowrun: Veiled Extraction (coming in 2020)
(published by Catalyst Game Labs)

HOUSE OF
STONE

ALASTAIR STONE CHRONICLES: BOOK EIGHTEEN

R.L. KING

MAGESPACE
PRESS

Copyright ©2019, R. L. King

House of Stone: Alastair Stone Chronicles Book Eighteen
First Edition, June 2019
Magespace Press
Edited by John Helfers
Cover Art by Streetlight Graphics

ISBN: 978-0-9994292-9-7

| PROLOGUE

DARKNESS.

Stillness.

The air smelled of age and neglect.

His eyes snapped open, but it didn't matter: the dark was so complete it was almost a tangible thing, pressing against his skull. His eyes burned with it, dry and unaccustomed to being open; he almost felt them scratching against their gritty sockets like old sandpaper as he shifted his gaze back and forth to no effect.

His breath caught in his ruined throat, hitching gasps trying to pull any air into his lungs from within the cramped, sealed prison.

His hands tried to scrabble at his sides, to find any purchase, any way out, but he was weak. So weak. He felt the accumulation of dust under him, but couldn't even raise his arms. The prison's walls touched his shoulders.

His body didn't seem to want to work properly. His diaphragm fluttered, his lungs refusing to inflate as he continued to gasp for the air that wasn't there.

Or was it? How could he be awake if there was no air? Where was he? What was he doing here? Who had put him here?

The thoughts, the memories, didn't come. Not right away. His brain was long out of practice for any kind of thought. His mental impulses zipped around, unformed and chaotic, flashing images across his mind's eye too fast to comprehend. When he tried to grab one, to pin it down long enough to study it, his effort got him nothing more than splintered fragments.

His fists clenched involuntarily, long nails digging into fleshless palms, gathering the dust and then releasing it again. Inside his chest, his long-dormant heart fluttered once again to life, beating a faint, weak, and disorganized rhythm.

When the thoughts finally did begin to come, when his erratic memories began to knit together to give him a clearer picture of what was happening here, his first response was rage. What had they done to him? *How* had they done it? That part wouldn't come yet, but it didn't need to. He didn't need the details. The exact methods they had used to accomplish their aims didn't matter, but only that they *had* accomplished them.

He didn't even try to pierce the darkness pressing in on him. Not yet. He could do it, he knew, but it would take time. Probably quite a lot of time. The processes, now that something had started them again (*what* had started them? He had no idea, but at this moment he had no intention of questioning it) were not fast. Especially not given what he suspected they would have to accomplish. He had no idea how long he had been here, but he did know it had to have been a very long time.

That was fine, though. He was patient. He could wait here in the dark for his strength to return. For his power to return. He could already feel it trickling in. Then, he could remove himself from this place and set about determining where—and *when*—he was.

He closed his dry eyes and relaxed his thin, weak arms. He was vulnerable here, but he was also safe, shrouded in his hidden cocoon. As long as no one found him before he was fully restored, he had no need for concern.

A small, cold smile crept across his sunken features. No, *he* would have no need for concern.

Certain others, however, would not be so fortunate.

| CHAPTER ONE

ALASTAIR STONE wasn't psychic in the way most of the world defined the word, but when his phone buzzed one lazy Thursday afternoon in mid-June, something told him he wouldn't like what he heard when he answered it.

He put aside the book he'd been reading in his Encantada study and picked it up, noting the familiar number. Maybe his premonition wouldn't end up being true after all. "Yes, hello, Verity."

"Hey, Doc. You busy?"

"Not really. What's up?" He glanced around the office, at the untidy stacks of books and papers around him. In truth, "busy" was a relative term. He'd arranged it so he wasn't teaching any regular classes for the summer quarter, only a couple of one-shot evening seminars in July, intending to use the time to catch up on some research for a couple papers he was trying to finish. Raider perched on top of one of the book stacks, primly licking his front paw and watching Stone with sudden interest.

Her long pause renewed his apprehension. "Well…" she said slowly, "Unfortunately, I have some bad news."

Ah. So he *was* right. "What sort of bad news?" He leaned back in his chair, and Raider immediately hopped down from the book stack and settled in his lap.

"Well…" she repeated, definitely sounding uncomfortable now. "I…won't be able to go to Imogen's wedding with you."

He tensed. "Why not?"

Imogen Desmond, daughter of his late master William Desmond, had called him to announce her upcoming wedding to Clifford Blakeley a few weeks ago, and the invitation had arrived a couple weeks after that. Verity hadn't been invited specifically—it was to be a small, intimate affair with only close friends and family—but Stone's invitation had included a plus-one along with a handwritten note from Imogen suggesting he ask her to accompany him. Not exactly protocol, but then again, Imogen had never been much for protocol when it didn't suit her.

"I'm sorry…" She sounded miserable. "Believe me, if there was any way around it, I'd be all over it. But Jason's got a case and he needs my help with it. It's a kidnapped child, only four years old, and Jason's certain he's in terrible danger. So far the cops are pretty sure he's in Texas, but they're afraid the kidnappers will try to smuggle him into Mexico. We need to go there so I can do a ritual to find him before that happens. We're leaving tomorrow morning."

Stone's sigh mirrored Verity's. The wedding was on Saturday evening, and they'd been planning to take the portal to the Surrey house tomorrow afternoon. It was highly unlikely she and Jason could fly to Texas, finish their business, and get back in time for her to make it, even if everything went perfectly and they found the boy right away. "I understand," he said. "Of course you've got to help if you can. Be careful, both of you."

"I'm sorry, Doc. If there was any other way around it—"

"No, no, it's fine."

"You sure?"

"Absolutely." What could he say? *No, you could find the child, but you should risk letting him die because I need you here to help me cope with my first love finally getting married?* No. Besides, it wasn't true. He'd come to terms with Imogen's upcoming wedding a long time ago, and spending a few hours in a formal suit helping her celebrate her happy day was the least he could do. Even if he had to do it alone.

"Absolutely," he said again. "I'll call you when I return, and you can tell me all about it. I'm sure you'll find the lad right away."

"Yeah." She still didn't sound convinced. "I'm sure we will. I don't think there's any magic involved, so it should be an open-and-shut thing. Thanks, Doc. Please give Imogen and Clifford my best."

"I will."

He hung up and tossed the phone back on the desk, looking down at Raider in his lap. "Well, mate," he said, scratching the tabby's head, "I suppose I should get on with it, shouldn't I? No reason to hang about here."

Raider purred, but said nothing.

Stone didn't need to pack much, since he kept a full wardrobe at the Surrey house. Aubrey had phoned a few days ago to let him know his suite had been opened and aired, but apologized that he might have to deal with some slight inconveniences such as noise and dust.

"I'm having the workers in as you instructed, to begin evaluating the east wing for renovation," he'd said. "It's bloody difficult to get on their schedule, so I had to take what I could get. They're starting in the cellar, in the area where the floor was buckling."

Ah, yes. The east wing. It had become a bit of a shared joke between them over the years. That part of the house had been closed off practically as long as Stone could remember; it suffered from a collection of minor problems, none of which ever grew serious enough to require immediate attention beyond occasional basic repairs, but when taken together they made that entire section undesirable for use as living space. Aubrey checked through its rooms every couple of weeks to make sure the windows were still in place, the doors hadn't stuck shut due to shifting, and the roof hadn't sprung any leaks, but all in all they'd both been content to leave it alone since the cost of renovation would have been far more than the modest trust fund covering repairs and Aubrey's salary could have handled.

That had all changed when William Desmond had died and left Stone a fortune in addition to the entirety of his collection of magical books and artifacts. One of the first things he'd done when he'd received the funds, aside from giving Aubrey both a substantial lump sum and a significant pay raise, was to earmark a large portion for repairs on the rambling old mansion, starting with the east wing. He'd given Aubrey access to the account and set him loose, asking him to handle arranging the various contractors and scheduling the work. The caretaker was far better at that sort of thing than he was, so Stone had instructed him to do what was necessary to get the place back up to presentable shape. He only wanted to be consulted for aesthetic matters when necessary, unless anything threatened to get too close to the magically hidden parts of the house.

He knew exactly the area Aubrey was talking about, where "the floor was buckling." It was a section of the cellar even less frequently checked than the upper portions of the wing, largely because it was bloody creepy down there. Aubrey went down only once every couple of months, reporting back that it was still as full of spiderwebs, grime, and dark shadows as it always was. It was only during his last check that he'd discovered something had shifted enough to cause a large crack in the stone floor, indicating that there might be a problem with the wall holding the whole thing up. He'd described the problem to Stone and the renovation efforts had immediately switched from the upper floors to the cellar, since sticking doors and broken windows didn't matter if the whole wall was about to cave in.

Stone had assured him the noise and dust wouldn't be a problem, since he probably wouldn't be staying long enough for it to make a difference. He might pop up to Caventhorne after the wedding, but he didn't plan to spend much time at the house.

As he finished tossing the few items he'd need into his overnight bag before heading down to Sunnyvale to take the portal, his thoughts turned, as they often did lately, to Ian.

It had been nearly two weeks since he and his son had last spoken, beyond a few hasty texts with vague reports of his current whereabouts, and a month since they'd met face to face when Ian had popped back to the Bay Area for a couple days through the portal before heading off to join some mage friends on a backpacking trip in Romania. Since then, his messages had come from various parts of Europe, Africa, and the Far East, where from the sound of things he'd spent most of his time soaking up the nightlife. They'd made tentative plans to meet in England at some point, but so far those plans hadn't solidified beyond "sometime soon."

On a whim, Stone pulled out his phone and punched Ian's number. His last location had been somewhere in Greece, which meant it would be the middle of the night where he was. Ian was even more of a night owl than Stone, though, so it shouldn't be a problem.

It rang several times. Stone was sure the familiar, flippant voicemail message would come on any second, but then a blast of high-energy music issued from the speaker followed by a muffled, "Hello?"

"Ian. It's your father. I hope I haven't interrupted anything." He didn't really hope that—at this moment, he didn't care too much about what he might have interrupted.

"Uh—oh, hi, Dad. Hold on." More muffled sounds. Stone thought he heard another male voice, and then the music dropped to barely audible. "Something wrong? You don't usually call this late."

"I thought I might find you awake if I called now." Stone forced his shoulders to relax; he hadn't realized how much tension he'd been carrying in them. "Are you still in Greece?"

"Uh—yeah. Athens. I'm at a club right now." He sounded sober, at least, which was something.

"Well, I won't keep you long. But I want to ask you something."

"Go for it." In the background, the male voice spoke again, but Stone couldn't make out any words. Ian's own muffled voice sounded, then cleared. "Sorry about that. What do you need?"

"I'll be heading to England tomorrow, to attend a wedding on Saturday night. And I'd like you to meet me there."

There was a pause. "Meet you...there? In England? You want me to come to this wedding?"

"No. I want you to come to England. We've been discussing it for some time now, but both of us keep putting it off for various reasons. I want you to come tomorrow, so I can show you around the house and the portals, and introduce you to Aubrey. He's been wanting very much to meet you."

Another pause.

Stone tightened his grip on the phone. "Ian—this is fairly important to me. I won't keep you long—you can head back to Athens or wherever else you're going after the weekend. But unless you've got something important planned for the next couple of days that you can't postpone, I'd appreciate it if you'd make the time for it."

He realized he had a bit of an edge in his voice, and quickly squelched it. Ian wasn't doing anything wrong—he was doing exactly what Stone had empowered him to do, by introducing him to the worldwide public portal network and setting up a healthy bank account for him to use while he traveled. Blaming him for wanting to see the world and have a little fun after his oppressive, abusive childhood and uncertain teen years as a runaway street hustler should be—and in fact was—the farthest thing from his mind.

But that didn't mean he couldn't impose a little parental suggestion now and then.

"What do you say? Will you come?"

The answer came faster this time. "Yeah. Of course I'll come, Dad."

More stress evaporated. "Excellent. Thank you, Ian. Just come through the London portal. I'm leaving now—suppose we meet tomorrow morning. I'll have to show you my private portal at the Surrey place—it's a bit tricky, so I want to do that before you use it. I can show you the house tomorrow before I head off to the wedding, and perhaps you and Aubrey can catch up a bit during the evening."

"Sounds good."

"Brilliant. I'll let you get back to your friends. I'll see you at the portal at, say, ten tomorrow?"

"See you there."

| CHAPTER TWO

A SMALL PART OF STONE WONDERED if Ian might be late, or even not show up at all. But no, his son popped out of the public portal in London, which was located in a back room of Tolliver's Magic Shop, a little before ten.

Stone looked him over. Not much had changed in the few months since they'd first met: he still wore the same kind of casually stylish clothes, his windblown dark hair was still tipped with white-blond and artfully spiked, and his slim physique still showed he managed to find time to hit the gym regularly. He hadn't added any new piercings beyond the ones in his ears and his left eyebrow, but he now sported several intricate tattoos on his forearms courtesy of Scuro. Stone hadn't asked how he got power—it wasn't any of his business—but Ian had assured him he had it under control and hadn't injured anyone.

Ian smiled when he spotted Stone. "Hey, Dad. How are you? It's good to see you."

Stone shifted to magical sight, taking in his son's blazing, silver-and-purple aura, and noticed another glow of magic near his chest. When he switched back, he identified the source immediately: a pendant on a silver chain around the boy's neck. "I'm doing well." He pointed. "Is that a new one?"

Ian glanced down. "Oh—yeah. My friend Mihas gave it to me, in Romania. He taught me a few things. Some of them were even related to magic," he added with a sly grin. "Says it means 'good fortune.'"

Stone recognized the rune, an ancient magical symbol. Whoever Ian was learning 'a few things' from no doubt knew his stuff. "It does indeed. You'll have to tell me about him some time. I'd like very much to hear about your travels in more detail."

"Sure, yeah, I'd like that too."

Stone noticed he didn't say anything about *when* he might like to do it, but he didn't push it. This wasn't the time for that. "Let's go—we don't have a lot of time today. The wedding starts at six tonight, so I've got to leave a couple of hours early if I'm to get to Canterbury on time, since there's no portal there. I'll show you the house today, and if you'll stay tomorrow as well, we can see the London place and Caventhorne. Give me a moment to calibrate this portal, and we'll go."

Ian paced the room, examining the walls covered with posters from old-time magic shows. "What's Caventhorne? Is that another one of your properties?"

Stone finished the calibrations before replying. "No. It belonged to my old master, William Desmond. Enormous old place, much larger than our ancestral home. When Desmond died, he left me in charge of arranging its conversion to a sort of magical library and resource center. Some friends of mine have been working on it for quite some time, and it's almost ready to open." He indicated the portal. "After you."

The journey from London to Surrey took nearly no time; only a few seconds passed in the foggy Overworld tunnel before they emerged into a small, stone room with a wooden table, a bookshelf, and a single door. "Is this in your house?" Ian asked.

"Not…exactly." He opened the door, led the way down a short hall, and pulled down a wooden staircase ladder. "Let me go first here—this is the tricky part I was telling you about."

Stone ascended the ladder, moved aside the fake top to the sarcophagus in the mausoleum, and leaped out. "Come on up," he called down to the curious Ian.

Ian scrambled up and looked around in wonder. "Wait…is this some kind of mausoleum?"

"Exactly." He used a light spell to illuminate the small space, shining it around so Ian could see the sealed alcoves set into the walls. "This is the Stone family crypt. Don't say it—I know it's a bit creepy to have a portal in a mausoleum, but it wasn't my idea. One of our ancestors must have had an odd sense of humor."

"It's kind of cool, actually." Ian moved around the sarcophagus as Stone returned the top to its spot, and examined the plaques below each sealed niche. "So these are my ancestors."

"Yes." Stone kept his tone even; this wasn't the time to give his son the whole sordid family history. He'd have to do it at some point, but they only had a few hours together today.

He stopped in front of one crypt. "Orion Stone. He only died around twenty years ago. Was he your father? My grandfather?"

"Yes." Stone walked toward the door, hoping Ian would do the same.

He remained next to the plaque. "He died young. What happened to him?"

"It was an…accident." Not the whole truth, but once again he didn't want to bring up the details until he had time to frame them properly. He'd already decided he would tell Ian the entire story, but like his son's travel accounts, it would happen at some unspecified later date when they had more time together. It wasn't a tale that should be rushed.

Ian pushed his hair off his forehead and rose from his crouch. "You must have been around my age when he died. That had to be rough."

"Bit of an understatement, yes." Stone opened the door and waved him out.

This time he followed, but he still looked contemplative. "Wait…before you said you were going through a rough patch when you met my mom. That was around the same time, wasn't it?"

Stone was surprised he'd remembered that, given everything he'd had to deal with during the early days of their acquaintance. "It was. Your mum helped me work through some of it during the short time we were together. I'll always be grateful to her for that."

Ian shot him an odd glance, almost as if trying to determine if he was telling the truth, then stepped outside the mausoleum and looked around the overgrown, windswept cemetery surrounding it. "So our family has its own graveyard. That's…different."

"We've got a long history." Stone pointed off to where the dark bulk of the mansion rose in the distance. "Come on—it's a bit of a walk to the house. You're welcome to come back here and look around whenever you like, but let's not keep Aubrey waiting."

As they trudged through the field, Ian took it all in. "So who's getting married tonight?"

"A dear old friend—William Desmond's daughter Imogen. I wish I could bring you along, but..." he paused. "I—er—haven't actually told her about you yet, and it might be a bit awkward if I turned up with you as my plus-one without any explanation. I'd originally planned to go with Verity, but she had something come up at the last minute."

Ian flashed his easy, sly smile. "Haven't told her about me yet? Keeping me a secret for some reason?"

"No, it's not that. I honestly haven't seen much of her since you turned up. But as I said, she's a dear friend—we almost married, many years ago—so it's not something I want to spring on her without proper...preparation."

"Got it. No problem—I don't really want to go to a fancy wedding with a lot of people I don't know anyway. Maybe I'll take the portal back up to London tonight and check out some clubs."

Stone didn't let his exasperation reach his face. He knew his son had been through a lot of unpleasantness in his life, and he didn't begrudge him some time to cut loose and explore a life of hedonism—for a while, at least. But at some point, he hoped the boy would settle down, take his magic studies seriously, and either find a job or choose a school instead of constantly globe-hopping in search of new sensual experiences. He'd certainly gotten up to his share of the same thing when he'd been Ian's age, but he'd also already finished his apprenticeship and his first year of university by that point. This was a talk he and Ian would have to have at some point as well. There seemed to be a lot of those turning up.

"I rather thought you might stay in tonight and spend some time with Aubrey," was all he said.

Ian's brow furrowed in a slight frown. "I know you want me to meet him, and I want to. But you want me to spend the evening with him, without you around? I'm not sure we'd have a lot in common, would we?"

They were approaching the house now. Surprisingly, Aubrey hadn't emerged from the house to greet them. Stone suspected the caretaker's sixth sense about his arrival was operating as well as it always did, which meant he was probably giving them space to show up when they were ready.

"You might be surprised. I'm not sure I explained Aubrey adequately. He's not just the caretaker of this place. He's my oldest and probably closest friend, and since my father traveled often when I was young, he served as perhaps more of a father figure to me than the real thing." He chuckled. "If you want to find out any embarrassing dirt about my childhood and early teenage years, he's the one to ask."

Ian's grin mirrored his. "Now that has possibilities."

As they approached the house, he slowed his long stride and tilted his head back to examine it. "Wow. This place is pretty impressive. Spooky as hell, but impressive. Even with the money you gave me, I'm still getting my head around what a big deal our family seems to be."

"There isn't much left of the family these days, actually. It's mostly me, you, and…a few others on my mother's side, up north." *Yes, let's not tell him about* that *barking mad side of the family yet…or perhaps ever.*

"So you aren't going to introduce me to a whole pack of aunts, uncles, and cousins?"

"Does that disappoint you?"

"Not sure," he admitted. "I suppose it would be weird to suddenly discover I'm part of a huge family, even if they weren't all mages." He indicated the house and started moving toward it again. "So it's just you knocking around this big old place? Are there a bunch of servants? I mean, this place does sort of look like *Downton Abbey* meets Castle Dracula."

Stone laughed. "I've never heard it described in quite that way before. But no, no bunch of servants. Aubrey looks after the place, but since I'm here so rarely and I don't do any formal entertaining, it doesn't need that much looking after beyond basic maintenance." He pointed toward the east wing as they mounted the stairs to the front door. "We're having some work done—renovations and whatnot—so you might see a few workmen around. I don't think they're here on the weekend, though." He opened the door and waved Ian inside, then led him into the massive great room. "Aubrey? Are you here?"

The old man appeared in the doorway on the other side. "Hello, sir. I didn't know when you'd get in." He stopped when he saw Ian standing behind Stone.

"Yes. Well..." he strode forward, motioning for Ian to follow. "Aubrey, this is Ian Woodward Stone. Ian, Aubrey Townes, who's the reason this place hasn't fallen down around my ears many years ago."

They approached each other slowly, like a pair of wary animals taking each other's measure. "Hello, Aubrey," Ian said, offering his hand. "Dad's told me a lot about you. Glad to finally meet you."

For a moment, Aubrey was speechless. Stone didn't blame him: he'd told the caretaker about Ian's existence quite some time ago, but being *told* your employer had a long-lost, nineteen-year-old son wasn't anything like the same thing as being presented with him in the flesh. Finally he swallowed, smiled, wiped his hand on the cloth again, and accepted Ian's handshake. "It's…such a pleasure, sir. I've likewise heard quite a lot about you, and I've been looking forward to finally meeting you."

"You don't need to call me 'sir,' you know."

"Good luck getting him to stop *that*," Stone muttered. "I've been trying for more than twenty years now."

"Are you hungry?" Aubrey asked both of them. "I've got some light refreshments ready, or I can put together an early lunch if you like."

Stone glanced at Ian. "No, I think we're good, Aubrey. We haven't got a lot of time today, since I'll need time to get ready and leave for the wedding this afternoon. I thought I'd show Ian around the place and the grounds a bit, and then we can sit down for lunch in a couple of hours and have a long chat, the three of us."

"Excellent, sir. I'll have something ready by noon, if that's acceptable. And I've prepared the suite near yours for Ian."

"Oh, I don't need a suite," Ian said. "I'll probably only be staying until tomorrow, right, Dad?"

"That's up to you. I've not got much going on at the University this summer, so if you'd like to stay longer that's fine. But come on—let's get you settled, and I'll give you the whirlwind tour."

The "whirlwind tour" took most of the two hours before lunch was ready. Stone showed Ian the inside of the house, beginning with the main living area and ending with the rooms in the west wing. "We won't go into the east wing," he said as they returned to the great room. "That's where they're doing the renovations, so it's probably not much to look at. What do you think so far?"

Ian had followed him around, examining the elegant, old-fashioned furnishings, artwork, and architecture in silence. "It's...a lot to take in," he said. "Definitely not the sort of thing I'm used to. It's beautiful. A little grim, though."

"It is that," Stone agreed. "It needs a lot of work, so I'm glad we're finally able to get started on that. But I suppose it suits me—I grew up here, so I'm used to it, warts and all. Wait until you see Caventhorne—it makes this place look quite shabby by comparison. That will probably have to be another time, though, unless you can stay longer. Anyway, come on—I want to show you the good stuff."

"Good stuff?"

"Everything I've shown you so far has been fairly mundane, hasn't it?"

"Ah, right. The magic. Should have guessed."

Stone led him downstairs. As they passed through the illusionary tapestry leading to the hidden staircase, he said casually, "Have you given any thought to what we've discussed, about your future plans?"

"You mean studying magic?"

"Well, that too, if you want to. But have you thought about whether you want to pursue going to university?"

Ian shrugged. "Not really—not yet. I've got plenty of time for that. And I *have* been learning magic. Some of my friends have been teaching me some techniques."

Stone picked up his stride so Ian couldn't see his face. "Ian—"

"What is it?"

He sighed. "Look—I know we haven't known each other very long, and I've no intention of going all parental with you. I doubt it would do any good even if I did, at this point. But if you'll listen to a bit of advice from someone with more experience…"

"Sure. Of course."

"It's not a good idea to pick up magic piecemeal, especially not from people who haven't been studying much longer than you have." He turned back around, keeping his aura carefully under control. "You've got such immense potential power, Ian. If it's trained properly, you could be a stronger mage than I am—and without bragging, that's saying something. It makes me angry every time I think about Trin buggering you up when you first discovered your power."

"Buggering me up? You mean making me into a black mage?" Ian's gaze was challenging. "You do all right, don't you?"

Stone let his breath out, considering his words. He couldn't afford to lose his cool with the boy—that would be the fastest way to drive him away. "No," he said. "Not making you into a black mage. That isn't what I meant. But she left out so much of your core training—the stuff most beginning mages get at the start of their apprenticeship—to focus only on the bits she wanted you to have to serve her ends. It means if you begin a proper apprenticeship, you'll have to unlearn some bad habits. It shouldn't delay your progress for long because you've got so much to work with, but…" He spread his hands. "If you're going to do it, you've got to think about getting started."

"I *will* get started. But…"

"But?"

Ian shrugged. "Things are changing, Dad. How much contact do you have with mages my age these days?"

"What's that supposed to mean?"

"Aside from Verity, I mean. I've met quite a few of them while I've been traveling around. Nowadays, a lot of them don't do formal apprenticeships. They learn as they go, figuring out what they want to know and finding teachers—or else getting together and teaching each other. Hell, in parts of Africa and Asia they don't even use the one-teacher, one-student model these days. It's more of a community thing, with a group of mages learning from a group of teachers, according to what they consider most important."

He passed through a hidden doorway behind Stone and descended the stairs downward. "I'm still learning a lot, since I didn't grow up with the idea that I'd train in magic when I turned eighteen. But I'm finding out that your way of doing it is very Western-European- and American-centric. It's a great way to learn, but it's not the *only* way. And…" he began.

"And what?" Stone turned back around, stopping in front of the door that led to his magical library and workroom.

"Well, don't take this wrong, because I promise I don't mean it that way—but in a way, what you're trying to get me to do is as restrictive as what Trin taught me."

Stone sighed. He had no idea what he expected when he'd met Ian—he supposed in the back of his mind, he assumed the boy would be a lot like Verity: highly intelligent, eager to learn, and full of questions, but still accepting the paradigm of modern Western magical teaching. Apparently, that wasn't to be the case.

This was exactly why parents didn't teach their own children. He hadn't internalized it before, but over the past few months he'd truly come around to the wisdom of it. After all, was this really any different than when Verity had decided she wanted to train with Edna Soren, to learn a more nature-based form of magic to complement his own more classical, formula-based approach? He'd not only approved of that, but helped Verity arrange alternative study methods.

"Look," he said at last. "This probably isn't something we should discuss now. I'm sure you have valid points—it's entirely possible that I'm out of touch with certain areas of modern magical teaching. I've got an open mind. All I want to do is make sure you have the chance to take your potential as far as you want to take it, and I hope you'll listen to me when I tell you that blundering about in the dark picking up random bits and bobs from a load of students who know as little as you do isn't the best way to do that."

Ian's eyes narrowed, but finally he nodded. "Yeah. I get that. And I agree it's probably something we should talk about later. Right now I want to see the rest of your place, and see if I can get Aubrey to tell me any funny stories about your childhood over lunch."

Stone chuckled. "Given half a chance, he'll talk your ear off." He pushed open the door and added softly, "This isn't just *my* place, Ian. It's yours, too. Or it will be someday, at any rate. But until then it's still your home, if you want it to be. You're welcome to stay here whenever you like. Hell, you can live here if you want. Aside from requesting you keep any wild parties elsewhere and treat Aubrey with respect, I want you to do as you like."

Ian shot him an odd look as they entered the magical library "Thanks, Dad. I appreciate it." He looked around, craning his neck up to get a glimpse of the top shelves of books high above. "Hard to get my mind around having all these magical ancestors all of a sudden. Do you know anything about them?"

Stone tensed. "I…know something about them, yes."

"Can you tell me? What were they like?"

"They were…" *You weren't going to hide anything from him, remember?* It was harder now that the hypothetical situation was standing directly in front of him. "I'll be honest with you, Ian—aside from my father, they weren't very nice people. That's something I'd appreciate you not spreading around. Sort of a…family secret."

His son looked intrigued, turning away from where he'd been studying a section of the shelves. "We have dark family secrets, too?"

"Quite a lot of them, as it happens. And I promise, I'll share them all with you—but not just now. It will take more than a few hours, and honestly I don't want to go into it right now. Won't put me in the right frame of mind for the wedding tonight."

"That's fine." He narrowed his eyes. "It sounds like they're pretty bad, though."

"They are. Our ancestors were the blackest sort of black mages—not like you and me, but the kind who did terrible things with their magic. I'm still coming to terms with it myself. There's probably a lot more to uncover, but I haven't been in any hurry to hunt it down."

Ian had levitated to the second level of the shelves and was scanning some books there. He floated back down, and when he faced Stone his expression was sober. "Sorry—I didn't mean to sound like I wasn't taking it seriously."

"It's quite all right—as I said, it's just not something I want getting around. Oh—and that reminds me," he said quickly. *Bloody hell, how had I forgotten to mention that?* "I'm—er—not exactly proud of this, but Aubrey doesn't know we're black mages. And I'd prefer it stay that way."

Ian frowned. "I thought you said he was your closest friend."

"He is. It's—complicated, trust me."

"You think he'll disapprove?"

Stone wasn't surprised he'd gone there, given his previous concerns about revealing other aspects of his life. "No. I don't think he'll disapprove. I just think it's best that we keep our magical status to ourselves."

"Okay, if that's what you want." He still looked troubled. "Does he know I'm gay?"

"He does, yes. I hope you don't mind that I told him."

"And...?"

"And what?"

"And how did he react?"

Stone shrugged. "He didn't 'react' at all." He chuckled. "He's older, Ian, but he's quite open-minded. He'd have to be, wouldn't he, with all the insanity he's had to cope with over the years?" He gripped his son's shoulder. "Your being gay is one of the more normal things I've dropped on him recently. Don't give it another thought. Anyway, we should go—he'll be waiting for us, and I want to show you the workshop and the ritual area before we finish up down here."

Ian took a last look around the library as they left. "This is all pretty impressive. Will I have access to this area?"

"You will, but not yet. I'm still treating you as an apprentice, even if your training has been…unconventional. And there are things in here you shouldn't be messing about with until you're farther along in your studies. But if you like, I'll set you up with a subset of the library, here and at Caventhorne."

"We'll see. Some of the reading has been interesting, but I find I'm more of a 'learn by doing' kind of mage."

"Fair enough." That amused Stone—it seemed the universe was conspiring to continue presenting him, the ultimate scholar and theory guy, with would-be students who'd rather jump in and get their feet thoroughly wet before bothering to learn the *why* of what they were doing. He supposed he'd been the same way in his youth, and perhaps that was the direction magical scholarship was headed these days.

When they arrived back upstairs, the pleasant aroma of something savory filled the air. "Ah, I see he's gone all out," Stone said, chuckling. "You don't need any more proof that he likes you. If he didn't, he'd probably have pizza delivered or something."

"You're kidding, right?"

"Well, yes, but he *can* be a bit on the passive-aggressive side when he's not on board with something. Think Jewish mother in the guise of an old British bloke."

"So, like, tea and crumpets instead of chicken soup?"

"More like toad in the hole and a nice ale, but yes, you've got the idea."

Aubrey came out of the kitchen, wearing oven mitts and a full apron over his rumpled sweater. "Ah, good, you're back. I've got the table set and everything's ready to go when you are."

Stone noticed immediately that he had only set two places. "You're joining us, Aubrey, and no argument."

"Yes, sir. Thank you. I didn't want to assume." Aubrey looked pleased to be included. He tucked the oven mitts under his arm and hurried to set another place.

Lunch was a pleasant, leisurely affair. It wasn't long before Stone began to relax, letting go of some of the tension he'd been feeling about whether either Ian or Aubrey would lead the conversation in unexpected directions by asking questions without easy answers. As it turned out, neither of them did that. Ian proved to be a surprisingly adept conversationalist, drawing Aubrey out with inquiries about his job, quirks of the house and grounds, and Stone's childhood. The caretaker, likewise, though clearly curious about everything to do with this newfound member of the family, seemed content to remain on safe paths. Even though Stone had confided some of his frustration at Ian's hedonistic ways, he didn't bring anything up beyond asking the boy about his travels. By the time they'd polished off the simple but excellent meal of roast beef, carrots, and Yorkshire pudding and sat sipping wine, Stone was feeling downright mellow. Another hurdle passed, and successfully.

Aubrey stood and began to clear the dishes, glancing out the window toward the overgrown garden. "I do apologize for the debris and dust. I hope they haven't disturbed you at all."

"I hadn't noticed any," Stone said. "Have the workmen been doing much yet?"

"A bit in the east cellar. I forgot to mention they discovered something odd yesterday, so they stopped work until they can get some more specialized equipment in on Monday."

"Odd?" Stone frowned. *Odd* was one word you didn't want to leave undefined around this house.

"Yes, sir. Remember I mentioned the floor buckling, and we thought it might indicate one of the walls was unstable?"

"Yes..."

"Well...they wanted to get a look underneath it, to see what kind of shape the foundation was in, so they broke through at the spot where it was already ruined."

"What did they find? I do hope the foundation isn't going. That will not only be bloody expensive, but the place will be crawling with workmen."

"They're not sure yet, sir. They...didn't find the foundation."

"What?" Both Stone and Ian looked up from their wineglasses. "What do you mean, they didn't find it?"

Aubrey paused in the act of stacking plates. "They expected to find a solid foundation beneath the cellar—of course they did. But instead, they discovered what appears to be an open area. They were afraid to go any further, since they had no idea what it is or how far it extends, so they reported it to me and said they'd be bringing in some bracing and other specialized apparatus at the beginning of the week."

Stone stared at him. "Way to bury the lede, Aubrey—shouldn't you have told me about this the moment you found out?"

"Sorry, sir. I was planning to tell you when you arrived, but things got a bit chaotic. In any case, I'm sure it's nothing to worry about—though you're correct that if it ends up that the foundation is compromised, that might lead to some inconvenience and expense."

"Brilliant." Stone tossed his napkin aside. "Though I suppose it shouldn't surprise me—this place has always been a bit of a money pit. I probably mentioned the inheritance from Desmond where it could hear me, so now it's decided it needs more attention."

Ian looked at him sideways, almost as if not quite determining if he was kidding. "We should go have a look at it."

"I wouldn't advise it, sir," Aubrey said quickly. "I'm not sure it's safe down there right now. They've got it all cordoned off and cautioned me not to go near it until they've had a chance to investigate further."

Stone stood. "Don't worry, Aubrey—we'll be fine. But I do want to see what we're dealing with. I've only got about an hour before I have to leave for Canterbury, so I'd best get on with it. Do you need any help with this?" He indicated the table.

"No, sir, of course not. But please be careful."

"I will." There was no point in telling Aubrey about all the far more dangerous situations he'd gotten himself into even within the last year—it would only dismay him further. "Come on, Ian. Let's have a look."

As they left the dining room, Ian chuckled. "You know you're not going to find a door to Narnia down there, right? It's probably just an old crawlspace or something."

"You're probably right. But in this house, you can never be certain of that. And odds are if there is a doorway down there, it's probably to Hell, not to Narnia."

| CHAPTER THREE

S TONE HADN'T BEEN IN THE EAST CELLAR for years, except when Aubrey had taken him down there recently to show him the ruined floor. He shined his flashlight around, taking in the grimy walls, years' worth of dust accumulation, and scattered tools lying around the floor in the back corner near the wall.

"This is...uh...rustic," Ian said from behind him. He too had a flashlight, and was examining the heavy wood beams of the ceiling. "Do you and Aubrey ever worry that people might sneak in here and set up housekeeping?"

"Down here? They'd have to be fairly desperate. But no, the wards keep people from sneaking into the house proper. We're sitting at the confluence of three powerful ley lines, which makes the wards even more potent than they should be. Aubrey's found a few squatters and poachers on the land now and again, but only one person ever got into the house without permission, and he was a special case."

"How so?"

"He works for an associate of mine. He's a wild talent, and the one thing he's very, very good at is getting through wards."

"That's convenient."

"Indeed it is. He used to be a worthless pothead a few years back. Your old friend Trin found out about him and used him to steal some books from my library, but we caught him. My associate, who is not what one might call forgiving, weaponized him."

"Weaponized?"

"Offered him a choice: either end up as a pile of ash on the floor, or take a magical oath and work for him. Naturally, he chose the option that let him stay alive. So now he's clean and sober, he's learned a load of new mundane spy skills, and my associate uses him for his own purposes."

"Huh. Sounds like a great guy. Your friend, I mean."

"He's all right. He's just one of those people you don't mess with. Not more than once, anyway."

Stone aimed the flashlight ahead of him, focusing on the ruined part of the floor. The last time he'd seen it, the plain gray surface, composed of large interlocking slabs of stone, had sported a long crack perhaps three feet long and an inch wide, a few feet back from the far wall. In spots near each end the two sides of the crack pressed against each other and drove the sections of floor slightly upward. It reminded Stone uncomfortably of tectonic plates, a topic he'd been trying not to think too hard about these days. Especially not in conjunction with Stefan Kolinsky.

Now, though, the workmen had clearly been busy. As Aubrey had said, the area around the crack had been cordoned off with sawhorses and yellow *CAUTION* tape. Within the confined area, they'd used tools to enlarge the opening so it was no longer a crack, but a small hole perhaps two feet long and a foot wide. From where he stood, Stone could see nothing but blackness inside the hole.

Ian crouched next to the tape and directed his flashlight beam toward it. "Can't see much—looks pretty dark down there."

"It does indeed. Let's see if we can't get a little light on it without causing a cave-in. Hang on." He lifted smoothly off the floor and floated over the hole, stretching out flat a few inches above it and poking his arm down into it. He didn't bother with the flashlight, but instead used a light spell to illuminate the area.

What he saw nearly made him lose control of the levitation spell. A cold chill ran down his back. "Bloody…hell…" he whispered.

"What is it?" Ian, clearly reluctant to walk past the tape, stood and leaned forward, trying to get his own glimpse.

Stone didn't answer right away. Instead, he continued to stare down into the small hole, where his light spell had revealed a much larger space than he'd expected. As Ian had suggested, he too thought he'd find a crawlspace perhaps two or three feet deep. That would have been odd, but it would have made sense.

What didn't make sense was the much larger open space that stretched downward to a shadowy, dust-strewn stone floor perhaps ten feet below.

"There's a room down there," he said.

"You're kidding." Ian inched forward, craning his neck to get a better look.

Stone backed up, twisting his body upright and touching down outside the cordoned area. "See for yourself."

Ian repeated his actions, levitating over the hole and using a light spell to look. "You *weren't* kidding. Looks like a pretty big space, too. I can't see the edges. And you knew nothing about this?"

"How would I? My father never mentioned anything about secret hidden rooms under the floor in the basement, and it wasn't exactly the sort of thing I could find by exploring."

"Why would there be a room hidden under the floor in your basement?"

"No idea." It was a damned good question, though. Stone's heart beat faster.

"Do you want to—go down there and have a look at it?" Ian sounded half-eager, half-doubtful.

Stone glanced at his watch. It was already after two p.m. He needed time to shower and dress for the wedding, and it would take at least an hour to drive up to Canterbury. Still…

"Let's take a quick look, yes. Stand back—let me widen this hole out a bit so we can get through."

Ian backed up against the wall, and Stone used careful magic to pry a few more sections of the stone floor away from the hole. He set them aside, stacked in a neat pile, until he'd widened the one-by-two-foot hole into one roughly three feet in diameter. A few small chunks broke loose and rained down, pattering on the floor below.

He took a step back, waiting to be sure everything had settled as Ian came forward. "Let me go first, and don't follow until I say so." He didn't even try to tell Ian to remain up here—it wouldn't have done any good, and they both knew it.

"Careful. You don't know what's down there."

"What are you expecting? The minotaur? Fortunato? It's probably just an old wine cellar or something."

When Ian didn't reply, Stone re-cast his levitation spell, this time dropping straight down through the hole. He kept his light spell up, shining it around as he descended.

When his feet touched the ground, he turned in place, directing the light around for a better view. He narrowed his eyes. He'd been expecting to find a stone-walled chamber, but instead the walls looked rough—more like a cavern than a room. Someone had clearly carved this space out on purpose, as its shape was too uniform to be natural. Perhaps he was right about its use as an old wine cellar. The air was chilly and smelled of dust and long disuse.

The oddest thing about it, though, was at the end farthest from him, on the other side of the space. A roughly shaped, human-sized doorway led out, the area beyond it wreathed in more darkness. If his sense of direction wasn't turned around, it led out past the edge of the house, toward the grounds to the east of the wing.

There was more to this hidden section of the house than this single room.

How *much* more?

"Do you see anything?" Ian's voice called from above.

"Yes. Come on down. Carefully."

A moment later, Ian had floated down and landed next to him. Immediately, he peered around, taking the place in as Stone had. "There's more down here. Not just the one room."

"So it appears."

"Come on—let's go see where it leads."

Stone's curiosity fought with his common sense. He had no idea what was down that hallway—it could be nothing, or caved in, or in danger of caving in. If the area was unstable enough that the floor was cracking, it was possible it wouldn't be safe to venture further. If the authorities found out about it, they'd probably forbid him to do it.

As always, though, curiosity won. After all, he couldn't allow some part of his own house to exist without exploring it, right?

"Fine," he said. "Not for long, though. I have to get going soon, and I don't want you, or anyone else, down here without me." He started toward the doorway, putting up his magical shield as he went. "I'll go first, and you stay behind me. Keep your shield up at all times—I'm not sure how stable it is down here."

"Yeah."

Content that Ian was treating this with the proper level of respect, Stone raised his flashlight and walked through the doorway.

Beyond, he discovered an uneven passageway, carved into the rock as the previous room had been. He cast the light around, pleased to find no obvious signs of instability. The floor was dusty but clear, and he didn't see any cracks or sections where pieces had fallen from the walls or ceiling.

His heart pounded harder as he picked his way down the hall, noting the rotting torches attached high up on the wall at regular intervals. The passageway twisted just enough that whatever was beyond it wasn't visible. Behind him, he heard Ian's quiet footsteps.

"This is pretty amazing," his son said, his voice as soft as his steps. "It's hard to believe this place has been in the family as long as it has, and you never knew anything about it."

"You're telling me." Stone wondered if his father had been aware of it, but doubted it. The floor, before it had cracked, looked as if it had lain undisturbed for decades, if not longer. Unless there was some other, as yet undiscovered way in, he and Ian were probably the first Stones who'd been down here since the place had been sealed.

The end of the twisting passageway came into view, the way forward blocked by a stout wooden door with iron fittings. Stone held up a hand and slowed his pace even more, creeping up to the door as if expecting someone to jump him. *That's absurd,* he told himself, though he didn't move any faster. *If anything was down here, it's been dead longer than you've been alive.*

The thought chilled him.

He reached the door and stopped, studying the old-fashioned locking mechanism.

"Can you open it?" Ian asked.

"It's probably rusted. Let me see if I can force it. Hold the light."

Ian took Stone's flashlight and pointed it, along with his own, at the lock.

Stone shifted to magical sight, looking for any signs of arcane energy holding it shut, but found none. The only magic he noticed down here was the same ley line power that suffused the entire house. He glanced around at the door and its frame.

"What are you looking for?" Ian asked. "Can't you open it?"

"I'm sure I can. But first I want to make sure it's not holding something in."

"Holding something in? Do you honestly think anything could be alive down here?"

"Not alive." He turned back to his son. "Quick magic lesson: any time you find a locked door, especially somewhere as old and strongly magical as this place, always check it over for sigils, seals, anything that might be holding it closed. There are all sorts of dangerous things out there that aren't technically alive."

Satisfied by Ian's sudden sober expression that he'd gotten his message through, he turned back to the door and finished his examination. As far as he could tell, it sported no carvings, painted symbols, or any other indication that the door might have been placed there to imprison some force. He wasn't sure whether he was relieved or disappointed—possibly a bit of both—but at least now he could get down to the business of breaking the lock. As much as he'd like to spend the rest of the day down here, he didn't have time. Imogen was counting on him to be there for her.

He took a centering breath, focused on the lock, and shaped the Calanarian energy around and through the stout iron. As he suspected, the primitive mechanism was thoroughly rusted, but it proved no match for his concentrated power. After a few seconds, it gave way with a loud *crack* that echoed back along the carved hallway.

"There we go…" he murmured. "Stand back."

Both of them retreated a few steps, and Stone used magic to pull the wooden door open. It swung outward, its old hinges squealing their protest. Beyond it stretched utter blackness.

Stone moved forward again, reclaiming his flashlight from Ian and holding it in front of him. "Bloody hell…" he whispered.

"What is it? Did you find something?" Ian came up behind him, peering over his shoulder. Stone heard a sharp intake of breath, and then a soft, "Wow."

Beyond the open doorway was a circular room perhaps thirty feet in diameter. Like the hallway, it appeared to have been carved from living rock. Stone didn't know where to look first, so he began by shining the light around, letting his gaze roam over the astonishing details one section at a time.

The room's central and most interesting feature was the large ritual circle set into the floor at its center. The circle itself, a combination of paint, carving, and even some bits set into the floor, took up roughly half the room—around fifteen feet across. Stone couldn't make out the details of its sigils from where he stood, and deliberately didn't move forward yet. He wanted to get the big picture before focusing on anything in particular.

In the middle of the circle stood a carved stone pedestal, seven feet long by three wide. It rose from the circle's center, its flat top elevated to a height of around four feet, and appeared to have something attached to it. Stone gave up on the flashlight, instead raising his hand to form a bright ball of light around it and then directing the light upward until it hovered at the room's ceiling some eight feet above them.

"Are those manacles?" Ian whispered from behind him.

"It appears they are," Stone murmured. The platform sported four iron manacles with stout chains snaking downward to rings set into the floor.

"It looks like…somebody was sacrificed here."

Stone didn't miss the slight tremor in his voice: this setup strongly resembled the one Trin Blackburn had used back in Los Gatos—the one she'd strapped Ian to in her sick attempt to recreate the long-ago sacrifice of Ethan Penrose.

"Yes," was all he said. There was no sign of a body on or near the pedestal, though the brighter glow from the magical light revealed rust-colored stains on its surface that could easily have been long-dried blood.

An ice-cold rush of dread ran up his spine. He'd found documentation, hidden in one of the crypts in his family mausoleum, verifying that his ancestors had been the blackest of black mages, performing human sacrifices of unwary travelers and other unfortunates to power their magic. Could they have done it *here,* under the very house he had called home for his entire life? And if so, what manner of rituals had they been powering? Barely aware he was doing it, he took a staggering step back as the implications hit him.

Ian gripped his shoulder. "Are you okay, Dad?"

"Yes. I'm fine." *And if you believe that, I've got some choice swampland you might be interested in...* But he only waved his son off. "I'm fine. Perhaps the air down here isn't good."

"Seems okay to me. Dusty, but that's understandable."

Stone didn't reply. Instead, he looked around the rest of the room, taking in what the sight of the circle and sacrificial pedestal had temporarily distracted him from. Several shadowy doorways led from the room: one each at the northwest, northeast, southwest, and southeast sides, and a final, narrower one to the north.

"How big *is* this place...?" he said under his breath.

Ian followed his gaze to one of the doorways. "Should we check them out?"

Stone wanted nothing more than to remain down here for the rest of the day—hell, for the rest of the *week* at least—bringing down more lights, magical examination gear, and perhaps his friends Eddie Monkton and Arthur Ward to help him study every inch of it. But he glanced at his watch and saw it was already two-thirty. Even if he cut a few corners and drove like a madman, he'd still have to leave soon or risk arriving late to Imogen's wedding. This had all been down here for at least a hundred years—it wouldn't be going anywhere for the next few days.

"Not much time right now. I need to get moving." He pointed at the doorway to the northwest. "Let's take a quick look at that one, and the odd one next to it. We can come back tomorrow and spend more time at it."

Ian looked disappointed—Stone was glad it seemed he'd inherited at least *some* of his father's curiosity—but nodded. "Let's do it."

Stone moved a little faster now, aware of the clock ticking away the few remaining minutes before he'd have to leave. Still, he paused to examine the doorway before passing through it, looking for wards, sigils, or other indications he should be careful. When he found none, he continued through the doorway with Ian close behind him.

Beyond stretched another carved passageway, eight feet wide with its arched ceiling perhaps seven feet at its highest point. Unlike the one they'd initially traversed, this one was arrow-straight, extending around twenty feet back before coming to an abrupt end. Along each of the walls, bricked-up alcoves were spaced two feet apart. The alcoves started at the floor and measured around four feet high and three feet wide.

"What are those?" Ian asked. "Did somebody hide something in there and then brick it up? Why so many of them, though?"

Another chill rose up Stone's spine. *Stop it,* he told himself. All he said was, "No idea." He continued pacing down to the end of the passageway, paused to examine the wall at the end with both magical and mundane sight, and then retraced his steps to where Ian stood in front of one of the alcoves closest to the entrance. "Still no indication of magic, and those bricks don't look strong enough to imprison any magical beasties."

"Shall we break one open and see what's inside?"

"Yes, but not now. No time. Let's check out the odd exit, and then we'll have to go."

Once again Ian looked reluctant, but he followed Stone out until they both stood in front of the single passageway leading north.

"This one looks different," Ian said. "Assuming the three others are like the first one, it's almost like they radiate out like wheel spokes. But this one doesn't have a mate on the other side."

Stone nodded, distracted. He'd shifted to magical sight again and was examining the doorway. He tensed. "Look at this," he said, shining the light around the edge.

Ian moved in closer. "They look like some kind of symbols." His vision fuzzed as he switched to magical sight. "Not magical, though, right? I don't see anything."

"Nor do I. But I wonder if they might not have been at some point." Moving with more care than before, he crept down the hallway. "Keep your shield up."

This passage was shorter than the others, stretching only ten feet back, but unlike the others, this one ended at another door. Instead of wood, though, it was composed of heavy stone, its entire surface covered in intricate carved symbols, sigils, runes, and images. Stone moved closer, holding the flashlight up for a better look. Despite the complex patterns, he still saw no trace of magic.

R. L. KING

"That's beautiful," Ian said. "Somebody must have spent years working on it."

"You may be right."

"No magic, though, unless I'm missing it."

"No, I don't see any either."

"Can you read any of those symbols? Some of them, especially around the outer edges, look like some kind of language to me."

Stone nodded. "I agree. But I can't read it. I could probably work out some of these symbols given time and research materials, but they definitely aren't any of the standard magical languages."

There was no point in asking Ian to help; he knew his son's training with Trin and the scattershot collection of friends he'd been learning from hadn't included much that covered any kind of magical languages or symbology. To be fair, most young mages these days were woefully lacking in those areas, unless their teachers were like Stone and valued them enough to insist on including them as part of their apprenticeships. He'd done it with Verity, but when he attended gatherings of mages these days he found more and more of the younger generation focusing on the more practical aspects of modern magic without bothering to learn its underpinnings. He thought it was a mistake, but he was becoming more of a minority every year.

Ian was studying the images, holding the light close. "The detail is amazing. I see humans, some birds, something that looks like a big lizard or a dragon or something…the artist was really talented."

Stone wondered if the person who'd created this masterpiece had been one of his relatives, or if they'd hired a craftsman to do it. He couldn't see a signature or creator's mark on it anywhere, but the carving was so complex it could easily have been hidden among the detail somewhere.

"Are you going to open it?" Ian asked, rising from a crouch. He'd been examining the seam at the bottom.

Stone shook his head. "No. Not now." He looked at his watch again. "I've got to go—I can't spend any more time down here if I don't want Imogen to flay me alive for turning up halfway through the wedding." As difficult as it was, he turned away from the stone door. "It will take some work anyway—I don't see a lock mechanism, and I'd prefer not to break the door if I can figure out how to get it out in one piece. There's time." He flashed Ian a wry smile. "Thinking of hanging about a bit longer to see how this sorts out?"

"Don't know yet. Maybe so. We can talk about it when you get back."

Stone didn't miss his son's obvious curiosity, and immediately sobered. He gripped Ian's arm. "Listen to me," he said, softly but firmly. "I don't know if you're considering it, but I don't want you down here while I'm gone. Do you understand?"

"I—"

"I mean it." He hardened his gaze and met Ian's gray eyes. "Give me your word, Ian. I don't want you down here at all, and I don't want you to tell Aubrey anything about what we found today. Promise me."

Ian's eyes narrowed, and for a moment Stone thought he'd push back. But then he shrugged. "Sure. I promise. I won't come down here without you. I mean, I know you said this is my home too, but you're still my dad, and it's your call."

"Good." Stone let himself relax. He trusted Ian enough to keep his word, and sensed no duplicity in the boy's aura. "Let's go."

They retraced their steps down the short hallway, through the circular ritual room, and out through the winding hallway to the entrance room. As they floated upward through the floor—Ian first, then Stone—the boy paused. "Why not tell Aubrey?"

"Because he'll worry. I'm going to tell him to stay out of here too, since it's potentially dangerous. I'll have him call the workmen and tell them not to come on Monday. There's no way any mundanes are getting near this place until I've thoroughly examined it."

"Probably smart." Ian followed him out the door, which he locked behind them. "But…that carved door worries me. Do you think there's something dangerous behind it?"

Stone paused, considering. "Who knows? It's possible, I suppose. But if it's been here this long, I doubt it's going anywhere overnight. We'll take a look tomorrow. But now I'll have to get moving fast. Remember what I said."

"Don't worry. I won't do any exploring without you."

CHAPTER FOUR

I MOGEN AND CLIFFORD'S WEDDING was held at Canterbury Cathedral in Kent. Stone had no idea how they'd managed to secure the venue on such relatively short notice, but Imogen had mentioned that Clifford had a country house in the area, so perhaps he or his family had some influence.

The portals wouldn't help him this time, since it didn't make sense to leave from London, so he chose to drive instead. He didn't mind; he enjoyed driving, and getting out on the road often helped him clear his head.

As he drove at steady speed but nearly on autopilot along the M25 motorway, his mind wasn't on the wedding, or even on Imogen. He couldn't stop thinking about the underground chamber with its ritual circle, obvious trappings of ritual sacrifices, and odd, catacomb-like chambers. He hadn't mentioned it to Ian—though he wondered if the boy hadn't figured it out for himself and likewise not said anything—but he wondered if they would find human remains inside each of those small, bricked-up alcoves. Had his ancestors used them to inter the bodies of their sacrificial victims, unmarked and unremembered? The thought sent another chill running down his spine.

Then there was the other sealed chamber, the one with the elaborate carvings. That one had been different. What was its purpose? Had it been built to imprison someone, or something? Was it a repository for more books or records—perhaps even more horrifying than the ones he'd already found inside one of his ancestors' crypts in the family mausoleum? What could be more horrifying than finding out your family members were murdering innocents to power their magic?

Stone wasn't sure he wanted to know. Whenever he speculated that things couldn't get any worse regarding his family's misadventures, history had a way of stepping in to say, "Hold my pint."

But of course he *had* to know. Were there other chambers like that one down there? How many brick-sealed alcoves were there? Did the other passageways branch out into more?

Enough, he admonished himself. No matter how much he wanted to get back to the new mystery beneath his home, today was Imogen's day. He owed it to her to put aside his own concerns and focus on her. Tomorrow would come soon enough.

He arrived with only minutes to spare. By the time he located parking and hurried to the church, most of the other guests had already been seated. He paused outside to straighten his formal suit, deliberately didn't attempt to organize his hair (he'd already done that as well as he could, and messing with it now would only make it worse), and then headed in.

"This way, sir," the usher said instantly when Stone announced his name. The young man handed him a program and led him to a pew in the second row on the bride's side. The front row was empty, left open for the bridesmaids. "Here we are." The few others already seated in the row— mostly older couples Stone didn't recognize along with a few longtime staff members—glanced at him with curiosity.

"In the front?" Stone asked, tilting his head.

"Yes, sir. Miss Desmond left clear instructions. She says you're family."

A twinge ran through Stone—*I could have been family, if things had gone differently*—but said nothing and took his seat at the end of the row. Glancing behind him at the other guests, he recognized only a few: some old friends of William Desmond's, mostly. The rest, he supposed, were friends or relatives of Imogen's mother, who had died before she and Stone met. Five rows back, he spotted Eddie Monkton and Arthur Ward, seated next to each other. They caught Stone looking and both smiled understandingly. They'd both spent a lot of time with Stone and Imogen when the two of them had been together, and they, more than anyone but Imogen herself, knew how hard this day would be for him.

The church was beautiful, decorated in a simple and elegant style in the manner of a couple who were comfortable enough with themselves, each other, and their circumstances to avoid anything resembling ostentation. Stone knew Imogen had grown up surrounded by immense wealth, but William Desmond had never treated it as anything special. As austere and draconian as he'd been with his apprentices, Desmond had loved his daughter dearly and provided her with every advantage she would need to succeed—but he'd also instilled in her both a deep sense of duty and compassion and a spine of pure steel. Stone had never worried about anyone taking advantage of Imogen Desmond, because she was both bright enough and determined enough to shut them down the instant she got a whiff of duplicity.

Stone bowed his head for a moment, a sudden twinge of grief slicing through him. Desmond should have been here, walking down the aisle with Imogen, and then seated in this very spot to see his only daughter get married. True, he'd made no secret of the fact that he'd have preferred the groom to be Stone, but that ship had sailed many years ago and he'd come to gracious terms with it, just as Stone himself had.

Stone could almost picture him sitting there, every line of his steel-gray hair and his formal suit perfect, casting the occasional gently askance glance at Stone's futile attempts to force his own unruly spikes to settle down. Desmond had never lowered himself to joking, but his opinion of Stone's tonsorial defiance had been a long source of good-natured ribbing between them.

A fanfare shook Stone from his melancholy, and he stood with the rest of the guests to direct his attention to the rear of the church. As the doors opened and Imogen appeared on the arm of Kerrick, Desmond's estate steward and longtime dear friend of the family, his breath caught.

Her white dress was not elaborate or showy, but it suited her so perfectly Stone wondered if she'd broken with her usual practical ways and had it custom-designed. Bold yet conservative, the dress managed to combine an old-world sophistication with a more modern sense of style. Imogen was small and slight of frame, but the way she stood there, pausing a moment to let her glittering gaze roam over the assembled guests, made her look as if she was ready to take on the world and claim it for her own. For just a second, her gaze met Stone's and they locked; he thought he saw the tiniest of impish, wistful smiles before her attention moved on and she began the procession toward Clifford, who, according to British custom, did not face her.

Stone couldn't help it—he switched to magical sight as he followed her progress toward the altar. Her strong blue aura blazed so brightly it seemed to light up the space around her, leaving little trails in her wake as she made her slow, steady approach. If he had any doubt of her happiness, that sight drove it away.

He closed his eyes for a moment, gripping the well-worn wood of the pew in front of him, overcome as he rarely was with a jumble of emotions: love, pride, happiness. Surprisingly, he felt no jealousy, no resentment. He could never truly love her if he objected to her clear and unmistakable pleasure at this day. Her face could lie, but her aura couldn't.

He sat straight and tall during the ceremony, continuing to watch with magical sight as Imogen and Clifford exchanged their vows. Mostly he focused on her, but now and then shifted his attention to Clifford Blakeley. Imogen's fiancé had always struck Stone as an unremarkable man, kindly and bland with his dark-blond hair, round, pleasant face, and conservative style of dress that bordered on frumpy. Today, though, as he stood facing Imogen in his beautifully tailored tuxedo, it wasn't only his aura that radiated joy. He looked like a man who couldn't quite believe he was where he was, and doing what he was doing. As he and Imogen held hands and spoke their promises to each other, his gaze never left her eyes. It was as if he'd forgotten about everyone else in the church, creating a bubble around himself and Imogen.

　　　　　　　　　　　　　　　　　　　　　　R. L. KING

Stone wasn't the type to tear up at weddings, and this one was no exception, but as the vicar at last pronounced the two of them husband and wife and they kissed, he once again tightened his grip on the pew and blinked away a persistent prickle behind his eyes. *Good for you, Imogen, love. I hope he makes you as happy as you've always deserved to be.* If there was indeed some sort of afterlife, he could almost picture William Desmond watching from there, his eyes shining with pride at his daughter.

Eddie and Ward caught up with him as he filed out of the church with the rest of the guests. "All right, Stone?" Eddie asked softly.

He nodded, putting on a cheerful smile. "Fine. Lovely ceremony, wasn't it?"

"Indeed," Ward said, eyeing Stone with a sideways glance indicating that neither he nor Eddie was fooled. He looked back over his shoulder at the wedding party as they filed out along with the photographer to take advantage of the beautiful summer evening with some photos on the grounds.

"We were startin' to worry you might not show," Eddie said. "Bit late, weren't you?"

"Yes. I was—dealing with some issues back at the house. Ian turned up, so I was giving him the tour and we lost track of time."

"Oh, 'e's finally come 'round, then? Does that mean we might finally get to meet 'im?"

"We'll see. I'm not sure how long he's staying." Ever since he'd told Eddie and Ward about Ian, they'd been teasing him about whether he'd at last succumbed to madness and the boy was merely a figment of his imagination.

"Right," Ward said, amused.

"Sod off," Stone muttered, chuckling. "You'll be at the reception, I assume?"

"Wouldn't miss it," Eddie said. "We'll see you there. You'd better save me a dance, though. I didn't get all done up in this penguin suit for nothin'." His grin nearly split his face as he and Ward waved and headed off toward their respective cars.

Stone had farther to walk, and he didn't move at his usual quick pace. He wasn't sure why he hadn't told his friends about the day's discovery. He knew he would eventually, since he planned to enlist their help in exploring and cataloging what might be down there. Eddie's position as keeper of the massive London magical library, as well as curator of the soon-to-be-opened magic resource center at Caventhorne made him, along with longtime arcane researcher Ward, ideal candidates to assist him. Besides, other than Verity, they were the only people who knew anything about Stone's sordid family history.

The reception was held at a small, elegant venue a short distance outside the town proper. Stone wondered why they hadn't chosen one of the offerings at the Cathedral itself, but thought he knew: Imogen was an intensely private person, and he'd gotten the impression Clifford was too, so they might have considered the Cathedral's facilities too "commercial."

The location they'd chosen looked to Stone as if it might have been a private manor house at some point. It was a lovely, two-story home about the same size as his place in Surrey but in much better repair, surrounded by manicured grounds and meandering, fairylike paths. Stone drove through the gates and surrendered his keys to the uniformed valet at the door. He took in the circular driveway with a fountain at its center and the twinkling lights along the paths, just beginning to come on as twilight fell, as he mounted the front steps along with several other chattering guests.

He didn't clearly remember too many details of the reception itself. Despite his preoccupation with the discovery back at his own house, he pulled his "charming" act around him like a cloak and circulated with a glass of wine in hand, chatting with various guests before retiring to one side to talk shop with Ward and Eddie while they waited for Imogen and Clifford to arrive. He'd informed Imogen of Verity's last-minute no-show as soon as he'd found out about it, and the planner had hastily rearranged the table settings so he wouldn't be seated next to an empty spot. Fortunately, she'd also been kind enough to seat Ward and Eddie at the same table, so at least he didn't have to spend the evening making small talk. That, especially tonight, would have been pure hell.

Imogen, Clifford, and the rest of the wedding entourage arrived before long, taking their seats at the head table as the dinner service began. Stone managed to keep his mind on the event, forcing himself not to continue his speculations about what was going on back at the house. He focused on listening to the speeches and enjoying the excellent meal, and tried not to think too hard about anything else. He could get back to what was happening at the house after this was over. He owed Imogen his attention tonight.

Speaking of Imogen, he hadn't noticed her leaving the head table, but now she was crossing the room and heading in his direction. Her smile wreathed her face as she approached, and her gaze was locked on him. There was no doubt as to her destination.

"Alastair," she said warmly when she reached him. "I'm so glad you came."

Stone rose and took her in. She looked even more radiantly beautiful up close. She'd removed her veil and her carefully coiffed, chestnut-brown hair had become ever so slightly disarranged, which in Stone's mind made her look even more appealing. More like her usual self, an irresistible combination of playful and serious, eyes sparkling with mirth. Clifford stood behind her, his expression more serene but no less heartfelt, obviously content to bask in his new wife's joy.

"I did say you couldn't keep me away," he murmured. He took her hands and gave them a gentle squeeze. "I'm so happy for both of you. It was a lovely ceremony, and you know you both have my best wishes."

She rose on tiptoe and planted a chaste, soft kiss on his cheek. "Thank you, Alastair."

Stone offered his hand to Clifford. "You're a lucky man, Blakeley."

His smile widened, faint crinkles of laugh lines appearing around his eyes. "Believe me, I know it. Imogen is one of a kind."

"Oh, you two." Imogen laughed and ducked her gaze. "You're talking about me as if I'm some kind of prize hunting trophy or something."

"No, no." Stone shook his head, taking her hand again. "That sells you short. What you are is an amazing woman, a dear friend, and a lovely bride. All I meant was that Clifford is lucky he met you, and lucky he gets to spend the rest of his life with you. I couldn't be happier."

She shot him a quick glance, but then smiled. "You're such a dear, Alastair, and you always will be." Apologetically, she gestured back at the group of tables. "We need to—keep going, do the mingling thing. But I hope we can talk later."

"Absolutely. Save me a dance?"

"Of course."

As they made their way along the narrow aisles toward the next table, Stone shifted to magical sight and watched not Imogen's aura, but Clifford's. Its steady, placid blue still flashed with happiness, but showed no hint of resentment or jealousy. Stone wouldn't have blamed him if it had—Clifford knew about the relationship the two of them had shared, and how close they'd come to marrying all those years ago.

But it didn't, and Stone relaxed. He hadn't wanted to admit it, not at first, but Imogen and Clifford *did* make a lovely and well-matched couple.

He didn't get his dance with Imogen until much later in the evening. Sitting back with Eddie, Ward, and the others he'd met at his table, he watched the reception progress through the toasts, the cutting of the cake, and Imogen and Clifford's first dance. Bittersweet melancholy stabbed him again as he thought about how she wouldn't have a dance with Desmond, picturing her tiny, white-clad form held protectively in her broad-shouldered, elegant father's arms.

"Stone?" Arthur was looking at him with concern.

Stone waved him off. The first dance was finishing now, Imogen and Clifford lingering a moment in the center of the floor before Clifford leaned in to kiss her and moved off to dance with his elderly mother. Stone rose smoothly and approached Imogen.

"May I have this dance?" he asked softly.

She turned from where she'd been watching Clifford depart, and a smile lit up her face. "Of course."

He'd deliberately gone easy on the champagne and stayed away from the bar, and not only because he'd have to drive home later that evening. He offered her his hand and they swung into a waltz as all around them couples moved onto the floor.

She looked him up and down, taking in his formal suit. "You look so handsome tonight. I know I've said it before, but you should dress up more. It really does suit you."

He chuckled. "Nobody's supposed to be looking at me, or any of the rest of us blokes. You're the star attraction tonight, love, and you look stunning as always."

She ducked her gaze. "You always did know the right thing to say."

"You wouldn't think so if you knew how many responses I consider and *don't* say." He nodded toward Clifford and his mother, a spry old woman in a conservative gold dress. "You two look so good together. I was watching your auras during the ceremony, and if I ever had any doubt—which I didn't—I don't anymore. He obviously worships the ground you walk on."

"Yes—I suppose I'll have to break him of that, won't I?" she said with a twinkle in her eye.

"Oh, I don't know. It's not so bad, really. I still do too, and you've put up with me all these years."

"Alastair—" She squeezed his hands, then glanced away.

"What is it?"

"Nothing."

"Moggy…"

Her gaze shifted back. "It really is nothing. Just a bit…overwhelmed. I'm so happy today, and I'm so glad you're happy for me. I know it shouldn't mean so much to me—not after all these years—but…well, it does."

Stone barely noticed the other dancers, and heard the music only enough to lead the dance with a confidence born of many years of instruction in his youth. "Listen," he said softly. "I know you can't read auras, but please, if you've never believed anything I've said before, believe this: I love you, Imogen. I will always love you, until the day I die. Possibly after that."

When she started to reply, he squeezed her hand again. "I don't mean that in a romantic way—I know we've moved beyond that a long time ago. But you've got to know you're one of the dearest people in my life, and I would do anything for you. I mean that. And because of that, I want nothing more than for you to be happy for the rest of your life. I can see Clifford makes you happy. I see it in the way you look at him, and the way he looks at you." He swallowed. "I see it in ways you can't."

She met his gaze and held it, then pulled him into a hug, burying her head in his shoulder. "Thank you, Alastair. I couldn't ask for a better friend."

Stone wasn't so sure about that, but he *was* sure he meant every word he'd said. "Come on now," he said, chuckling and gently breaking the hug. "People will talk. You don't want Clifford challenging me to a duel or anything, do you?"

She laughed. "I don't think he'd win a duel with you. Maybe a round of golf."

"I wouldn't have a chance. Perhaps we'd better—"

He stopped, feeling the sudden buzz of his phone inside his breast pocket.

"What is it?" Imogen asked. "Is something wrong?"

"No, no—I thought I'd turned this bloody thing off. Let me just—" He pulled it out and glanced at the display, freezing an instant before thumbing the button to shut it off.

The familiar number was Ian's.

Why would Ian call him now? His son knew where he'd be, and that he wouldn't want to be interrupted, unless—

Imogen must have noticed something change on his face. "Alastair?"

The song was ending now. "I'm so sorry," he said. "I need to take this. Will you excuse me for a moment?"

"Of course. Is everything all right?"

"I'm sure it is," he said with a certainty he didn't feel. He leaned in to kiss the top of her head, smiled, and hurried off to a quiet corner of the hall, already hitting the button to answer the call.

"Hello, Ian. Is something wrong? Why are you—"

"Dad, please." Ian cut him off, speaking fast, voice shaking.

A cold bolt of dread froze Stone in place. "Ian. What's wrong? Calm down and tell me."

He heard a couple of deep, shuddering breaths. "Dad. You have to come back. I'm in London. Something's wrong at the house."

| CHAPTER FIVE

B Y EARLY THAT EVENING, Ian had already begun to regret promising his father he'd remain at the Surrey house instead of going into London to hit up some clubs.

After Stone had departed for Kent, taking the little black convertible he kept covered in the garage for the rare occasions when he'd need to drive somewhere, Aubrey had done his best to entertain Ian for the afternoon and early evening.

He'd started by giving a more elaborate tour of the grounds, driving Ian around the wild, mostly forested acreage on a little vehicle that looked like something halfway between a golf cart and a tiny gardener's pickup truck.

"I didn't know my dad owned so much land," Ian said as the little contraption bumped and jounced along a narrow dirt path through a thick patch of trees.

Aubrey chuckled. "I'm not so sure he knows himself, sir." He gestured around the area. "I can't remember the last time he's come out here, as far as I know, at least. He used to wander the grounds quite a lot when he was a child, but—"

"But he's not a wilderness kind of guy," Ian finished.

"Er—no, sir. Not really."

Ian could sympathize with that. During his travels, some of the guys he'd met had been into that kind of thing, and had convinced him to accompany them on several excursions ranging from afternoon hikes to his recent backpacking trip in the wilds of Romania. He'd been a good sport about them—especially the Romanian trip, since Mihas had been smoking hot and great in bed, even if the bed was a sleeping bag in an old tent—but he couldn't deny the truth: he was, at his core, a city boy. He liked the bright lights and frenetic energy of nightclubs and bars, the intrigue of narrow, shadowed alleyways, and the cultural diversity of museums, art galleries, and concerts.

"So why does he have all this land if he never wants to do anything with it?" he asked, as Aubrey slowed the cart to point out a family of deer barely visible through the thick foliage.

"It's part of the estate, sir. This place has been in the Stone family for generations."

"Huh." That was something else Ian had no real experience with. He'd spent most of his early childhood years in a tiny, shabby two-bedroom apartment with his single mother. When she'd married Bobby Tanner, her new husband had moved the family to a much nicer and more spacious two-story home in Winthrop, Ohio, and when Ian had finally had enough of Bobby and run away at sixteen, he'd had to make do with a series of less-than-homelike places that sometimes included friends' couches when he'd been particularly down on his luck. He'd seen luxury—plenty of it—during his time as a street hustler, attending hot parties nearly every weekend and going home with everything from actors to studio executives to buttoned-down bankers and lawyers who would have died before admitting they'd sought out his services. But all of it had been temporary, and he'd never dreamed of attaining that standard of living on his own.

And now, here he was tooling around the vast grounds of an English country estate with its caretaker, a man who'd been in his father's family longer than his father himself had. Life was funny sometimes, that was certain.

"So…" he ventured once they were moving again. "What do you *do* with it? Do you have to take care of all this land? That seems like a big job for one guy. Especially when Dad doesn't even care about it." He didn't mention the fact that Aubrey was clearly getting on in years; the man had the healthy, robust look of someone who spent a lot of time outside doing physical work, but he still had to be at least sixty.

Aubrey chuckled, the deep lines around his eyes crinkling. "I enjoy it, sir. I find it very peaceful out here. Your father isn't fond of carefully tended gardens, so mostly we just leave it wild. I drive around once a week or so checking for signs of problems, but aside from that, it doesn't require a great deal of care."

"Problems?" He nodded in the direction of the house. "I'd think you'd have more of those inside. That house has *got* to be haunted. Before I would have been joking, but knowing Dad…"

"No, sir, I can say with certainty that I've never seen a ghost inside the house. I'm more likely to encounter poachers or squatters out here, honestly. I occasionally see the leftovers of their abandoned camps, and now and then I have to encourage them to go on their way." He patted the stock of the shotgun he kept next to him in a specially designed holder.

Ian wondered if Aubrey had ever needed to actually shoot anyone, but didn't ask. "So, no ghosts? That surprises me. With all those generations living in the house, you'd think *somebody* would have stuck around."

"Perhaps not, sir. Your father tried to explain it to me once—he said that the magically talented, for whatever reason, rarely leave ghosts, or 'echoes,' as he calls them. And since the house has been occupied by magically talented men for at least six generations..."

"Well, yeah, but there had to be a lot of people who *weren't* magically talented too, right? Wives, other kids, servants—this place must have had more servants back in the day."

"True," Aubrey admitted, then shrugged. "I'm sorry, sir—I wish I could tell you thrilling stories of hauntings and other eerie happenings, but the truth is, at least as long as I've been here, the place has been fairly...well...mundane. At least as far as ghostly presences are concerned."

Ian didn't answer, and the caretaker finished his loop around the grounds and headed back toward the house. As he passed the low wall separating the small cemetery from the field leading back up toward the house, Ian pointed at it. "Still getting my mind around the fact that our family has its own graveyard."

Aubrey nodded. "Unlike the grounds as a whole, your father does spend time there when he's home for more than a day or so. I think he finds being surrounded by his ancestors comforting, in a way."

"He didn't seem too comforted when he told me about them. He said they were a bad bunch."

R. L. KING

"Yes, sir," Aubrey said, looking uneasy. "I suppose many of them were, from what he's told me. At least his—well, yours too, of course—direct ancestors, starting with your great-grandfather. But there are other family members and staff buried there as well."

Ian couldn't quite understand why household servants would want to be buried in a cemetery with their masters—he supposed a lot of his ideas about how rich Brits interacted with their household staffs weren't exactly based in reality—but once again he didn't ask.

Aubrey pulled the little cart up in front of the main house. "Here we are, sir. Let me just put this away and then I'll come in and get dinner started. You're free to wander about the house and grounds as you like, of course—the areas your father prefers to keep closed are behind wards, so you needn't worry about accidentally going somewhere you shouldn't."

Ian leaped out. "Thanks, Aubrey. Seriously, though—no need for you to cook dinner. I can entertain myself if you've got things of your own you want to do. Or we could just order a pizza or something." He shot a glance toward the house's imposing façade. "Do they even *deliver* pizza out here?"

"Oh, yes, sir. There's a place in the village that's quite good, actually. Or we could go into the village if you like. I trust you've never visited a genuine English pub?"

Ian chuckled. "Nope. But that's okay—if you don't mind, I think I'd rather just stay here. The pizza sounds good, though. Don't cook for me, unless you want to for yourself. And anyway, please don't feel like you have to keep entertaining me just because Dad said so."

"Of course not, sir." His eyes twinkled. "Just between you and me, I rarely do anything just because your father says so—but that said, our intentions usually align fairly well."

"You're quite a guy, Aubrey—pretty much nothing like I expected, to be honest."

"Indeed? And what *did* you expect, if you don't mind my asking?"

Ian considered. "I guess I thought you'd be more...formal. Stuffy, even. Kind of like Alfred in the *Batman* comics."

"Well, I'm glad you don't consider me 'stuffy,'" Aubrey seemed amused by his words. "And in any case, I'll take your comparison to Alfred as a compliment, though I doubt I'll live to see the day when your father goes gallivanting about London in a skintight bat suit."

"Hell, I haven't even known Dad very long and I already doubt that would be the strangest thing he's ever done."

"You're quite likely correct, sir. If you'll permit me just a bit of sentimentality, though, I'm very glad your father's finally brought you here. I was beginning to think there would never be another Stone in the family."

"Well, you never know." Ian waved at the cart. "Anyway, don't let me keep you."

Aubrey shot him an odd look, almost as if wondering if he were being dismissed, but then nodded. "Yes, sir. I'll put this away and then ring Mama Giovanni's."

By the time the pizza arrived and Ian and Aubrey had polished it off with pints of ale at the scarred kitchen table, the sun had gone down. They chatted about neutral topics over the meal, but as the caretaker gathered the remains into the box to throw them away, he said reflectively, "I wonder how your father is doing tonight."

Ian lounged in his chair, finishing off his pint. "He went to a wedding, right?"

"Yes, sir. But…not just any wedding."

"Oh?"

"Imogen Desmond is the daughter of your father's master, William Desmond, who passed away last year."

"Oh. Right. He did mention something about that."

"I'm not sure he would have wanted me to tell you this, but he didn't ask me not to. He and Imogen were to be married themselves, several years ago."

"He mentioned that too, but he didn't say much more about it. What happened? Did her father not approve or something?"

"Oh, no, sir. To the contrary." Aubrey retrieved a damp cloth and wiped down the table. "Mr. Desmond considered your father to be the closest thing he had to a son of his own. He felt his daughter and your father were a perfect match, and actively encouraged their relationship."

"But…it didn't work out?"

Aubrey shook his head ruefully. "No, sir. I won't go into the details—I don't even know them all, since your father never told me—but from what I understand, Miss Desmond, who isn't magically talented, felt your father cared more for his magical studies than he did for her. She broke it off. Quite reluctantly, to be sure, but she did. That was the catalyst for your father deciding to take the position at Stanford and relocate to the United States."

"Wow." Ian had wondered for a while what would have caused Stone to leave all of this to move halfway around the world, but he'd never have guessed the true reason. "But...now he's going to her wedding? He stayed friends with her after she dumped him?"

Aubrey's eyes glittered, and his smile was gentle. "Your father loves Imogen Desmond deeply, and he always will. He understood and respected her concerns, and came to agree with her that they wouldn't have been a good match. But yes, they've remained dear friends for all these years." He turned away, returning the rag to its hook. "That doesn't mean I expect he's having an easy time of it tonight, though."

"Yeah...I guess I can see that. It's too bad Verity had something come up so she couldn't go with him. It probably would have been easier with her there."

"He'll be fine, sir." His tone changed, growing more brisk. "Are you staying for a while? I expect your father will want to show you more of the magically warded areas of the house, his library..."

"We'll see. I haven't actually started my formal magical training yet. I'm still getting used to all of this. Remember, I've only known I'm a mage for a couple of years now. It wasn't like I grew up my whole life expecting it."

"True enough. That must have been quite a shock for you."

"Yeah...in more ways than one." Ian had no idea how much Stone had shared with Aubrey about the circumstances of their meeting, and suddenly he had no desire to go into it himself. That could lead to a very long conversation of the type he didn't want to have. He glanced out the window; the sun was well on its way down now, wreathing the overgrown gardens behind the house in shadows. "Listen, Aubrey—I hope you won't mind, but I'm a little tired. I think I just want to go up to my room for a while."

"Of course, sir. It's been a long day, and I'm sure your father has some things planned for tomorrow."

I'll just bet he has, Ian thought. It was probably driving his father crazy, knowing something mysterious waited under the house and being prevented from exploring it. He wondered if Dad would head back down there immediately when he returned that night, or if he could manage to wait until morning.

"Can you find your way back to your room on your own, or do you need me to show you?" Aubrey was asking.

"I'm fine. Thanks. I'll see you tomorrow. Thanks for everything—the tour, and the stories about Dad's childhood…I feel like I know him a little better now."

Aubrey beamed. "I'm so happy to hear it, sir. If you need anything, please don't hesitate to come by. My flat is above the garage."

"Got it." Ian vaguely remembered his father pointing out the large, free-standing former carriage house when they'd arrived, as they walked past it from the graveyard toward the house. But he didn't think he'd be giving Aubrey any calls tonight. He wondered what time his father would be home.

He did head back toward his room, mostly so he wouldn't arouse Aubrey's suspicions, but he didn't intend to stay there. Already restless, he once again regretted agreeing not to go into London.

You can put up with it for one night, he told himself in disgust. After everything his father had done for him—got him away from Trin, saved him from being sacrificed to some extradimensional demon, hell, even trusted him enough to give him a hefty bank account and set him loose to travel the world without (much) protest, the least he could do was tone down his hunger for constant stimulation and settle down until tomorrow. Maybe he might even stay around for a while if Dad wanted—with the understanding that he wouldn't be spending his nights lurking around the drafty old mansion like some kind of vampire hermit.

He made a detour on the way back to his room, stopping by the library—at least the part of it that wasn't downstairs behind wards—to look for something to read. He used to like reading when he was a kid, preferring lurid horror novels and action-adventure stories with a hint of the gory super-natural. All that had changed after his mother had married Bobby Tanner, though: Bobby had considered such books "ungodly" and cleaned out Ian's small library, tossing the books in the fireplace and forbidding him to bring more of them into the house. He'd still done some reading at the school library, but gave it up after he'd run away to Los Angeles.

Stone's library didn't include any horror novels or super-natural thrillers. In fact, most of the books were old and didn't look as if they'd been removed from the shelves in years—some possibly before Stone was born—and the re-mainder appeared to be scholarly volumes on cultural anthropology and world occult traditions. Many of the oth-ers were histories, biographies, a few ancient encyclopedias, and a whole lot of tomes about magic. Ian examined the shelves with magical sight, not surprised he didn't find a hint of arcane power anywhere among the stacks. He was sure the good stuff was in the warded library.

Still, he supposed it couldn't hurt to get a bit of grounding in magical history, even if it was from mundane sources. Eventually he'd have to settle down and start studying magic in earnest. Despite his words to his father earlier in the day, he knew if he was to get anywhere with his powers, he'd have to do something other than compare notes with an eclectic group of students who weren't much farther along than he was. Sure, he got plenty of useful and interesting techniques from them—probably ones his father had never even seen—but Dad was right, he needed a solid background. Just...not quite yet. Maybe he'd think about it in a few months, when he needed a break from seeing the world.

He selected a couple books and carried them upstairs to his room, where he kicked off his boots and stretched out on the bed. There wasn't a TV set in here, or even a radio. Now that he thought of it, Ian didn't remember seeing a TV anywhere in the house, not even in the massive great room downstairs. If he hadn't seen Stone's place back in the States, with its full complement of modern electronic conveniences, he'd have wondered if his father was going for some kind of Hogwarts aesthetic here. Maybe they kept the home theater hidden away somewhere behind closed doors, to maintain the place's old-fashioned appearance. In any case, if he was going to spend any time here at all, he'd have to convince Dad to let him add a few modern upgrades. He grinned as he cracked open one of the books and an imaged flashed in his mind: Aubrey, back at his apartment over the garage, kicked back in a sleek leather chair watching his big-screen TV with full surround sound and Dolby stereo.

Yeah, probably not.

The house was quiet, with only the occasional call of a far-off bird and the *skreek-skreek* of crickets breaking the silence. It sounded strange to Ian, who was used to being surrounded by sound: the electronic hums of devices, the soft hubbub of distant voices, the rumble of traffic and trains. He wondered whether, if he opened his door, he could hear Aubrey puttering around downstairs, or if the caretaker had already left. He decided there was no point in checking, since it wouldn't change what he did.

He switched on the bedside lamp and began to read, but soon found his mind wandering. *Damn, this stuff is dry.* If this was the kind of thing his father would expect him to be reading in order to learn magic, he could already see potential problems.

Trin, as bad as she'd been, had never made him read anything. All the techniques she'd taught him had been face to face, with her showing him how they worked followed by a few practice sessions to make sure he'd gotten them down. True, she'd only taught him what she thought he needed to know—hell, she hadn't even told him of the *existence* of the teleportation portals, let alone instructed him on their use— but she'd been a good teacher. He couldn't deny that.

Dad was a good teacher too, patient and great at explaining complex concepts in a way that made them easy to understand. Ian sometimes regretted that he couldn't simply apprentice himself to his father, but even their brief time together had convinced them both it wouldn't be a good idea. Dad had promised to find him a teacher when he was ready, but made it clear he'd have to decide that on his own.

"I'm not going to waste everyone's time lining up a master for you if you're not ready to apply yourself," he'd said shortly before Ian had embarked on his explorations. "You let me know when you want to get started, and I'll find someone you can get on with, who can handle your power level."

Ian realized he'd read the same line at least four times and it still hadn't sunk in. His mind began to wander further, returning to earlier that day when he and his father had discovered the secret catacomb-like space beneath the mansion. He wondered, given his father's catlike curiosity, if Dad would be disappointed that he wasn't more excited about going down there—so much so that he might even be tempted to break his promise and explore the area on his own.

He wasn't, though. It wasn't he didn't find the discovery interesting, but ancient ruins didn't hold the same fascination for him that they did for Stone. He wanted to see what was down there, but he could wait until tomorrow. His father was obviously jazzed about whatever they might uncover behind those bricked alcoves and the intricately carved stone door— let him have his fun.

One thing Ian *did* know, though—as long as he stayed up here, stretched out on the bed trying to read these dull books, he was certain he'd drop off to sleep any minute now. Since he wanted to talk with Dad more when he got home, that wouldn't work. Maybe if he went back downstairs he could find something a bit more interesting to read, give one of his friends a call, or possibly even take a moonlight stroll outside for a while.

It was every bit as quiet on the ground floor as it was in his bedroom. He headed out to the kitchen and retrieved a beer from the refrigerator (he'd thought Brits drank their beer warm, and was relieved to discover it wasn't universally true), took the two books back to the library and re-shelved them, then scanned the shelves for anything that looked more interesting. When he didn't find anything, he briefly considered hunting down Aubrey to see if the caretaker had any more compelling reading material.

Finally, he grabbed a tome on ancient Egyptian magic and returned to the great room, stretching out on the leather couch in front of the unlit fireplace. He glanced at his watch: nine-thirty. It would still be at least three hours before Dad was home.

It was going to be a long night.

The book, at least, was more interesting than the others had been. It included sections on the various gods and their magical traditions, as well as several full-color plates showing the details of discoveries inside the Pyramids and other tombs. Not exactly Ian's usual choice of reading material, but apparently beggars couldn't be choosers around here.

He'd lost track of time again when he thought he heard something: a far-off noise that sounded like a heavy object crashing to a hard floor.

He jerked his head up and sat very still, closing his eyes and craning his ears. Had he heard it at all, or had it been merely a figment of his imagination? Perhaps he'd dropped off again, and the sound had been part of a micro-dream.

After thirty seconds of stillness that seemed to stretch into many times that long, the sound didn't repeat. Ian closed the book and sat up straight, looking around. Since he hadn't even been certain he'd heard it at all, he hadn't gotten a good bead on where it had originated.

Probably just a cat or something outside, he thought. *If it was anything at all.*

He got up and went back to the kitchen, looking for something he could put together for a snack and another beer. Inexplicably, he felt uneasy, realizing how alone he was in this large, unfamiliar, and forbidding house.

Don't be stupid. What do you think is going to happen—a ghost jumping out at you?

He thought it was possible, despite Aubrey's statement to the contrary, but the thought of ghosts, or echoes, or whatever they were called didn't bother him. Hell, a ghost or two might liven the place up a bit.

He found some bread and cheese and made a hasty sandwich, pairing it with another bottle of beer, and munched it as he headed back to the great room. His stocking-clad feet made no sound on the gray slate floor.

The feeling of unease intensified as suddenly the rock-solid certainty hit him that someone was watching him.

He paused a moment, just long enough to convince any watchers that he hadn't noticed them, then spun around.

Nothing.

He snorted, angry with himself for letting the place get to him. Nobody was in here—the only other person on the entire property was Aubrey, and the caretaker wouldn't sneak into the house and spy on him. One thing he was sure about after spending the day with Aubrey: the old man was about as straightforward as they came. If he had something on his mind, he'd say it.

Nonetheless, Ian focused on keeping his aura steady as he pondered his next move. Perhaps he should finish his snack and go back to his room. Even if he fell asleep before Dad got home, he could always talk to him tomorrow. Maybe he was more tired than he thought. He *had* been doing a lot of running around, staying up late partying with his friends many nights in a row. Maybe this old, silent mansion would be a good place to take it easy for a while.

Another crash sounded, far away and muffled.

Ian tensed, gripping his beer bottle tighter.

He had *not* imagined that one.

Nor had he imagined his sudden certainty—strong enough that he would have staked his life on it—that the sound had come from the east-wing cellar.

Hang on. That is *stupid.* The house was huge and constructed like a fortress—there was no way he could have heard *anything* coming from that far away, unless the whole east wing had collapsed.

So why was he so sure?

He thought about finding Aubrey to tell him about it, but discarded the thought. The old man was probably fast asleep by now, and wouldn't be too happy to be awakened with some vague and foolish suspicion.

No—he'd go check it out, just to set his own mind at ease. If something *had* fallen down there, or the walls had collapsed, or the floor had fallen down into the catacomb, he'd head right back out and find Aubrey. He might even call his father. He'd want to know, even if it did mean having to leave his old girlfriend's wedding early.

He set the beer and half-eaten sandwich on a nearby side table and hurried off toward the east side of the house, moving silently and listening with care for any further sounds. When he reached the stairway down to the cellar he switched to magical sight, peering down into the dark expanse, and then turned the light on and headed down.

The place looked much as he'd remembered it from earlier that day. The sawhorses were still in place with the tape stretched between them, cordoning off a hole that appeared no different than before. Ian glanced up at the ceiling, holding up a light spell for a better look, but it was as solid as ever, with no cracks or signs it had shifted. Same with the walls.

He paused a moment, staring down into the black hole. He heard nothing, saw nothing, but still that persistent feeling nagged at him: whatever the sound had been, it had originated down there.

He had two choices, then: he could ignore it and go back to his room, waiting for his father to return home so he could tell him either tonight or tomorrow morning. Or he could go down there and have a look around to reassure himself that the whole thing had been his imagination. Dad wouldn't even have to know he'd done it if he found nothing, and if he *did* find something, he'd be too busy wanting to examine it himself to be angry about Ian breaking his promise.

The decision—if it had truly been a decision—took him mere seconds. Apparently he *had* inherited some of his father's curiosity after all. He pulled a shield around him and cast a levitation spell, floating upward over the barriers and dropping neatly down through the hole to the stone floor below.

The flashlights they'd used earlier that day still lay on the floor nearby. He picked one up and flicked it on, then stuck the other one in his pocket. No point wasting energy using magic if he didn't need to.

He crept down the winding passageway, shining the light around. No cracks here; the floor was clear and obviously nothing had fallen along this stretch. When he reached the other end he paused, dousing the light and studying the area with magical sight.

Nothing.

When he turned the flashlight back on, the large, circular ritual area remained as quiet and unchanged as ever. The circle was still on the floor, as was the large pedestal in its center with its rusting manacles and unsettling bloodstains. Once again, Ian directed the flashlight upward, but the ceiling looked undisturbed as well.

He remained where he was, thinking. He had no idea how big this place was, or how far the passageways radiating out from the center room stretched. The one he and his father had examined earlier had only gone back around twenty feet, but he had no way to be sure the others would do likewise. And then there was the odd, singular hallway leading to the carved stone door. Should he try checking them all out? How long would that take? If Dad returned home before he finished, he knew it would lead to an uncomfortable conversation.

He crept forward, shining the light in front of him.

As soon as he stepped into the circular room, the overwhelming feeling that someone was watching him intensified. He stopped again, casting quick glances around in front of him, behind him, and off to the sides, but neither magical nor mundane sight revealed anything out of the ordinary.

Damn it, calm down, he told himself in annoyance. *You're a mage, not some scared kid. Dad probably deals with this kind of stuff all the time.*

Once again, Trin's teachings had not prepared him for this kind of situation. Despite her sneaky, manipulative ways, most of her magic had been straightforward in its focus. Ian wondered how many other holes there were in his magical repertoire.

He cast the light around again, looking for signs of movement. "Is anybody down here?" he called, his voice echoing along the gray stone walls.

There was no response, but that nagging sensation of being watched didn't depart.

"Okay…" he muttered. "There's nothing here. It's just a spooky bunch of old tunnels. Not everything is magical."

He'd been in catacombs before; he and some mage friends had taken a trip through part of the ones in Paris a few weeks ago. They'd spotted hints of old magic—it would have been difficult not to in such a place—but never had he gotten the same feeling of observation.

"If somebody's here, show yourself," he shouted. The echoes came back even louder, bouncing back and forth as if mocking him. But nothing else appeared.

Fine. He'd just do a quick scan of the hallways he and his father had already examined. If there was anything else, it obviously didn't present an immediate danger. It could wait until later tonight, or tomorrow morning.

Decision made, he picked up his pace, holding the flashlight beam in front of him as he approached the hall leading to the stone door. As he passed the first alcove space, he shined the light down that way for a quick look, relieved that the bricked-in niches remained sealed and silent. Emboldened, he strode forward and poked the beam down the next hallway.

And stopped, dread slicing through his body and rooting his feet to the floor. He gripped the flashlight tighter as it slipped in his hand.

Earlier that day when they'd examined it before, the door had been pristine, its intricate carvings seemingly unmarred by the passage of time. Even the strange language his father couldn't read had been clear and easy to make out around the outer edges.

Now, it looked as if a bolt of lightning had struck it.

A massive crack extended diagonally across it about halfway up, reaching from one side to the other. The upper part of the door had broken free of the substantial stone frame, falling into the hallway in front of it and shattering into several pieces. The lower portion was still intact, but as Ian crept closer and pointed the flashlight beam at it, he could see a darkening at the edge that looked almost as if it had been burned. A faint, acrid smell filled the space, along with the dust hovering in the air.

Whatever had happened here, it had happened recently—and could easily have been the source of the crash Ian had heard from upstairs.

Except…how could it have been? How could he possibly have heard even something this heavy hitting the ground from halfway across the house?

Unable to stop himself, even though he knew his wisest course of action now would be to go back upstairs and call his father, Ian took another tentative step forward, holding the flashlight out in front of him like a sword. His shield flickered around him; he hoped it would be sufficient to handle anything that might choose to attack him. He felt suddenly cold, and the "watching" sensation increased even further. Was it coming from inside whatever was behind the broken door?

Beyond the door, the room was nearly empty.

Ian shined the light around, picking out the confines of a small room, its walls made of the same rough stone as the rest of the cavern. In the center lay the blasted remains of what looked like a featureless stone box.

Ian swallowed. A coffin? It looked about the right size, but there was nothing ornate or fancy about it. Merely a possibly human-sized stone box, its shattered pieces spread out over the floor as if someone had set off a bomb inside it.

He took another step forward, but didn't enter the chamber. Something else caught his eye: it was difficult to see, but it appeared that all the surfaces in the chamber—walls, floor, and ceiling—were covered with writing. Small, precisely drawn symbols, sigils, and runes had been carefully placed in straight vertical lines, as if someone had run out of paper and decided to write out their thoughts on the walls around them.

"What the hell…" Ian breathed, leaning in to try to get a better look. Almost an afterthought, he switched to magical sight.

The writing didn't light up, which was what he'd expected, but faint traces of magic floated around the interior of the chamber. Something magical had been here. But what?

Behind him, an ear-splitting shriek rang out.

Ian whirled around, reinforcing his shield and raising his hands to prepare a spell. What was going on? Who had screamed?

More screams joined the first. It sounded like a cacophony of tortured souls all shrieking their agony at once. They bounced off the walls, reverberated, sometimes joining for a moment into a head-cracking blast of sound before each veered back off into its own key of misery.

Ian jammed his hands to his ears, but it didn't help. The unrelenting noise penetrated his head and rose once again in volume, almost as if they'd originated from there. Sometimes he thought he could pick out words, but not intelligibly enough to understand them.

He had only one thought now: he had to get out of here. Perhaps if he could get back upstairs, the shrieking would cease. He could call Dad and tell him what was going on, and the two of them could check it out together. Dad would know what to do.

Loud banging joined the shrieks. Ian picked up his pace, erupting back into the circular center room and flinging the flashlight beam wildly around to search for the passage that would take him back to the way upstairs.

Something was wrong with the floor. It was black instead of gray, and it was—

Moving?

The beam stilled on one spot long enough for him to get a good look, and his whole body went rigid.

The entire room was full of spiders.

They seethed along the ground like a black carpet, climbed up the walls, nearly covered the pedestal in the middle of the circle. Where the light picked them out, Ian could see glowing, multi-faceted eyes on some of the larger ones as they oriented on the beam and began crawling over each other in their haste to reach him.

"No!" he shouted, unwilling to wade into that roiling, multi-legged mass of terror in his stocking feet. He raised his hands, gathering magical energy to him, and then flung it out in a wide beam.

The smell was horrific. The energy drove the spiders backward in a wave, burning them until the stench of their cooking bodies made Ian's eyes water and his gorge rise. Too late, he remembered his levitation spell, and used it to lift him over the smoldering carpet, trying not to look at their twitching legs as the live ones tried to stand on top of the dead ones to reach him. Several more dropped from the ceiling, getting in his hair, dropping down his shirt, even landing on his face.

He clawed at them, flinging them aside.

How could they get past his shield?

Were they illusions?

It didn't matter. Even if they were, he couldn't break through them. His heart pounded harder as he floated past the first alcove on his way to the passageway.

More shrieks tumbled out of the alcove—and then blood poured out as well. As if some giant had emptied a bucket of the stuff down at the far end, it flowed out of the narrow opening and engulfed the closest wave of spiders, bearing them upward, forming a grotesque spider soup as the creatures waved their legs in a desperate attempt to swim.

Ian, fighting the urge to panic, didn't spend much time looking at them. Instead, he propelled himself forward into the passage leading back to the entrance chamber. Miraculously, he'd still managed to hang on to the flashlight; as he floated by, he couldn't help noticing the blood was following him. It crawled up the walls, forming interlocking words that kept pace with him, almost as if they wanted him to see them. He caught glimpses of some of the words as he flew by:

GET OUT
MURDERERS
DIE

The words kept forming, dripping like something out of a horror movie as he at last reached the entrance chamber. Without hesitating, he launched himself upward through the hole in the floor, nearly slamming into the ceiling in his haste to escape.

As soon as his feet hit solid ground, he leaped over the barrier tape and backed up, unable to resist the temptation to look back and see if anything had followed him up out of the hole.

The blood, as impossible as it had to be, was crawling out behind him, its red tendrils creeping, seeking, flowing across the floor.

Panting, his whole body surging with adrenaline and terror, Ian dashed out of the room, slammed the door shut, and took off at a run toward the stairway leading to the ground floor.

The shrieks did not stop.

They didn't even decrease in volume.

They came from all around him now—inside his head, echoing from the walls, swirling and racing around him.

Along the hall where he ran, doors opened and slammed shut repeatedly. As he ran by, he caught glimpses of unearthly glows from inside some of the rooms.

What the hell is going on?

He burst free of the east hallway into the great room and skidded to a stop, looking around wildly for some idea of what to do, but the shrieking in his head prevented coherent thought. He could make out some of the words now, the same ones that had appeared in blood on the walls of the downstairs passageway: *"Get out!"* and *"Murderers!"* and *"Evil!"* and *"Die!"* but the words were nearly lost amid the incoherent screaming. From somewhere far away, crazy, tuneless piano notes began to sound—*did his father even* own *a piano?* A freezing wind whipped from the hallway behind Ian, chilling the fear-sweat that bathed his body.

A loud *pop* sounded ahead as one of the chandeliers that lit the great room exploded, pattering shards of glass down on Ian like deadly rain. His shield blocked them, but he quickly leaped aside so he wasn't standing beneath the others in case they did the same. A moment later both did, plunging the room into near-darkness. In Ian's hand, his flashlight flickered as its batteries failed.

Still panting, he flung it aside and pulled the other one from his pocket. "Stop it!" he screamed, trying to get over the other shrieks, but they only grew louder to compensate. A series of books flew off the shelves and pelted him, their covers flapping like insane birds around his head. Ahead, a pair of crossed swords yanked free from a wall display and streaked toward him. He dived behind a heavy couch, not trusting his shield to fully stop them, and one of them embedded itself in the other side, its point poking through and missing Ian by scant inches.

Get out!

Go!

You don't belong here!

Murderers!

Ian crouched there behind the sofa, his hands jammed to his ears. *That's it,* he thought desperately. *They want me out, I'm out. Dad can deal with this.*

More books pelted him, followed by a series of logs from the cold fireplace, as he ran toward the front door. He was half afraid the shrieking horrors wouldn't let him out as he scrabbled at the knob, but the door opened so readily that he nearly fell over backward when he encountered no resistance.

Half-crazed with fear and confusion as the voices still did not quiet, Ian did the first thing he thought of: he took off across the yard toward the cemetery, throwing desperate glances over his shoulder as if expecting a pack of fiends to be following him. All he saw was the hulking house, eerie lights flickering off and on from all the windows. He thought he caught a brief glimpse of more blood running down from the eaves, but he didn't stop long enough to verify it.

Instead, he flung open the door to the mausoleum, pulled the cover off the center crypt, and threw himself down the stairs to the portal. To his relief it was there, beautiful as ever, its pastel colors shifting and dancing as if nothing was out of the ordinary.

For a moment his panic rose as the shrieking prevented him from visualizing the calibration, but then he remembered his father resetting it to the London house after they'd arrived earlier today. Hoping that was still true but certain he'd go crazy if he couldn't get away from the hellish screams, he plunged into the portal.

Instantly, the shrieks stopped, replaced by the familiar foggy, silent tunnel. Still, he didn't stop. He kept running until he reached the other end and popped free, staggering and dropping to his knees to the floor.

He fell forward to lean on his arms, his back heaving with his terrified breathing. He didn't recognize the room, since he'd never been to Stone's London house before, but he didn't care where he was as long as the insanity back at the mansion had stopped. Wherever he was now it was quiet, so quiet after the previous noise that Ian's head pounded with it.

He wasn't sure how long he remained there on his hands and knees, panting, letting his heart rate return to something close to normal and his breathing calm. It was cold here; his sweating body shivered in it, but he didn't care about that right now.

I've got to call Dad. That was the only thought that reliably poked through his jumble of confusion and terror. *He'll know what to do.*

God, I hope *he knows what to do.*

CHAPTER SIX

"WHAT DO YOU MEAN, there's something wrong at the house?"

Stone turned away from the wedding guests, hoping no one had noticed the sudden concern on his face. "Ian, calm down. What are you talking about? Why are you in London?"

"It's...the house..." Ian still spoke between panting breaths. "Something's wrong. In the basement."

"The basement?" Stone clenched his hand around the phone and hardened his voice. "Ian. Calm down. Now. Tell me what's going on."

Silence crackled on the line for a few seconds, and Stone could almost picture his son pulling himself together.

"I heard something," Ian said at last. "I got up to get something from the kitchen, and I heard a crash. Sounded like it came from the east wing. So I went to investigate."

"What did you find?" Stone glanced around at the hall. So far, it didn't seem that anyone had noticed him, but he hurried to calm his aura. Eddie and Ward would spot trouble immediately, and he didn't want anything to distract him from Ian now. "Did someone try to break in?"

"No. Well—I don't think so." More puffing breaths. "It was in the basement, Dad. Down where we were today. Something broke that carved door. Broke it right in half."

"Bloody hell." Stone's blood chilled. "You went down there? I thought you promised—"

"I *did*. I'm sorry—I just wanted to make sure nothing was wrong down there. But Dad—something *is* wrong. Very wrong. Screaming, illusions, spiders, blood—"

"Ian!" Once again Stone cut him off sharply, even though his own terror was growing. "Explain!"

"I can't!" He sounded miserable now. "They were screaming in my head. Blood running down the walls, and they were throwing things at me—I got out of there. I didn't know what else to do. I couldn't fight them with magic. I ran. Took the portal up here to your London place. That's where I am now."

"All right—all right. I'll—" As Stone cast another glance around, looking for Imogen, another thought struck him, sending more terror slicing through his body. "Ian! Where's Aubrey?"

"What?"

"Aubrey!" He was practically yelling now, his heart pounding. "Does he know about this? Did you leave him there?"

"Dad, I—"

"You *left* him *behind*?" Stone felt as if something was squeezing his head. "Something's attacking the house and you didn't think to *warn* him?" He knew he sounded harsh, but right now, the thought of the defenseless Aubrey being savaged by some kind of magical threat nearly paralyzed him with fear.

"Dad—"

"Stay there. Stay right there. Do *not* do anything else, and don't leave the house. Do you understand?"

"Dad—"

"*Do you understand, Ian?*" His voice had pitched louder now, and nearby people were throwing odd, concerned looks his way.

"Yes. I understand." Resignation and misery shot through his voice.

"All right. Good. I'll call you in a few minutes. I'm leaving here now, but it will take me some time to get back."

Without waiting for a reply, he hit the button to end the call, then immediately made another one. Heart thudding like a drum solo in his chest, he forced himself to drive down the horrific images that kept rising in his mind. He moved off down an unused hallway, hoping Imogen's crowd would be too genteel and well-bred to follow him when he obviously wanted privacy.

The phone rang once, twice, three times, and in the few seconds' space between each ring Stone's terror grew with exponential intensity. "Come on…come on…" he muttered. "Answer…please answer…"

"Hello?" The voice on the other end sounded bleary and confused, as if its owner had just been awakened from sleep.

"Aubrey!" He *was* yelling now as relief overwhelmed him.

"Sir? Is that you?" The caretaker still sounded drowsy.

"Oh, dear gods, Aubrey, it's good to hear your voice! Are you all right?"

"Sir? Er—of course. Why wouldn't I be?" A pause. "Where are you? Are you still at Miss Desmond's wedding? Is something wrong?"

Stone sagged against the wall. "You're all right? Nothing's going on?"

"Sir, please. I don't understand. Of course I'm all right. I was doing some reading in my flat, and I must have dozed off. Please tell me what's going on."

"You didn't hear anything? Screams? Breaking glass? Nothing?"

Silence hung in the air again. "Er—no. No, sir, nothing like that. Are you all right? What makes you think—"

"Ian rang me. He's in London now. He said something went wrong in the cellar, and it drove him out of the house. He took the portal to London and contacted me from there."

"*What*?"

"I don't know. I'm bloody angry with him right now, to be honest—that he'd run off and leave you there if there was danger."

"But sir—there isn't any danger. At least not here. Do you want me to go to the house and—"

"*No!*" Stone was shouting again. "No," he repeated, more quietly this time. "Don't go anywhere near that house. Just— I'm leaving now." He glanced at his watch: it was barely after ten-thirty. "I need to go to London to find Ian. Should take me an hour and a half or so. Traffic shouldn't be bad this time of night. Listen, Aubrey: I want you to pack an overnight bag and go down to the village. Get yourself a room for the night, or call one of your mates. Have a drink, enjoy yourself, but stay away from the house. Will you do that for me? I'll ring you again as soon as I can."

"Sir—"

"No arguments. I mean it. I can't get a clear story out of Ian, but he's terrified. I don't want you anywhere near whatever's going on up there. Do it now. Can I count on you?"

"Of course, sir." Aubrey sounded resigned, and not at all happy about it.

"Promise me you won't pop over to the house for a look."

"I—I promise. I'll go now."

"Good man. And take your mobile with you. Is it even charged?"

"Yes, sir, I just put it on before I settled in to read."

"Good, good. I'll see you soon."

He jammed the phone in his pocket and hurried back out into the main hall. Everything looked so *normal,* with people dancing, standing around in little groups drinking champagne, or seated at the small, elegantly-decorated tables dotting the area to the side of the dance floor.

He quickly spotted Imogen on the other side of the room, near the head table. She stood next to Clifford, chatting with a small group of elderly guests. He hurried over to them, slowing as he approached, forcing himself to project calm. Whatever catastrophe was currently unfolding back home, he didn't need to disturb Imogen's evening with it.

She looked up as he approached, and despite his efforts, he could see from her expression she'd caught on that something was wrong. She said something to the group of guests, patted Clifford's arm, and moved off toward the other end of the table to meet Stone.

"Alastair, are you all right?"

"I'm—fine. But I'm afraid something's come up back at the house, and I need to see to it. I'm terribly sorry to dash out early, but—"

"Something's come up?" Her eyes narrowed. "Is it serious? Is there anything I can—"

He forced a smile. "You're a dear to offer, Moggy, but it's nothing you can help with. I was just talking to Aubrey, and I've got to go."

She didn't look as if she entirely believed him, but she dropped her gaze. "I understand, of course. Thank you so much for coming. It meant so much to me, and to Clifford, to have you here."

Stone doubted his presence had registered on Clifford Blakeley much at all, but he took her hand. "You two have a lovely honeymoon. We'll talk again when you return. I've got some things I want to share with you, but they can wait."

Imogen tilted her head. "I'm looking forward to hearing them." She pulled him into a hug, her slim arms going around his waist and squeezing hard. "You take care of yourself, Alastair. Promise me. You haven't had too much to drink, have you?"

He chuckled, returning the hug more gently. "No, I've been good tonight." He bent to kiss the top of her head, the old, fond gesture that always used to amuse and exasperate her because it emphasized how much taller he was. "I'll see you soon."

Pulling back, he caught Clifford's eye and nodded a farewell, then hurried off. With luck, he could get out before anyone else tried to stop him to chat again.

"Oi, Stone!"

Stone sighed, slowing again as Eddie Monkton came up next to him. He held a pint from the bar, and his tie was already beginning to wilt. Eddie was not the sort who coped well with formal wear. "Hello, Eddie. I was just leaving, I'm afraid. Something's come up back home."

"Oh?" He nodded toward Arthur Ward, who was watching them from nearby while chatting with a woman in a green cocktail dress. "You're not foolin' anybody, mate. Ward and I both saw your aura before you 'id it. This is more than 'somethin's come up,' innit?"

Damn his perceptive friends, anyway. But there was no point in trying to lie about it. "Bit more, yes. I was actually planning to talk to you both about it tomorrow, but it seems it's got other ideas." He checked his watch, then threw another glance toward the door. "But I can't do it now. No time. The short version is that we discovered a hidden area under the house. Sort of like catacombs. And now something's apparently gone wrong in it."

The way Eddie's eyes lit up with curiosity, both professional and personal, was almost comical. "That right? Magic down there?"

"Quite probably. Eddie, I can't stay. Something attacked Ian while I was out. He's in London now, and I need to get to him while the story's still fresh. I'll ring you tomorrow. I could use some help when I go back there to have a look around."

"Try to keep me away, mate." Eddie clapped him on the shoulder. "I'll give Ward the details and we'll be waiting to 'ear from you."

Nobody else tried to intercept Stone as he departed the hall. He waited with growing impatience for the valet to bring his car around, then practically hustled the young man out of the driver's seat, shoving a large tip into his hand before roaring off through the gate.

As soon as he got on the road, he called Ian back and put the phone on speaker as it rang.

The boy answered nearly instantly, as if he had been staring at his phone waiting for Stone's call. "Dad? Is Aubrey all right?"

A little of Stone's anger at Ian's thoughtlessness abated at his words. "He's fine. I told him to go into the village and get a room for the night. But he claims not to have seen or heard anything."

"That's—hard to believe. Whatever was down there was screaming so loud I couldn't even block it out by covering my ears." His voice still shook a little, but he sounded calmer than he had before.

"All right. Tell me what happened. Don't leave anything out. I'm driving now—should be there in a couple of hours." Not for the first time, Stone wished magical science provided the means to teleport from any location to any other. The portals were convenient if you were near them, but they did him no good when traveling from somewhere that didn't have any.

"I told you, I went downstairs to get something to eat, and I heard a crash. So I decided to—"

A loud crackle of static obscured his next words.

"—screaming."

Damn. "Ian, I didn't get that. Can you say again?"

"I said, I went down through the hole to take a quick look, and—"

More static.

Bugger it. Mobiles were useful things…until they weren't. "Ian, listen—we've got a dodgy connection here. Just sit tight and wait for me, and you can tell me the whole story when I get there."

"Yeah. Okay." Disappointment and frustration laced his voice. "I—"

The line beeped as the connection broke.

Stone glared at the device on the passenger seat and goosed the accelerator, nudging the little convertible up to significantly above the speed limit. As he drove, he tried not to entertain the thought that something other than the usual patchy cellular coverage had caused the interference on the line.

| CHAPTER SEVEN

I T TOOK STONE NEARLY TWO HOURS to get back to London, and by the time he pulled the convertible into the underground garage at the Kensington house, he was nearly seething with tension and impatience. He dashed up the stairs, already yelling, "Ian!"

Ian emerged into the hall from the main sitting room. Even after all this time he still looked disheveled and pale, but relief wreathed his features. "Dad. Damn, I'm glad to see you."

"Are you all right?" Stone looked him over, using both mundane and magical sight. One of Ian's strongest talents was aura manipulation, but right now he was making no effort to use it. His potent silver-and-purple aura roiled and sparked with red flashes of disturbance. Whatever he'd seen back at the house had spooked him hard.

"Yeah. Dad, I'm sorry—I shouldn't have left Aubrey there. But—"

"You're right. You shouldn't. But he's fine, so no harm this time. Come on." He stalked off down the hall.

"Come on—where?"

"Back to the Surrey house. I want to see what's going on down there."

"Dad—wait!"

Stone stopped and turned back. Ian hadn't moved. "What?"

"You—want to go *back* there? Tonight?"

"Of course I do." He struggled to keep the impatience from his tone. "If something's going on in my house, I want to know what it is."

"Yeah. I get that. But—shouldn't you sit down for a few minutes? Let me tell you what happened? Shouldn't you be prepared before you go down there?"

Stone didn't miss the fact that Ian had said 'you' instead of 'we,' but he let it go for now. "Fine. I need a drink anyway." He changed direction, heading for the liquor cabinet. "Talk fast, though. I *am* going down there tonight, and you're coming with me."

Ian waited until Stone had gotten a drink, then joined his father in pacing the room. "This is—I don't even know where to start."

"Start at the beginning. And don't leave anything out."

Stone listened with growing tension as Ian described his trip down to the subterranean chamber, the cracked stone door, the spiders and blood and screaming, and his final desperate escape through the portal. By the time the boy finished, obviously trying to keep his voice from shaking and just as obviously still rattled by the evening's events, Stone was willing to cut him a little more slack for leaving Aubrey behind. He had to keep reminding himself that despite his two years of training, Ian had very little experience with dangerous real-world magic beyond the limited bits Trin Blackburn had taught him to further her own vengeful plans.

"Okay," he said, resisting the urge to pour another drink. He'd need to have his wits about him tonight. "So you're saying whatever was there was throwing things at you? Are you sure they were real? The spiders and blood and whatnot sound like illusion to me."

"I don't know." Ian flung himself down on the nearest sofa. "I don't know if some of it was illusion, or all of it, or none. But it doesn't make sense to have that much blood and that many spiders showing up. I mean, the whole floor in that circular room was a solid carpet of them."

Stone thought back to his and Zack Beeler's ill-fated trip to Thalassa Nera's New York City apartment. "The spiders probably were illusions. I've seen similar ones. But I won't know for sure until I've seen it for myself." He slammed the glass down on a table. "You said you made out some words in the screams?"

"Yeah. I think so, anyway. It sounded like they were saying things like *'Get out,'* and *'You don't belong here,'* and *'Murderer.'* I didn't get a good look at what they were writing in the blood, but I did see similar stuff."

"So they were trying to drive you off."

"Not just drive me off. They blew up the chandeliers in the main hall, and threw books and logs from the fireplace at me. If I hadn't had my shield up, I'd probably be dead." Ian clenched his fists and met Stone's gaze. "Dad, is it possible the place is haunted? I was talking to Aubrey earlier and he said he's never seen any ghosts, or—he called them something else."

"Echoes. And no, it's not. I've lived in that house since I was born, and I've never seen an echo there. Neither has Aubrey, and he's been there a lot longer than I have."

"Yeah, but…" Ian sounded troubled.

"But what?"

"Well—what if there *are* ghosts, or echoes, or whatever, and they were stuck behind that broken door? What if they got out when it broke, and now they're pissed about something?"

Stone was about to dismiss the idea, but stopped before he spoke. *Was* it possible? After all, Thaddeus Benchley's echo had lain dormant for years in his home back in Encantada, only showing himself when a magically talented resident moved in. Echoes could be imprisoned, with the proper magic. If some powerful entity had been entombed behind that elaborately carved door, breaking the door could have released it.

But who—or what—had broken the door?

"Ian…" he said carefully, moving to stand over his son.

"Yeah?"

"Are you sure you didn't go down into those passageways tonight? Just to have a quick look around?"

"No, Dad. I already told you—I didn't go until I heard the noise. I just wanted to figure out where it came from."

"I promise, I won't say anything if you did. But if you disturbed that door—"

Ian glared at him. "I *told* you," he insisted, "I didn't. Check my aura if you don't believe me. That door was already broken when I went down. I think that was what I heard."

Stone waved him off, and didn't check his aura. "No, I believe you. Come on. Let's go have a look." When Ian hesitated, he waved him up from the sofa. "Come on—it will be fine. I know this all looks fairly terrifying, but I can handle echoes."

"If that's what they are."

"True. But even if they're not, I need to figure out what they are so we can get rid of them. I'm not handing my house over to a pack of magical bullies."

"What about Aubrey? Should you call him?"

"Let him sleep. As far as he knows, nothing's wrong and I've gone mad for waking him up and sending him away in the middle of the night."

"Why do you suppose that is?" Ian mused as he followed Stone back to the portal room.

"What?"

"Why do you think they didn't attack Aubrey?"

"No idea. He didn't enter the house, or the underground chamber. Maybe that's what triggered it."

They reached the portal, and once again Ian hesitated.

Stone paused in front of the shifting pastel doorway and turned back to his son. With reluctance, he said, "Look—you can stay here if you like. I'm expecting a lot of you when you've got no experience with this kind of thing. It's up to you."

For just a second, it appeared Ian would take him up on the offer. But then he pulled himself up straight and his expression hardened. "No. I'm coming. This is the kind of thing I have to learn to deal with. And I'm still pissed at myself that I freaked out and didn't even think about Aubrey. Let's go."

Stone clapped him on the shoulder. "Brilliant. Keep your shield up and stay close to me."

The Overworld didn't look any different as they stepped through the portal. Stone half expected something to jump them the instant they exited a few seconds later into the room below the mausoleum, but nothing did. He took point, shield at full strength as he mounted the ladder upward, noting that the cover was off the crypt in the room's center. "Did you leave this open?"

"Yeah. Sorry. Like I said, I was a little freaked out."

Stone scrambled out and stood aside for Ian to do likewise, then moved the cover back into place. "I don't see anything yet. Do you?"

"No." He looked around. "You don't think it was...all in my head, do you? Could that be why Aubrey didn't hear anything?"

"That's part of what I want to find out."

Outside in the chilly, pre-dawn air, the small cemetery looked peaceful and undisturbed. Stone buttoned his jacket; he wished he'd paused to change out of his evening clothes before heading down here, but it couldn't be helped now. "Do you see anything? Hear anything?"

"Nothing."

"Right, then. Stay close."

Stone set off at a fast stride toward the house, his shield glowing around him, and Ian followed. As they drew up closer to the structure, he switched to magical sight.

And stopped, so quickly that Ian nearly slammed into him from behind.

"Bloody hell..." he breathed.

All around the massive bulk of the mansion, an eerie, sickly pale-green glow flickered and danced, picking out the outlines of the roof, the chimneys, and the walls. A brighter version of the same glow issued from the windows. As he continued to watch, bits of red seeped around the edges and crawled outward.

"That's...not my imagination, is it?" Ian asked softly from behind him.

"No. No, that is not."

Stone sharpened his arcane vision, trying to make sense of the glow. It had been a while since he'd studied his house with magical sight, but he was certain whatever this was hadn't been there before. Even being near it made him uncomfortable, his skin prickling and the little hairs on the back of his neck standing at full attention.

"What are you going to do?"

"Stay here. I'm going inside to have a look around."

"No way am I staying here," Ian protested. "I'm not letting you go in there by yourself. Besides, I don't really want to stand out in the yard like an idiot either."

Pleased at his son's newfound courage, Stone nodded. "All right. We'll go in together. Quick magic lesson: shield is priority one. Do *not* let it slip, no matter what you see. If it's real, the shield will block it. If it's illusion and you believe it, the shield will still block it. And if it's illusion and you *don't* believe it, it won't matter anyway."

"Got it. Let's go before I lose my nerve."

Together, they walked forward toward the front door. Stone wasn't striding fast now, but maintaining a steady pace. He continued to watch with magical sight as they approached, and immediately noticed that the closer they got to the door, the more the creeping red continued to replace the eerie green. By the time they reached the top of the steps, the green had faded entirely.

"You see that, right?" Ian asked. "The way it's changing color?"

"I do." Stone made no move to open the door yet.

"What do you think it means?"

"Nothing good, most likely. Keep your eyes open."

He used magic to open the front-door lock, once again half expecting something to resist him. Once again, nothing did. The door swung open on the dark entryway. Stone scanned the area beyond first with mundane sight and saw nothing but darkness. When he shifted back to magical sight, though, the red glow sprang up all around inside.

"Hmm. Stops at the threshold. Another data point. Let me go in first."

Ian didn't seem inclined to argue with that, so he took a careful step across the threshold and moved into the entry hall.

Immediately, the house erupted with shrieks and screams, seeming to come from everywhere at once. A pair of vases rocketed from tables on either side of the room and slammed into Stone's shield, then hit the floor and exploded into shards.

"Shit!" Ian snapped, backpedaling. "It's not just my imagination!"

Stone didn't back up. His shield seemed to be holding against the physical attacks, though the screaming voices grew louder with each step he took. He couldn't tell if they were in his head or coming from inside the house, but either way they threatened to split his brain.

He paused, trying to fight past the cacophony in his mind to make sense of the screams. It was difficult, but after a few seconds the caterwauling wails resolved themselves into coherent speech:

Get out!

You don't belong here!

Murderer!

Betrayer!

A curse on your line!

Evil!

GO!

Both entryway windows shattered in an explosion of glass, and then the entire room was drenched in blood. It poured from the ceiling, crawled down the walls, and coated Stone's shield. From the floor, the rug rose up and snaked around him, pressing against the shield.

"Dad! Get out of there!"

Get out!

Murrrrdererrrrrr!

Oouuuuutttt!

Stone lashed out with magical energy, projecting pure waves of Calanarian power outward from the shield. The blood-soaked rug shredded into pieces, flying out and slapping with wet *thwack*s into the walls, mingling with the shards of glass from the blown windows and the shattered vases.

"Dad, look out!"

Stone ducked just in time to avoid a heavy end table streaking toward him. It crashed into the far wall and it too fell to pieces. Another small table shot out the door and smacked into Ian's shield, staggering him backward and sending him tumbling down the steps.

"Ian!" Stone spun, dashing to where his son had fallen. More objects, smaller now, flew through the open door and crashed around them.

Ian was already scrambling back up. "What the hell is going *on* in there?" he demanded, throwing himself sideways to dodge a heavy flying lamp. Off to their right, another window exploded outward.

"Come on." Stone grabbed Ian's arm and set off at a fast walk back toward the cemetery. The screaming voices still pounded in his head, but no more objects pelted them as they moved further from the house.

"Are we *leaving*? I thought you said you wanted to—"

"I do. But we're not going to get anywhere without more preparation. We'll head back to London tonight, and ring Eddie and Ward in the morning." Stone kept moving; when it was obvious Ian was following, he let go of his arm.

Ian eyed the cemetery nervously, but nothing rose from any of the graves and attacked them. It wasn't until they'd descended the steps in the mausoleum and stepped out of the portal at the London house that he spoke again. "Do you have any idea what caused that? I mean, aside from the obvious—it's got to have something to do with opening that space under the house, right?"

"Almost certainly." Stone paused, trying to think now that the voices weren't shrieking in his head anymore. "But what I'm more interested in is what caused that heavy door to crack. It was clearly holding *something* prisoner, but what? And why would it get out after all these years it's been buried? Just because we broke through the floor into the chamber doesn't mean we broke the seal on that chamber.

Unless there was some magic holding the whole thing together, and we disturbed it."

"Sounded like a lot of somethings in there." Ian pulled a comb from his back pocket and ran it through his hair. "You heard the voices, right? It didn't sound like just one."

"No, you're right. It sounded like quite a lot of them."

"So you think they were *all* imprisoned behind that door?"

Stone sighed. "I have no bloody idea. What I want is to get down there and have a look, without having the house fall down around my ears."

"Don't you have any kind of magical protection you can use to keep them from attacking us?"

"Possibly, but it will take some research. I've never encountered echoes this violent before, nor in these kinds of numbers."

They headed upstairs, and Ian began to pace. "What do you think they want? I thought I heard them saying things like 'Murderers,' and 'Get out.' Do they think *we're* murderers?" He froze. "I killed Bobby—so I guess I *am* a murderer. But how would they know about that?"

"Both of us are, by those standards," Stone said grimly. "But you're right—why would a load of echoes that have been buried possibly for centuries care about that sort of thing?" He paused, stiffening. "Wait a moment."

"What?"

His knees went weak as another thought hit him. He staggered over to the liquor cabinet and poured a stiff shot, then let himself sink down to the nearest chair. "I don't know if you heard it, but right before we got out of there, one of them said something different. Something like, 'A curse on your line.'"

"I must have missed that one. It felt like my head was going to crack in two. But what do you think it means?"

Stone stared into the golden liquid, swirling it in the glass before tossing it back. "Remember I told you before that our ancestors weren't very nice people?"

"Yeah. You said they were really dark mages. But—"

"I didn't tell you everything." This wasn't the way Stone would have wanted to reveal this information to his son, but at this point he had little choice. Without meeting Ian's gaze, he said, "Our ancestors—everyone from my grandfather back at least six generations, were very powerful, and very nasty. They did a lot of dark rituals to power their magic, and at least some of them involved human sacrifices."

Ian stared at him in shock. "You're kidding." But then he quickly added, "No, you're not. So…you think these ghosts, or echoes, or whatever, are what's left of the people they sacrificed?"

"It makes sense." Unable to remain still, Stone got up and began pacing again. "They said 'a curse on your line'…that makes sense if my family—*our* family—murdered them in black-magic rituals."

Ian swallowed. "Are…you sure? How do you know this?"

"I found some papers a while back, hidden in one of the crypts in the mausoleum. They detailed a lot of what happened back around the time the house was built. Back then, not many people noticed or cared when foreign travelers or poor people or prostitutes went missing. Nobody looked for them, and even if they did, they rarely found them. Apparently, our ancestors took advantage of that to provide a steady stream of sacrificial victims for the rituals they used to gain more power."

"Wow." Ian ran both hands back through his spiky hair. "So…you're thinking they must have killed them in these rituals and then buried their bodies in that hidden area under the house? Maybe in those little bricked-up alcoves?"

"Possibly. But that doesn't make sense. Did you notice any of those broken when you went down there?"

"No. I only went down the hallway we checked today, though, and then checked the one with the carved door. That's when things started happening and I got my ass out of there."

Stone contemplated pouring another drink, but decided against it. It was already almost dawn—not exactly the time to be getting drunk. "If you're right about that carved door being broken—"

"I saw it, Dad. I'm sure of it."

"Yes, but illusions can be tricky. Anyway, let's assume for the moment that you're right—you really *did* see it broken. If so, then it makes sense whatever's in the house came out of there, not from the alcoves."

"Maybe it's both. Maybe whatever was behind the door was part of what kept the stuff in the alcoves under wraps."

Stone nodded in approval. "Good thought, and definitely worth investigating—*if* we can even get in there to have a look." He sighed and glanced at his watch. "For now, though, it makes sense to try getting a bit of sleep. I don't want to wake Eddie and Ward at the crack of dawn, and it seems the place is only causing trouble when someone's around. I think it's safe to wait until morning."

"What about Verity? Do you want to get her involved in this?"

"I don't want to take her attention off the case she's on with Jason. She said she'd call me when she's done." He waved Ian off. "Go on, now. Find one of the bedrooms you like and try to sleep. I know this whole night's been a bit harrowing for you."

"That's kind of an understatement. But—and don't take this wrong—it's kind of intriguing, too, don't you think?"

Stone turned away to hide his smile. This night might have gone to hell in a serious way, but it was nice to see that apparently Ian truly *was* turning out to be his son.

| CHAPTER EIGHT

S URPRISINGLY, Stone did manage to get some sleep. He woke to his phone buzzing on the nightstand, and for a moment the unfamiliar location confused him until he remembered he was at the London house. He snatched it up and instantly recognized the number.

"Aubrey." He glanced at his watch: a little after eight a.m. "Are you all right?"

"Yes, sir. Are *you*? Where are you?"

"In London, with Ian."

"Are you...feeling better today, sir?"

"That's a hard question to answer."

"I trust you took care of whatever the problem was at the house? You must have been there last night."

"I was, and no, not yet. Something's up, Aubrey. I want you to stay away from there until I let you know it's safe. Perhaps it's a good time for you to take a holiday, or go visit some relatives for a while."

There was a pause. "Sir..."

"No arguments, Aubrey. Whatever's there is dangerous, and I don't want you getting hurt."

Another pause. "Dangerous, sir? I...I don't know what you mean. I was just there this morning."

"*What?*" Stone gripped the phone harder. "Aubrey, I told you to stay away—"

"I know, sir. And I'm sorry. But I left so quickly last night that I forgot several things I needed, and I remembered one of the gardeners was supposed to be there this morning. He doesn't have a mobile, and I didn't want him walking in on something that might injure him, so I decided to risk a quick trip."

Stone sighed. Aubrey was a stubborn old man, and he'd have a good laugh at anybody who thought he followed "orders". "Are you there now?"

"No, I'm back in the village. But I was there less than an hour ago, and…sir, I didn't encounter anything out of the ordinary."

"You didn't?"

"Not a thing, sir."

"Did you go up to the house?"

"Yes, sir, through the back door near the kitchen."

Stone's blood chilled. "And nothing attacked you? You didn't hear screams, or feel odd in any way?"

"Sir—no. Nothing like that. I picked up what I needed from the kitchen and left the same way. Nothing seemed out of the ordinary at all."

"You didn't go near the great room or the front entryway?"

"No. I didn't need to. Should I have?"

"No," Stone said quickly. "What did you do then?"

Aubrey sounded like he wasn't sure what to make of Stone's strange questions. "I went back to my truck and left. I was able to intercept the gardener just as he came in the front gate. I told him he'd have to come back later, and I'd ring him when it was convenient."

Stone let his breath out and sat up. "Well…that's good news, at least."

"What did *you* see in there, sir?"

"I'm not entirely sure. For all I know, it could have all been illusion. I'm sure some of it was." He got up and pushed aside the heavy drapes to peer out the window. It was a gray day, but he didn't see any sign of rain.

"Sir…can you tell me anything else about what's going on? You said something about the cellar—"

"I don't know yet. Ian thought he heard something last night. He went down to the cellar to check, and discovered a door we'd found down there yesterday—a heavy, carved stone door—was broken in two."

"In…the cellar? I don't remember seeing any doors like that."

"Er—yes. I didn't tell you yet, but we found a whole network of passageways—catacombs, and some kind of ritual area, hidden under the floor down there."

"Dear *God*, sir!"

"I know. I'm sorry—I was trying to keep it under wraps until I had more time to explore it. Please don't mention it to anyone else. But after Ian went down there to investigate last night, he was attacked."

"Attacked? By what?"

"We don't know that either. My working theory is echoes."

"Echoes? You mean…ghosts, sir?" Aubrey sounded astonished.

"That's exactly what I mean. I'm not sure if the damage they've done is real, illusionary, or a combination of both. But it doesn't matter—either way, it's dangerous, and I don't want you in the middle of it."

Aubrey sighed. "What...are you going to do, sir? We can't simply avoid the house."

"No. We can't. I don't care what these things are, that place is mine and they're not driving me out of it. But I've got to figure out what they are, what they want, and how to get rid of them. Based on what they were screaming, I'm thinking they may have something to do with what my ancestors got up to."

"Your ancestors?"

"They said something to do with 'a curse on my line.' That makes me think it's related to my family somehow."

The line was silent for several seconds. "Perhaps that's why I wasn't affected, then."

Stone frowned. "What do you mean?"

"Well, sir, if whatever's going on up there is related to your family, perhaps that's why they attacked you and Ian, but not me."

He almost brushed that off, but then a tingle went through him. "Bloody hell, Aubrey, you might be on to something there. But I don't want to put you in danger by testing it."

"I was already inside the house, and nothing attacked me. I'm willing to chance it again, if you want to find out for sure."

"I'll—let you know. I don't like it. Listen, Aubrey—I need to make some other calls. Promise me you won't go anywhere near that house until I'm there. I need your word. I'd be gutted if anything happened to you because of my buggered-up family."

"I…promise, sir. I locked the gates, and I'm not expecting anyone else up there today. I'll ring the workmen and let them know they shouldn't come back to deal with the cellar tomorrow."

Stone pictured a flock of angry echoes pelting the innocent workers with household debris, and blood cascading down the walls. Even if they didn't get hurt, if that story got out to the world the place would be surrounded by camera crews before the day was over. "Good man. I'll see you soon."

He found Ian downstairs, seated at the dining room table with a large, white paper bag and two steaming to-go cups in front of him. He wore a snug-fitting T-shirt and jeans, and his hair was tousled. "Morning," he said. "I was just about to go looking for you." He nodded toward the items on the table. "I couldn't find anything in the kitchen, so I went out for some coffee. Have a croissant. They're still warm."

Stone frowned at the bag, which had a Paris address on the side. "Where did you go?"

Ian grinned. "Paris. There's this great little *pâtisserie* just down the street from where the portal is, so I just popped through. It was faster than trying to drive around here."

Stone shook his head in wonder and dropped down across from his son. He dragged a cup over and pulled a warm, sweet-smelling pastry from the bag.

"So," Ian said, "what's the plan?"

"I was just talking with Aubrey. He's bloody stubborn, but in this case it might have done us some good."

"How so?" Ian liberated a second croissant and took a big bite.

"He went to the house this morning, even though I told him not to. Said he needed to retrieve some things from the kitchen, so he went in through the back door. And nothing attacked him. He didn't see anything unusual at all."

"Huh. That's weird."

"It might not be. If the echoes have issue with our family, it might be that others who aren't related to us can go inside safely."

"You want to test that with Aubrey?"

"No, of course not. But *he* wants to. And I think he might have a point. You saw the energy around the place—it wasn't just at the front door, but covering the whole house. And he went right inside, neat as you please."

Ian tilted his head. "Maybe so. But even if he can do that, how will that help us? He can't go down in that hidden basement and look around. He'd break a leg or something trying to get down through the hole."

Before Stone could answer, his mobile rang again. He held up a finger as he pulled the phone out and recognized Verity's number. "Hello, Verity. How are you?"

"Hey, Doc. Doing great. How about you?"

Stone didn't reply. "How did your case go? Are you still in Texas?"

"No, we're back home now. It went *fantastic*. Couldn't ask for better. I used a ritual and it led us right to the kid. The kidnappers were trying to smuggle him into Mexico in the toolbox of a truck, but we called the cops, and the Mexican authorities nailed them as they tried to cross the border. The kid's fine, just a little shook up. He's back with his parents now."

Stone couldn't miss the wide grin in her tone. "That's brilliant, Verity. I'm so happy to hear it. And proud, too. Am I still allowed to be proud of you even though you're not my apprentice anymore?"

She laughed. "Sure. In this case, anyway. *I'm* proud of me, and so is Jason. He did good too—some great detective work to get us to the point where we could do the ritual, and coming up with a good cover story for how we figured out where the kid was. We were gonna go out and celebrate tonight. You want to join us? You can tell us all about Imogen's wedding."

"Er. Actually, something's come up. I'm still in England. I was wondering if you might come over here, if you don't have anything else planned in the next day or two."

"Is everybody okay?" Now concern laced her voice.

"Yes, everyone's fine. The wedding was lovely—it's not related to that. Imogen and Clifford are probably well on their way to the French Riviera by now. It's something at the house. We've discovered something nasty in the cellar."

"Something nasty? We?"

"Ian's here. We're at the London place right now. If you've got a few minutes, I'll catch you up."

"Sure, let's hear it."

He watched Ian nibble a croissant and sip coffee as he gave Verity an abbreviated rundown of what had occurred since yesterday afternoon. He left out the specifics about his family; she already knew they were a bad bunch, but he'd never given her all the details about the papers he'd found in the crypt at the mausoleum. He'd probably have to now, but thought it might be better to do it in person.

"Wow," she said at last, when he finished. "That's...pretty scary. So you can't go back to the house without getting attacked and screamed at?"

"Apparently not. But Aubrey went in without triggering anything. He thinks it might be related to my family, since he can get in and Ian and I can't. I'm inclined to believe him. He wants to test the hypothesis, but I'd rather not have him do it alone. I'd be much more comfortable if he had some backup. Specifically, magical backup."

"Uh—sure. I don't have anything with Scuro for a couple days, and I can postpone my lesson with Hezzie for a while. Want Jason to come too?"

"If he wants to. Do you think you can get him to come through the portal? I haven't got time to wait for you two to take a conventional flight."

"I'll see," she said dryly. "You know how he freaks out when we even mention it. Either way, I'll be there in a few hours. London portal?"

"Yes, don't take the one at the Surrey place until we're sure it's safe." He glanced at Ian again. "Thank you, Verity. I appreciate it."

"Hey, this is interesting stuff. I wouldn't miss it. See you soon."

| CHAPTER NINE

VERITY ARRIVED TWO HOURS LATER, with a nervous Jason gripping her shoulder as if expecting to plummet to his death if he let go.

She'd called just before they left, so Stone and Ian waited for them in the portal room. "Bravo, Jason," Stone said with a grin, offering an amused golf clap. "You must finally be developing some of your sister's curiosity."

"Shut up, Al," Jason muttered, sweeping a hand across his sweat-dotted forehead. "I don't like that fucking thing *one bit*." Like Verity he carried an overnight bag, and he also had a camera bag slung over his shoulder.

"You didn't have any trouble, did you?" Stone shifted to magical sight, examining Jason's aura. It looked disturbed, but within normal parameters for what he'd just done.

"It was fine," Verity assured him. "No problems at all. Jason's just a big scaredy-cat with no sense of adventure." She tugged herself away. "You can let go now, big bro. We're all safe and cozy in London."

He glared at her, but released his grip. Taking a deep breath, he scanned the room. "Hey, Ian," he greeted, and then his gaze settled on Stone. "So, what's the deal here? You dug up a secret hidden basement, and now your house is haunted?"

"That's about the size of it." He gave them both a few more details he hadn't told Verity over the phone as they trooped upstairs. "So," he finished when they reached the sitting room, "I'm thinking Verity and Aubrey can go in and check things out. Since the echoes don't seem to want Ian and me there, if they likewise don't want you two there I doubt you'll have much trouble getting out."

"What about me?" Jason asked. "You want me to go too?"

"Wait a sec," Verity said, laughing. "I can barely drag you through a perfectly safe travel portal, but exploring a haunted house is no problem?"

"I can fight back against stuff getting thrown at me," he growled. "We get stuck in that portal with those *things* and there's not much I can do about it."

"Hardly any *things* to worry about anymore," Stone said. "If you come along, though, you'll have to brave the portal again. I don't want to waste time taking the train down."

"Yeah, fine." He glanced at Ian. "You do this all the time, right?"

Ian looked amused. "Yeah. I've been all over the world. Nothing's eaten me yet." He waggled his eyebrows suggestively. "Not this week, anyway."

"Right, then," Stone said quickly. "Verity, are you up for it?"

"Oh, sure." She couldn't hide her sly smile at her brother's sudden uneasiness. "Jason, will you trust me? It takes about ten seconds to get from here to Surrey, and you'll have three mages with you. You'll barely notice it."

"Fine." He glared in Ian's direction, then shrugged and rolled his eyes. "Let's do it."

"Brilliant. I'll ring Aubrey and let him know we're coming."

❖

Aubrey met them outside the mausoleum. "Is everything all right, sir?"

"Fine." He nodded toward the tiny building, where Ian was following Verity and Jason out. "Looks like a bloody clown car in there. Have you seen anything odd since we spoke last?"

"No, sir. But I haven't been up to the house. Nothing's wrong at my flat, and I did a bit of work outside to keep busy. I haven't heard anyone screaming, and no one's thrown anything at me yet. I did take a look at the front of the house, though—from a reasonable distance," he added hastily when Stone opened his mouth to protest. "I saw some evidence of broken windows, and the front door is open."

"So it's likely not *all* illusion, then. Are you sure you want to do this? Jason and Verity could—"

A quiet dignity settled over the old caretaker as he shook his head. "No, sir. I want to. I've been looking after this place since before you were born. I'm taking it as a bit of a personal affront that something's trying to drive its master away. I want to get to the bottom of this as much as you do."

They walked through the cemetery and up to the circular driveway in front of the house. As Aubrey had said, half of the double front door yawned open, and the two windows on either side of it were both shattered. Stone switched to magical sight and was not at all surprised to see the green energy creeping around the edges and glowing from inside.

"Wow," Verity said. She'd obviously been doing the same thing. "That's freaky looking."

"What do you see?" Jason asked.

"It's like the place has its own weird aura. Like radioactive green. And it's worse inside." She turned away from the house and back toward Stone. "Echoes can do that?"

"There hasn't been a lot of definitive study about what echoes can and can't do. They're generally fairly mercurial, and don't like answering questions. But I've never seen an aura like that before, so that's new." He studied the house again and took a deep breath. The pulsing green light seemed unhealthy somehow, and he couldn't help envisioning it going red and swallowing his friends up if they went in there. "Perhaps we should take a few more readings before we—"

Verity touched his arm. "We'll be careful, Doc," she said softly. "But if you want to figure out what's going on in there, you need more data."

He knew she was right, even though he didn't want to admit it. "All right," he said with reluctance. "Just…take a quick look around. Keep going if nothing happens, but if you sense *anything* malevolent, get yourselves out. Promise me."

"Yeah. No problem."

"And stay in contact." Stone pulled out his mobile. "I want to know what you're seeing."

Aubrey produced his own phone, which Stone had insisted he get a few months ago. "I'll do that, sir. Best to let Miss Thayer focus on dealing with any magic that might arise. Though if my theory is correct, there might not be any to deal with."

"I hope so," Stone said. He glanced at Jason, who was opening his camera bag. "What have you got there?"

Jason pulled out digital camera on a strap, followed by an SLR, and slung both around his neck. "If I'm gonna be the mundane in the crowd, I might as well make myself useful in mundane ways. I figure you might want some photos if anything weird is going on."

"Good thought," Stone said in approval.

"I'll be right back, sir," Aubrey said. He hurried off toward the garage, and returned a few moments later carrying two stout wooden objects. As he drew closer, Stone chuckled. "A cricket bat and a shillelagh? Aubrey, you are *full* of surprises."

Aubrey offered the scarred cricket bat to Jason. "Best if we can defend ourselves, sir. I didn't think you'd approve of my discharging a shotgun inside the house."

Verity grinned. "Give me that camera, Jason. This needs documenting." When he handed it over, she backed off. "Smile, both of you. The two mighty hunters ready to battle the forces of darkness with sporting equipment."

Neither of them did, but she snapped the photo anyway and returned the camera. "Okay. Let's go."

Stone backed off, motioning for Ian to follow him, and called Aubrey's mobile. When the caretaker answered, he put the call on speaker and nodded toward the house. "Be careful," he called again, trying not to visualize a ceiling beam falling on their heads. "And do *not* go downstairs in the east wing. We'll save that for the next experiment."

He watched with growing tension as the three of them mounted the front steps. Verity held up a hand and paused before they crossed the threshold, obviously scanning with magical sight. After a few moments, she nodded and stepped inside, and then a few seconds after that waved the others in.

"Is anything happening?" Stone demanded, pacing. "What do you see?"

"It's a bit of a mess in here, sir," Aubrey's crackling voice came through immediately. "The entryway is in quite a lot of disarray. The lamps have exploded, there's a broken table on its side, and it looks like something slammed into the door to the great room at rather high velocity. And something has blown the rug to pieces."

"Yes, that was me. It attacked me when I tried to enter. Verity, can you tell if any of it's illusion?"

"Doesn't look like it." She sounded farther away, as if she might be turned away from the phone. "It's just a mess, like Aubrey said."

"Any blood on the walls?" Ian called over Stone's shoulder.

"Nope." Jason this time. "No blood. I've got some pics for you."

"Good. All right," Stone said. "Keep going." His heart beat faster. "What about the aura, Verity? It still looks green from here. Any sign of red?"

"Nope. All green. It's freakin' weird-looking, but it seems calm enough at the moment."

"We're opening the door to the great room now, sir," Aubrey said. "It's quite dark in here."

"The chandeliers are on the floor," Verity said. "Three of them, it looks like. There's glass all over the place."

"That matches with what I saw," Ian murmured to Stone.

"Careful," Stone said again. "But you don't hear any-thing? No screaming? Nothing's moving?"

"Nothing," Jason said. "Place looks like somebody came in here and tossed it. Books on the floor—holy shit, is that a sword poking through the back of one of the sofas?"

"Yeah, that happened last night," Ian said, leaning in to be heard. "It's from the wall. Scared the hell out of me."

"All right," Stone said. "So at least so far, it doesn't seem you lot are setting the echoes off."

"You sure you don't want us to check out the east wing?" Verity asked.

"I'm sure," he answered quickly. "I want a bit more time to study the situation before we go there—I'm still hoping to work out a way Ian and I can go in with you, or if nothing else I want to ask Eddie and Ward to accompany you so you'll have more magical protection. Check out the kitchen and the west wing. Ian, you ran directly from the east wing to the front door, right?"

"Yeah. Through the great room. I didn't go anywhere else. I wanted to get my ass out of there before something smashed me into a wall or drove me crazy with all that screaming."

"Right, then," Stone said more loudly. "You heard that, right? Check the areas where neither Ian nor I went, and see if they're disturbed."

"Okay," Jason said. "We're heading upstairs."

Stone didn't realize he was holding his breath until Verity's voice came through again a few seconds later. "Everything looks fine up here, Doc. Nothing disturbed as far as I can tell. Nothing's moving except us."

Stone pondered. "Looks like Aubrey's theory is holding up so far," he said under his breath to Ian. "The damage is confined to areas where you and I went, which certainly sounds like the echoes have some issue with the Stone family specifically." Louder, he said, "All right—come on out. Keep your eyes open, though. I wouldn't put it past those things to try something when they don't think you're paying attention."

When Verity, Jason, and Aubrey emerged through the front door a few moments later, though, the echoes had remained dormant. Stone ceased his pacing and hurried over to them, tension draining from him as he did. "Everything all right?"

"Yeah," Jason said. "Nothing bothered us. Like I said, it looked to me like somebody broke in hunting for something."

"Except for the sword," Verity added. "And the radioactive green glow."

"Here, see for yourself." Jason pulled out the digital camera, fiddled with it, and offered it to Stone.

Stone paged through the photos on the tiny screen, with Ian looking over his shoulder. They showed exactly what his friends had described: the broken chandeliers, scattered books, destroyed rug, and shattered windows. "I'd half expected the photos to be buggered up," he commented, handing the camera back. "Echoes can do that sometimes."

"I'm not sure they were even there," Verity said.

"What do you mean? Of course they were there," Ian protested. "You saw what they did in there."

"No, that's not what I mean. I don't mean they don't *exist*—just that I didn't get any sense of being watched while we were in there. Did either of you?" she asked Jason and Aubrey.

The caretaker shook his head. "No. I'd like to think I'm rather well attuned to that house for someone with no magical ability. I didn't feel anything odd or disturbing—other than dismay at the thought of having to clean up all that disarray in there."

"You won't," Stone said, only half paying attention as he once again studied the house with magical sight. "We'll have a crew in to do the cleaning once this is sorted." He frowned. "I'm going to try going in again. Perhaps they *are* dormant right now. Perhaps they spent all their energy on the little show they put on last night, and now they've got to rest before they put on another one."

"Do you think that's wise, sir?" Aubrey asked, brow furrowing.

"Not really. But I've got to know. I'm already bloody sick of being run out of my own house by a load of supernatural squatters."

"You want me to go with you?" Ian asked.

"No. If they're still active, it shouldn't take long to verify it." He held up his phone. "I'll keep the line open."

Verity looked as if she might say something, but then signed and nodded. "Be careful. Don't get yourself run through with any medieval weapons or anything."

"That's always been my aim." Stone shot her an amused sideways glance.

The others remained clustered in a little knot near the circular driveway, their attention riveted on him as he trudged back toward the house.

It didn't take long to determine the echoes were most decidedly *not* dormant. As soon as he stepped over the threshold, the screams began anew, and all around him, the broken glass, books, bits of shattered furniture, and swatches of destroyed rug began whirling around him like a tornado.

Get out!

You don't belong here!

Murrrrrdererrrrrrr!

GO!

The voices shrieked and wailed, falling over each other and competing for which could be louder and more head-splitting. Stone spun around, shield up and magical senses active. He heard a liquid *whoosh* from above him a split-second before something warm and wet cascaded down on him from the ceiling. As it bypassed his shield and drenched him to the skin, he realized with horror that he was soaked in bright red blood. It ran down his neck, creeping down his chest and back, and dripped from his sodden hair into his face. His feet squelched and slipped in it as he whirled and darted back through the door. He'd barely stepped through and closed it behind him before a heavy fireplace log slammed into it with a rattling, ear-shattering *thud.* He lost his balance in the slippery blood and staggered forward, tripping over his feet at the top of the steps. Both Ian and Verity caught him with magic and lowered him to the ground before he took a hard tumble.

Panting, he dropped to his knees. His heart thudded so hard he thought he might pass out. Still in the grip of panic, he tore his blood-soaked coat off and flung it aside.

Except it *wasn't* blood-soaked.

The long black coat was dry and clean, aside from a light dusting of dirt from where he'd thrown it.

"Doc?" Verity hurried over to him. "What's wrong? Are you okay? You went so pale—"

Stone rocked back, still on his knees in the dirt. He stared at his hands, half expecting to see them caked in sticky red blood, but all he saw was a bit of grime from the ground.

"Bloody hell..." he got out, breathless.

"What happened?" Jason demanded, as Aubrey came over to grip Stone's shoulders. "What did you see?"

"They're...not dormant." He paused a moment to get himself back under control, then accepted a hand up from Aubrey. "They are most certainly *not* dormant. And they've definitely got something against me."

He held out his arms, inspecting himself for any leftover signs of blood, but saw none. It was as if the blood had never been there—which, of course, it couldn't have been.

"What happened? We didn't see anything," Jason said. "Didn't hear anything, either. You just suddenly freaked out and took off, then tripped over your own feet and did a header down the front steps."

Stone retrieved his coat, shook the dirt off it, and shrugged back into it. "Blood," he said. "I felt like an extra in a bad *Carrie* revival. Those things were screaming at me like before, and suddenly something dumped a big bucket of blood on me from above my head. Illusion, but...damned convincing."

"My God..." Aubrey whispered. He gripped Stone's arm. "Sir...what are you going to do? If you can't get inside—"

Suddenly, Stone's momentary fear burned away, replaced by cold anger. How *dare* these renegade echoes, or whatever the hell they were, try to drive him out of his own home? Even if his ancestors had been less than saintly, *he'd* never done anything to them, and there was no way he planned to take on this guilt by association without fighting back.

"What I'm going to do," he said, clenching his fists, "is make a few calls. Before I can do anything else, I need more data."

| CHAPTER TEN

STONE, IAN, VERITY, AND JASON were already at the London house when Eddie Monkton and Arthur Ward arrived through the portal an hour later.

"Some problem you've got, mate," Eddie said after Stone introduced them to Ian. He carried a large leather satchel slung over one shoulder and couldn't hide his excitement. "I've been waitin' for you to give a ring ever since you ducked out last night."

Ward, at least, had the grace to look concerned. "Where is Aubrey?"

"He stayed back at the house." Stone led them upstairs to the sitting room, where one of the house's skeleton staff offered them refreshments and then departed. "I asked him not to, but you know Aubrey. He's more stubborn than I am, and as he pointed out, whatever's going on there doesn't seem interested in *him*."

"Sounds like it," Eddie said. "So you've got some kind of family-related 'aunting, or curse, or summat." He settled back with cup of coffee. "Why don't you start by tellin' us the whole story?"

Stone couldn't sit still, so he paced and prowled the large room while catching his two friends up with everything that had gone on so far. Both of them listened with close attention, and by the time he finished Eddie was practically wriggling in his seat, and Ward wore an expression somewhere between fascination and horror.

"Okay," Eddie said. "So you 'aven't been downstairs again since you took that first look 'round yesterday afternoon?"

"I was, briefly," Ian said. He sat perched on the end of one of the antique brocade sofas. "I didn't stay long, though, after everything went to hell."

"It seems a reasonable assumption that the carved door breaking disturbed the echoes," Ward said contemplatively, rubbing his chin. "But if that's so, what broke the door in the first place?"

"Are you sure you didn't see any cracks when you examined it, Stone?" Eddie asked.

"Nothing obvious." Stone glanced at Ian, who shook his head. "If they were there, they were well hidden."

"And no magic around it?"

"Not a bit. Ian and I both looked carefully. If there ever was any, either it's gone by now or the door was blocking it."

"Okay…" Eddie opened his satchel and removed several books and stacks of papers, which he laid across the coffee table but didn't open yet. "Ward's probably right about the door, but it's also possible that we're lookin' at this thing wrong side 'round."

"What do you mean?" Verity asked.

"Well, I'm willin' to bet quite a lot that the door and the echoes are related somehow—but there's two ways of lookin' at 'em. Maybe the broken door caused the echoes, either by stirrin' 'em up or by releasin' 'em from some kind o' stasis or captivity…or else the echoes were there all along, and did somethin' to break the door."

"That doesn't make as much sense, though," Ward pointed out. "Stone and Ian went down there to look around yesterday afternoon and nothing bothered them then. Right, Stone? Did you sense anything unusual?"

"Not a thing. Well, other than the fact that there's been a ritual room and network of bloody catacombs hidden under my house for at least a couple hundred years. That's a bit unusual."

"Ian said he heard the crack late last night," Verity said. "It doesn't make sense that something that heavy would just…fail like that, so suddenly, after being there that long. Especially if it was reinforced with magic. I know you said you didn't see any, Doc, but like you said, maybe it was shielded from the other side or something."

"Maybe the earth shifted," Jason said. "Same thing that caused the crack in the floor in the first place. Maybe it happened again."

"A good thought," Stone said. He wondered briefly if this could be related to the rifts he'd found earlier that year, but even aside from the fact that his home didn't correspond to any of the dots on Desmond's globe, his gut told him it wasn't. "But since it coincided so closely with our presence in the chamber—probably the first human presence down there since it was sealed…"

"And definitely the first *Stone* family presence," Eddie added.

"—I'm more inclined to suspect that our breaking through the floor into the chamber was the catalyst," Stone finished.

"But I thought you said it was the workmen who broke through and found the space underneath," Jason said.

"Yes, but the workmen weren't Stones."

"No," Verity said. "But nothing attacked you the first time you went down there, either."

"Perhaps that's because the vault wasn't cracked yet," Ward said. "From the sound of it, the whole thing down there was a system: the carved vault door, the passages, the ritual room, and the fact that it was all sealed off."

"Yeah," Eddie said, leaning forward with enthusiasm. "I think you're on to something, mate. Stone, once the workers breached the initial protective enchantments by breaking through the floor, maybe that released enough power for whatever was behind that vault door to break out, which in turn let the echoes out to play."

"Or the combination of the floor breach and the presence of two powerful Stone family members in the vicinity was enough energy to set it off," Ward added.

"That's all great," Jason said, "but indulge the mundane for a minute here, okay? Regardless of what started it, what are you going to *do* about it? I'm guessing Al doesn't plan to sell his house because it's full of pissed-off ghosts. Do we even have any idea who these ghosts *are,* or what pissed them off in the first place?"

Stone had almost forgotten that he hadn't told Jason anything about his family. "Er," he said uncomfortably. "I've got some idea, yes. I don't want to go into the details right now, but let's just suffice it to say I found out not too long ago that my ancestors got up to some fairly ghastly things. Including human sacrifices, apparently."

"*What?*" Jason gaped at him. He rubbed his face. "You're sayin'…you think somebody in your family was sacrificing people in your basement?"

"That's exactly what I think. The ritual area seemed set up for that sort of thing, and our theory is that the bricked-in alcoves were where they interred the bodies when they were…finished with them. You can't ash a dead body, and if they were hidden away in a sealed chamber, there was no chance they'd ever be found."

He met Jason's gaze, then dropped his own as shame gripped him. "I know, Jason. You don't have to say it. I'm not too happy about it myself, but what's done is done. And now, apparently, the proverbial chickens have come home to roost."

"We'd be in better shape if they were nought but chickens," Eddie said. When nobody seemed amused, he shrugged. "Sorry, sorry. But at any rate, I don't think we'll be gettin' too much farther along without takin' a shufty at the place."

"You want to go *down* there?" Jason asked.

"I think we have to," Ward said.

"Nobody *has* to do anything," Stone said with a sigh, resuming his pacing and trying to block out the mental images of innocent prisoners screaming as they died to fuel his ancestors' power. "But if you two wanted to take a look, I wouldn't turn down the offer. I clearly can't do it, and neither can Ian—and Verity doesn't have the background to make sense of what she might find down there."

"That doesn't mean I'm not going with them," Verity said firmly. "Even though I can't read ancient Mesopotamian or whatever, I can still help out."

"Yeah, me too," Jason said. He still looked pale from what Stone had told him, but also resolute. "You magical types are gonna need somebody to take notes and document this stuff while you're pokin' around. And I swing a pretty mean cricket bat if the shit hits the fan."

"There's still one other question," Ian said.

"What's that?" Eddie finished his coffee, picked up one of his books, and began riffling through it.

"We still don't know what's up with the carved door. Why is it there? What was it holding, if anything? It makes sense that those bricked alcoves were used for burying sacrifice victims, but why was there a separate passageway ending in a completely different, tougher door with a lot of weird carvings on it? That sure sounds to me like it was imprisoning something that's out now, doesn't it?"

"It certainly does," Eddie agreed.

Ward nodded. "And if that's so, where's that prisoner now? If it was nothing but powerful energy, it might just be what gave the echoes enough of a jolt to start functioning. But if there actually is—or was—some sort of entity down there…"

Stone stopped behind the sofa as his frustration rose. He gripped the soft fabric until he feared he might rip it, then backed off. "Damn it, I don't like this at all. I don't like any of it. It's *my* house these things are causing trouble in. I should be down there myself."

"It's your house, and your curiosity's killing you," Verity said with sympathy. "I get it. I think we all do. But—"

"But I haven't got a bloody choice, do I?" Stone didn't even try to mask the bitterness in his tone. "Who knows what those things might get up to if Ian or I tried to go down into the heart of their domain? They might bring the whole place down around our ears."

"Hate to agree with you," Eddie said ruefully, "but I think you're gonna need to sit this one out, mate. But the good news is, assuming those things don't go after Ward and me, we should be able to gather some good data to be gettin' on with."

"Yeah," Jason said. "I'll take lots of photos and video, and make notes and sketches. It'll be the closest thing to being down there yourself. Well, without a live video feed anyway. We could probably set something like that up, but it'd take time."

"We don't *have* time," Stone said. "Whatever's going on down there, who's to say it won't get worse if we put our heads in the sand and let it keep getting on with whatever it's up to?" He turned back toward his friends, picking each of them out with his gaze. "But I've got to say this: it's entirely possible there's something dangerous down there. I've always been rubbish at accepting help, but this time there aren't too many other options. If you go, though, I want you all to be sure you know what you might be getting into."

Eddie waved him off. "Come on, mate. You know I'm dyin' to get myself down there. Normally I'm not fond of the kinds of adventures you get into, but this is the stuff researchers have naughty dreams about. An untouched catacomb system under the 'ouse of a powerful magical family? I'm 'avin' a 'ard time stayin' put and not runnin' down there right now."

Ward gave a rueful smile. "I'm not quite as enthusiastic as Eddie—to be fair, I rarely am about anything—but yes. I'm in agreement."

"Doc, you're stalling," Verity said. "The sooner we get down there and have a look around, the sooner you'll know what you have to deal with."

Stone studied them all for a few more seconds, fighting his growing frustration. Part of it was worry about his friends—without any particular pride, he knew he was by far the most potent mage among the group, and also the most experienced with unexpected magical danger. But a large chunk of it was simple annoyance that he couldn't accompany them into a situation that was uniquely *his,* or at least his and Ian's. What would they find out about his family and the atrocious things they did? What he already knew was bad enough, but what if they found something *worse*?

Finally, though, he sighed. "You're right, of course. Let's gather a few things before we go, though. This needs to be treated as a potentially dangerous expedition—we can take another hour or two to pick up some supplies before we go." He pulled out a notepad and began listing items; after a moment, the others joined in.

At least if he was going to send them down there, he'd do as much as he could to make sure they were safe.

| CHAPTER ELEVEN

THREE HOURS LATER, the leftmost bay in the three-car garage beneath Aubrey's apartment bore little resemblance to its usual self.

Stone had moved his little black convertible outside, and in its place the group had set up a makeshift "command center." A table in the middle held several large notepads, pens, books, and a collection of items the group had purchased earlier in London.

"Looks like we're going on some kind of archaeological expedition," Jason said as he checked his cameras—the digital and SLR he'd brought with him, along with a small video camera they'd bought today.

"In a way we are," Ward said. "Stone and Ian barely got a look at what was down there, but whatever it is, it's likely been down there for at least two hundred years. It will be fascinating to see what's revealed."

"As long as it doesn't try to eat our faces," Jason muttered.

"That's why you're going with three mages," Verity said, grinning.

"Not bloody likely," Eddie said, matching her grin. "If the shit 'its the fan down there, the lot of us will be 'idin' behind you, Verity. Stone's the nasty one in this bunch. Ward and I're just a couple of magic boffins, so I 'ope 'e's taught you everything 'e knows."

"All right, enough of that," Stone growled. "I'm feeling guilty enough sending you lot down there without me, and I want you all to promise you'll get out immediately if anything goes wrong."

"I don't think you have anything to worry about there," Ward said. "As interesting as this is, I have no illusions about my ability to deal with it if it decides it wants us out."

Verity picked up a black skateboard helmet from a stack of several. "Are you sure we need these? We'll have magical shields."

"Well, we couldn't find hard hats on such short notice, and anything heavier might bugger up your peripheral vision," Stone said. "Put it on. You'll be grateful for it if you drop your shield and something comes down on your head."

She looked dubious, but donned the helmet along with a pair of safety glasses, then pulled on her leather jacket. "Fine. Everybody know the plan?"

They all nodded. They'd discussed it at length once they arrived, and everyone in the group had their specific job. Verity would take point, using magical sight to spot any threats and hopefully dealing with them. Jason would take photos with all three cameras for multiple redundancy in case anything went wrong with any of them, and maintain communication with Stone, Ian, and Aubrey at the command post using his cell phone and a short-range radio. Eddie and Ward would make sketches of any writing or symbols they found, scan the area with their own magical sight, and help out with communication when Jason was busy taking photos.

All of them wore heavy jackets and boots along with their helmets and glasses, and each carried two flashlights with fresh batteries. Next to the table, another box contained a long extension cord and more powerful electric lights on folding stands, which they planned to plug in upstairs and set up in the ritual room.

"Let's do this, then," Stone said. "Remember—stay in constant communication. I want to know everything you're seeing as soon as you see it."

"You got it, Doc."

Stone watched them as they trudged out and headed toward the house, the box floating along next to Verity. "I don't like this," he muttered.

"Nor do I, sir," Aubrey said. He sat in a folding chair next to the table, looking dejected. He hadn't contributed much to the planning, and seemed to be there only because he didn't want to be alone in his apartment.

Ian prowled the area, examining the middle part of the garage where Aubrey had a workshop set up. He picked up a hacksaw, studied it, then set it back down. "I just wish we could go with them. I hate sitting out here on my ass when the action's happening up there."

"Well, if we're lucky, they'll get us some information to go on, and we can start working out how to deal with the echoes." Stone returned to the table and pulled out his phone. "Anyway, they should be getting to the house any moment now."

The three of them waited tensely for several more minutes, and then Stone's phone buzzed. He punched the button immediately, with more force than necessary.

"Jason?"

"Yeah. We're here, in the upper basement room. Standing in front of the hole right now. We've got the extension cord plugged in and the lamps ready to take down. V's going first, then Eddie and Arthur, and then me last so they can levitate me."

"Good," Stone said. He put the phone on speaker and set it on the table. "Any problems so far?"

"Not a thing. Everything looked fine, except for the stuff that was messed up before. V says the aura around the place is still that weird green."

"Well, that's something, anyway." Stone couldn't shake the feeling that the echoes were waiting for his friends to go down into the sub-basement before springing whatever trap they had planned.

"Okay," Jason said after a moment. "V's down."

"Nothing's attacking her?" Stone gripped the edge of the table, leaning forward. His one major concern had been that the echoes wouldn't take kindly to *anyone* down in their domain, and particularly not any mages.

"Nope. I'm shining a flashlight on her now, and she looks fine. We're sending the lights down now, and then Eddie's going."

By now, Ian had drifted back over and stood on the opposite side of the table from Stone, looking every bit as tense as his father. The two of them stared at the little device on the table as if it were the most important thing in the world—which, at that moment, it might have been.

"Eddie's down," Jason said. "Everything fine so far. Arthur's getting ready to go, and then it'll just be me."

"All right. Keep talking."

"Yeah." A rustling sound came over the line, and then a sharp intake of breath.

"Jason?" Stone demanded.

"Sorry, I'm okay. Just still not used to that damned levitation spell."

"What do you see?"

"We're in what looks like a stone hallway."

"You saw this part before, right, Doc?" Verity spoke from farther away.

"Yes. There should be a door at the other end."

"It should be open," Ian added. "I didn't close it when I was running out of there."

"Yeah, it's open," Jason said.

"Do you see anything weird? Blood on the floor? Words written on the walls in it? Dead spiders?"

"Nothin' like that," Eddie said. "Place looks a bit dusty, but that's all."

"All right," Stone said. "Go on through the door, to the ritual room."

"Yeah," Jason said. "We'll set up the lights there. The extension cords are long enough we should be able to spread them out a little. We—"

The line crackled several times.

"Jason?" Stone snatched up the phone. "Jason, can you hear me?"

More crackles, followed by a loud pop.

"Bugger!"

Ian was already scrambling for the radio. He keyed it. "Jason? Are you there? The phone's cutting out."

A blast of static erupted from the tiny speaker, along with a few disjointed words:

"—fine—"

"—cutting out—"

"—keep going—"

"Damn it!" Stone snapped, slamming his fist down on the table.

Ian tried the radio a few more times, but got nothing but static—even the voices weren't coming through anymore. "They sounded okay…" he said uncertainly. "Should we go check on them?"

Stone shook his head. "There's no point. The echoes won't let us near the place." He agreed with Ian—before they'd faded, the voices hadn't sounded agitated or distressed, which probably just meant that either the group had moved far enough underground that the signals weren't getting through, or else the echoes were interfering with them.

"Do you want me to go up there, sir?" Aubrey rose from his chair and came over to the table, looking concerned. "I could call down to them, and relay messages that way."

"No, Aubrey." Stone tossed the phone back on the table with a sigh and swiped his hand through his hair. "Echoes are generally fairly single-minded. Obviously they don't want Ian or me up there, but so far they haven't had any issue with the others. We'll just have to trust that to remain true."

"But—" Ian began.

Stone waved him off. "Verity's damned good, and despite all their talk about being boffins, Ward and Eddie can handle themselves if they have to. They'll get themselves out of there if there's any danger, just like you did." He wasn't sure how much of that he actually believed, but it didn't matter at this point. Unless he wanted to go up there himself, they were out of communication. He'd have to trust his friends to handle things on their own.

CHAPTER TWELVE

J ASON GLARED AT HIS PHONE in disgust. "Signal's fucked."

He hadn't needed to say it—everybody in the group could hear Stone's and Ian's fragmented, staticky voices coming through the speaker, and everybody heard when they stopped.

They gathered around, waiting as Jason tried his radio and got the same result. "I 'alf expected that to 'appen," Eddie admitted, not looking concerned. "Even if the echoes aren't interferin' with the signal, bein' down this far's gonna do it anyway. I didn't say anythin' to Stone because he's wound up enough as it is."

"So do we keep going?" Jason glanced around nervously, taking in the rough-carved gray stone walls and the heavy wooden door ahead of them. It was open, and beyond it was nothing but darkness. Despite his talk about swinging a mean cricket bat earlier that day, he'd picked up a good solid baseball bat in London and felt a lot more comfortable with it. He tightened his grip on it, wishing he'd brought his gun—but guns were no good against ghosts.

"Of course we do," Verity said. She had a light spell up and was shining it around. "Doc's counting on us to get a

152 |

R. L. KING

look around down here. I say as long as nothing's attacking us, we should try to get as much as we can."

"I agree," Eddie said. "'Ang on a tick, though. Jason, bung me that radio for a sec."

Jason handed it over. "Why?"

"Just gonna let Stone know we're okay, before the lot of 'em, Aubrey included, get themselves killed tryin' to rescue us." He levitated back up through the hole, and returned a few moments later.

"We good?" Verity asked.

"Yeah. 'E's not 'appy about bein' out o' communication, but 'e says to keep goin' and be careful."

"Does he want regular reports?" Ward asked.

"'E *wants* us to report back every five minutes." Eddie chuckled. "But 'e said don't worry about it, we should just get on with it." He waggled his finger at Jason. "But take lots of good pics, mate. Trust me."

"Yeah. Let's go. The sooner we're out of here, the happier I'll be." He shivered a little; despite his leather jacket and the summer warmth outside, the air down here was colder than it should have been. The others were doing the same, and when he looked closely he could make out the faint steamy trails of their breath.

Verity, still holding up her light spell, passed through the door first, stepping aside to let the others follow. "Wow," she said, shining the light around. "This is pretty impressive."

"Impressive" wouldn't have been the word Jason used. More like "fucking creepy," but he kept that to himself. He brought up the rear, pausing to scan the large, circular room. He took in the circle on the floor, the pedestal in the middle with its manacles, and the open doorways to other passageways, trying to spot anything moving. Nothing was, as far as he could tell.

"I don't see any sign of blood or spiders," Ward said, pacing the room and directing his own light spell around. He approached the circle but didn't cross it. "A few bloodstains on this altar, but they look quite old."

"Let's get those lights set up," Verity said. "We can look around in here and get some photos and sketches before we move on."

Jason unfolded the stands, plugged the two lamps into the extension cords, and flipped one of the switches, wondering if the lamps would even work. He let his breath out with relief when bright white light flooded the chamber, chasing away the shadows and illuminating the stone ceiling eight feet above them.

Verity levitated the second lamp across the room and turned it on, adding even more light. "Well," she said. "This place is freaky. It's not every day you find a hidden ritual circle in your basement."

Eddie didn't answer. He had the fuzzed-out expression that indicated magical sight, and was carefully scanning the circle. After a few moments, he summoned a shield around himself and tentatively stepped across it, looking as if he thought something would jump him or zap him. When nothing did, he walked closer to the altar/pedestal and began examining the manacles. "Looks like somebody was sacrificed 'ere for sure," he said soberly.

"Probably more than one," Ward agreed, coming up next to him. "I don't see any signs of magic now, but this is a classic sacrificial ritual configuration."

"I'm not even gonna ask how you know that," Jason said. "Don't mind me—I'm just gonna take some pictures while you three get your magic geek on."

"You *two*," Verity corrected. "Eddie and Arthur are the experts. I'm mostly just the magical muscle. You take your photos, and I'll keep an eye out for anything that might want to cause trouble."

By now, Jason had grown used to the fact that in situations like this, his small, slim younger sister was a far more effective protector than he was with his strength and his mundane weapons. It still bothered him a bit, but it was what it was, and he had a job to do. He pulled out the video camera and began pacing the room, filming the walls, the circle, and the pedestal.

"Is it safe to come in there?" he asked Eddie and Ward, who were examining it more closely and muttering to each other. Eddie had a notebook open and was scribbling furiously on a page.

"What?" Eddie's head snapped up. "Oh—uh, yeah, should be," he said offhandedly, then returned to his discussion.

Verity must have noticed her brother's look of dismay, because she gripped his arm. "Don't mind them," she said with a grin. "When they find something interesting to study, they make Doc look like the kid eating paste in the back row of class. Just ignore them and get your shots."

"Yeah…" Jason gingerly stepped into the circle, letting his breath out when he made it safely. He took some video of the pedestal, the manacles, and the bloodstains, then pulled out his two still cameras and got some shots with both.

"Okay," Eddie said twenty minutes later, snapping his notebook shut and stowing it in his satchel. "That's about all we can get from this room right now—I'll want to take a closer look later, but we'd best get a once-over of the whole area so we can get back before ol' Stone's 'ead pops off from curiosity. We can always come back for another look."

His words relieved Jason. As uneasy as he felt down here, once he'd finished documenting the area he had little else to do but stand around waiting for the others to finish. "I assume we're gonna stay together."

"Oh, yes," Ward said with an amused smile. "This is a scientific examination, not a horror movie."

Verity laughed. "From what Ian said, it sounded kind of like a horror movie to me. I'm just glad we missed the spiders floating in blood." She pointed at the open arch to the southeast hallway. "I think this is the one Doc looked at. Want to start there?"

"Might as well," Eddie said. "We'll start there and work our way 'round counterclockwise, ending up at the odd one to the south. If any of the chambers branch, we'll leave those until after we've checked out all the main ones. Sound good?"

Without waiting for a reply, he headed toward the indicated archway, a light spell flaring around his hand. "Let's save the torches in case we need 'em."

Once again, Jason brought up the rear, glancing over his shoulder to make sure they hadn't picked up any ghostly stragglers. Every minute they spent down here without anything attacking them increased his tension; he knew Stone believed the echoes posed a threat only to members of his own family, but he wasn't basing that belief on too much evidence. Jason couldn't help picturing a whole flock of echoes

156 | R. L. KING

lining the hallways, watching with spectral amusement as they waited for their hapless prey to blunder into their trap.

As Stone had indicated, the hallway extended back around twenty feet, with several bricked alcoves lining both sides. None of the alcoves appeared disturbed; whatever had caused the heavy carved door to break obviously hadn't affected them.

Eddie and Ward held up their light spells, each examining one of the alcoves. Verity paced around, peering at the others and keeping an eye on the end of the hallway.

"These look like burial or interment chambers," Ward said, leaning in closer. "I don't see any markings or writing on this one, with either magical or mundane sight. Do you, Eddie?"

"Nope. I think you're right. My guess is they used these to hold the bodies from whatever sacrifices they were gettin' up to out in the ritual room. Odd that they separated them, though—would have been easier to do some sort of mass interment."

Jason snapped photos of several of the alcoves, but didn't bother to get them all since they were essentially identical. As he walked up and down the hallway taking video, the chill that ran through him had nothing to do with the cold. Nobody had told him about Stone's relatives conducting ritual human sacrifices, even though not only Eddie and Ward but Verity apparently knew it and had for quite some time. He knew it wasn't fair to blame Stone for things his ancestors had done more than a century ago, but he still couldn't help feeling…wrong about it. Almost as if he shouldn't be here, his presence violating the dignity of these unfortunate victims yet again.

"Should we break one of these open?" Verity asked. "See what's inside?"

"I think we know what's inside," Ward said gently. "As much as I'd like to verify our hypothesis, ethically I'm not sure we should be breaking open burial chambers to satisfy our curiosity."

"Let's keep going," Eddie said. He sounded disappointed, but also resolute, as if he agreed with Ward. "Maybe we'll get lucky in one of the other 'alls and find one that's already crumbled. Brickwork like this can get a bit fragile as time goes on, so if there's been any sort of seismic disturbance..." He let that trail off as he exited back into the circular chamber.

The next two hallways, to the northeast and northwest, looked identical to the first one: roughly twenty feet long, lined on both sides with more sealed brick alcoves. All of them were intact, to Eddie and Ward's obvious dismay. Jason dutifully took photos while the mages scanned for magical anomalies, any carvings or writing, or anything else out of the ordinary.

"I guess it's good these don't branch," Verity said. She still looked interested in the proceedings, but Jason noticed that, like him, she appeared to be getting impatient with Eddie and Ward's slower progress as they paused to study everything along the hallways. "How many of these little chambers have we found so far?"

"Thirty-two," Eddie said, looking up from his notebook.

Thirty-two. Jason suppressed an involuntary shudder. If the mages were right and each one of the niches contained a body, that meant Stone's ancestors had murdered nearly three dozen people to power their unholy rituals. That also assumed they were correct that each alcove housed only one body, and they still had one remaining hallway to examine before they checked out the one with the formerly sealed vault.

Verity touched his arm. "You okay?"

He started to say he was fine, then glanced at Eddie and Ward at the other end of the hallway and shook his head. "I'm not sure. This is…why didn't you tell me about this? About Al's relatives performing human sacrifices?"

She looked down. "I don't know. It wasn't really my thing to tell, I guess. I know he's really upset about it—ever since he found out last year, he's had trouble coming to terms with it. I don't think he wants anyone else to know. The only reason Eddie and Arthur do is because he asked them to research his family line and they turned up some bad stuff."

When he still looked troubled, she touched his arm to stop him as Eddie and Ward continued on to what was presumably the final hallway of alcoves. "There's something else, isn't there?"

"Isn't that enough?" he asked with some bitterness. He didn't want to say what else was on his mind aloud, but he knew perceptive Verity wouldn't let him alone until he did. "But yeah, there is."

"What is it?" She nodded toward the hallway. "We should go with them—I'm supposed to be helping with security if anything jumps out."

"I know. We can go in a sec. But…V, if there really *are* a bunch of bodies buried under this house…somebody needs to know about it."

Her expression suggested she'd already thought of that. "Yeah. It'd be like one of those mass Native American gravesites they discover sometimes back home. I'm not sure whether after all this time it would be considered a murder scene or an archaeological find, but either way…"

"Either way, the authorities have to be notified."

"Doc's not gonna like that."

Jason didn't answer. That was the crux of his dilemma. Verity was almost certainly correct: Stone wouldn't want to let anybody know about any bodies they might find buried beneath his home. There would be no way to keep such a find quiet; once it got out, the place would be mobbed with police, reporters, researchers, and herds of curious lookie-loos trying to get a glimpse of the "murder house." Shining that kind of public light on Stone and his affairs could cause him a lot of trouble, especially if any smart reporters started putting to-gether the other pieces of his life.

But on the other hand, if there *were* remains in those nooks, they belonged to innocent human beings who'd been slaughtered by a monstrous family to serve their lust for power. Sure, Stone hadn't had anything to do with it directly, but how much did that matter?

Verity took his hand. "Come on," she said gently. "Let's go. Maybe we're wrong. Maybe there aren't any bodies at all."

"Oi, you two!" Eddie called from somewhere down the final hallway. "Come 'ave a look at this."

They jogged over, avoiding the circle. Eddie and Ward stood back from one of the alcoves halfway down the hall. The light spells they held up illuminated the hallway itself, along with the outside of the nook.

Jason didn't have to ask what they'd found; it was easy to see. Unlike all the other niches so far, this one's brickwork had crumbled, uncovering the top two feet of space that had blocked whatever was inside.

"What's in there?" Verity asked, excited.

"Didn't look yet. Waited for you two." It was obvious to everyone that it hadn't been easy for him to wait even that short a time. "Get some photos, will you, Jason? Then we'll shine the light inside and see what these things are 'idin'."

Heart pounding, Jason quickly snapped off two photos each with the SLR and the digital, then stood back and trained the video camera on the black opening. "Okay, ready. Go for it."

In the glare of the light spell, both Eddie's and Ward's faces showed both excitement and fear. Slowly, as if realizing this was a kind of reveal, they moved their glowing hands past the broken brickwork and lit up the space inside.

"Bloody hell…" Ward whispered.

Jason leaned in closer with the camera, and his grip tightened on it. "Shit…" he murmured.

He'd hoped they would find something other than human remains in the alcove; what he saw drove that hope away instantly. That part didn't surprise him. But—

"Were they…*chained up* in there?" Verity peered over Eddie's shoulder, face pale and eyes wide.

"Sure as 'ell looks like it." The normally cheerful Eddie looked serious to the point of grimness.

For a moment, they did nothing but stare. The alcove, formed of the same stone floor and living rock walls as the rest of the chambers down here, extended back from the entrance around four feet. Attached to the rear walls with stout bolts were a set of heavy manacles, rusting now but still substantial.

Trapped in each of the manacles, skeletal hands and forearms dangled against the wall. Below them, the rest of the skeleton lay in disarray, barely held together by the decaying shreds of clothing.

Something cold began to grow in the pit of Jason's stomach. "Wait a minute," he said in a monotone. "Nobody would bother burying a body chained to a wall like that. If they shut them up in there like that, does that mean…"

"That they probably weren't dead when they were interred," Ward said. He sounded every bit as grim as Eddie had.

| CHAPTER THIRTEEN

J ASON SAGGED BACK against the opposite wall, letting the hand holding the camera drop. "You're saying...they bricked people up down here *alive*?"

"Why would they do that?" Verity demanded. She'd gone even paler, and was still staring into the alcove with horror. "I thought they used all these people for human sacrifices, on that altar out there. That's bad enough, but—"

Eddie took a step back, swiping his hand over his forehead and letting out a long breath. He exchanged a somber look with Ward. "I've got a theory...but I'm gonna keep it to m'self for the moment. We need to talk to Stone first."

"Eddie..." Verity began.

He shook his head. "No, luv. Stone needs to 'ear this."

"Should we go back, then?"

"Let's take a look at the rest of his hallway, and the other one," Ward said. "I'm not certain I want to come back down here any time soon once we leave." He pulled a bottle of water from his satchel and took a healthy swallow.

Jason took a last look at the unfortunate pile of bones in the alcove before following the others. "It's like that Poe story."

"'The Cask of Amontillado,'" Verity said. "Yeah. Except that guy only bricked *one* guy up in the wine cellar. Eddie," she called, "I know you didn't want to break any of the rest of these, but we should check at least one other. Maybe they're not all like that."

"Oh, so you think we just got lucky and found the one that is, then?"

She didn't answer.

"I'll put big money that there's more than one," Jason said. "At least now we know where the ghosts are coming from. I'd be pretty pissed too if somebody sealed me up in a hole while I was still alive."

The sudden sound of something crumbling and hitting the ground, followed by Ward's yelp of surprise, jerked their heads up.

"Arthur?" Verity called, hurrying down the hallway. "You okay?"

"I'm fine." Ward sounded a bit breathless. "But—look at this."

By the time they reached him, Eddie was already there. The two of them were staring in shocked horror at one of the alcoves at the end. As with the other one they'd found earlier, the mortar holding the bricks together at the top had eroded away, releasing the bricks and revealing a smaller hole. The broken pieces lay in the passageway.

"Did that just happen?" Jason demanded. "Just now?"

Ward nodded. "Just as I reached the end. They shifted and broke free."

A chill ran up his spine, horror-movie visions of shuffling animated skeletons filling his mind. "Holy shit. Is something in there?" He gripped his baseball bat.

"I don't think so," Eddie said. "Don't get yerselves all wound up about the walkin' dead or summat. I don't 'ear anything else. Probably just weak mortar breakin' loose. 'Appens sometimes in places like this. It was likely ready to go, and Ward knocked it free walkin' past. You eat a big breakfast today, Arthur?"

Ward ignored him, still staring at the alcove. "This one looks a bit different to the others."

Jason and Verity hurried to join him, examining the final nook on the right side.

"You're right," Eddie said. "The bricks are a darker color. Maybe this one was done later."

"Is there another body in it?" Verity asked.

Ward stuck his hand with its light spell in through the hole, which was much smaller this time, and peered after it. "I don't see any bones or manacles," he said after a moment. "It looks like there's something on the floor, though. A box, perhaps? It's hard to see."

"Back up," Jason said. "And hold that light up." He shoved the video camera into Verity's hands and drew the baseball bat all the way out of the makeshift sling he'd fashioned so he could carry it on his back. When neither Eddie nor Ward objected to his obvious intentions, he began poking at the bricks near the hole. He worked tentatively at first, but then applied more strength until he'd knocked out enough of the crumbling structure to make rough-edged hole around two feet in diameter. He stepped aside and re-holstered the bat. "Try that."

Eddie and Ward moved back in, both holding light spells. "It *is* a box," Eddie said. "Metal. Looks pretty 'eavy."

"Should we bring it out?" Verity asked. "Doc will want to see it, I'm sure."

"Yeah, probably." He offered a self-deprecating grin. "Muscle was never my strong point, though, nor Ward's neither. Care to do the honors?"

They backed off, and Verity took her place in front of the hole. She concentrated a moment, and everyone remained silent as she slowly levitated the substantial metal box up and out. Even so, she nearly dropped it before settling it to the floor. "Wow, that thing weighs a ton. I wonder what's in there—gold bars or something?"

They all gathered around to peer at it. It was around three feet long by two high and two deep, made entirely of metal with more metal straps reinforcing its structure. Various symbols and sigils were etched into its top, sides, and front. A fist-sized padlock, its shackle as big around as a child's finger, held a stout clasp shut. Although the whole thing showed minor rusting, it appeared in remarkably good shape for a box that had spent the last two hundred-plus years in a damp underground cavern.

"It might just be the box itself." Ward crouched next to it, examining it with his light spell and then his expression fuzzed. "Interesting. It's got both a heavy mundane lock and some kind of magical one."

"A magical lock? And it's still active after all this time?" Jason asked, astonished.

"Doesn't surprise me, 'round here," Eddie said. "Verity, if we 'elp you, can you bring it out to the ritual room? We'll take it back with us when we leave."

"You don't want to try to open it?"

"Not here. It's Stone's family, so he should get the first go at it. I don't see anything else in 'ere. We should probably pick up our pace a bit—Stone's got to be frantic with curiosity by now."

"Just the one area left," Verity said, her voice strained with the effort of levitating the box.

Jason preceded the three of them to the ritual room, glancing around to make sure nothing lay in wait for them. As far as he could tell, nothing had changed: the lights still blazed, the circle and pedestal remained quiet, and aside from a faint electrical buzz and the far-off sound of water dripping, he couldn't hear anything out of the ordinary.

All of a sudden he wanted to get out of here, though. "Let's hurry this up," he urged. "You're right, Eddie—Al's gonna want to see this stuff. And this place is giving me an extra-large helping of the creeps."

"You and me both, mate," Eddie said. "Right, then—let's check out that last hallway. Take lots of pictures, will you?"

"Hopefully we won't find any more bodies," Verity said.

All of them paused a moment before stepping into the final passage. This time, Verity held the light spell as Eddie and Ward examined the walls.

"No alcoves this time," Eddie said, and pointed. "Just that big door at the end. That thing must've been impressive before it was broken."

As Ian had reported, the heavy stone door had cracked in the middle, at a slight diagonal. Broken chunks, ranging in size from a couple of inches to nearly a foot long, littered the hallway in front of it, and as Verity held the light closer, they could all see the charring along the intact part of the door.

Carefully stepping around the debris, Eddie and Ward moved in for a closer look.

"Can you read any of the symbols on the door?" Verity asked.

"Maybe. I'd need more time and research, though," Eddie said.

"We need to make some sketches. With those and the photos, we should be able to take a good stab at it," Ward said. "But let's look inside first. We—"

He stopped.

"What is it?" Jason demanded, reaching for the baseball bat. "Is something in there?"

But Eddie was looking now too. "Bloody *'ell.*"

Jason moved in, looking over the shorter man's shoulder. "What...the hell is *that?*"

Beyond the door, the chamber was larger than the alcoves—perhaps eight by eight feet—but that was where the resemblance ended. Instead of rough-carved stone walls and floor, it had a significantly more "finished" look—more a room than a crude burial niche. The granite floor was inlaid with more symbols, and a smaller version of the circle out front lay in its center. Where the larger circle had included a pedestal or altar with manacles, obviously designed to chain an unfortunate sacrificial victim to its top, this one contained a pale, stone box, the size and shape of a coffin.

The top of the box had been broken open—not just broken, but *blasted.* Bits of rubble littered the floor all around the room, and when Verity moved her illuminated hand inside, Jason could see what looked like fresh pits in all three visible walls, all of which were likewise covered in neat rows of carved and painted symbols.

"What *happened* in there?" Verity whispered. "This is no sacrifice. This looks like they carefully put something in here."

"And whatever it is, it looks like it got out," Eddie added in the same strangled tone.

All of them looked around nervously again as if expecting to be attacked now that they'd discovered the secret, but the area remained as quiet as ever.

"It does," Jason said. He pointed at the scattered chunks of door. "These are on the outside. If somebody had broken in from outside, the pieces would be inside the room, not out here."

"So...where *is* it?" Verity asked softly, still looking around.

"I'm more interested in *what* it is," Ward said. He crouched, examining the edges of the intact portion of the door. "Because I don't think this is a door."

"What else would it be?" Jason asked. He'd climbed, with some trepidation, over the remainder of the door and inside the room, following Eddie. When nothing attacked him he began turning in place, filming the markings on the walls.

"I don't see any sign of a knob, a handle—anything holding it closed." Ward rose to stand and likewise clambered into the room. "If I had to guess, I'd say this wasn't a door, but a seal."

"You mean—they shut somebody else up in here?" Verity bent to pick up one of the blasted pieces of the coffin-like box and examined it. "I do sense faint magic, but—"

"Wait," Jason said, growing cold again. "So they sealed somebody up in here inside a stone coffin, behind a heavy door carved with magic stuff, in a room with more magic stuff on every inch of the walls." He swallowed. "I know I'm just the mundane here, but I'm not an idiot. That sounds to me like whatever it was, it was pretty powerful and whoever sealed it up was worried about it getting out. Somebody please tell me I'm wrong."

"I don't think you're wrong," Eddie said. He sounded even more sober than he had before, and was scribbling away at a rapid pace in his notebook. "Like I said, I can't read all this right now—I'll 'ave to take it back to the London library for some serious research time—but I know enough to get the gist of it. Ward, you too?"

Ward nodded. "These are protective sigils. The sort one might use for imprisonment."

"But…" Verity stepped forward for a look inside the main part of the stone coffin, which was still mostly intact. "This is a casket, right? For a dead body? Why would you need to imprison a dead body?"

"That's another good question," Eddie said.

"I've got some better ones," Jason said. "If whatever was in there's been down here for like two hundred years, what happened to it? Why did it pick now to break out? Did it—I don't know—bust out if its coffin and take off, or did somebody else break it out? And…" He glanced back down the hall toward the ritual room. "Where the hell is it *now*?"

Ward let his breath out. "We should document all these inscriptions on the walls," he said, "but suddenly I'm not terribly keen on staying down here much longer."

"'Ate to say it, but I've got the same feelin'," Eddie said. "We should get back to Stone anyway—maybe 'e's got some thoughts about this mess, and 'e's likely goin' spare up there waitin' for news. Tell you what—Jason, take some good shots of all four walls and the bottom part of the door. We'll gather up the largest chunks of it along with a few samples of the broken coffin and take them back along with the box. Maybe that'll be enough to at least get us started. Sound good?"

"Yeah. If it means getting out of here faster, that sounds very good." Jason noticed he wasn't the only one constantly casting nervous glances around. "Just give me a sec to get the last of this."

He took the photos and video with more speed than he had before, and less than five minutes later he had the cameras stowed away. "Okay, let's get the fuck out of here."

Suddenly, he couldn't shake the feeling that someone—or some*thing*—was watching them.

CHAPTER FOURTEEN

"WHERE THE HELL *ARE* THEY?" Stone demanded. He paced the garage again, striding around like a tiger someone had locked in a cage. "They've been gone for over an hour." He returned to the table, gripping it with both hands until he feared he might break either it or his fingers. "I should go up there. They could all be dead down in that hole for all we know."

"Sir—" Aubrey began. He sat across from Stone, where he'd remained for most of the time except when he'd headed up to his apartment a while ago and brought back a collection of refreshments neither Stone nor Ian had touched.

"I know. I *know*. There's no point in it. But I can't just *stay* here sitting on my arse while gods know what is going on under my house!"

"We don't have a lot of choice." Ian leaned against the wall, almost as tense and frustrated as his father. "We have to trust that they can handle whatever's there."

Stone glared at him. "And how long are we to do that? Another hour? The rest of the day? Will we hang about here for a week?"

"Sir—" Aubrey said again.

"*What*, Aubrey?" Stone took a deep breath and let it out in a loud *whoosh*. "I'm sorry," he said, more softly. "I don't mean to take this out on you. If it's anyone's fault, it's mine. I'm the one whose accursed family started this whole dog's dinner."

"None of that," Aubrey said. "I was just going to say—would you like me to pop up there and take a look? I could try calling down to them, and—"

Stone's phone buzzed on the table.

For a second, none of them moved. Then Stone dashed over and snatched it up. "Yes? What's happening? Are you all right?" He punched the speaker button as Ian came back to the table.

"Yeah," Verity said. Her voice sounded crackly and indistinct, but at least it was intelligible this time. "We're out of the chamber, and coming back over. We're all fine."

"Nothing attacked you?" Stone's heart pounded as a hundred questions jostled against each other in his brain, fighting for their turn.

"No. Nothing attacked us. We didn't see any sign of the echoes or…anything else moving."

Stone frowned. "Verity…I know you well enough that I can tell you're keeping something from me, even over this dodgy connection. What is it?"

"We…found some things. Doc, we're coming out there. Please, just wait. You need to see for yourself."

Stone, Ian, and Aubrey exchanged glances, and Stone wanted nothing more than to run out of the garage and intercept them on their way over. He didn't do that, though. Instead, he said, "Fine. But hurry up. You do realize you've been gone over an hour, right?"

"Time got away from us a little. We're leaving the house now—we'll be there in a minute."

Stone broke the connection, looked at Ian and Aubrey again, and hurried out into the yard where he could see the front of the house. It was a mild, overcast day—at least it wasn't raining. In a few moments, the door opened and four figures emerged, pausing to close it behind them.

"What's that they've got floating between them?" Ian asked.

Stone had been so focused on watching the group at the house that he hadn't even heard his son approach. But Ian was right: Jason's tall figure took point, while Eddie and Ward flanked something the size and shape of a large box or chest levitating between them. Verity brought up the rear.

Unable to restrain himself any longer, Stone dashed toward them, meeting them halfway. "What's that?" he demanded, pointing at the box. As he drew closer, he immediately spotted the magical sigils and symbols on its sides and top.

"Come on, Stone, it's not a 'ard one," Eddie said. "That right there's what we call a box."

Stone glared at him. "Not in the mood for jokes, Eddie. Where did you find it? And what else did you find in there?" Looking up from the box, he noticed that all four of the satchels they'd taken in with them were now bulging where they hadn't been before. "Tell me everything."

"We will," Ward assured him, still focused on doing his part to levitate the box. "Let's get inside so we can put this thing down, and we'll give you the whole story."

"Fine, fine." He hurried back inside the garage and used magic to sweep everything to the side of the table, making room for the box and whatever else his friends had brought with them.

The group arrived a moment later, more slowly due to the effort of levitation. They lowered the heavy box to the table with audible sighs and stepped back, panting.

"*Damn,* that thing's 'eavy," Eddie said. He wrenched off his helmet and safety glasses, tossed them aside, and swiped his hand across his damp forehead. "Anybody got a beer?"

Aubrey retrieved the refreshments and offered them around. He appeared as curious as Stone and Ian about the contents of the box, but faded back and resumed his chair.

"Okay," Stone said. "Out with it. And what's weighing down those bags?"

Eddie opened his and laid several chunks of the broken door on the table next to the box. "'Ang on, let us tell this in order. Verity, suppose you do it?"

Slowly, with several interruptions from Eddie and Ward to fill in details, Verity described their explorations, starting as they entered the ritual chamber.

For the most part, Stone listened silently, once again gripping the table and forcing himself to focus on Verity's tale instead of trying to decipher the inscriptions on the box. When she got to the part about the broken brick alcove and the manacled skeleton inside, a cold chill ran up his back.

"So you're saying the skeleton was still in the manacles?" he demanded. "You're sure about that?"

"Oh, yeah. Its hands and forearms were, anyway. Jason documented everything. Jase, show him the pics you took."

Jason, uncharacteristically silent throughout the exchange, pulled out the video camera and tried to rewind the footage to the section with the skeleton.

His hand tightened on the camera, and his face went pale under his tan. "Oh...fuck..." he whispered.

"What is it?" It was all Stone could do not to snatch the camera from his hands.

"Oh fuck..." He set the video camera on the table with a shaking hand and pulled out the digital. Everybody stared at him as he flicked through several of the photos, and then his hand dropped.

"What's wrong?" Verity asked, coming around to take it from him.

"Nothing," Jason said dully.

"Nothing?" Stone grabbed the video camera. "If nothing's wrong, then—"

"No, you don't get it." Jason spoke with more force now. "*Nothing*. There's fucking *nothing* on the film—not on the video camera or the digital. It's all blank. Gray, like I took a couple hundred photos of a fogbank."

"Bloody 'ell," Eddie said.

"What about the other one?" Verity asked. "Maybe that one's okay—"

"I doubt it," Ward said. "Film cameras are more sensitive to arcane energy. Sometimes they'll show things the human eye can't see, but if the digital footage is corrupted, I'll wager quite a lot that is too."

"We can't exactly take it down to the corner chemist and get it developed," Eddie said. "Not with what's on there."

"I can develop it," Jason said. "Back home, anyway. But I think Arthur's probably right. Fuck!"

Verity touched his arm. "Don't worry about it, Jason. None of us thought to check. And Eddie and Arthur did take a lot of notes and sketches, so we're not totally messed up."

Stone cleared his throat loudly. "Oi! Any chance one of you lot might stop banging on about cameras and finish telling me what's going on?"

"Sorry, mate," Eddie said. "Verity, keep going. We'll sort this out once Stone has the whole story."

Verity and Jason exchanged glances, and then Verity resumed the story, describing what they found in the southernmost hall and the formerly sealed chamber. She didn't look at Stone while she spoke, but every few seconds she shot a quick glance at him, nervous under his burning, steady gaze.

When she finished, Stone remained silent for several seconds, then bowed his head. "I...don't even know where to start," he said. He rubbed his face with both hands.

"Doc—" Verity began.

"I need a moment. Just—talk among yourselves, will you? And don't touch that box yet."

Without waiting for a reply, Stone trudged outside the garage. A light rain fell now, casting an eerie pall over the yard as the sun began its descent. He jammed his hands into his pockets and walked for several moments, then stopped and looked at the dark, forbidding form of his ancestral home.

Forty-one people.

That had been the final count, with the alcoves in the final hallway added in.

His family had murdered forty-one people in their rituals. Not only murdered them, but imprisoned them alive.

For more than two hundred years, his ancestors, his father, and he had carried out their day-to-day tasks while sitting atop the remains of forty-one innocents whose only crime had been to be in the wrong place at the wrong time when a family of monsters were on the prowl for victims.

And that assumed there *were* only forty-one victims. His friends had examined only two of the alcoves, finding a single body in one and the mysterious box in the other. That wasn't enough data to verify that each of the others contained only one body—or that there weren't other hidden chambers under the house that they hadn't found yet.

He closed his eyes and let his breath out. He'd have to go back to the garage. To face the others. Even though all he wanted to do right now was keep walking, to get as far away from this place as he could, he knew he couldn't do that. His friends were waiting for him. His son, heir to his family's horrific legacy, was waiting for him. He wondered bitterly if Ian would have been so keen to be part of the Stone family if he'd know what he was signing on for.

"Doc?" came a soft voice from behind him.

He turned with some reluctance. Verity stood a few feet back, her hands in the pockets of her leather jacket. She'd removed her helmet, leaving her dark hair tousled.

"You okay?" she asked.

He shrugged.

She walked forward and touched his arm. "Anything I can do to help?"

"Can't really think of anything. Unless you can change the past. I don't think I taught you that one, though."

Her arm went around him, and she snuggled her head into his shoulder. "None of this is your fault, you know."

"I know that. But it doesn't make it much easier, does it?" He realized with no real surprise that his legendary curiosity had all but deserted him. He didn't *want* to know what was in that box. He didn't want to see what was in the chamber below the house, even if the echoes were to allow him access. Hell, he wasn't even sure he ever wanted to enter that house again.

"We should go back," Verity said gently.

"Why?" He gave a bitter snort. "So I can find out even *more* horrible truths about my family?"

She squeezed him again. "It sucks, I know it does. But…not finding out isn't going to change anything. At least this way, you'll know exactly what you're working with. You won't be able to deal with those echoes if you don't know more about them."

"Who says I *want* to deal with them?" he snapped, pulling away from her.

"What do you mean?"

He sighed and shook his head. "Never mind, Verity. Never mind. You're right. I've got to have the whole story. That much is true, at least. I can't make decisions based on partial data. Come on—let's go back."

Without waiting for a reply, he turned and set off with long strides back toward the garage. Regret gripped him—he shouldn't treat Verity like that, especially since all she wanted to do was help—but it didn't change the fact that what he truly wanted to do right now, if he couldn't simply go somewhere far away, drink himself into oblivion, and forget about the whole thing, was to gather up all of the items his friends had brought back, take them somewhere, and examine them on his own.

At least that way, the people who respected and cared about him wouldn't have to see any more of his family's shame.

But he couldn't do that either. Ten years ago, he would have. Hell, *five* years ago he probably would have. But maybe he'd grown—just a little—in those ten years.

It was one small thing to hold on to, at least.

He found Eddie, Ward, Ian, and Aubrey back in the garage, milling around in various attitudes of discomfort. None of them were anywhere near the table. They all looked up when he came in.

"All right, mate?" Eddie asked softly.

"No. But let's get on with this anyway." He nodded toward the items on the table. "I assume those chunks are what's left of the door blocking the south hallway."

"Yeah," Jason said. "And a few pieces of the coffin or whatever, but there weren't any markings or carvings on that."

Stone picked up one of the larger chunks, forcing himself to compartmentalize his whirling thoughts. If he let the guilt and shame overwhelm him, he'd never accomplish anything. If nothing else, he owed the people who'd died beneath his home some kind of closure, and he wouldn't get that without figuring out how to deal with their echoes.

He addressed Eddie and Ward. "Did you make anything of the carvings on the door, or the inscriptions inside the chamber?"

Eddie flipped to a page in his notebook and turned it so Stone could see the series of sketches. "We think the inscriptions are protective—or more precisely, imprisoning. The language is bloody old—some of this structure goes back thousands of years. I'd have to take the sketches back to the library to do some research, but my initial thought is that whoever sealed that thing in that room, they were very concerned about it getting out."

"I still don't get it, though," Jason said. "If that *was* a coffin, doesn't that mean whatever it was, it was dead?"

"Not necessarily," Ward said. "As we've seen with the bricked alcoves, it wasn't unheard of to seal living beings away. It's possible the chamber could have been another form of that same thing."

"So they shut him, or her, or whatever, up inside a stone coffin and then sealed them behind protective enchantments in that room?" Verity asked. "That sounds like whoever they were, they weren't some poor mundane homeless person or prostitute."

"And where are they *now*?" Jason demanded. "This is starting to sound like some kind of bad vampire story. You know, they lock Count Dracula up but he gets out and starts causing trouble? Do you think the ghosts—sorry, I can't get used to calling them 'echoes'—are connected with whatever was locked in that room? Hell, *could* it be Dracula? *Are* there vampires?"

"Can't say there aren't," Eddie said. "I've personally never encountered any, but I've heard stories. We all have. But," he added when Jason started to reply, "even if there are creatures who drink human blood to survive, that doesn't mean that's what we're dealing with here."

"Then what *are* we dealing with?" Verity asked. "And what, if anything, is its connection with the echoes? Where is it now?"

Once again, all of them looked around as if expecting it to be lurking nearby.

"We can't say at present," Ward said. "We don't have enough data. All we know for certain is that at least one person was likely interred alive in the crypt, that something either broke out of that sealed room itself or had inside help, and that some number of echoes have a vendetta against Stone's family to the point where they won't allow any of them to set foot inside the house. What we *don't* know is if any of those three things are connected."

"Maybe we should look in the box," Ian said. He narrowed his eyes. "Hey, I just thought of something."

"What's that?" Eddie asked.

He pointed at it. "Arthur, you said the bricks just sort of popped out of that alcove when you got near it?"

"Yes. Eddie is probably correct—the mortar was—"

"But what if that *isn't* what happened?" Ian interrupted.

"What do you mean?" Verity asked.

He gripped the box's edges. "The echoes obviously don't like our family, right? And we're assuming for now that the reason people were bricked up down there was for some ritual purpose, and it was done by our ancestors. Right?"

"Yes…" Eddie said slowly. "What are you gettin' at?"

Ian began to pace, looking eerily like his father when he was working something out in his mind. "Echoes can move things around—we know that. It's not all just illusion. They can affect the physical world."

"Right…" Verity said. She looked as confused as Eddie did.

But Stone didn't. "Yes!" he snapped, raising a hand in triumph. Some of the shame burned away, replaced by a new energy as he caught on to Ian's train of thought. "Ian, you're thinking perhaps the echoes *wanted* this lot to find that box.

That they knocked the bricks out just as Ward passed by, trying to catch his attention."

"Yeah. Especially if the echoes don't know these guys are connected with our family—or maybe they don't even care. You said echoes are pretty single-minded, right, Dad?"

"Yes, generally they are."

"That could make sense, then. If their obsession is with punishing the Stones, maybe they don't even *care* that these guys are working with us. What if they just wanted somebody who isn't connected with the family to find out the truth of what happened? If it's in that box…"

"Then they took their shot, bringing it to the attention of somebody who isn't a Stone," Verity said with enthusiasm. "You might be on to something, Ian."

"I only see one problem with that hypothesis," Ward said. He'd pulled the chair over and was now sitting in it, leaning in close to the box as he examined it with a magnifying glass he'd removed from his bag.

"What's that?" Stone asked.

"This box has a mundane lock on it, which should be easy to deal with. But it also has a magical one. And unless I'm reading these sigils wrong, only a Stone can open it."

CHAPTER FIFTEEN

ALL SEVEN OF THE OBSERVERS stood around the table, looking down at the metal box.

"Do you want to try opening it, Stone?" Eddie asked. "Or do you think Ward or I should give it a go?"

"Why would the echoes point it out to us, if we couldn't open it?" Jason asked.

Stone pondered. "I think it's that single-minded thing again, honestly. If Ian's on to something and they do want it found, maybe they haven't worked out the rest of their plan yet." He leaned forward, studying the sigils. "In any case, from the look of these protective sigils, Ward's right—only a Stone can safely open this."

"What does that mean, 'safely'?" Verity asked. "If somebody else tries, will it explode, or turn them into a frog, or just destroy what's inside?"

"No way to tell. I think that's on purpose." He pointed at some of the symbols near the mundane lock. "Aha...oh, this is bloody tricky."

"What is?" Eddie asked, leaning in for a closer look.

Stone lifted the lock, holding a light spell so he could see its rear side. It, too, was covered in tiny, precisely carved sigils. "Good thing you *didn't* try opening this."

"Bloody hell…"

"What is it?" Jason demanded. "What's going on?"

Stone pointed at the lock. "The mundane lock is a trap. A diversion. If anyone—even a Stone—tried to force it open…well, I'm honestly not sure what might happen. It doesn't say here, precisely, except to imply it's not pleasant. And given what my ancestors have obviously gotten up to, 'not pleasant' probably doesn't mean a little flag with *'Bang!'* on it will pop out."

"So how do we open it?" Verity asked. "Does it say anything else on the back of the lock?"

Eddie tilted his head to get a better angle on the upside-down inscription. "This isn't nearly as old as the writing inside the chamber. Fairly bog-standard old-style magical script. Something about *'Only one with the true blood of a Stone can gain safe entry. All others beware.'*"

"But Al, you said even you couldn't break the lock," Jason said. "Do you have to do some kind of magical ritual to—"

Stone was only half-listening to him as he continued to study the inscription. Then, in spite of the gravity of their situation, he couldn't help but flash a manic smile. "Of course…" he murmured. "Tricky indeed, my horrible old ancestors were." He glanced around at his friends. "One of you lot got a pocket knife?"

Ian, Aubrey, and Jason all pulled one from their pockets at once and offered them. "What are you gonna do with it?" Jason asked.

Stone took Ian's knife and popped it open. He summoned a small jet of blue flame from his fingertip, held the blade in it for a few seconds, and then made a small slice across his finger.

Jason, Verity, Ian, and Aubrey gaped at him in astonishment, but Eddie and Ward nodded in sudden understanding as he lifted the lock, turned his hand over, and dripped several drops of blood into the lock's large keyhole. As he did so, he muttered an incantation under his breath.

The lock emitted a faint sizzling sound. An acrid odor wafted out over the table, and a moment later a small puff of red smoke issued from the keyhole. With a *pop,* the lock burst open.

"Holy shit…" Jason breathed.

"True blood of a Stone, indeed." Stone paused to heal the cut on his finger, then pulled the lock free from the hasp and tossed it aside. "Handy little thing."

"I've heard of blood locks," Eddie said, looking at it in wonder. "Haven't seen many, though. I think Desmond had a couple old ones buried in his stuff up at Caventhorne, but we couldn't get 'em open because the lines have died out." He waved at the box. "Go on, then—open it."

Stone stood facing the box and summoned a shield around himself. "Stand back, all of you, just in case we've missed something."

The others drew a few steps back, all of them as focused on the metal box as Stone himself was.

Stone drew a deep breath, his heart hammering. What would he find inside the box? Valuables? Body parts? Potent magical items? Or, more likely, more records of the terrible deeds his family had committed. As he'd discovered from previous documents, they were nothing if not meticulous in their record-keeping.

Do I even want to know?

The others watched him in silence. He wondered if they were giving him space, allowing him to do this at his own pace, or if they were as concerned as he was about what might be inside.

Just do it, damn you. Leaving it in there won't change anything, and you don't have the right to hide from this.

With a flick of magic, he pulled the heavy metal hasp free and lifted the box's lid.

Neither the hasp nor the hinges made any noise. The lid came free without sticking, once again showing remarkably good preservation despite its age. Stone moved forward with tentative steps, peering into the revealed space.

"What is it?" Eddie asked, but didn't approach the table.

The box wasn't full. In fact, it contained only a few items: a leatherbound ledger, a thick journal, and two large, rolled sheaves of vellum lay in the bottom. Placed neatly alongside them was a bundle of soft leather, wrapped in several loops of twine.

Stone studied the space with magical sight, checking for any lingering traps. He didn't find any, though, and didn't expect to. The blood lock and the powerful enchantment on it had ensured only those of the Stone line could gain access, so it didn't make sense to include additional hazards for any who did.

"What's in the box, mate?" Eddie asked again, softly.

Stone still didn't answer. He set aside the wrapped leather bundle, picked up one of the rolled vellum sheaves, and unrolled it on the table in front of the box, using Ian's knife and three beer bottles to hold down its edges.

The others moved closer. "That looks like an old building plan," Jason said. "Like whatever they had before blueprints."

"Yes, sir," Aubrey said, peering at it. "If I don't miss my guess, it appears to be the plan for this very house."

"It does indeed," Stone said. He pulled up the topmost page, which displayed the structure's third floor and attic. As he expected, the other pages contained detailed plans for the second and ground floors, with the bottom-most one showing the basement level. He moved this one to the top and examined it more closely. "Look—it even includes the hidden areas where the library and workroom are."

Ward had come forward too, and was looking at the legend at the bottom of the ground-floor plan. He pointed at the date there. "Is that around when the house was constructed, Stone?"

"Far as I know, yes. That sounds about right."

"What about the other rolled paper?" Jason asked. "More plans?"

Stone left the first set where they were and unrolled the second. This one was as large as the other, but included only a single sheet. The sketching on this one looked cruder than the house plan, drawn with a heavy black pen but without the mathematical precision of the other. Someone had obviously treated all of them with the technique mages used to keep ancient paper supple and free of decay.

"It's the underground chamber," Verity said. "It's got to be." She pointed. "Look, there's the circular ritual room, and the hallways branching out in four directions."

"I don't see the other room, though," Jason said. "The one with the coffin. It should be to the south, but it isn't."

"Look," Eddie said. He pulled out a capped pen and pointed at one of the hallways. "Each one of those alcoves is labeled with a number."

"So they are." Stone examined them until he located the alcove labeled *1,* then followed them around, tracing each one in turn with his finger. "Forty-one in all."

"The chamber where we found the box isn't labeled," Eddie said. "See there it is at the end of the 'all. Aside from no number, it doesn't look any different."

"What's it mean?" Verity asked. "Why are they numbered? And why isn't the sealed chamber here?"

"Maybe they hadn't built it yet," Ian said. "Look at the date on this one."

It took a moment to find it, scrawled near the bottom right corner of the map. "That's a year before the date on the other one," Ward said. "So this was built first. I suppose it makes sense—if you want to include a secret, hidden network of passages under a house, the best time to excavate it is before the other parts are built."

"Why the numbers, though?" Verity asked. "Just so they could keep track of the individual alcoves?"

Stone had barely been listening to his friends' speculations. As they continued to pore over the plans, he had withdrawn the ledger from the box and begun flipping through it. "No," he said dully in response to Verity's question. "It's not the alcoves they were keeping track of."

He opened it to a random page and laid it on the table on top of the plans, and everyone crowded around for a closer look.

At the top of the page, encircled, was the number *15.* Beneath it, filling approximately half the page, were several lines of old-fashioned script written in black ink. Like the plans, the page appeared as fresh and new as if it had been written yesterday.

"That's not English," Jason said, his brow furrowing as he tried to make sense of it. "Is it more of the magical language?"

"And...what are those at the top?" Verity pointed to a pair of shorter lines just beneath the circled number.

"It's a name," Stone said. "And a location. '*Thomas D.*,' I think it says. '*Spitalfield*.'"

"Where's that?" Jason asked.

"It's part of London," Eddie told him. He looked grim. "Back 'round the time when this 'ouse was built, it was one o' the more notorious slum areas."

"Wait..." Verity said, pulling the map from under the ledger. She levitated the box to the floor and spread the map out on the table in its place. "Doc, how many numbered entries are there in that ledger?"

"Forty-one," Stone said softly. "Yes, Verity, I think you've worked it out."

She pointed at the alcove marked *15*. "So...that's Thomas D." Her voice shook a little.

"Quite likely." He examined the text below the name and location. "Apparently he was a beggar, encountered outside a pub late one night in August of 1716 and given a promise of work."

"So..." Jason said in a dull tone, "they lured him down here and...what? *Did* they give him work, helping to build this place, and then killed him? Why would they bury him alive, though? That's the part I don't get. If he was killed as part of a sacrifice, then why would he be bricked up alive?

Assuming he was, of course. We don't know what's going on inside the alcoves that are still sealed, just the one we saw into."

"That's a damned good question," Stone said. He stared dully down at the ledger, flipping through the pages. Each one contained a number, a name, and a location, followed by a note about the person. Some pages included full names, some partials, and even a few nicknames. A couple had only descriptions: "a middle-aged trollop," or "an elderly traveler." Both men and women were represented, though the men outnumbered the women by nearly two to one, and a small subset of the entries included approximate ages marking the victims as children as young as ten years old. The locations were spread all over the country, from unsavory dockside districts in London all the way up to Manchester.

He couldn't be sure, of course, but he didn't need to be sure. Something deep in his bones told him he was correct: each and every one of these entries represented a human being, either a poor unfortunate trying to eke out a living in a brutal age, or perhaps in some cases a wealthier individual who'd somehow landed on the wrong side of his family of monsters and paid the ultimate price for it.

"I could see why they might do that with a small number of people," he said. "Perhaps enemies of some sort. But...*all* of them? It doesn't make sense."

"I think I might be able to answer that." Eddie's tone was even grimmer than Jason's. He pointed down at the box Verity had placed on the floor to make room. "Stone, d'you mind if I 'ave a look at that other book?"

Stone narrowed his eyes. "What are you getting at, Eddie?"

"Please. It's not something I want to say unless I've got some proof. It's—" He shook his head. "May I?"

"Yes, all right. Do it." Stone didn't want to let him look— didn't want to let him find something even worse so he could share it with everyone in the room. It was bad enough his family had been so thoroughly reprehensible, without having their crimes put on display in front of an entire audience.

But they aren't just an audience. They're your friends, and none of them have been anything but loyal to you. He drove down the fear he didn't even want to acknowledge: not that they would reveal his family's sins to the world, but that they would begin to see *him* through the same lens.

They all watched Eddie as he picked up the remaining tome and began paging through it. Stone moved around behind him, looking over his shoulder.

Instead of more narrow, old-style text, the book mostly appeared to be full of complex ritual diagrams. Eddie turned the pages too fast for Stone to get a good look at them, so instead he watched his friend's face. The librarian's jaw set and his brow furrowed as he flipped through; he looked he had to force himself to keep reading.

"Eddie…" Stone murmured. "Give me something. Please. Was your suspicion correct?"

Eddie handed the book to Ward, then turned back to Stone and let his breath out. "Looks that way. You're not gonna like this, mate. You sure you don't want me to tell you in private first?"

He almost took the offered chance. If it was something truly horrible, he could count on his old friend to keep it quiet. That was what he *did,* as a researcher and curator of one of the largest collections of magical literature in the western world. Discretion was a cornerstone of his job, and the reason why so many mages trusted him with their personal business.

But yet…

"No," he said firmly. He looked around, taking in the serious faces of his friends, of his son. They were all looking at him, serious and tense, ready to accept his decision even if they didn't like it. "No, you all deserve to know. Tell us, Eddie. What happened down there?"

Eddie almost looked sympathetic. He glanced at closed book Ward held, then back at Stone. "'Ave you ever 'eard of a foundation sacrifice?"

CHAPTER SIXTEEN

EVERYONE EXCEPT WARD looked at Eddie blankly.

"Can't say I have," Stone said, but another chill began creeping up his back. It wasn't hard to guess at least the gist of what his friend referred to.

"What is it, Eddie?" Verity asked. Her voice was soft, tentative, almost as if she wasn't sure she wanted to know.

Eddie let out a long sigh and began pacing. "It's a very old practice—mundanes mostly gave it up centuries ago. The idea is that you sacrifice living beings—often animals, but sometimes 'umans—to your deity, then entomb their bodies in the foundation stones of buildings as they're being constructed. They believed that by doin' this, the spirits of the sacrificed beings would serve as kind o' guardians for the building, the city, whatever, and also that their gods would bless the project."

"That's...horrible," Verity said, going pale.

"It is, which is why they stopped doin' it as people got more enlightened. But you've got to remember, we're mostly talkin' about very religious people 'ere. They believed the souls they interred were immortal, so all that 'appened when their bodies were sacrificed for this ceremony was that their souls were freed to be re-inserted into another body. Believe

R. L. KING

it or not, some people actually fought for the honor of servin'
as a sacrifice."

"You're kidding," Jason said. He looked as pale as his
sister. "People *wanted* this?"

"Not all of them did," Ward said. "In many cases, slaves,
prisoners, or other low-status people were sacrificed and interred against their will, especially in the later years of the
practice."

"But wait," Ian said. "This is all terrible, but what's it got
to do with us? You said they sacrificed people and *then* put
them in the foundation, right? They didn't bury them alive."

"Not generally," Eddie agreed. "I've read accounts where
animals were imprisoned alive, but not 'umans. Not by mundanes, anyway."

"But mages did…" Stone said. He stood still, his body
suddenly leaden. "Or at least…my ancestors did."

"I'd be very surprised if it was just your ancestors," Eddie
said gently. "Most of our lot, especially the powerful ones,
weren't exactly saintly back in those days."

"But they weren't religious, either," Stone said. "So why
would they—"

"I don't think it's about religion," Ward said. "I think it's
about power."

Stone stared at him, then took a step back and dropped
into Aubrey's vacated chair as the truth he didn't want to
acknowledge hit him. "Dear gods…" he murmured. "Yes.
You've got to be right."

"What are you talking about?" Jason demanded. "What's
he mean, power?"

Stone spoke in a plodding monotone, and didn't look at
him. "It's a basic principle of magic that the energies of birth

and death are the sources of the most potent power. That's why human sacrifices are so dangerous, and why they can add immense punch to rituals if properly handled. We already know my ancestors used sacrifices to power their rituals, but apparently that wasn't enough for them."

"So...just to be clear," Ian said slowly, "what we're talking about here is that our ancestors actively went out looking for people who wouldn't be missed, or enemies, shackled them in specially prepared holes, and bricked them up so the energy of their deaths could...what? Power some ritual?"

Eddie nodded. "I don't know about a ritual, but I think you've got the rest correct." He indicated the book Ward held. "I'll wager if we read through that thoroughly, we'll get the rest of the story. My guess is they set something up in advance, probably as part of the design of the 'idden area. They placed the sacrifices in their alcoves, closed them up, and then covered the chamber and began buildin' the rest. They probably worked out a way for the death energy to strengthen the magical protections on the 'ouse. Or possibly bound the spirits *to* the area, to provide perpetual reinforcement."

"But *why*?" Stone flung himself up from the chair, unable to remain seated as restless energy surged within him. He waved his hand, encompassing the area around them. "This place is built on *three bloody ley lines*. It's one of the most magically powerful locations in all of Britain. The wards are some of the strongest around, so much that they've never needed to be refreshed since they were originally cast. What the hell were these people trying to guard against, that they'd have to torture and kill forty-one people to do it?"

Verity must have heard something in his voice. She intercepted him, putting a gentle hand on his shoulder. "It's okay, Doc—" she began.

"No, Verity." He shook free of her hand. "It's most certainly *not* okay. This is about as far from 'okay' as it's possible to be." He jerked his head toward the house. "I'm not sure I'll ever be able to go back into that place again even if we *do* get rid of the echoes. I'm not even sure we *should.*"

"Dad—" Ian began.

"No, Ian. No. Just—don't." Stone resumed his mad pacing. His mind spun, sending him image after image of manacled people—men, women, even children—screaming in vain for someone to help them, to release them from their tiny, dark prisons. He pictured the cold, uncaring faces of his ancestors, ignoring their desperate and fading pleas as they finally succumbed to starvation and died dangling from their bonds.

"Why should we get rid of them?" he demanded. He could hear the edge of mania in his voice, but did nothing to alter it. "They've got as much right to be here as we do. More, maybe. They didn't ask for their lives to be sacrificed so our damnable family could gain more power. Of *course* they're angry! Wouldn't you be? I'm surprised they haven't pulled the whole accursed place down around our ears—and I'm not sure I'd blame them if they did!"

"Stone. *Alastair.*" Ward's tone was calm, though it still shook a little, and his dark skin bore a hint of gray pallor. "Please. We can discuss all of this, but—there's something else."

Stone pulled up short. "Something *worse*?" He'd stopped asking how anything could have been worse.

But Ward shook his head. "No. Not worse. Just...something you might not have known." He still held the book, open to one of the earlier pages. He turned it around so Stone could see.

"What is it now?" Stone didn't want to look, but as always his curiosity got the better of him. He took a couple of deep breaths and tried to slow his heart's mad thundering.

Ward pointed. "It's possible that I'm reading this wrong—the script is difficult to make out, and the language is archaic—but it appears your house here was not the first to stand on this land."

"*What?*" Stone strode forward, examining the page. "There was another house here? When? What happened to it?"

"I'm not certain. Sometime shortly before this one was built, obviously. They don't mention much about it—apparently it was common knowledge at the time so they didn't need to discuss it—but from what I can gather, it was destroyed, and violently."

"Violently?" Jason came over and looked at the page, even though it was obvious he couldn't read a bit of it. "What, like somebody blew it up?"

"Magic was almost certainly involved," Ward said. "If my translation of this passage is correct, the place was literally razed to the ground."

"Bloody 'ell," Eddie said, moving over to look at the pages too. "I've never seen anything about this in any of the library's references. Not even when I was researchin' Stone's family tree last year." He lifted his gaze to settle on Stone. "This could mean your line goes back farther than we thought it did. If the records beyond what I already showed you were lost…"

"Or destroyed," Ward added. "If someone hated your family enough to level their ancestral home to the ground, it's possible either they or your own family did something to obscure the earlier records."

"That sounds like there was something nobody wanted anyone to find out about," Ian said.

"It does indeed," Eddie agreed. "Stone, do you want me to look into this in more depth? I can dig into the oldest reference material back in London, and…"

Stone didn't know what he wanted to do. He continued staring with a kind of numb shock, shifting his gaze between the maps on the table, the open ledger with its pages of dispassionately numbered sacrificial victims, and the tome in Ward's hands. "Do what you like," he said. "Just…I think I need to go somewhere for a while, and be alone with my thoughts."

"No, you don't," Verity said firmly. "That's the last thing you need right now." She approached him again, slowly, the way she might have approached a wary young animal. When he didn't move away, she put her hand on his arm. "And anyway, you're not fooling anybody: what you want to be alone with is a big bottle of booze. It's not going to do you any good at all to go off somewhere and drink yourself into a stupor, or destroy yourself thinking about all this stuff on your own. Stay here with us. We can help."

Stone snorted. "You can help?" His tone dripped with despair. "How? How can you help? Can you change any of this? Can you appease these echoes, who have every right in the world *not* to be appeased?"

The others remained silent, looking discreetly away so as not to intrude. Verity pulled Stone into a hug and buried her face in his shoulder.

"No," she said, muffled by his coat. "No, we can't do that. But we can listen. We can be here with you."

He almost pulled away again. His body felt as if someone were running a current through it, urging him to move, to run, to get away from here before it shook itself to pieces. His brain wouldn't settle on a thought, fighting through more images of screaming, pleading victims.

"Fine," he said at last. "Fine. I'll stay. For now, at least. But I'm not sure what good it will do any of us. I'm hardly fit company at present." He raised his head, patted Verity's back, and turned back to the box. "There's one more thing in there. Let's have a look at it, shall we? Might as well get all the nasty little secrets out at once."

Nobody moved for a moment, all of them exchanging glances and not wanting to make the first move. Finally, Ian bent and lifted the leather-wrapped bundle from the box. As the rest gathered around the table, he laid it on top of the map, undid the twine wrapped around it, and unrolled it.

Stone bowed his head. "No…" he whispered.

He didn't need any help from Eddie or Ward to know what he was looking at.

Spread across the dark-brown leather surface were several small objects, glittering in the overhead light: gold rings, some set with colorful gemstones; a pair of glimmering golden necklaces with jeweled pendants; an intricately carved cameo featuring the image of a beautiful woman; a handful of gold coins. The final item was a dagger with an elaborately carved and jewel-encrusted hilt, and an equally ornate scabbard.

Everyone looked at the items in silence, and then Jason said, "Did these belong to the victims? They seem fairly fancy for poor people."

Stone scanned the small treasure with magical sight and saw no sign of arcane energy. "This reinforces the idea that the sacrifices weren't all paupers. I suspect the murderers took this opportunity to rid themselves of a few enemies of the family. Possibly even the people who destroyed the house in the first place." He looked at Eddie for confirmation.

"It's possible. Which means if we examine that ledger carefully, we might get some ideas about who it might have been." He pointed at it. "If you'll trust me with this and the other one, I'll take 'em back to London and see what I can find out. If nothin' else, Ward and I can get you full translations."

"Fine," Stone said. "Do what you like. Of course I trust you."

"Hey," Jason said. "Let me try to get some photos before you take those, if that's okay, Al. That way if you need to consult something, you'll have something to look at."

"You're welcome to give it a try. No idea if it'll work, though."

Jason snapped a sample photo of one of the pages with his digital camera, then checked the photo roll and flashed a thumbs-up. "Looks like we're good here."

Stone nodded, not terribly interested in the process of photographing the ledger and journal. Instead, he gripped the table and gazed down at the small pile of valuables. "I don't feel right about keeping these," he said to no one in particular. "If nothing else, they should go to a museum or something."

"Or to their descendants, if we can find them," Verity said. She looked away, then met his eyes with reluctance. "And...Doc...I hate to say this now, but there's something else you need to think about."

"What's that?"

She swallowed. "The...victims. The skeletons, assuming there's one in each of those alcoves. You...can't just leave them there."

Stone had already thought of that. "I know," he said with a sigh. "I know, Verity. Something's got to be done. They need to be properly buried, if nothing else, and...commemorated somehow."

"But...what about the authorities? Are you going to keep this secret?"

Ian and Aubrey drifted over, catching the end of the conversation. "You can't keep it secret, sir," Aubrey said. He, too, looked reluctant. "It's...not right."

Stone clenched his fists. "I *know*," he said again. "I get that. And I suppose I shouldn't be complaining about how inconvenient all this is likely to be for me. It can hardly beat dying alone in manacles, can it?" Bitterness once again tinged his tone. "But...first we need to sort this out. We need to deal with the echoes. And I haven't got any idea how to do that."

"I think I do."

Stone turned. Eddie and Ward, who'd been talking quietly on the other side of the room, had approached him. He narrowed his eyes at Eddie. "You do?"

"Yeah. The valuables there gave me the idea."

"And what do you propose we do, then?"

"I think we should have a séance. And as soon as possible."

| CHAPTER SEVENTEEN

I F ANYONE AT THE THE KING'S ARMS Inn and Public House in the village near Stone's home thought the collection of individuals who showed up later that evening and commandeered a large table in the back room looked strangely stressed, they didn't say anything about it. Not within their earshot, anyway. The group did have to endure the not-so-discreet glances of more people than usual walking by, though.

Stone barely noticed. He was aware that many of the villagers, despite being friendly with Aubrey, considered him odd. Hell, the villagers had likely thought *all* the Stones over the years to be odd, but because he was absent from his house far more often than he was present, that added an extra dimension of mystery. Tonight, though, he had more pressing issues weighing on his mind than a bunch of small-town busybodies trying to catch an earful of what he and his collection of mad friends were discussing.

They couldn't have anyway—a simple spell took care of that, obscuring their words just enough to make them unintelligible to anyone standing more than two feet from the table.

R. L. KING

"Are you sure about this, Eddie?" Stone asked. "I've got to say I still don't like it. Even if this woman knows what she's doing, it's got the potential to backfire rather spectacularly. If we set off those echoes any further, they might decide to bring the place down around us."

"No guarantees—you know as well as I do there aren't ever guarantees in stuff like this—but Poppy is the best medium I know. She's the real deal. If anybody can get to the bottom of what those echoes want, it's 'er."

They had adjourned to the village on Aubrey's suggestion, and Stone was grateful for it. He needed to get away from that place for a while, and Aubrey's flat, though large, wasn't big enough for them to all be comfortable. He hadn't eaten much, but he was already on his third Guinness. Verity flashed him a concerned glance when he ordered it, but he waved her off. Even though he had no intention of getting drunk tonight—not yet, anyway—that didn't mean he intended to abstain entirely. He needed *something* to take the edge off the crushing guilt that wouldn't leave him alone.

When Eddie had first suggested the séance, he'd nixed the idea. The last thing he wanted to do right now was bring in some stranger and make her privy to his family's darkest and most embarrassing secrets. That, and he didn't have a lot of respect for most so-called "spirit mediums," largely because the vast majority of them were frauds. With most magic, the practitioner could demonstrate their power in a way others could observe and quantify, but mediums, by the very nature of their work, had to be taken with a certain degree of trust. In all his life, he'd met only one practitioner of divination whom he not only believed could do what she claimed, but that he trusted—and right now, for reasons of his own, he wasn't keen on trying to track down Madame Huan.

Eddie had assured him, though, that the woman he recommended was not only highly talented, but could also be counted on to exercise utmost discretion. "You wouldn't believe some o' the things she gets up to," he said, waving off Stone's objections. "Some o' the folks she's worked for, your eyes'd pop clean outta your 'ead if you knew. I can't say who, but trust me. She does work for the Library occasionally, when I'm tryin' to get some insight into some particular event or location."

"I don't know, Eddie." He glanced at Ward. "What do you think? Are you behind this insane idea, too?"

"It's up to you, of course. But if I were you, I'd try it. You need to find out what's going on here before you can decide your next steps. If the echoes won't talk to you, perhaps they'll talk to her."

Still, Stone hesitated. "Let me think about it," he said as they all sorted themselves into three cabs to head down to the village.

"Don't think too long, mate," Eddie warned. "If you want 'er to come tonight, I'll 'ave to give 'er a ring soon. And just so you know, she doesn't work cheap."

Stone didn't say anything else about it until after they'd finished their meals. He picked at his risotto, pushing it around on the plate until he'd finally given up and ordered the third Guinness. The others gave him space; they talked about inconsequential topics, dominated by Eddie's football stories and Ian's accounts of some of his portal-based world tour.

Finally, as the meal wound down and everyone was sipping pints or cups of coffee, Stone sighed. "All right, Eddie," he said, hoping he wasn't making a big mistake. "Give this woman a call, if you think she can help. Don't give her too many details until I get a chance to talk to her, but make sure she knows what she's getting into. This could be dangerous."

"You got it." Eddie immediately leaped up from his chair and pulled out his phone. "Give me two ticks to pop outside where it's quieter, and I'll let you know what she says."

He hurried out, and returned ten minutes later to drop down next to Stone. "All right. She's coming. I gave 'er the minimum amount of info necessary, but she's already intrigued. Says she needs a bit to prepare, so she'll meet us at the Tolliver's portal at eleven and we can go through from there."

"Where is she planning to do this?" Stone asked. "I insist on being present, and Ian and I can't enter the house."

"We'll work that out when she gets 'ere."

"Sir, forgive me for interrupting," Aubrey said, "but of course you're welcome to use my flat if you like. We can push the furniture against the walls in the sitting room."

"Thanks, Aubrey. It might come to that, but I'd rather not have a load of angry echoes tearing *your* place apart. Let's see what she has to say."

He drained his pint and considered ordering another one. In the back of his mind, he couldn't help thinking this was a bad decision, and one not only he but his friends might end up paying dearly for.

| CHAPTER EIGHTEEN

BECAUSE IT DIDN'T MAKE SENSE for the whole group of them to mob Tolliver's to meet the medium, they decided Stone, Eddie, and Verity would go while the others waited back at Aubrey's place.

The magic shop had several customers, which didn't surprise Stone—they were open twenty-four hours and did most of their business after dark. Fortunately, when they arrived at the portal room they found it deserted. Stone paced, unable to remain still.

Verity caught up with him. "I know you don't like this," she said, touching his arm. "But maybe if you can talk to the echoes, you might be able to reason with them."

He shook his head. "Would you be willing to reason, if you were them? *I* certainly wouldn't want anything to do with any descendants of the people who did that to me."

"Well...maybe they'll at least tell you what they want. Right now, we're just guessing. That can't be any help."

"I suppose not. I just want to get on with it." He glanced at his watch. "Five after eleven. She's late."

"She'll be 'ere," Eddie said. He leaned against the wall, watching the portal's shifting pastel colors.

At that moment, almost as if waiting to make a proper entrance, a figure emerged from the swirling doorway. When she saw Eddie, her face broke into a wide smile. "Eddie! How are you, luv?"

Eddie returned her grin, striding over to accept an enthusiastic hug. "Poppy! Good to see you again. You're looking well, as always."

Stone and Verity exchanged glances.

Eddie waved one hand at them, and one at the woman. "Poppy, these two miscreants are my mates, Alastair Stone and Verity Thayer. And this is Penelope Willoughby, but she'll bite your 'eads off if you try callin 'er that."

"Poppy" Willoughby was clearly not what either of them had been expecting. Stone wasn't sure what he *had* been expecting, but to start with, she couldn't have been a day over twenty-five years old, which was the first bit of strangeness. Most of the mediums he'd met, for whatever reason, were older—women more often than men, but rarely below their forties. Also, aside from Madame Huan, all of them possessed a vaguely ethereal, loopy quality, as if they either hadn't quite synced up properly with the real world or were perpetually baked. Possibly both, in some cases.

This woman, on the other hand, looked like she'd just left one of the hotter London clubs to fulfill this appointment. Tall and well-padded without being chubby, she had light brown skin, an impressive figure, and open, friendly features. She also had a tall, bright-blue Mohawk, an abundant quantity of makeup, and she wore a trendy outfit featuring skintight jeans, low-cut top, and a bright blue leather moto jacket that matched her hair. Her black, stiletto-heeled boots made her almost as tall as Stone—taller, if you counted the Mohawk.

Rounding out her ensemble was a capacious satchel of purple leather.

Her startlingly green gaze settled on Stone and Verity. "Alastair Stone, is it? I've heard about you."

"Er—have you?" Stone asked. He felt suddenly as if he had been engulfed in a cheerful whirlwind.

"Oh, yeah. Quite the celebrity, you are." She turned to Verity with approval. "And Verity Thayer. Don't think I've heard of you."

"Uh—I'm Dr. Stone's apprentice." Verity, usually good at rolling with anything that came up, seemed almost as taken aback as Stone.

"*Former* apprentice," Stone added. He took a deep breath and tried to fit this new bit of unexpected information into his increasingly teetering worldview. "Er—it's a pleasure to meet you, at any rate. I hope you can help us."

"Oh, I do too. Eddie says you've got quite a dilemma. Whole infestation of hostile echoes, is it?"

"So it would seem."

Her expression sobered, making her look less like a drunken club girl and more like a competent professional. "Nasty stuff, that. I've heard of a couple cases like that, but never seen one m'self. Are you wantin' me to contact anyone in particular, or just reach out to whoever's willin' to talk?"

"I'll...take what I can get at this point," Stone said. "But I'm not sure Eddie warned you—none of them are terribly happy with me, or my son. They've got some perfectly reasonable issues with the Stone family in general."

"Ah, yeah." She nodded knowingly. "Eddie did say somethin' about that, though he didn't say why. Is that part of what you want me to try findin' out?"

"We think we already know that bit," Eddie said. "What we're really lookin' for, I think, is what Stone can do to placate 'em so they'll take off and let 'im back in 'is 'ouse."

Poppy narrowed her eyes. "How many o' these things are we talkin' about here? Four? Five, maybe?"

"Forty-one," Stone said dully, once again regretting his decision to call in outside help.

She almost did a classic double-take. "Hang on? Did I hear you right? Did you say *forty-one*?"

"It's…a unique situation. Listen, maybe this was a bad idea. If you don't think you can—"

She waved him off. "No, no, I didn't say I couldn't help. But forty-one spirits…that's… that's a new one," she finished. "I'm not sure I want to know what you lot did to piss off that many people, but I suppose I'm gonna find out."

"We're not sure all forty-one of them are there," Eddie said, glancing at Stone. "It's possible some o' them might've already moved on, innit?"

"I guess we'll find that out too, won't we?" Poppy said. To Stone, she added, "This is gonna increase the price, though. Sorry—I hope Eddie told you what I do doesn't come cheap, and tryin' to contact that many hostile echoes could be bloody dangerous."

"If you can do it, name your price," Stone said. "Perhaps you—or they—can identify one of their number to speak for them. That might make things easier."

Poppy laughed and patted Stone's shoulder. "Oh, luv, you might be a big noise in the magical world, but it's obvious you haven't dealt with too many spirits. Trust me— they're almost never that organized. Especially if they're angry. If I make contact, I'll have a hard time makin' most of 'em shut their gobs long enough to get a coherent word out o' the rest."

Stone glanced at Eddie, but didn't say anything. He still didn't think this was a good idea, and felt as if the whole situation was getting away from him, but he didn't see an alternative unless he wanted to abandon his ancestral home—including his priceless magical library and innumerable arcane objects—to the echoes.

"So," Poppy was saying, looking at her tiny gold watch. "Do you want to go for it? We can do it tonight if you like. It's a little after eleven now. Midnight's a good time for these things. Can we get there by then?" She patted her satchel. "I've got everything I need here."

Verity squeezed Stone's arm, and he nodded. "Yes—might as well get on with it. We can take the portal straight to my place."

"Private portal. Nice and handy." She flashed Stone a smile. "Don't worry—I haven't met a spirit yet I couldn't get through to."

Jason, Ward, Ian, and Aubrey were waiting in Aubrey's sitting room when they returned, lounging around the homey, comfortable space sipping coffee and ignoring the television droning in the background.

Poppy greeted Ward with enthusiasm, and Eddie introduced her to the remaining group members. "Okay," she said briskly, all business now. "I assume that monster of a house up the way is where the problem is?"

"That's right," Stone said. "Ian and I can't even pass the threshold without being attacked."

"So there's physical manifestations?"

"Oh, yeah," Ian said. "One of those 'physical manifestations' almost took my head off before I got out of there, and there's a sword sticking through one of the sofas."

"It's a combination," Stone said. "Physical, illusionary, and auditory."

"Means they're powerful," Poppy said. "But you probably already knew that. Any idea how old they are, and what caused them to manifest now? Eddie didn't give me much detail."

Stone hesitated, still reluctant to reveal his family's shame to an outsider.

She must have picked up on it, because she shot him a sympathetic look. "Don't worry, luv—you can count on my discretion. Ask Eddie here if you don't believe me. You'd be surprised at some of the reasons spirits get their backs up."

He sighed, and didn't look at her. "We were doing some renovation, and uncovered their remains in a series of secret, sealed chambers under the house. We think they were used in a rather massive foundation sacrifice nearly three hundred years ago."

She whistled. "Wow. That's, uh…wow. I can see how they're pissed—and powerful. But don't worry—I'll do my best to get you sorted."

"Do you think you can convince them to leave Dr. Stone alone?" Verity asked. "I mean, yeah, his ancestors did terrible things, but *he* didn't. Can you help them…pass on, or whatever they need to do?"

"We'll see." Poppy hefted her bag and faced Stone again. "So you say it's safe to go up there for anyone who isn't related to you?"

"So far. But if at all possible, I want to be present during the séance. Can you manage that? Perhaps broker a…temporary truce?"

"We'll see," she said again. "I'll need to go up there without you first, to set things up. Eddie and Ward can come with me to help, and I'll see if I can get them to let you join. If not, do you want me to keep going anyway, with the others?"

Stone wanted to say no. This was *his* house, and *his* family. The idea of his friends talking to the echoes without him raised irrational, almost childish feelings of stubbornness. But that was all it was—irrational. He needed to do whatever was necessary to deal with the situation, even if he couldn't be part of it.

"Yes," he said at last. "Do it anyway. But please—try to make them see I mean them no harm. I'm sympathetic to their plight, and only want to help them."

"I'll do my best." She patted his arm, and he noticed she seemed even more serious than before. Apparently forty-one sacrificial victims interred under a house were more than even she was used to dealing with. "Wait here, and I'll call you as soon as we know anything."

Stone didn't sit down after she, Eddie, and Ward trooped out of the apartment and headed off. Instead, he prowled Aubrey's living room, pausing occasionally to stare out the window at the darkened house.

During one of these times, Aubrey approached him. "May I…get you something, sir?"

He barked a soft, harsh laugh. "So many ways to answer that, aren't there? But…no. Thank you, Aubrey. All I want just now is to get this over with."

"It isn't your fault, sir. You know that, of course."

He nodded without looking at the caretaker. "I do. But that doesn't change much, does it? As far as those echoes are concerned, it *is* my fault. Blood matters, especially in cases like this. Can you imagine how it must have been for them, trapped behind some kind of magical seal for all these years, just…*steeping* in hatred? What else did they have to do? And now that they're out, they want somewhere to vent it. I can hardly blame them for that."

"No…I suppose not. But it's not fair for them to vent it at you and Ian. You had nothing to do with what happened to them." He sounded almost indignant.

"You'd think so. But echoes aren't like classic ghosts in stories—not exactly. Except for very rare cases, they're not fully-functioning beings. They don't retain all the thoughts and memories they had when they were alive. The *reason* they remain behind and don't pass on to wherever spirits go when they die is *because* they've got some obsession they need to work out." He gave a bitter laugh. "Happy, contented people who die of old age don't leave echoes, Aubrey. And the ones who *do* hang about are driven by those obsessions. Single-minded sorts, most of them are."

"Most of them?" Verity asked, coming up alongside them. "Sorry, didn't mean to eavesdrop."

"It's quite all right. I need something to take my mind off what's going on up there, anyway."

She nodded and joined them at the window. "What did you mean, *most* of them? Are some not like that?"

Stone shrugged. "It's quite rare. Usually when you see a more fully-formed personality in an echo, it's someone who's magically talented. And that almost never happens. I've liter-ally never heard a credible example of a mage leaving an echo. If anyone had both a reason and the power to do it, Desmond would have been an ideal candidate. But he didn't."

"So…you're saying it's probably a myth."

"I'm saying it's unlikely in this case."

"What about…whatever was in the coffin in the sealed room?"

"Damned good question."

"Do you think it might have stirred the others up?"

"It's possible, certainly. But one interpretation of the maps we found in the box today is that whatever was in that chamber might have been imprisoned later, after the sacrifices were already made. Maybe even after they were long dead."

"But we don't know that. Maybe they just didn't include the chamber on the map because they wanted to keep it even more of a secret than the rest of what they did in there."

"Could be. With any luck, Ms. Willoughby will be able to make contact with some of them, and they can give us more data."

"Sir…" Aubrey ventured. "Do you think she might make contact with whatever was in that chamber you mentioned?"

Stone considered. "I'm not sure whether I hope that does happen, or it doesn't." He pushed off from where he'd been gripping the window frame and yanked his phone from his pocket. "Bugger it, I just want them to *tell* me something."

But the phone remained silent for nearly another thirty minutes. When it finally buzzed, startling Jason from his light doze and Ian and Verity from the card game they'd begun at the kitchen table, Stone jerked it from his pocket. "Yes? What did you find out?"

"Poppy's livin' up to her reputation," Eddie said. "Those echoes are 'oppin' mad, every last one of 'em. But she had a little chat with 'em and they've agreed to give you and Ian safe passage into the 'ouse until sunrise. They promise to leave you alone until then, but they won't let you down in the chamber. We'll have to do the séance upstairs."

"Is that all right? Can she do it from there?"

"Oh, yeah. She says it doesn't matter, long as it's inside the 'ouse. We've already got something set up in the great 'all. C'mon up and we'll get this party started. Oh—and bring the items we found in the box today. The jewelry and whatnot."

Stone looked at his friends, who were watching him. He looked at Ian, who had been staring out the window. This whole thing could be a trap—he could be leading them all exactly where the echoes wanted them to be, and gathering them into a neat little group.

"This could be dangerous," he said. "Anyone who wants to stay behind—"

"Come on, Dad," Ian said, already heading for the door. "You know that won't work, right?"

He sighed. "I know. But I had to try, didn't I?"

CHAPTER NINETEEN

D ESPITE EDDIE'S ASSURANCES, Stone hesitated as he stepped over the threshold and into the house, expecting something to jump him. Magical sight had revealed the same green aura he'd spotted before; when he walked inside, it remained green with no signs of the angry red from before. A definite, palpable sense of psychic tension pervaded the area, as if they were being watched, but nothing moved or screamed.

"I guess the echoes weren't lying, for now at least." He glanced at the broken furniture, shattered glass, and the remains of the rug littering the entryway floor. "If we manage to sort this out, I have *no* idea how I'm going to explain to a cleaning crew what went on in here."

"Just tell them you had a really wild party," Ian said. "I've seen *way* worse than this on the morning after some of the ones I've been to."

Stone didn't favor that with a reply, but continued crunching through the broken glass into the great room. The others followed.

Eddie, Ward, and Poppy had already moved some of the heavy furniture against the wall. A large, round wooden table stood in the middle of the floor, circled with mismatched chairs—Stone recognized several of them from the dining room, and a few more from various downstairs chambers. The only light in the vast room came from candles; the remains of the three broken chandeliers had been gathered into a large pile and shoved against another wall. Near the cluster of furniture he saw the sofa Ian had referred to, with one of the swords from the wall shoved completely through it. He tried not to think about the kind of force required to do that, and how easily that force could be redirected against softer human bodies.

As they approached closer, Stone spotted a large ritual circle beneath the table. "You didn't need to do that," he said. "We could have used my workroom."

"It's okay," Poppy said. "I find in situations like this, I'm more comfortable when I set everything up myself. No offense. I'm sure your circle is quite nice, but I like the personal touch."

"None taken." Actually, her words increased Stone's respect for her and her abilities. He studied as much of the circle as he could see from where he stood; it looked much different from the types he usually employed, but then again, he didn't often try to communicate with spirits. "What do you need us to do?"

"Nothing, just yet. Let me just finish up here, and then we'll see what we can find out."

The others, including Eddie and Ward, stood back while she placed items from her purple satchel on the table. She spread an intricately patterned cloth, then arranged a small group of white candles in wooden holders in the center, with a larger one at their heart. Around these, she added a pair of incense burners and three small bowls in a triangular pattern which she filled with water from a bottle in her bag, and then scattered several rocks and crystals of varying hues.

Then she looked up at Stone. "Eddie said you had some items that might have belonged to some of the spirits."

"Er—yes." He put the bundle down on a nearby table and opened it so she could choose what she wanted.

She stood next to the table, closing her eyes and running her hands over the items. "Oh, yes," she murmured. "These have powerful resonance. They'll do fine." After a pause, she selected one of the necklaces, the cameo, the dagger, and two of the rings, and arranged them in a grouping within the triangular space she'd delineated with the three bowls.

"There," she said, satisfied, and then faced the group. "This is a big group, which can be good, but it can also be dangerous if we're not all on the same page. If any of you are skeptical or don't truly believe in what we're about to do, best if you step out now." She settled her gaze on Jason.

He looked startled, and shook his head. "Me? No way. I'm fine. Yeah, I *used* to be skeptical about this kind of stuff. But I've seen too much of the real deal—I'd be an idiot not to believe it now."

"Fair enough. Are any of you frightened? Nervous about anything?"

"Well, having forty-one angry spirits in my house doesn't make me overly happy," Stone said dryly. "But I expect they already know that."

She waved him off. "You're all right. But once we start this, we can't break the circle. You know how dangerous that can be. No getting off once the ride starts. I can't tell you what we might see or hear tonight, but I doubt it'll be pleasant. I can't have anyone breaking free and running—it could put all of us at risk. Me, especially, which is why I'm such a stickler about it." Her expression fuzzed as she scanned the group, paying particular attention to Jason and Aubrey. "No shame in knowing your limitations, folks."

Aubrey looked as if he might say something, but tightened his jaw and stiffened his shoulders. "I want to see this through, sir," he said to Stone.

"He'll be fine," Stone told Poppy. "They all will."

"All right, then. Everyone please take a seat. Dr. Stone, you and Ian have the closest connection to the spirits here, so you sit at my right, and Ian at my left."

Everyone arranged themselves around the table. Verity sat next to Stone, with Jason next to her and Aubrey, Eddie, and Ward rounding out the group. "What do you use to communicate with the spirits?" Verity asked. "Do you have a…board or something?"

Poppy chuckled. "No, luv. I've never worked with a spirit board. I won't say it's not a valid method of communication, but I will say a lot of mediums who aren't…well, let's say the best at what they do…tend to use them as a crutch. Besides, this group is too big for everyone to reach the pointer."

"Poppy's a true medium," Eddie said. "The spirits inhabit her body, and speak through her. It's right fascinatin' to watch, the few times I've seen it in action."

Stone frowned. "And you're sure this is safe for you?" he asked her. "With so many angry echoes here—"

"I'll be fine," she assured him. "I'm not planning on letting them all in at once. From my brief communication earlier when I convinced them to let you in here, I get the impression they want their stories told. Let's see what we find out. If any of them begin to channel through me, any of you can speak to them, but it's best if only one or two people do. They might get agitated if too many people are yammering away at them."

"Got it," Eddie said. "This is Stone's show—he can do the talkin'."

"Unless they don't want to talk to me," Stone said. "You two will have to do it if they don't."

"Yeah. Lucky us. Let's 'ope they're in a friendly mood."

Poppy smiled at the group. "Okay. That's settled, then. If anybody needs to use the bathroom, this is the time to do it. Last call before we get started."

When no one got up, she gave a brisk nod. "All right, then. Here we go." With a brief hand wave, she extinguished the other candles illuminating the area, and lit the ones in the center of the table. Their flames cast flickering glows, reflected in each of the participants' eyes. Another gesture lit the incense burners, sending tiny columns of dark, aromatic smoke wafting upward.

"All right," she murmured. "Everyone join hands. From the moment we create the circle, it must not be broken for any reason. I know I keep saying that, but I can't stress it enough. There'll be a force holding us together, but it's not so strong you couldn't break it if you tried. I'm putting my trust in all of you."

All around the table, each person clasped the hands of those on either side. As soon as Poppy's long-nailed fingers curled around his hand, Stone felt a tingle of energy. The tingle intensified as the connections locked into place until finally, at the end, a faint and steady current surged through all of them. He wondered if the others felt the same thing he was.

"Good…good…" Poppy murmured. "Everyone take a few deep, cleansing breaths, and let them out slowly. Try to clear your mind of any thoughts not related to what we're doing here. This is the time to let the outside world fade away. Nothing is important now except our circle, the spirits around us, and our purpose for being here tonight."

Stone was glad he had extensive training in meditation, because even with that training he had a hard time clearing his mind. He felt Poppy's warm, dry hand on one side; on the other, Verity gave him a brief squeeze. He cast a quick glance at Poppy, noting she didn't have her eyes closed. Instead, she was scanning the group with magical sight.

Stone did the same, continuing his meditation. All around the circle, the various auras flared and danced: Verity's emerald green, Aubrey's and Jason's clear blue, Ian's silver-purple, Eddie's bright orange, and Ward's plum. Although they retained their distinct hues, as Stone continued to watch, the colors began to merge, to become a pure ring, separate but combined. All of them, including his own tri-toned purple, gold, and silver, flowed into Poppy's electric turquoise, feeding her energy. It was a beautiful thing to see, and once again Stone's opinion of the young medium's talent rose.

"Good…good…" Poppy whispered again, clear in the silence. "We're prepared, so let's begin."

She began what sounded halfway between a prayer and a chant, low and soothing. The words were in a language Stone didn't understand, but his bond with her and the rest of the circle members gave him the intent: it was a prayer to invoke the spirits, to assure them they were safe and that the group meant them no harm, and to encourage them to reveal themselves. When she switched to English, he barely noticed the change.

"Honored spirits," she murmured in a low, musical tone. "We have gathered together tonight, in the presence of those objects that resonate with your energy, to invite you to join us. We know you have suffered great pain and great fear, and we know you seek vengeance upon those who've wronged you. But tonight we ask only that you speak to us, in hope that we might reach an understanding. Please, spirits, join our gathering and share your thoughts with us. I invite you to speak through me. Be welcome. You will suffer no more harm here. We only wish to hear from you."

For almost a minute, nothing happened. Stone continued to scan the faces of his friends, watching the auras blending together and feeling the humming connection passing between them. As Poppy dropped into her soothing chant again, not seeming disturbed by the spirits' lack of response, Stone wondered if they would deign to speak to them at all, and also whether he'd made a mistake by insisting on including himself and Ian in the séance.

In the center of the table, the candles flickered.

Stone shifted his gaze. Had he seen that from the corner of his eye, or was it merely wishful thinking? He tightened his hands slightly on Poppy's and Verity's.

The candles flickered again. This time, there was no mistaking it: the tiny flames danced in the unmoving air, growing and writhing. The smoke from the incense burners did likewise, their dark, ropy tendrils growing thicker as they wafted around the table.

"Yes, spirits," Poppy intoned. "We can feel your presence. We can feel you here with us. Welcome. We mean you no harm."

Stone did his best to project benign, welcoming thoughts as all around him the air seemed to take on an electric charge. He couldn't describe it any other way: now it wasn't only the connection holding the group together that hummed, but everything around them. The temperature dropped noticeably, and across the room a heavy curtain drawn over a window rippled. A sudden image popped into his mind from a horror film he'd watched long ago at Barrow, featuring a little girl sitting in front of a snowy TV, gravely stating, "*They're heeeerrre....*"

No doubt about it: they *were* here. The candles flickered even more madly, and the room grew so cold Stone could see everyone's breath in little puffs in front of them. Eddie's and Ward's auras remained steady, but Jason's, Aubrey's, Ian's, and even Verity's showed red flashes of nervousness. Nobody attempted to break the circle, though. Everyone continued to stare into the center of the table, occasionally glancing at each other.

"Welcome, spirits," Poppy said, raising her voice a bit louder. "Welcome. We have here the master of this house, the descendant of those who've wronged you. But he means you no harm. He is grateful you have offered him this brief respite, and he feels great sorrow over what was done to you. He begs you to join us tonight, to speak to us, to help him to help you find peace and cross over to the next world." She nodded toward Stone, shooting him a significant glance.

"Er—" Stone began. He wasn't entirely sure how to speak to the spirits of people his family had buried alive. "Yes.

Thank you all for allowing me to speak with you here. I know I can't erase the terrible things my ancestors did to you, but for what it's worth, I'm truly sorry for it, and I want to make amends. Please—tell me what you want, and I'll do my best to see it done."

The temperature dropped again, and a faint wind began to stir around the table. The candle flames grew taller, flickering even more madly, and Stone began to sense a feeling of pressure around them, joining the electric hum. Even though he couldn't see them with either magical or mundane sight, he sensed the spirits pressing in closer, jostling for space, squabbling over who would be the one to speak for the group. It was a fanciful notion, and he had no idea whether it was correct.

Despite the cold, beads of sweat stood out on Poppy's smooth forehead, and the shaved sides. Her hand in his began to tremble, then tightened.

Her eyes, which had been closed, flew open.

Next to Stone, Verity made a soft gasp.

It had been impossible in the faint candlelight to see Poppy's green eyes, but now they definitely weren't green anymore. They glowed a pale yellow, and her gaze settled on Stone.

"You…" she growled. Her voice no longer had the pleasant, feminine lilt; now, it sounded deep and masculine, with an odd accent. "*Murderer…*"

Stone's heartbeat increased, and he tensed. "Please," he said. "I mean you no harm. I didn't do this to you. Please tell me how I can help you."

"Murderer…" the gravelly voice said again. Poppy jerked, closing her eyes and tossing her head backward.

When she opened them again, the glowing yellow was gone, replaced by a pale blue.

"Mother?" The voice was different too—high and frightened. "Mother? Where are you? It's so dark…"

Before Stone could respond, Poppy's head jerked again and her eyes went a different shade of green—more like the one that suffused the house itself. "Stone, you damnable bastard!" A different masculine voice this time, reedy and patrician. "I'll see you in hell for this! I'll see your entire accursed *family* in hell for this!"

Stone didn't even see the others in the circle anymore. His shocked gaze was fixed on Poppy's face, watching her attractive features subtly shifting to give the impression of whichever spirit spoke through her. If he hadn't known what was going on here, he would have considered her a masterful actor, adjusting her face to the requirements of the series of roles she played. "Who are you?" he whispered. "What's your name?"

Poppy's features shifted again, revealing a frightened, wide-eyed face. "Please!" she screamed, pounding both hands on the table without releasing her hold on Stone or Ian. "Let me out! I beg you, let me out!"

Stone tightened his jaw. "I didn't do it," he said. "I'm not responsible for any of this. It wasn't me. But I want to help you. I want to set this right. Please—tell me what you want."

"Blasphemer!" said a male voice.

"Murderer!" said another man.

"A thousand curses upon your blood!" said a woman.

"What's happening? Why have you done this?" pleaded a child.

"I only wanted honest work…" sobbed a teenage boy.

"Bloody hell…" Stone breathed, his tension growing. "I don't know what to do. I don't know what to tell them." He felt himself losing control; the sudden urge to break free, to run, to get away from this place and never come back gripped him so hard he could barely keep himself from succumbing to it. All around him, he felt the increasing pressure of unseen forces crowding around him, collapsing his aura, their centuries-long hatred almost visible in the air. Every last one of them wanted him to die in agony—wanted his entire family to suffer eternal torment. He'd never felt this kind of hatred directed at him in his life, and now it washed over him, threatening to submerge him. "I…can't—"

With obvious effort next to him, Poppy gathered herself, her whole body growing taut. "Enough…" she grated through clenched teeth. More sweat beads sprang from her forehead, and her stiff, electric-blue Mohawk began to wilt sideways. When she raised her head again, her eyes no longer glowed. She squeezed Stone's hand and took several breaths, then said in her own voice, shaking but strong and confident, "Enough. Please. Spirits, friends, you've come here to commune with us in good faith. Please. Alastair Stone is a good man. He doesn't share the sins of his forbears. He is strong and powerful, and he wants to help you. Please—tell us what you want. Tell him what he can do."

Stone swallowed, watching her as she blinked several times, twitching her head back and forth. In the table's center, the candle flames likewise whipped to and fro as if caught in a windstorm, though only a faint breeze blew through the room. The smoke from the incense burners was so thick now that he couldn't see the others across the table, and the temperature had to have dropped at least twenty degrees since they'd begun the séance. He waited in silence, turning his attention back to Poppy as she struggled with the waves of angry spirits jockeying to be heard.

"Put us to rest..." she whispered.

"What?" Stone leaned in closer. "What did you say?"

"Put us to rest...all of us...You must..."

He stared at her. "Put you to rest?"

"All of us...We must have proper rest...We must be...remembered..."

"Remembered..." Stone murmured.

"Their bones..." Eddie said softly from across the table. "They want to be properly buried, on 'oly ground... identified..."

Stone swallowed. There were potentially forty-one sets of bones in those alcoves, and the ledger they'd found identified many of them only by initials, nicknames, or partial names. How was he ever going to—

Nobody said this was going to be easy... a little voice in his head said.

But even so—"I—" he began, looking at Poppy in desperation. "I—don't know if I can do that. I don't know if it's *possible* to identify them all anymore. The records—aren't complete. Are they saying if I can't do that—"

Poppy's head jerked again. Her eyes glowed once more, and her expression went sly. "There is another way..." It was the gravelly voice that had begun their interaction with the spirits.

"Another...way?" Stone leaned forward again, gripping Poppy's and Verity's hands, his attention fixed on Poppy's steady gaze and unpleasant smile. "Tell me, then. Please."

"Sacrifice." Her smile broadened, and its effect on her normally cheerful face was chilling as she met Stone's gaze with her eerie yellow eyes.

"Sacrifice? Of what?"

"The Stones committed this atrocity. If you cannot lay us to rest and set our souls free from this hell, then Stone blood must atone for the sins committed against us."

Across the table, Eddie gasped.

"Stone...blood?" A shot of ice ran through Stone's veins. "What...are you talking about?"

Poppy gripped his hand tighter, but her face was still twisted into the spirit's grim visage. "You took our lives. If you can atone in no other way, then we will have yours in return. We shall see if you speak truth, or if your words are as empty as those of your accursed kin."

"Poppy," Ward said in a strangled tone. "Stop this. Now. End it."

Poppy threw her head back and laughed in the man's voice, the sound echoing into the great room's rafters. The wind picked up, blowing the candle flames and the incense smoke around even harder, but the candles didn't go out.

"Stop it," Eddie demanded. "Break the circle, Poppy!"

Stone felt the medium's hand jerk in his, but whatever force held them together had intensified to the point where it was no longer possible for them to separate. He too tried to pull free, but it was as if someone had glued their fingers together. All around the table, the others were doing the same thing, with the same result.

And then, suddenly, the laugh cut off, as abruptly as if someone had flipped a switch.

Poppy's chin dropped down until it rested on her chest, her head shaking back and forth like a dog after a bath.

"Something…else…is here…" she got out between gasps.

| CHAPTER TWENTY

"**S**OMETHING ELSE?**" Stone instantly switched to magical sight, trying to spot anything new around the table. He didn't see anything, but he did *feel* it: a gathering of magical force around them, spinning and whirling. It settled over Poppy and poked at her.

"It's trying to take 'er over!" Eddie shouted. His hands were still gripped fast in Ward's and Aubrey's, but he raised their joined arms in clear alarm.

Stone wasn't sure *how* he knew it, but he was certain whatever was here now was not any of the unfortunates whose remains were shut up inside the brick alcoves. He couldn't see the growing magical energy, but he didn't need to: it pressed against him, malevolent and brimming with power, trying to find a way past Poppy's formidable mental defenses.

A thought came with a sudden shock: "Could it be whatever was in the sealed room?"

"Whatever the 'ell it is, we've got to stop it!" Eddie yelled. "'Elp 'er! If it takes 'er over—"

Stone didn't wait to hear what might happen if the strange, potent force took control of the medium's body. Gripping Poppy's and Verity's hands tightly, he reached out to Calanar for power, focusing on augmenting Poppy's fading shield with one of his own. "Help me," he snapped.

From all around the table, he felt Eddie's, Ward's, Verity's, and even Ian's energy gathering. Their auras joined together with a singular shared purpose: protect Poppy from the force trying to get in.

Poppy slumped forward, her head hitting the table with a *thunk,* still twisting and bucking as if overcome by a seizure. Pink froth bubbled at her lips, and her long fingernails dug into Stone's palm until they drew blood.

He barely noticed. As soon as he felt his friends' energy joining his, he focused on melding it all together, forming it into a barrier he hoped the new intruder couldn't pass. "Go..." he snapped, casting his gaze around and trying to spot whatever the thing was. "Get out! We won't let you have her!"

At the outer edges of his awareness, he sensed more entities nearby. The echoes? He thought so, but now they seemed frightened—as frightened of this interloper as he and his friends were. "Get out!" he shouted again. "Whoever you are, you won't take over this woman's body. We won't allow it. So go!"

He shifted some of his power away from the shield; now that the others were augmenting it, he had to take a chance. They wouldn't be able to hold it forever, and this thing could be strong enough to wait them out, chipping away at them until their own endurance faded. He had to go on the offensive.

In his head, he felt rather than heard laughter, but it wasn't the gravel-voiced laughter of the echo. It still sounded like a man, but it also carried a brittle edge of insanity. Stone clenched his hands tighter around Poppy's and Verity's, holding the medium's arm against the table to prevent it from thrashing around. He couldn't see Ian on her other side, but he seemed to be doing the same thing.

"Dad, do something!" his son shouted. "I can't hold her forever! She'll break her arm!"

Rage overwhelmed Stone. How *dare* this intruder make such an audacious attack within the walls of his ancestral sanctum? The echoes might have reason, and they might have justification, but whatever this thing was, it wasn't one of the sacrificial victims. Not with magical power like that! The hatred was every bit as strong—he could feel that, too—but any guilt Stone might have felt burned away at the thought of it causing harm to the woman he'd brought in to attempt peaceful negotiation. The echoes had agreed to a truce, so even if the intruder *was* one of them, it had broken the agreement.

"Get...*out!*" he thundered, forming a pure blast of magical energy from the Calanarian force flowing through him, and sending it lashing out in an unfocused blast aimed at the vortex whirling around Poppy. He kept the conduit open, letting the force rip through his body until it lit him up with the familiar combination of pain and ecstasy.

For a moment, he thought it wouldn't work. Its power met his and resisted—but only for a few seconds, and then, with no sound, no surge of energy, it vanished as if it had never been there.

All around the table, the force holding the séance participants locked together also vanished, and all of them sagged back in their chairs. Poppy, who had been wrenching at Stone and Ian like a madwoman, slumped and went still.

"Bloody 'ell!" Eddie got out. "Is everybody all right? I—Poppy!" He leaped from his chair and hurried around the table.

Stone had already acted, though. He gathered the medium in his arms—she wasn't light, but between his newfound strength and a hard shot of adrenaline, he barely noticed her weight—and lowered her to the floor.

Verity used magic to snatch a pillow from a nearby sofa and put it under her head, and Eddie and Ward both raised light spells, revealing their own pale faces and those of the others.

"Holy shit…" Jason breathed, dropping to his knees next to her. "Is she alive?"

"We need to get 'er the 'ell *out* of this place," Eddie said. His voice shook as his gaze darted around the room. So far, the other echoes seemed to be keeping their bargain: despite Stone's and Ian's presence, they had not renewed their assault.

Verity was scanning Poppy's aura. "She's taken quite a shock," she said grimly. "I think she'll be all right—I'll take care of her. But Eddie's right, we should get her out of here. If that thing comes back—"

Everyone except Stone and Verity scanned the area nervously.

"Sir," Aubrey spoke up for the first time. He was breathing hard, his face pale and sweating from fear, but he swallowed and his voice came out firm. "We can take the young lady to my flat, if you like. Will that be sufficient, Miss Thayer?"

She looked at Stone. "Doc? How sure are you that you got rid of it?"

"I—don't know," Stone said. And he *didn't* know. How could he, when he didn't even know what it *was?* He sensed he'd driven it off, but he didn't think he'd destroyed it. "I—think it will be all right, though. So far, this madness all seems confined to the house itself."

Poppy moaned. Her legs moved, and she raised one bloody hand to her forehead.

"It's okay…" Verity said. "You're all right." To the others, she added, "Let's get her out of here. Jason, can you carry her? I think all the mages are pretty tired out right now."

"Yeah. I got her." Jason bent and hefted her with little effort, and together the group trooped out of the great room and into the entrance hall toward the door.

Stone brought up the rear, magical sight active in case any of the echoes decided to try any sneak attacks, but none did. They made it outside and up the stairs to Aubrey's apartment without any further incident.

As Verity and Eddie tended to Poppy and Aubrey adjourned to the kitchen to make tea for everyone, Stone stood in the middle of the room, heart still pounding and adrenaline still pumping. He didn't think he could sit still now if his life depended on it.

Ian approached him slowly, as if not sure he should. "Dad? You okay?"

Stone studied his son who, like the others, looked pale and tired. Not for the first time, he wondered if it might have been best—or at least safer—for Ian never to have found out about his magical heritage. He wondered how regular mundane problems might compare to being targeted by a flock of vengeful echoes, or some powerful force that had apparently been imprisoned along with them.

He offered a bitter chuckle. "Damn good question, isn't it?"

"You're bleeding."

"Am I?" He glanced down at his left hand, which was covered with dried blood from where Poppy's nails had pierced his palm. "Fair trade, wouldn't you say, compared to what Poppy got?" Nonetheless, he summoned a simple healing spell and sealed the wounds, then drifted toward the bathroom to wash his hands.

Ian was still waiting when he came out, joined now by Jason. "What was all that about back there?" he asked.

"Did I understand that right?" Jason added. "Those things...those...echoes wanted their bones to be moved out of there and buried?"

"Yes." More than anything right now, Stone wanted a drink—and not the tea Aubrey was offering. "They want their remains to be removed and buried on holy ground—at a cemetery, or a churchyard, or—I don't know—perhaps they'll settle for having a priest pray over them. But it doesn't matter, does it?"

"Why not?" Ian asked.

"Because they must have been put down there nearly three hundred *years* ago." He spread his hands. "You saw the ledger, where all of them were listed. I doubt my ancestors even *knew* who most of them were. They didn't care."

"Al—" Jason began.

"Well, they didn't." Stone paced back and forth, bleeding off restless energy even though his body and mind were both exhausted. "That's fairly clear. They prowled the streets, looking for people no one would miss, and either lured them into a trap or simply snatched them. It would have been easy, with their level of magic. Those poor sods would vanish without a trace, and no one would ever see them again." He sighed, gripping the back of a nearby chair. "The only ones we might have a chance of tracking down are those with a full name listed—and after all this time even that will be difficult."

"What about Poppy?' Ian asked. "Could she—I don't know—contact them individually and ask them?"

"I don't think it works like that. We're not even sure they're all still here. Surely some of them must have crossed over by now. And at any rate—" He waved toward the sofa, where Verity crouched next to the unconscious medium while Eddie and Ward hovered nearby looking worried. "—it's not like she'll want to go anywhere near my house again, even if I were to ask her. Which I wouldn't."

"So...then...what happens?" Jason looked troubled. "I know I'm just a mundane and I probably missed half of what went on back there, but did that one guy—the one with the deep voice—say something about...sacrificing yourself to get rid of them?"

Another chill ran through Stone. "Yes," he said grimly. "That's exactly what he said. That if we can't properly lay the remains to rest, it will take the blood of a Stone to convince them to vacate the premises. And I doubt they'd settle for a finger-slice, or even a pint or two."

"He wants you to kill yourself," Jason said. "Al, you can't—"

"Of course I can't. And neither can you," he said sternly to Ian.

Ian raised his hands. "Hey, no problem. Wasn't going to offer. It's a nice house and everything, but I'm not dying to run a bunch of ghosts out of it."

"But if that's off the table and we can't identify the remains sufficiently to do as the echoes ask, then that leaves us—well, me, anyway—with a problem."

"What's that?" Jason asked.

"Well…I've got to work out what to do—what I *want* to do—about the house, and the echoes. If they won't leave and the options they offer us aren't feasible, then I've got to find others. And as far as I can see right now, I've only got two: I can work out a way to fight them, either on my own or by bringing in help, or I can concede."

"Concede?" Ian demanded, eyebrows lifting. "You mean, just—go away and let them have the house?"

"It's an option. Not one I like very much—this place *is* my ancestral home, even if my ancestors were a reprehensible bunch, and it's part of your inheritance. But on the other hand, it was built on the literal backs of forty-one brutal murders. Possibly more than that. Do I even have a *right* to claim it?"

When Jason started to say something, he held up his hand. "That was a rhetorical question, at least for now. I'm far too shattered to think clearly about anything at present."

Verity rose from her crouch and approached, with Eddie and Ward behind her. "Think about what?" she asked. "Sorry to interrupt again."

"How is Poppy?" Stone glanced over at the medium; she still appeared unconscious, but some of the gray pallor had receded from her face. They'd covered her with the patchwork quilt Aubrey kept over the back of his sofa.

"She'll be okay, I think. I healed the physical damage, and she's sleeping. But her mental defenses were tough. I think hers, combined with ours, made it so whatever that thing was didn't get in very far before we kicked it out. What *was* that thing, anyway? Do you have any idea?"

They were all looking at him now—even Aubrey, who'd come back bearing a tray full of steaming teacups and a plate of cookies and crackers.

They all think you have the answers, he thought with dismay.

He shook his head. "I don't know. I've got no idea. I don't think it was one of the echoes, though." He accepted a cup from Aubrey's tray, but didn't touch the cookies.

"Why not?" Jason asked. "Whatever it was, it seemed pretty pissed."

"Because it clearly had strong magical ability. Echoes can do a lot of things, as we've seen—they can affect the physical world, if sufficiently motivated. Some of them can even possess living beings, as we saw with Raider and Dr. Benchley."

"Wait, what now?" Eddie asked, tilting his head. "Somethin' possessed your *cat* and you didn't bother to tell us about it?"

"Some other time, Eddie," Stone said quickly. "At any rate—Poppy's mental defenses are formidable. I could see that, and they'd have to be for her to do what she does. Possessing a fully-trained mage with a specialty in mental techniques would be a hell of a lot harder than popping into a cat."

"Fair enough," Ward said. "Are you suggesting your ancestors interred a powerful mage down there?"

"The sealed chamber," Eddie said, his expression growing suddenly grim. "Whatever it is, either it broke out on its own or somebody broke it out. You think that's what it was?"

Stone shrugged. "That was my hypothesis, yes. But all that does is bring up *more* questions. If the plans were correct and that chamber wasn't constructed until some later date, after the tunnels were dug and the foundation sacrifice was made, then what *was* in there, and why? And if the chamber *was* constructed at the same time but kept from the plans, there had to be a reason for that too."

"Yeah…" Ian said, rubbing his jaw. "And it sounds like even if Poppy was willing to give it a try, talking to that thing probably isn't a good idea."

"No, probably not. Which means we need to find another way to figure out what the hell it is and what it's doing there." He turned to Eddie and Ward. "You two made extensive sketches of the walls inside that chamber, and what's left of the door. You have bits and pieces of the destroyed part, and both of the books from the box. Do you think those will be enough to get started with some research? Even if we can't get the whole story, maybe we can get some of it."

"Sure, mate," Eddie said. "We'll get started tomorrow. Can Poppy stay here tonight if she's not ready to—"

"Oh, I'm ready," came a voice from the other side of the room.

Everyone turned. Poppy had propped herself against her pillows and was now half-sitting up. "I'm definitely ready. But first I'd love a cup o' that tea, if you've got one. With something a bit stronger in it, if you've got that."

Stone hurried over to her. She still looked pale and tired, her Mohawk still drooping dejectedly to one side and her makeup smeared, but some of the spark had returned to her green eyes and her voice sounded stronger. "I am so sorry…" he began. "Poppy, please forgive me. If I'd known—"

She waved him off. "Don't worry about it, luv. It happens sometimes, even in situations where there's only one or two echoes." She shuddered. "But blimey, whatever that thing was there at the end, it packed a punch." Her gaze settled on Stone as she carefully took a cup of tea from Aubrey. "And I'll tell you this, too—I didn't get much from it, unfortunately, but I did get one thing, loud and clear."

"What's that?" Stone wasn't sure he wanted to know.

"It hates you. I mean, *really* hates you. Makes the rest of those tossers back there look like a bunch of kids playin' at bein' spooks."

| CHAPTER TWENTY-ONE

A N HOUR LATER, Aubrey's apartment felt much quieter and more subdued.

Eddie and Ward had left through the portal a short time ago, taking Poppy with them.

"You're sure you're all right?" Stone asked before she departed. "I feel dreadful about this. If you've got any doubt—"

She patted his arm. "No, luv, no. I'll be fine. Just got a bit of a headache, but that's normal. You're the one who should be careful. You've got quite the infestation on your hands, and I'm just sorry I can't be more help with it."

Stone didn't even consider asking her to try again, and she didn't sound as if she wanted to anyway. "I'm grateful for what you did do, and I completely understand."

He'd paid her handsomely, nearly twice what she'd originally asked for, which had gone a long way toward cheering her up. "Let me know what happens, if you can," she said. "I'll be curious to know what that nasty thing ends up being."

"If I can," he'd agreed, knowing full well he didn't intend to share anything else, no matter what he found.

"Take care, mate," Eddie said. He carried a large bag stuffed full of the pieces from the broken door. Ward had a similar satchel containing the journal, the ledger, and the notebooks where they'd made sketches of the sigils and symbols on the chamber walls. "We'll get a few hours' kip and then start right in on this first thing tomorrow. We'll give you a ring if we get anything."

And then they were gone, disappeared through the portal. Stone trudged back up to Aubrey's apartment, throwing himself down on the couch with a stiff shot of Scotch the caretaker had poured for him when he'd turned down more tea.

"So," he said. "Here we are."

"Yeah." Verity sat next to him, leaning against his shoulder. "What do we do now?"

"Now? Eddie's got the right idea: we get some sleep. If you lot are half as tired as I am, any decisions we make tonight will be rubbish anyway." Stone wondered if he'd even be *able* to sleep with all the mad thoughts running through his mind, but he at least needed to try. This wasn't the kind of stuff you wanted to take chances with, running on liquor fumes and the ragged edge of exhaustion.

"Where are we gonna do that?" Jason looked around Aubrey's sitting room. "Sleep on the floor here? Or go through the portal to London or back home?" He didn't look too thrilled about that latter suggestion.

"No." Stone stood and finished off his drink. "I'm not, at least. I'm going to sleep in my own bedroom."

They all gaped at him. "Your own bedroom, sir?" Aubrey asked. "At the house? But—"

"But nothing. You all heard Eddie and Ward: the echoes have given us safe passage until sunrise tomorrow morning. I plan to hold them to that. I'll get a couple hours' sleep, then use the rest of the time to rescue a few things from my library, just in case we can't get back in again."

"What about that other thing?" Ian asked. "The one that attacked Poppy?"

Stone shrugged. "I'm not bothered about it. That séance was set up specifically to be receptive to communication from the spirit world, and Poppy was particularly sensitive to that sort of thing. Also, you might not have noticed, but I did: the other echoes didn't like that thing any more than we did. They don't want it there. I'm certain we drove it off. I doubt we destroyed it, but we did hurt it. And I suspect the echoes will join forces to keep it out as long as they can. Especially since they don't have to waste their energy having a go at us until tomorrow."

"Doc, are you sure—" Verity began. She looked troubled.

"Subject's closed." Stone set the glass on the table. "You lot can stay here or go back to London if you like. But I'll be damned if some ectoplasmic wanker who doesn't even have a dog in this race is going to keep me out of my own house."

They all exchanged glances, and then Ian's gaze hardened. "Okay, then. If you're staying, so am I."

"Us too," Verity said, nodding toward Jason. "I don't think we'd be in any danger either way, though. The echoes don't care about us. And we're not leaving you alone in that place."

"Are you sure?" Stone asked, touched by their courage and their loyalty. "I'm willing to take this risk for myself, but—"

"Like you said, subject's closed," Jason insisted.

"We can even help you with your library tomorrow," Verity said. "You can get more stuff out if we help carry it."

"Let's go, though," Ian said, looking at his watch. "If we don't get up there soon, there won't even be any point in *trying* to sleep, and we might as well just start on the library now."

"Right, then. Aubrey, do you need any help cleaning up before we leave?"

"No, sir. I think I'll head to bed too, and tidy up in the morning." He took a deep breath, clearly steeling himself for something. "Would...you like me to accompany you as well?"

"To the house?" Even more than before, a warm feeling of pride struck Stone. He truly didn't deserve friends this loyal. "No, Aubrey," he said gently. "No. You don't need to be part of any of this. You just get yourself a good night's sleep and we'll talk about our next steps tomorrow."

"Yes, sir. Thank you, sir."

Stone didn't miss the relief in the old man's voice. Aubrey would bravely stand, shoulders squared and shotgun at the ready, between Stone and any mundane threat with the audacity to come after him, but even after all these years, he'd never grown fully comfortable around the supernatural world. Stone shielded him from it as much as possible, and regretted that he'd been unable to do that in this case.

"Good night," he said. "With any luck, we'll all get a good, restful sleep and we'll have clearer minds in the morning."

| CHAPTER TWENTY-TWO

S TONE ENTERED THE HOUSE FIRST, half expecting something to start flinging furniture at him when he stepped back over the threshold, but nothing did. The aura remained green and pulsing—the echoes were clearly still there, and probably watching, but as yet they kept their agreement and didn't attempt to prevent him or Ian from entering.

"All right," he said. "We'll need to clear out of here before sunrise—at least Ian and I will." He glanced at his watch. "It's one-thirty now, so to be safe that gives us three hours. Ian, please show Jason to the room next door to yours. Verity, you know where your usual is. I'm planning to set an alarm for two hours so I've got time to gather a few things before we go back to Aubrey's. I'll see you all soon. Good luck getting some sleep."

Verity lingered behind as Ian and Jason trooped upstairs. "You really want me to sleep in my old bedroom?" she asked with an amused smile.

Despite everything that had happened tonight, he had to return the smile. He'd hoped she'd say that, but had no intention of asking. "Well…not particularly, to be honest. But no point in waving the fact in front of your brother."

"You really want to sleep?" she asked with a sly, sidelong glance. She took his hand and started up the stairs.

"We should…"

"Yeah, I know we should. But that's not what I asked you."

"What about the echoes?" He allowed her to lead him upstairs and down the hall to his suite. Ian's and Jason's doors along the way were already closed.

"What about them? They can watch if they want to. I've got nothing to hide."

"Well…if you put it that way…" A twinge of guilt made him hesitate, but for once he shoved it aside. "I'm glad you're here, Verity," he said softly, squeezing her hand. "You're making a horrible situation…a bit less horrible."

"Only a bit?" But her smile was understanding as she led him into his suite.

He found he couldn't sleep afterward—not entirely, anyway—but being with Verity did relax him enough that he dozed, drifting along on the afterglow of their time together. Even though it ended up being more about taking comfort from each other than the actual lovemaking, the guilt tried to poke its head up again: what right did he have to experience pleasure in the middle of all this pain and misery? But once again he submerged it. Yes, he'd have to figure out a way to atone for his ancestors' sins—but they weren't *his* sins.

The echoes seemed not to object, or at least if they did, they didn't do anything about it. Stone tightened his arm around the sleeping Verity, and she snuggled into his shoulder with a contented little mumble.

Far away, a faint sound broke the house's silence.

Stone tensed, sitting up a little in bed. He'd left his watch on and looked at it now: three-fifty a.m. He still had almost half an hour before the alarm he'd set would go off.

Had he heard something at all, or had he dropped off to sleep without realizing it and dreamed it? It was certainly possible, given the night's events.

Next to him, Verity muttered a vague question and snuggled in closer, her arm draped over his chest.

He stroked her back. "Go to sleep. It's nothing."

He almost believed it—but then came another sound, too faint and distant to identify. It almost sounded like some small item crashing to the floor and breaking.

Stone sat up further, looking around with magical sight. Nothing looked out of the ordinary. It was odd that he'd heard anything; his suite was at the end of the hall on the second floor of the west wing, and the substantial closed door should have blocked out anything that wasn't nearby.

Idly, he shifted to magical sight again, figuring the same eerie green glow would still be present in the room.

The glow was still there, and it was still green—but now it was a *different* green. Sicklier, with a yellow cast that wasn't there before. The change was subtle, but he didn't miss it.

"What's wrong…?" Verity mumbled.

"I'm not sure. Probably nothing. Stay here." He extricated himself from beneath her arm and sat up, using magic to pick up his jeans from the floor.

He was almost certainly being paranoid. The echoes had showed no sign of breaking their agreement. If he *had* heard a noise, it was probably Jason getting up to use the bathroom and knocking something over in the unfamiliar house. But still, it couldn't hurt to take a quick look around. He pulled his jeans on, shivering a bit as the cool air hit his skin. Even in the mid-summer, this place never really got warm without cranking the heaters and lighting the fireplaces, and they hadn't done either of those things.

Stone crossed the room to the door and eased it open, peering out. The dim sconces revealed nothing but the other closed doors along the hallway.

Another *crash* sounded, faint but louder. It sounded as if it had come from downstairs, perhaps in the great room. A second later, he heard something scrabbling at the stone floor.

What the hell—?

"What is it?" Verity whispered from directly behind him, making him jump.

"Don't *do* that!"

"Did you hear something?" She'd hastily pulled on her T-shirt and jeans.

"I think so. I was about to go check."

"I'll come with you."

There was no point in trying to convince her to remain in the room, so he didn't bother. "It's probably nothing, but—"

This time, the crash was loud and unmistakable, followed once again by the scrabbling sound.

Stone and Verity exchanged grim glances. "Come on," Stone said. "We need to wake the others. Something's going on down there."

"Should we just get out? Go back to Aubrey's place again until morning?"

"I want to see—"

Downstairs, glass shattered.

"Bloody hell!" Stone snapped. "You get Jason. I'll get Ian."

He didn't wait for her to respond, but instead strode down the hallway and pounded on his son's door. "Ian! Wake up!"

The door flung open, revealing Ian dressed only in black boxer briefs. His hair was tousled and he looked as if he'd just awakened. "Dad? What time is it? What's going on?"

"Not sure yet." Another crash punctuated his words, followed by more glass breaking.

Across the hall, Jason emerged, looking equally disheveled and gripping his baseball bat. Like Stone, he wore only his jeans. He and Verity quickly joined the group. "What's happening?" he demanded. "Are the ghosts back?"

"*Something's* back," Stone said. "Not sure what it is, but I'm about to go check."

"Shouldn't we—" Verity began.

Downstairs, it sounded like someone had pulled one of the bookcases over.

Stone didn't wait any longer. He took off at a run toward the staircase, stopping at the top and scanning the area below with magical sight. No lights were on down there, but if any living beings were present, their auras should glow bright and clear.

At first, he thought what he saw *was* auras—auras of the same sickly green as the glow suffusing the house. Whatever they were, there were a lot of them, their forms humanoid but not quite human.

Next to him, Verity gasped. "Doc…" Her voice shook.

"You see them too?"

"Yeah." She spoke barely above a whisper.

"See what?" Jason demanded. "Somebody turn a damn light on."

Unlike the others, he'd spoken in a normal tone, fear making it sharp.

Downstairs, the closest of the shuffling humanoid figures stopped at the sound of his voice. In unison, they all turned toward it, their heads swiveling upward to lock in on it.

Only then did Stone get a good look at them, and an ice-water rush of terror shot up through his body.

"Shit…" Ian muttered next to him. "Are those—"

"—*Skeletons?*" Verity finished, gripping Stone's arm.

Stone didn't have too many other guesses. As soon as he identified the strange, shuffling human-like forms, the answer locked into place: they were exactly that.

Human skeletons.

And suddenly, they weren't shuffling anymore.

CHAPTER TWENTY-THREE

WITH THE BURNING GREEN LIGHTS in their yawning eye sockets flashing hatred, the skeletons all began to ascend the stairs. Their bony feet scraped against the floor, their shambling forms moving faster than it seemed possible. Aside from that, the only sound they made came from the clanking of the rusting manacles still wrapped around their wrists. They raised their arms, their long, spindly fingers reaching toward the group at the top of the stairs.

Stone was the first to shake free of the horror gripping him. "Stand back," he ordered, gathering magic.

As soon as the others were clear, he pointed his hands down the stairs and let loose with a wide blast of pure arcane energy. He'd worry about what these things were and where they'd come from later. Right now, all he wanted was to see them in pieces on the floor.

The magical blast hit the leading edge of the fast-moving skeletons, lighting them up. Stone hadn't held back: it should have driven them all backward at minimum, tumbling them down the stairs and halfway across the great hall, if not blown them into bits.

It did neither. The skeletons braced themselves as the magic washed over them, looking like sailors on a ship's deck in a storm. They jerked and shuddered until it passed, then resumed their upward climb, eyes burning with even more malevolent light than before.

And now they were all fixed on Stone.

"What happened?" Verity yelled. "Why didn't—"

"They're resistant to magic!" Stone snapped. "Back up."

He looked around, trying to find some kind of weapon, but up here at the top of the stairway weapons were in short supply. What the hell *were* these things? Were they really skeletons? Were they illusions? Where had they come from? Had the echoes sent them?

Whatever they were, they were almost at the top of the stairs now. Two of them had taken the lead, moving faster than the others. They wore the tattered remains of rotting clothes along with their manacles; their bones weren't the bleached white of horror-movie skeletons, but rather brown and discolored, as if they had recently emerged from the grave. As if—

Oh, bloody hell.

A quick vision rose in Stone's mind: a series of bricked-in alcoves, their bricks crumbling as *something* ripped itself free from the wall and emerged from each of them to begin their slow climb upstairs.

But that was absurd! Scattered skeletons didn't simply rise from their piles and go gallivanting about. That didn't *happen!*

But it *was* happening—either that or someone was casting a hell of an illusion.

"I got this!" came a booming voice from behind him. "Get back, all of you!"

Before Stone could stop him, Jason surged forward, both hands knotted around the handle of the baseball bat he'd bought in London today. "Jason! No!"

But Jason didn't even seem to hear him. He stood, legs apart, and dropped into a classic batting stance. When the first skeleton reached him, its blazing gaze still fixed on Stone, he drew back and swung for the fences.

The bat connected with the skeleton's head with a *crack*, knocking it free of the creature's body. It sailed down the stairs and landed somewhere in the great room, rolling away. The headless bones collapsed in a heap.

"You guys want some more of that?" Jason yelled, raising the bat again. "Come on! Try me! Bring it on!"

Several more skeletons had almost reached the top of the stairs now. Surprisingly, they hesitated, slowing as they approached. Below, Stone's magical sight spotted more joining them, pouring out from the direction of the east wing.

He grabbed Jason's arm. "Jason, we've got to get away from there. There are too many of them."

Next to him, both Ian and Verity threw spells at the skeletons, but they seemed even less affected than they had been by Stone's blast.

"You're right—magic's not hitting them!" Verity cried.

The skeletons were gathering courage again. They separated, spreading out and moving wide of Jason's bat, and resumed their steady climb toward the top.

Stone thought fast. He'd fought magic-resistant enemies before—but nothing was *truly* resistant to all of magic's effects. It just meant he couldn't hit them directly.

Stepping back, he reached out with his power and grabbed hold of the rug on the stairs. *I needed to renovate this place anyway,* he thought as he wrenched it upward, ripping it free and flinging it backward.

The rug rippled like a storm-tossed sea, lifting the skeletons with it and sending them flying back down toward the floor. "Yes!" he yelled, settling the end of the ripped rug around them.

If he'd entertained any hope of smashing them to pieces as Jason had with his home-run shot, though, their next action dashed it. They struggled beneath the old rug, throwing it free and erupting back to their feet with surprising speed. Still more new ones crowded in behind them, and still all of them fixed their green-flamed, hate-filled gazes up toward Stone and the others.

"What do we do?" Ian demanded. Already, the things were starting back up the stairs.

"We can't hit them all with baseball bats," Verity added. She looked pale, but her eyes were steady. "And if we can't hit them with magic—"

"How many of those things *are* there?" Jason was at a clear disadvantage without magical sight.

"My guess is forty-one."

His friend looked at him in shock, obviously not expecting an answer. "That's an oddly specific number, Al. What—" And then he got it. "Wait—those are from—"

"I think they might be. Come on—back up. We need to make a plan."

From down below came the sound of more crashing, breaking glass, and shuffling, skeletal feet.

"Where?" Ian asked.

"My suite. Come on. I've got an idea."

They hurried down the hall to Stone's suite, where the door still stood open. "Inside," Stone urged, waving them all ahead of him while keeping watch toward the stairs. Several of the skeletons had already reached the top, and when they spotted the open door they picked up speed.

As soon as everyone had slipped through, Stone followed them, slammed the door shut, and engaged the lock, then looked around the room.

"Will that hold them?" Verity asked. She was still watching the door. Only seconds later, the knob began to rattle, and bony fists began pounding on the heavy wood.

Stone wasn't sure it would. The pounding was a lot more forceful than he would have expected from relatively fragile human bones, rattling the door in its frame as the uneven, drumlike pattern of *thuds* echoed around the room. "Something's augmenting them," he muttered. He spun and waved his hand, levitating the substantial wooden armoire over and settling it in front of the door.

"There," he said. "That might not hold them long, but it doesn't need to."

"Holy shit, Al," Jason said. "That thing must weigh a couple hundred pounds at least."

"So what now?" Ian asked. "Do you have any weapons in here?"

Stone gave him a look, amused in spite of himself. "I'm a mage, Ian. I hardly need to keep baseball bats in my room for home defense."

"Well, I sure as hell don't see any. Are you planning to throw the armoire at them?"

"No. I'm planning for us to get the hell out of here."

"How?" Verity asked.

Stone pointed at the high, drape-covered window on the other side of the room. "There. We'll go out onto the roof, float down, and come at them from the back."

"Why not just get away?" Ian didn't look frightened, but he did look determined. "You want to fight a bunch of magic-resistant skeletons? Will they follow us if we leave the house?"

"Who knows?" The pounding on the door intensified, and Stone thought he saw it move above the top of the armoire. "But I'll be damned if I let them take over my house. And we've got to check on Aubrey anyway. If any of them went after him—" The sudden thought chilled him.

"Why don't you call him and ask?" Jason asked.

"Bloody hell, I'm an idiot." He dashed across the room to his nightstand and snatched up his phone. "Jason, keep an eye on that door. Ian, you help. If they come through—er—throw the armoire at them. Verity, get the window open."

"On it."

Stone punched Aubrey's number and listened with growing impatience as it rang once, twice, three times before the old man answered. "Yes, sir?" He sounded as if he'd just woken up.

At least one *of us is getting some sleep.* "Aubrey! Are you all right?"

"Er…is there some reason I wouldn't be, sir?"

"Nothing's trying to get in over there?"

"I…don't believe so. Sir—are *you* all right?"

"Been better. Listen—Aubrey—I want you to stay right where you are. Lock your doors, load up your shotgun, and wait. We'll be over there shortly."

"Sir?" Now Aubrey's voice was louder, clearer, and more full of concern. "What's going on over there? Are the...spirits back?"

"Not...exactly. Just do what I told you. Please. And stay indoors." He shot a glance back over his shoulder when he felt a blast of air, and was pleased to see Verity had gotten the window open. "We'll be there soon."

Without waiting for Aubrey to reply, he shoved the phone in his pocket. An instant later, the door broke with a shattering *crack* and something began beating against the heavy armoire.

"Go!" Stone shouted, waving the others toward the window. "Out! Verity, levitate Jason down. We'll head for Aubrey's place."

If anyone other than the skeletons had been watching from outside, Stone's group must have looked like quite a ragged assemblage as they scrambled out through the window onto the slate roof: all of them barefoot, two clad only in jeans and one in his underwear. Only Verity, in her jeans and T-shirt, looked even moderately prepared for this kind of adventure.

"Careful," Jason called as his feet slipped on the damp roof. "It's a long drop." Like Stone, he kept switching his gaze back and forth between the edge of the roof and the open window.

Behind them, a loud *crash* split the air. "That'll be the armoire," Stone shouted. "Go! Go!" He barely noticed the early-morning chill now as his heart pounded. How the hell were they going to get rid of forty-one magic-resistant, pre-ternaturally tough animated skeletons? With all his experience with the magical arts, this was a new one on him.

There wasn't supposed to *be* any magic that could raise the dead. He'd heard rumors of necromancy in his early days of study—it was a favorite sensationalistic topic of discussion among young mages—but those rumors had all come with the certainty that if necromantic practices had ever even existed, the techniques had died out hundreds of years ago.

So did whatever was in that chamber under the house, his little interior voice reminded him helpfully. *If it ever even died at all...*

They touched down on the ground together, and Stone spun to see if the skeletons were following. Up on the second floor, two of them poked their heads out the window of his suite, their hateful gazes fixed downward. A second later, they began clambering out onto the roof, and others appeared in their place.

"Go!" Stone urged. He wondered if, like the echoes, the skeletons would remain within the confines of the house, but didn't plan to take chances. In case the things weren't bound by the same strictures, his group needed a defensible area. It would be too easy for the skeletons to surround them out here on the grounds.

The others followed him without question, heading toward the garage and Aubrey's apartment. He barely felt the cold, dew-covered ground or the driveway's gravel beneath his bare feet, the adrenaline surging through him submerging any potential pain.

Up ahead, a square of light appeared at the top of the garage stairs, and a moment later Aubrey's stout figure came into view. He looked like he'd dressed hastily, wearing his trousers along with a striped pajama top, a robe, and leather slippers. He held something in his hands, and as they drew closer Stone realized it was his hunting rifle. "Hurry," he called, snatching a glance back over his shoulder.

To his horror, several of the skeletons were on the ground now, and they didn't seem at all deterred by the fact that they weren't inside the house anymore. Several more of the monsters scrambled across the roof, and as Stone looked again, three more dropped over the edge and landed without damage on the grass below.

"Those things are bloody tough!" he panted.

"Doc, we can't lead them up into Aubrey's place!" Verity caught up with him, grabbing his arm.

With a chill, Stone realized she was right. The skeletons would overrun the old man's apartment, and there wouldn't be enough space to fight effectively. "Aubrey!" he yelled. "Come down here. To the garage."

Aubrey didn't move.

"Aubrey!" In the glow of the light above the door, Stone caught sight of Aubrey's face. The old man wasn't looking at Stone and his friends; instead, his gaze was directed past them. His eyes had gone wide with terror.

He's spotted them. Damn.

"Aubrey!" he yelled again, louder. "Come down here! We're going to the garage!" Had he made a mistake, bringing them all out here? Would the skeletons have concentrated on them if they'd remained inside the house, and ignored Aubrey? But they couldn't stay up there too much longer—sunrise wasn't far off, and with it the return of the echoes. That assumed, of course, that the echoes weren't the forces driving these skeletons in the first place.

"We should just go!" Jason said. "Get the hell out of here. Take the portal."

"And do what?" Stone dashed up the stairs and gripped Aubrey's arm, trying to lead him down the stairs. "Leave these things to overrun the place? What will they do if we're gone? They could leave here and go after the village." That wasn't an option. These things were his problem, and somehow they'd have to figure out a way to deal with them while they were still on his property.

But first he had to get Aubrey moving. The old man still ignored him, his terrified gaze still fixed on the horde of skeletons shambling across the gravel driveway. "Aubrey!" he yelled a third time. "Damn you, man, snap out of it!"

When Aubrey still didn't acknowledge him, he sighed. "I'm sorry for this, Aubrey, I truly am." And then he slapped the caretaker's face.

Aubrey jerked, throwing a quick glare at Stone and bringing his rifle around, but as Stone had hoped, the slap broke his paralysis. "Sir," he breathed, pointing toward the crowd of skeletons with his rifle barrel. "Are those—are—those—"

"Come on!" Stone grabbed his arm and pulled harder. "Before they get any closer. We're going to the garage."

Aubrey's face was pale and his hands shook so hard he nearly dropped the rifle, but he allowed Stone to lead him down the stairs. By the time they reached the bottom and the others crowded around them, the leading edge of the skeleton mob was only a couple dozen yards away.

Jason had already gotten one of the garage's three doors open. "Come on!" he urged. "Go! Go!"

With Stone on one side and Ian on the other, they dragged Aubrey inside. Jason slammed the door down behind them and engaged the lock.

Verity, already inside, flipped a switch and a pair of harsh overhead lights threw sharp illumination over the space. "What are we gonna do in here?" she demanded.

Stone looked quickly around. He didn't enter the garage often, and when he did, it was usually only for long enough to retrieve his little black MG convertible. The car was there now, shrouded under its usual gray cover. In the next bay over was Aubrey's old, battered pickup truck, and beyond that was the space the old man had converted into a combination workshop and tool shed. The whole thing smelled pleasantly of oil, wood shavings, and old tires.

"Sir," Aubrey breathed, still clutching his rifle and obviously trying to get himself under control. "Dear God, sir, what's happening? Are those—"

"Animated skeletons, yes." Stone regretted that he didn't have more time to be gentle with his old friend, but already some of the creatures were pounding on the door. "They're highly resistant to magic, and they're bloody strong and hard to hurt. So in short, we've got a problem."

"We need weapons," Jason said. He held up his baseball bat. "Physical things. Everybody look around." He ducked around the back of the truck and headed for the workshop.

Aubrey clearly had questions, but he didn't ask them. Instead, he hurried after Jason. "They're resistant to magic, you said, sir?"

"Direct magic, yes." Stone, Verity, and Ian followed them. "Physical damage affects them, but we need a lot of it. Jason took one out by braining it with his baseball bat, but knocking them down a flight of stairs barely fazed them." Stone looked around, glad the garage had no windows the skeletons could break.

Fortunately for them, Aubrey kept his workshop neat and organized. "There's a lot of good stuff here," Jason said, scanning the row of saws and other tools hung on pegs on one wall. He snatched up a chainsaw. "This should do some damage."

Outside, the pounding grew louder. A loud *crack* sounded and a stained skeletal hand punched through the wooden garage door.

With the truck between himself and the threat, Aubrey seemed to be recovering at least some of his courage. He pointed to the far side of the workshop. "There's a can of petrol for the chainsaw over there, sir."

Another hand burst through the garage door in a different spot. "Right, then," Stone said grimly. "We can't stay in here. These things might be strong, but they can't fly. If we can get to the roof with some weapons, we might be able to pick them off. Aubrey, have you got more ammunition for that rifle?"

The caretaker pulled a box from the pocket of his robe. "Yes, sir. Just the one box, though. Twenty rounds."

"What about the truck?" Verity asked. "Can we get in there and run them over?"

"It won't fit all of us," Ian said. He'd joined the others in the workshop and was now holding a saw in one hand and a crowbar in the other. "But if we need to get out, that might be the way to do it."

More hands crashed through the garage doors. Stone pictured all the skeletons lined up along the front of the structure, battering away until they broke through. With that many of them, it wouldn't take long before they did. They had to do something.

He looked around again, and spotted a stack of stout two-by-fours on the far side near the workbench. "Jason, how good are you with a rifle?"

"Pretty good. Better with a pistol, but I've practiced."

"Sir—" Aubrey began.

Stone knew where he was going—he didn't want to give up his weapon. "I know, Aubrey," he said gently. "But I've got a more important—and safer—job for you, at least until we get up on the roof." He nodded to the truck. "Get in. We can fit three in the cab, so Verity, you're in the middle and Ian, you'll be on the other side."

"What are you thinking, Al?" Jason asked.

"Why am I in the middle?" Verity protested.

"Just do it." Stone levitated the stack of two-by-fours into the truck's bed. There were five of them, each one six feet long. "We don't have much time. Grab whatever other weapons you want and hurry." He talked fast, explaining his plan, but he had to cut it off when the section of garage door in front of the convertible splintered. Two skeletons poked their heads and upper bodies through, their long fingers ripping at the wood to make a larger hole.

"Go!" Jason yelled, grabbing the rifle and box of ammo from Aubrey and leaping into the bed.

Aubrey and Verity clambered into the truck. Ian fired up the chainsaw he'd taken from Jason and got in last, slamming the door shut and hanging the running saw out through the open window.

"Now, Verity!" Stone yelled.

She grabbed two of the two-by-fours with her magic and hovered them over the front of the truck, as more skeletal hands poked through in front of them.

"Three...two...one..." Stone called. "Go!"

He gathered magic and sent it out in a punishing wave, blowing the wooden garage door outward in splinters of fast-moving shrapnel. Several of the skeletons, caught by surprise, staggered backward and fell.

At the same moment, Aubrey gunned the accelerator. The truck erupted out of the garage bay, slamming into several more skeletons with hard *thumps*. The impact hit harder than Stone would have expected—how much could a human skeleton *weigh?*—jerking both him and Jason to the side. Still, he managed to grab a magical hold on the pair of two-by-fours. He sent them out in front of the truck, one at approximately neck height on the creatures and the other at pelvis height. They acted as battering rams, driving more of the things back and tumbling.

Meanwhile, two of the skeletons had skittered around the truck's side, seeking Ian's open window. With a roar, Ian swept the growling chainsaw in a downward angle, taking the head off the first skeleton and slicing the second's spine. Both collapsed soundlessly to the ground and dropped away. Ian whooped in triumph.

Following the plan, Aubrey drove the truck only twenty feet or so into the yard, then stopped. "Now, sir!" he called.

Jason, standing in the truck's bed, concentrated on picking off any skeletons getting too near Aubrey's side of the truck. Ian seemed to have things well in hand with his chainsaw, which the creatures on his side were avoiding. Verity had taken hold of another two-by-four from the back and was now using magic to swing it like an oversized baseball bat, bowling over skeletons in twos and threes.

"We're not killing them!" Ian yelled. "They keep getting back up!"

Stone had both noticed and expected that. Of all the creatures they'd taken down on their escape from the garage, only two seemed to be permanently down: the one Ian had cut the head off, and one Jason had beaned between the eye sockets with a rifle shot. "Come on," he yelled. "Let's get out and get to the roof. We need to destroy their heads to take them out!"

This was the most dangerous part of the plan. They were surrounded now; even though many of the skeletons were still struggling back to their feet, they moved fast and their single-minded devotion to reaching the group hadn't abated in the slightest. Stone and the others could use magical shields to protect themselves, but they were tricky to maintain around more than one person, especially when they were moving around as much as they were. The best option was to drive the skeletons back, scramble out of the truck as fast as possible, and levitate to the roof before they could recover. From there, they'd have a better angle to take them out one at a time. Forty-one was a big number, but it was a finite number. If the skeletons couldn't reach them, all his group had to do was pick them off. Time would be on their side.

But first they had to get up there.

"All right," Stone called. "Just like we planned it. Three...two...one...*go!*"

As one they lifted off the ground, with Stone levitating Aubrey and Verity lifting Jason. The levitation spell wasn't fast, but once they got out of range they should be safe for a while. Even if the skeletons were agile enough to climb up on the roof, between the five of them they should be able to keep them under control on all four sides of the two-story structure.

They'd made it halfway up when two of the skeletons surged out of the crowd and leaped upward, extending their arms. One missed and fell back to the ground, but the other one's grasping fingers closed around Verity's ankle. She yelped in surprise and pain, and for a second she bobbled her levitation spell. Jason dropped a couple of feet in the air, and more skeletons scrambled forward.

"Verity!" Stone yelled. Without conscious thought he split his concentration, lifting Aubrey up and dropping him on the roof while simultaneously using the two-by-four he'd carried with him to pulverize the dangling skeleton's pelvis.

It lost its precarious hold on Verity's leg and dropped back, but already others were leaping upward. Ian barely managed to jerk his legs up to avoid a lunge from another one. A moment later, he too dropped onto the roof, followed by a panting Verity and Jason.

Stone landed last, keeping an eye on the skeletons from higher up until he was sure his friends were safely in place. He took a fast look around at their perch: the roof was more steeply pitched than he remembered, meaning they'd have to stay near the edges or risk losing their balance and tumbling down, especially since everyone but Aubrey was barefoot. "Are you all right, Verity?"

"Yeah." Her voice sounded shaky from the other end of the roof. "Mostly freaked out, but at least that thing didn't mess up my ankle."

Two more skeletons leaped up, catching the edge of the roof, and tried to scramble onto it. Ian darted over and sliced

one of them with the chainsaw, and Jason took aim and pul-
verized the other's head with a rifle shot.

"Al," he said between panting breaths. "They're gonna
get up here. Did you see how high they jumped?"

He was right. So far, the one thing working in their favor
was that the things seemed mostly mindless—if they started
coordinating attacks, Stone and his friends would be in
trouble.

"I think we can hold them off," he said. "Everyone pick a
side of the roof. Aubrey, take your rifle back and go with Jason." He levitated the second two-by-four to Verity. "We've
already taken down three of them permanently. Even if there
are thirty-eight left, we know how to deal with them now,
and we've got the high ground. Aubrey, make those twenty
rounds count."

"It's like a damn real-life zombie movie," Jason muttered,
hefting his baseball bat. Another skeleton caught hold of the
roof edge; he smashed its hands and it fell.

"How are they doing this?" Ian demanded. "Are the echoes controlling them?"

"Lousy way to leave us alone until sunrise if they are,"
Verity said.

"Is it that thing from the basement?" Jason asked.

Stone crouched near the edge and looked down, taking
careful aim with his two-by-four and forcing five of the skeletons across the yard. Their questions were good ones; he'd
been turning over the same ones in the back of his mind
since they left the house.

The skeletons didn't have auras, but they *did* glow on
magical sight with the same sickly green light that filled the
house—the same green that formed the flames in their eyes.

He didn't think the echoes were driving them, though. For one thing, a group of echoes that large, even one this single-minded of purpose, wouldn't all suddenly decide to take control of their decaying bodies and attack. Even back at the house, they'd chosen different ways to show their anger: some threw objects, some created illusions, some screamed curses. For all of them to simultaneously possess their skeletons, break free of their prisons, and form into a mob implied either that something or someone was controlling them, or that it wasn't them at all, but rather some other force.

Stone's money was on the thing from the basement chamber. But who—or what—*was* it? He couldn't begin to stop it if he didn't know that.

He looked at his watch again. Four-thirty. The sun would be up soon, not that it would matter. He didn't intend to go back to the house again, at least not until he figured out more of this puzzle. Maybe Eddie and Ward would come up with something, but that wouldn't be until later today at least. They were probably fast asleep now.

From the other side of the roof came the *crack* of a rifle shot, followed by a whoop of triumph from Aubrey. "Got one!" the old man shouted. He seemed more confident now that he had an effective weapon in his hands. Around the corner, Ian stood, feet braced confidently on the roof's uneven surface, holding the chainsaw in front of him.

Stone shivered in the early-morning cold. Now that the skeletons seemed to be exercising more caution about attacking and his surging adrenaline had begun to fade, he had a moment to consider his surroundings. With faint amusement, he imagined the conversation that might take place when he rolled in to the Stanford department office before his upcoming seminar.

"*What have you been doing with your summer, Dr. Stone?*" Laura the admin aide would ask him.

"*Not much, really—just holding off murderous animated skeletons trying to take over my house, along with a pack of vengeful ghosts that hated my ancestors for burying them alive in our basement.*"

"*Oh, that's nice—I had a fun cookout on the Fourth...*"

Another rifle shot broke the silence, startling Stone from his absurd reverie. Almost idly, he smacked a skeleton trying to clamber over the edge and carefully moved down to get a look at what Verity was up to, glancing down as he did. Too many of the things still milled around down there—his efforts and those of his friends were doing the job of keeping them off the roof, but they were largely ineffectual in taking them down permanently. It was too hard to get a solid shot on them from this angle. Only Aubrey's precise rifle shots seemed to be doing any good, and they only had twenty rounds of ammo—less, now. What would they do when they ran out? They couldn't very well ring up 999 and have the police around to mop up.

Verity seemed to be holding her own with her swinging two-by-four, so Stone sidled back the other way to check on Ian. He could still hear the roar of the chainsaw, and wondered how long it would go before it ran out of gas. They hadn't brought any extra with them. Would fire take the skeletons out? It didn't matter, unless he wanted to destroy the garage and Aubrey's apartment as well.

Just as he rounded the corner, Ian lunged forward with the saw, swinging it with graceful confidence at a skeleton that had poked its head too far up while trying to climb onto the roof. The blade sliced neatly through its neck, sending head and body crashing back to the ground. It was weird how soundlessly they "died"—no screams or shouts of pain. Did animated skeletons even *feel* pain?

"Nice one!" Stone called. "You've got—" His blood chilled. "*Ian! Behind you!*"

Ian spun, but not fast enough. Another skeleton, possibly smarter than its companions or more likely just luckier, had been hanging on just below the roof line beyond where Ian stood. When he'd moved forward to slice the first one, the second one flung itself upward, grabbed hold of Ian's ankle, and yanked.

For a moment, Stone saw the world in slow motion as his son teetered on the edge, flailing his arms in a desperate attempt to regain his balance. Before he could react, Ian disappeared into the darkness. Unlike the skeletons, his descent was not silent—his scream echoed through the night air until a crash stilled it, and then came the scramble of bony bodies as they rushed in to claim their prize.

Stone didn't hesitate, nor did he consider the consequences of his actions. "*Ian!*" he screamed. His mind filled with images of the skeletal hands ripping his only son apart, he leaped from the roof, using magic to slow his descent, and dropped down in the middle of the growing crowd of scrambling, grasping creatures.

"*Al!*" Jason cried from somewhere up above, but he barely heard it. Before he even touched down he was already gathering magic, sending out a punishing wave of concussive energy, blowing the skeletons out in all directions and back nearly fifty feet.

R. L. KING

He didn't check to see whether he'd taken them down, stunned them, or barely affected them at all. His gaze was focused wholly on the sprawled form on the ground in front of him. "Ian!" he yelled, shaking the boy's shoulder. "Ian! Wake up!"

Ian must have gotten his shield up at the last second, because Stone didn't see any blood and none of his limbs were bent at odd angles, but his eyes were closed and his face was pale. *Stunned?* The chainsaw lay a few feet away, still growling but the chain on its blade no longer spinning.

"Al! Look out!" Above him, Jason had moved around to the closest side of the roof and now crouched there, looking down in horror. "Aubrey! Bring that rifle over here!"

Ian moaned. His eyes fluttered open, but no awareness showed in them yet.

Stone rose to his feet, standing over his son, only now noticing the scene around him.

The skeletons had recovered and moved fast. They surrounded Stone and Ian now in a loose circle, crowding in. The spaces between them grew smaller and smaller until the bony bodies nearly blocked them completely.

"Doc!" Verity yelled. "Get out of there!"

Stone thought fast, knowing he had time for only one action before they were upon him. He could raise his shield around himself and Ian, letting them pile on to buy time. He could grab Ian and try to levitate back to the roof before the skeletons leaped up and dragged them back down. Or he could send out another concussive wave to blow them back again. All three choices had their downsides, but he didn't have time to consider them.

He chose the shield, erecting a bubble around the two of them. It would allow them time—with his Calanarian power he could hold it for a while, long enough to make sure Ian hadn't been badly hurt. If he could get the boy awake, they could—

Bony bodies piled on top of the shield, pressing against it, climbing over each other. Stone felt an odd psychic pressure, as if the physical act of pushing the barrier created a corresponding push in his mind.

A skeletal hand punched through the barrier, reaching for him.

Bloody hell! They're getting through! They shouldn't be able to do that!

"Doc!" Verity screamed again. He heard her, but couldn't see her past the writhing bodies.

The shield didn't pop like a balloon. That was normally how it happened when something was strong enough to get through it: it would vanish, sending painful psychic backlash into the caster. This time, though, it was more as if the thing were suddenly made of a thick membrane instead of a solid surface. More hands pushed through, tearing holes until big chunks of it simply tore away, revealing stained, grinning, burning-eyed faces.

Aubrey and Jason both yelled something.

The *cracks* of rifle shots filled the air.

The bodies bulled their way forward, grasping, grabbing, pounding—

Skeletal fingers closed around Stone's throat—

And then a shrieking, unearthly scream rose into the air.

The skeletons staggered backward, jerking, their single-minded movements suddenly disoriented and unfocused. Their bony hands fell away from Stone, from Ian.

And then, with a loud *whoosh* like dropping a lit match into a massive bundle of oily rags, every last one of the writhing creatures vanished.

What the hell—?

For a moment, Stone was disoriented too, crouched over Ian, trying to protect his son from attack long enough to give his friends time to come up with a solution. But when nothing *did* attack—when he could no longer hear the clicking and clattering of bony bodies crowding against each other—he stood and looked around.

He and the still-stunned Ian were the only things remaining in the area in front of the garage. Except for his friends' yells from above, nothing made a sound.

Verity landed next to him, grabbing him by the shoulders. "Doc! Are you all right? They disappeared! Is Ian—"

Jason, not waiting for Verity to levitate him, clambered over the edge of the roof and dropped down, scanning the area. "Where'd they go? They were just there, and then—"

Ian sat up, panting, his gaze still a little unfocused but more coherent. "Shit," he said. "I slipped off, and—"

Stone wasn't looking at him. Instead, he stared out across the yard. "Bloody hell…" he murmured.

"What?" Jason gave Ian a hand up, and stood with him and Verity, confused. "Where are they?"

"Sunrise," Stone said. He pointed to the east, where the faint rays of the dawn sun rose over the horizon. "They're still here."

"Where?" Verity demanded.

He pointed down. "There. All around us."

And indeed they were: numerous small piles of gray-brown dust mingled with the damp, dew-soaked ground, already seeping through the gravel driveway. The rusty manacles lay in heaps near them.

"Wait…" Jason said. "You're saying they…just turned to *dust* at sunrise?"

"So it would appear, wouldn't it?"

"Did you know they were going to do that?" Verity poked at one of the dwindling piles with a black-painted toenail, almost as if expecting it to reconstitute and come after them again.

Stone shook his head. "No idea." His heart still pounded hard, and he shivered as the cool morning air met the cold sweat streaking his body. For the first time, he consciously realized he and his friends were barely dressed. "If I'd known, we could have waited them out."

"Sir?" Aubrey called from the roof. "Could I get a little help down, please, if those creatures are gone?"

"I got it," Verity said, and used a levitation spell to carefully lower the caretaker to the ground next to them.

Stone focused on his son, who looked more aware. The boy had streaks of blood on his chest and shoulders from where the skeletons' fingers had clawed at him, but didn't look seriously injured. "I'm sorry, Ian. I didn't act fast enough—"

Ian waved him off. "It's fine. My fault. I slipped when that thing grabbed me, but I got my shield up before I hit. I'm okay." He still looked pale, though.

"So…what do we do now, sir?" Aubrey asked. He still clutched his rifle like an anchor, his gaze never still as he continued watching for surprise attacks.

Stone considered. "Now…we go back to London and consider our next moves. See if Eddie and Ward have come up with anything from those inscriptions and journals. We take showers and get dressed." He let his breath out. "And I figure out what to do about our new problem."

"What new problem?" Verity asked.

"Well…" He indicated the yard. A light rain had begun to fall, further washing away the dust piles that had been the skeletons. "If those truly *were* the remains of the people imprisoned under the house, they're gone now. Their dust all pooled together and washed away in the rain. Which means we can't properly bury them even if we *did* work out all of their identities."

"Oh, no…" she breathed, catching on.

"You see the problem. Unless I come up with another idea for how to get rid of the echoes, the only options left on the table are vacate the house permanently, find a bloody good exorcist, or sacrifice myself in atonement."

| CHAPTER TWENTY-FOUR

"**Y**OU SHOULD TRY TO SLEEP," Verity said.

"Wouldn't do any good. I've never felt less like sleeping." Stone stood in front of one of the tall windows at the front of the London house, looking out over the street. It was still early, but a steady stream of traffic drove by in the light morning rain. *They're going to work*, he thought with some wonder. *They've got their briefcases and their cups of coffee, and all they've got to worry about is sales reports and unpleasant customers. Not walking skeletons trying to rip them to pieces.*

They'd adjourned here shortly after dawn had turned the skeletons to dust. They stopped only long enough to collect the manacles, and for Jason and Verity to run back inside the main house and retrieve their bags, along with clothes for Stone and Ian. Nothing or no one bothered them when they did so; the echoes still apparently still had no issue with anyone not related to Stone. Stone had thought—hoped— that perhaps the skeletons' destruction would mean the end to the echoes as well, but as soon as he put one foot past the house's threshold, the aura went red again and the screams began anew.

"I was tempted to go down into the basement and see if those brick alcoves had been broken open," Verity said when she returned. "I didn't, though. We can look later."

"I think those manacles were a fairly good indication," Stone told her.

They could have left earlier, as soon as they'd all gotten dressed, but Stone had to convince a reluctant Aubrey to leave as well. "Go visit your sister, or your nephew," he told the caretaker. "I know nothing's gone after you so far, but I don't want you alone here with all this madness going on."

"But sir—" Aubrey had protested.

Stone knew where he was coming from. Aubrey considered the estate as much his home as it was Stone's, and a large part of his self-image had always been tied up in his ability to look after it, protect it from threats, and contribute to its sense of quiet peace. To be driven away from it, especially when it was in such a state, would be to admit defeat— something the old man was no better at than Stone was.

Still, he insisted. "Aubrey, no argument. I've got a lot to be getting on with here, and I don't want to be worrying about what's happening to you while I do it. I hope it won't be for long—we need to get this sorted before those things settle in and decide they like the place."

"Yes, sir," he'd said with a loud, long-suffering sigh. "I'll pack a bag and leave this morning."

"Give me your word, Aubrey. And ring me when you arrive."

"I promise, sir."

Stone didn't say anything about it, but when he looked at the old man with magical sight, he spotted the obvious signs of relief in his aura. He was loyal, but he was also terrified of the supernatural unknown.

Jason didn't even complain when they entered the portal. When they stepped through on the other side, all of them breathed relieved sighs. Unless the echoes or any straggling skeletons could navigate the Overworld, they were probably safe here. "Everyone choose a bedroom on the third floor," Stone told them, "and try to get some sleep. I'll ring Eddie a little later this morning and we'll see where we can go from here."

Verity had drifted back down after her shower, finding Stone where he currently was. "Have you got a plan yet?"

He shook his head, still staring out the window. "Not yet. We need more information. We still haven't got a bloody idea what stirred up those skeletons. I've never seen magic like that before."

"So the echoes couldn't have possessed them?" She perched on the edge of a nearby sofa.

"Who knows? It's possible, of course. But I don't think it's likely."

"Okay...so what *do* you think is likely? Do you really think whatever was in that chamber did it?"

He began pacing back and forth in front of the window. "I don't *know*, Verity. We don't know what was in there. Hell, we don't even know if anything *was* in there."

"If not, then what broke the door? It sure looked like whatever it was, it broke out from the inside. Or else something or somebody wanted us to *think* it did. Could the echoes have broken the door?"

He chuckled mirthlessly. "You've always been good at asking the right questions. I wish I had some answers for you. I'm hoping Eddie and Ward will turn something up."

"Why don't you call them, then? You aren't doing yourself or anybody any good spinning your wheels. Have you even had anything to eat?"

"Not hungry."

She came up behind him, taking his shoulders in a gentle grip and turning him around to face her. "Hey…" she said softly. "I know you're having trouble with this. It's like your whole world has turned upside-down on you, and I know how much you hate not being able to figure things out. But you'll get it. *We'll* get it. I know we will. You've got a good team on your side, but you need to let us support you. Don't try to take this all on yourself. Okay?"

She always seemed to know the right thing to say without effort, but this time even that wasn't enough to shake his unease. "I'll call Eddie," he said at last. "But…I think right now what I need is a little time to myself. Try to get some sleep, Verity. I appreciate your help—everyone's help. You know I do. But—"

"I know." She pulled him into a hug. "I'll leave you alone. But not for long. I really don't think it's good for you to be alone too much right now, and if you were thinking clearly, you'd know it too."

He leaned against the wall and watched her go. When she reached the sitting room's doorway he wanted to call her back. He almost did. But in the end, he turned back around and continued to gaze morosely out the window into the rainy street.

☐

Eddie and Ward listened with wide-eyed astonishment to Stone's account of what had occurred the previous night.

"Bloody...'*ell*," Eddie breathed when the tale, supplemented with extra details from Verity, Jason, and Ian, was finished. His expression, warring between terror and fascination, was almost comical in its intensity.

"Indeed," Ward said, calmer as always but still obviously affected by Stone's story.

They sat at the big table in the dining room, three open boxes of pizza in front of them. Stone didn't keep much of a staff at the London house since he was rarely in residence, and by the time Eddie and Ward had arrived, both Jason and Ian had insisted on ordering something to eat. It was a little early for pizza, but considering how messed up all their schedules had been over the last couple of days, nobody minded.

"So you've got no idea what stirred them up?" Eddie asked, pausing to munch a slice. The bag containing the journals, along with another small stack of books, stood on the other end of the table, away from greasy fingers. "They just...started 'avin' a go at you for no reason? You didn't try goin' down into the chamber, did you?"

"No. We all went straight to bed after you left." Stone swept his gaze around the table at his friends for confirmation, but all of them shook their heads.

"No way," Jason said. "You think I'd go down there by myself? I don't trust those things to keep their word about not messin' with us."

"How's Poppy, by the way?" Stone asked, embarrassed that he'd been so keen on telling his story to his friends that he hadn't remembered to ask as soon as they arrived.

"She's fine. A little spooked, naturally, but remember, that kind o' thing's what she does. We made sure she got 'ome all right, and by the time we got there she seemed right as rain." He threw Stone a grin. "But I wouldn't count on 'avin' 'er back in for any repeat visits, though."

Stone *had* wondered if the medium would be willing to come back and try again with proper precautions in place, but he respected her wishes. "Fair enough."

"It sounds like we don't need a medium," Jason said. "We need an exorcist."

"That's definitely an option," Ward agreed.

"Did you find out anything from those books and your notes?" Stone asked, indicating the stack at the end of the table. "I know you two—you probably didn't sleep any more than we did last night, did you? You'd have been gagging to bury your noses in them."

Eddie and Ward exchanged sheepish glances, telling Stone everything he needed to know. "We did," Eddie admitted. "We went to the library directly after droppin' Poppy off and got started." He finished his pizza slice, wiped his hands on a napkin, then held them up and muttered a spell. Satisfied they were clean, he summoned the stack of books and the satchel to him and opened his notebook.

"The journal and the ledger weren't terribly interesting," he said, pointing at the pair of tomes. "Well—that's not true. They were *very* interesting to us, but not any more 'elpful to our current predicament than they were last night. They were exactly what we expected them to be: an annotated list of all the foundation sacrifices, and a detailed series of ritual diagrams and instructions."

Ward nodded toward the journal. "Not all the rituals were related to the foundation sacrifice. Many were—the rituals to strengthen the magical and mundane protections on the house were quite complicated, and required several days to cast. The victims were chained in those niches and allowed to die over those several days. Naturally, some succumbed sooner than others, and the constant influx of death energy fueled the workings and provided significant extra power."

Stone had only eaten a single slice of pizza, and his friend's words turned it to a hard ball in his stomach. He let his breath out and took a drink. "What about the other rituals?"

Eddie shrugged. "They were nasty, to be sure. 'Uman sacrifices always are. No surprise what they got up to, though—they used most of 'em to gain more power, either temporarily to add punch to something they were tryin' to do, or more permanently. The others were for strikin' back at enemies from a distance, either directly or through curses. I 'ate to say they weren't interestin', but we didn't see anything to do with skeletons." He dropped his volume, glancing around as if expecting someone else to be listening to their conversation. "That's a whole different kind o' magic, that is."

"What kind?" Verity asked.

"Necromancy," Stone said before either of his friends could respond. Then he shot them a questioning glance. "Right?"

"Got it in one." Eddie sounded grim. "But I gotta tell you, mate—there's no credible evidence that necromancy *ever* existed, let alone that somebody's gettin' up to it now."

"You can't raise the dead," Ward added. "It's simply not possible."

"What about echoes?" Verity asked. "They can possess things, right? Is there any reason they couldn't possess their own bodies?"

"No, I suppose not." Eddie flipped through his notebook, searching for something. "But—"

"But it's not likely," Stone finished. "I was thinking about this last night. It's certainly possible that *some* of the echoes might have got the idea to try it. But *all* of them? They're not a monolithic entity."

"Unless something else is controlling them," Ward said.

"Exactly." Stone slapped the table. "That's my thought as well."

"Mine too," Eddie said. "Because there's somethin' else you're not thinkin' about."

"What's that?"

"Echoes can possess inanimate objects, yes, or even living beings if they're strong enough to overcome the being's resistance."

"Or if it were to allow them in, for whatever reason," Ward added.

"Yes, exactly. But you're forgettin' that when they do, the fundamental nature of the object or being doesn't change."

"What's that mean?" Jason asked. Unlike the others, he was still devouring the pizza.

"What it means," Ward said, "is that if an echo were to take over, say, a coffee maker, that doesn't make it any less a coffee maker. The echo could use it to make coffee. It might be able to spray hot coffee on people nearby, or possibly strangle someone with its cord. But it couldn't suddenly leap across the room and walk out the door. And it would still be as easy to destroy as any other coffee maker."

"Or Stone's cat," Eddie said. "Blimey, I still wish I coulda seen *that*. But 'e didn't start carryin' on conversations in Latin, or takin' your car out for a spin, did 'e, mate?"

"No," Stone said. "He...mostly just acted like a normal cat, with a bit of extra intelligence driving. But what are you—"

And then he caught on. "Ah, I see what you're saying. If the echoes had possessed the skeletons, they'd still be three-hundred-year-old skeletons, and probably in pieces."

"Exactly right." Eddie nodded vigorously. "You said these things were strong and hard to hurt, right?"

"*Damn* hard," Jason said. "Even when we took 'em down, they got right back up and kept coming. It took a head shot to take 'em down permanently."

"Or a sunrise," Ian said.

"Right, right." Ward spoke with more enthusiasm now. "The sort of ritual necessary to do something like that would require a lot of power." He looked at Jason. "I don't know how much Stone's told you about magic, but it's quite common for a ritual's power to wane at sunrise or sunset."

"So..." Verity said, "you think someone *is* practicing necromancy?"

"Maybe," Eddie said. "But I wouldn't go there yet. I'd sooner look at some kind of strengthening ritual. Think of it less as raising the dead and more as a sort of mass animation spell, with an extra component tossed in so the bloody things didn't collapse under their own weight before they could do what they were meant to do."

"But..." Stone began, speaking slowly, turning his ideas over in his mind before he gave them voice. "That would mean someone would have had to break all of them out of their alcoves. Otherwise, the ritual would've had to reach them *inside* those sealed chambers. That's some pretty complicated spellwork, there."

"You got that right," Eddie agreed.

"What about the stuff from the chamber?" Ian asked. "Did you get anything from that?"

"Yeah," Verity said. "Do you have any idea who or what was in there? Could they have been strong enough to do that ritual?"

Eddie had been about to reach for another slice of pizza, but let it hover in midair for a few seconds before returning it to the box. "*That's* where things get interesting."

"How so?" Stone asked, leaning forward. "Did you get something?"

"Nothing specific," Ward said. "We still don't know who was sealed in that chamber."

"But you know it's a *who,* not a *what*?" Jason asked.

"We think so," Eddie said. "And the other thing we know is that it was bloody powerful. Really, *really* powerful."

Stone frowned. "How do you know that? And can you be more specific?"

Ward brought his satchel to him and pulled out his own notebook, along with a few of the larger chunks from the carved door. He pushed his plate aside and laid the chunks out in front of him. "Every one of the sigils, symbols, and inscriptions, on both these pieces of the door and the sketches we made, were for a single purpose."

"Yes?"

"Protection," Eddie said. All traces of the normal mischievous twinkle in his eyes had departed. "Binding. Warding."

Stone had never seen his two friends look so serious. "So...you're saying whatever they locked up in there, they might have been afraid it would get away from them?"

"Exactly," Ward said. "We'd have to go back and look at the chamber again now that we've worked out more of the symbols, but I'd say that we're looking at multiple levels of redundancy here. The magical equivalent of putting several locks on a box and then wrapping it with welded metal straps. Whatever was inside that room, whoever put it there didn't want it getting out."

Verity gripped the table. "Does that mean...it wasn't dead in the first place?"

"Like a vampire or something?" Jason asked.

"Probably not a vampire," Eddie said.

"*Are* there vampires?" Ian contemplated the pizza boxes, then snagged another slice.

"Sort of," Stone said. "Not the way the media portrays them, though. And they're rare. Most of what people might think of as 'vampires' were really some of the nastier black mages."

"So, what, then?" Verity asked. "Something magically talented, right?"

"Oh, without a doubt," Ward said. "Some of those sigils were designed to create a sort of magical nullification field around the space inside—either the whole room or that stone coffin." He pondered. "If I had to guess—and mind you, this is just a guess, with very little to back it up—I'd venture to say whatever was in there was in a sort of...suspended anima-tion. The construction probably shook something loose, giving it the tiny opening it needed to break free."

Stone stared at him. "Do you have any idea what kind of power that would have taken? Not just to do the ritual in the first place, but to sustain it until now?"

Eddied nodded. "Yeah, mate. We do. That's why this is all so terrifyin'."

"And now it's out there somewhere," Verity said. "And we have no idea who or what it is, or whether it hates Doc's family as much as the echoes do."

"That's about it," Eddie said.

"Was there anything in the journal about that sort of ritual?" Stone asked, pointing at it. "Anything even close?"

"That was our first thought," Ward said. "But no. Nothing. There are warding rituals, of course, but they're more concerned with protecting large structures, like the house. Nothing about keeping something imprisoned."

"Well. This is bloody brilliant, isn't it?" Stone stared at his hands on the table. He'd hoped Eddie and Ward could give him answers—and to some extent, they had. But those answers had come with a heaping helping of additional questions. "Now not only do I have to work out how to get the echoes out of my house without sacrificing myself because we don't have the bones to bury, but I've also got to track down whatever super-powerful entity was shut up in a containment chamber in the basement." He jerked his head up, knowing how manic he must look. "Anybody want a drink?"

Nobody answered. Jason and Ian continued eating pizza while Eddie and Ward paged through their notebooks and Verity studied the chunks of door spread out on the table. She looked up, obviously about to say something, when someone's phone buzzed.

"That's me," Eddie said, pulling it from his pocket. He glanced at the number, his eyes widening in surprise. "'Ello, Poppy. Didn't expect to 'ear from you this soon. Are you all right? Nothing's come after you, 'as it?"

He listened a moment, then nodded. "Well, that's good, at least. Wait, you've got what?" He shifted his gaze between Stone and Ward, his brow furrowing. "Wait, Poppy. 'Ang on a tick, will you? We're at Stone's place in London. I've got 'im and 'is lot 'ere, along with Ward. They'll want to 'ear this too. Let me put you on speaker."

He punched a button and laid the phone in the middle of the table, moving a pizza box out of the way. To Stone, he said, "She said she's been 'avin' odd dreams last night, and she thinks they might mean somethin'. Go ahead, Poppy," he added in a louder voice.

"Hello?" she called.

"Morning," Stone said. "I hope you're doing all right. Is something wrong?"

"I don't know yet." She sounded odd, as if she couldn't quite make sense of her own thoughts. "It might be nothing, but I figured I'd give Eddie a ring and let him know, just in case it isn't."

"I appreciate that. What's going on?"

"Well—last night, after Eddie and Arthur took me home, I had trouble sleeping."

"Not surprised. I think we all did."

"Yeah. Well, I had a little drink and finally went to bed around three-thirty. I didn't think I'd get any sleep, but I figured I'd at least try to rest for a bit. Anyway, I didn't think I'd nodded off, but the next thing I knew I was havin' this vivid dream."

"Is that unusual?" Stone asked.

"Dreams aren't, but this one was…different. I get them sometimes—part of my work, you know? But this one was about your house."

Stone leaned forward, gripping the table's edge, his attention focused on Eddie's phone. "Did you dream about the echoes? The spirits?"

"No. That wouldn't have surprised me at all after what happened. I'm not even sure how I knew I was *at* your house, because I was…shut up inside something."

All around the table, everyone exchanged glances. "Inside what?" Stone asked. "Do you know?"

"I don't. It was dark, and there wasn't much space. I…I didn't feel like me, though. I felt like somebody else. A man, I think. And I was…angry. Like, *really* angry. Murderous. I wanted to kill the people who put me inside that dark space. And there was this overwhelming sense of betrayal."

A chill ran up Stone's back. "What happened next?" He was very much afraid he might know the answer.

"The rage kept getting stronger and stronger, until I thought I'd just explode with it. I felt like I was drifting up through something, and then I was in this strange room."

"Strange room?" The chill settled at the base of his neck, fluttering outward. "Was it small and square? Did it have carvings or sigils of any kind on the walls?"

"I…don't think so. You have to realize, all of this was…well…dreamlike. Everything was dark and swirling around and hard to make out. It almost seemed like I was in a big round room, not a small square one. But that's crazy, right? It's probably just that I was spinning around."

"What did you do next?" Eddie asked. "Do you remember anything else? Were there any other spirits around?"

"No...I don't think so. Just me. That was when I woke up. I was soaked with sweat, and my whole body hurt. I think I was...clenching my muscles in my sleep, to go along with the rage in the dream." She paused. "When I woke up, I was still feeling that rage. I wanted to kill somebody. It scared me, until I got myself calmed down." She drew a deep, audible breath. "Did that help you? Do you know the place I'm talking about? Do you recognize it?"

Once more, the group around the table looked at each other. "I think we do," Eddie said after a moment. "Poppy, I'm sorry. I never should've brought you into this. Will you be all right? 'Ave you got somebody to look after you?"

"Yeah, I'm fine. I've got a couple of mates coming over in a bit, and we're gonna go indulge in some retail therapy with all that money Alastair paid me. And get really drunk tonight." She gave an unsteady chuckle. "Don't you worry, Eddie. I'll be fine."

"Thank you, Poppy," Stone said. "If there's anything I can do for you—"

"That's all right, luv. I think if you don't mind I'll just stay away from you and your lot for a while. A year or so from now, we can all have a drink and a laugh over this, but right now—"

"I understand. Thanks for letting us know about the dream, though."

When Eddie had put the phone back in his pocket, Ian spoke for the first time. "Do you think she's talking about the sealed room?"

"It would make sense," Jason said. "Like she said, she was disoriented in the dream. And that feeling like she was shut up inside something—that would be that box, right?"

"And whoever it is, it sounds like they hate the Stone family even more than the echoes do," Verity added.

"But what do we *do* with that information?" Ian took the last slice from one of the pizza boxes and closed it. "Whoever was in that box is gone now—how do we find out who it was?"

"There wasn't anything in the ledger about it, was there?" Jason asked Ward. "You know—records of any extra sacrifices, pages that didn't have numbers, anything like that?"

"No, nothing like that. The ledger was very precise: forty-one sacrificial victims, each one corresponding to one of the alcoves in the chamber. Nothing extra."

"We even examined all the pages with magical sight," Eddie said. "In case there were any secret records. We're fairly sure what you see is what you get."

Verity frowned, glancing at Stone. "Doc? You've been really quiet. And you look like you've got something on your mind. What is it?"

Stone looked up from where he'd been gazing down at the table, ignoring most of what his friends had been discussing. Poppy's words swirled in his mind. "I wonder…" he said, almost to himself.

"What do you wonder, mate? Did we miss something?" Eddie asked.

He stood with sudden intensity. "We've got to go back to the house."

"Back?" Jason and Ian said in unison.

"Why?" Verity added.

"Because I don't think Poppy *was* disoriented. I think she meant exactly what she said."

"What are you talking about?" Ward asked.

Stone made a *come on* gesture, urging his friends up. "She mentioned feeling like she was in a large round room, not a small square one. Does that sound like anything familiar?"

"Are you talkin' about the central ritual chamber?" Eddie frowned. "You think there might've been another sacrifice on that altar—one that wasn't recorded for whatever reason? Maybe that whatever was shut up in that sealed room might've been prepared there first?"

"No," Stone said, snatching his overcoat from the back of the chair. "I might be wrong—I hope I am, because it will add yet *another* unknown variable to our little puzzle—but I wonder if there might still be something, or someone, interred *inside* that altar."

| CHAPTER TWENTY-FIVE

"**Y**OU THERE, DOC?**" Verity stood in the basement room, looking at the dark hole in the floor while she straightened her jacket. "We're ready to go down."

"I'm here," Stone's voice came back instantly through the radio. "Where else would I be?" Even over the connection, she couldn't miss the bitter frustration in his voice. "Just—be careful, all right? If there *is* anything down there, it might not want to be disturbed. And keep the connection open."

"Yeah, we will." She glanced at the others. "Ready?"

"As we'll ever be," Eddie said.

When they'd returned through the portal to the house, Aubrey had already departed, his truck gone from the yard where they'd left it in their hasty retreat. The group had set up their command center in the garage again, with an impatient Stone and Ian remaining behind as the others set off for the house.

Eddie and Ward had both been skeptical about the idea that there might be something hidden within the pedestal in the ritual room, but they hadn't argued much about the trip back because they both wanted to see the broken alcoves and have another look in the sealed room now that they knew better what they were looking at.

"Just don't be disappointed if we don't find anything, mate," Eddie had told Stone before they left the garage. "I've never heard of anyone bein' shut up inside a sacrificial altar before."

Stone shrugged. "You're probably right. But we can eliminate another data point. Just don't take all day down there, all right?"

Now, Verity snapped her helmet into place and tightened her grip on her flashlight. "I'll go down first, in case anything's waiting for us down there. Send Jason down next, and then you guys come." She glanced at her brother; he was watching her grimly, his hands wrapped around the handle of his baseball bat. This time he also had a sledgehammer strapped to his back.

When she reached the stone floor below, she scanned the area quickly with both magical and mundane sight. Nothing unusual stood out, except that the wooden door was open. Had they left it open before, or had the skeletons done it when they poured out?

"Okay. Looks safe. Come on down."

A few seconds later, the others stood next to her. "Nothing so far, Doc," she said over the radio. "We're heading to the ritual room now."

The circular room looked no different than they remembered it from their visit yesterday. The altar and the ritual circle beneath it remained untouched, with no sign of tampering. The rusting manacles lay quiet and undisturbed on top.

All three of the mages scanned the altar with magical sight, taking positions all around it. "Anything?" Verity asked.

"Not a thing," Eddie said, shaking his head. "Looks as dull as ever."

"Yes," Ward agreed. "If there's been any magical activity here, I certainly don't see it."

"Should we just...break it open?" Jason asked. "I don't see any hatches or openings or anything."

"Yes," came Stone's voice over the radio. For the moment it was still working. "If you can't find a way in, break it open if you can. If it's solid, things will be more difficult, but we need to know that."

"Right." Jason pulled the sledgehammer from his back and paced around the altar, looking for a good spot.

"Wait," Eddie said, holding up a hand. "I want to look at the alcoves and the sealed room first, just in case Stone's right and something nasty 'appens when we open that thing up."

"Eddie—" Verity began. Now that they were here, she found herself caught up in Stone's curiosity. She wanted to see if he was right as much as he did.

"No, he's right," Stone said. "Have a look around, but don't take too long."

They stayed together again, none of them willing to wander off alone and make the search go faster, but even so it only took a few minutes to determine that their hypothesis about the skeletons had been at least partially correct: every one of the bricked alcoves had been blasted open from the inside, with bricks and pieces of bricks littering all four of the hallways. Their spot checks inside the alcoves found no evidence of skeletal remains, and some of the manacles holding the bones to the wall had been broken.

Verity relayed that information back to Stone as they trooped back to the center room and checked the remaining hallway with the formerly sealed chamber.

"No surprise there," he said. "If you hadn't found that, I'd have wondered where all those skeletons *came* from. Would have needed to check the cemetery, I suppose. What about the sealed room?"

His voice carried well to the others, and Eddie, who'd gone ahead, answered. "Everything looks fine here. No sign of disturbance. I want to get some more notes, but that can wait until after we've examined the altar."

"Assuming something doesn't jump out and eat us," Jason muttered.

Verity ignored him. "Come on. Let's do this. The suspense is killing me."

They'd lowered the stand lights back down through the hole from upstairs, and Ward switched them on, bathing the chamber in bright light. Eddie crouched next to the altar, pressing his ear against it and rapping with his knuckles.

"Anything?" Ward asked.

"'Ard to say. If it's 'ollow, the sides are too thick to resonate. I think we're gonna 'ave to crack it."

"Okay. Stand back," Jason said, handing the bat to Verity and hefting the sledgehammer.

The others retreated to the edge of the room, keeping a close watch on him. Verity noticed that, like her, both Eddie and Ward had magical sight up and stood tensely, ready to spring up shields around Jason if anything should leap free of the pedestal and attack him. "Here goes, Doc," she said. "Keep your fingers crossed."

Jason paused, sizing up the space, and then cocked the hammer back and swung.

Everyone held their breath.

The hammer's substantial head hit the side of the pedestal and cracked through, leaving a ragged hole six inches in diameter and scattering bits of crumbling stone around the edges.

"Yes!" Verity called through the radio. "It's hollow. Jason just busted through."

"Is anything inside?" Now Stone sounded eager, all his frustration gone.

"Don't know yet. Hang on."

She, Eddie, and Ward hastily approached as Jason pulled the hammer head free of the hole and began poking at its edges to widen it.

"Can you see anything?" Eddie thrust his hand, surrounded by a bright light spell, forward.

Verity used magic to help clear the hole, and after a moment Ward and Eddie did too. In only a few minutes they'd cleared it to a diameter of one foot.

Jason backed off with the sledgehammer. "You guys look. I break things—you analyze 'em."

"What do you see?" Stone demanded from the radio. "Tell me! Is anything in there?"

After a quick exchanged glance between Eddie, Verity, and Ward, the latter two backed up. "Go on," Verity said with a chuckle. "Take a look, before Doc's head explodes from curiosity."

Moving slowly, almost as if he didn't want the suspense to end, Eddie crouched in front of the ragged hole and pressed his face to it, moving his head to the side so he could get his light spell in as well.

"Well?" Jason called.

"Bloody 'ell," Eddie breathed, his shoulders tensing.

"What is it?" Verity crowded in closer.

He stepped back, pulling off his safety glasses to wipe sweat off his forehead. "Stone was right. There *is* somebody in there."

"Somebody? Who?" Stone's voice from the radio was louder. "Damn it, Eddie, give me *details*. Is it a body? A skeleton? A mummy? What?"

Eddie put his glasses back on. "We need to open this up more. It looks like a decayed male body. I can't get a good look because the hole's too small."

"Is there a catch inside?" Ward asked.

Eddie moved back in and directed the light upward. "Doesn't look like it. Whoever this is, they were sealed inside, and probably after they were dead. Don't think it was ever intended for anybody to get 'em out."

"Well, damn," Verity said, frustrated. "We can't just have Jason bash away at it—if the top collapses, it'll crush the body."

"How old does it look?" Ward gripped Eddie's shoulder. "Let me have a look. Perhaps we can determine when it was interred by the clothing style."

Eddie vacated his space and Ward leaned in, stuffing his hand through the opening to get better light on the subject. "The body's desiccated," he said. "but not skeletal. Probably the tomb preserved it to some extent."

"How old is it?" Stone said.

"The clothes are fairly rotted, but it looks like…late eighteenth, early nineteenth century, most likely. He—wait a moment!"

"What?" Stone, Verity, and Eddie all shouted at the same time.

Ward leaned back, poking his arm through the hole and feeling around. After a moment, he carefully withdrew it. In his hand was a small book bound in dusty black leather.

"It's a book," Verity said for Stone's benefit. "A little black book about the size of a personal journal."

"It was in his inner pocket," Ward said. "I wouldn't have spotted it if the fabric hadn't rotted away." Both he and Eddie were staring at it with hungry expressions, as if they'd just unearthed the Holy Grail.

"Bring it back here," Stone ordered. "I want to see it. But—look in the front now. See if there's a name in it, or any way to identify it."

Everyone crowded around the altar as Eddie carefully laid the book on top of it. "Doesn't look preserved," he said. "So we'll have to be careful."

He pulled a pair of thin gloves from his pocket and donned them, then gently pulled open the leather cover to expose the flyleaf.

"There's writing on it," Verity said. "I can't make it out, though. It's faded and old-fashioned."

"Eddie?" Stone urged.

"'Ang on…" Eddie leaned in closer, holding up his light spell, fully focused on the narrow, fussy script. "There's definitely a name 'ere, but it's damned 'ard to read. Joseph something, maybe, or…"

"James," Ward said. "I think it's James. And the surname's first initial looks like a *B* or a *P...*"

Eddie's shoulders suddenly went stiff, and he staggered a step backward, ripping off his safety glasses again. His face, in the harsh overhead light, was pale. "Bloody 'ell..." he whispered. "It can't be."

"*What*?" Stone yelled over the radio. "Eddie, what is it? Tell me!"

"Who is it?" Verity demanded.

Eddie swallowed, nodding toward the journal. "You're not gonna believe this, mate. *I* don't believe it. Remember before, when you 'ad Ward and me check into your family 'istory, and we found that partial journal from a bloke called James Brathwaite? 'E was a mage and an associate of one o' your ancestors, but he disappeared without a trace?"

"Yes..." Stone said.

"Well...I'm thinkin' maybe we might've found 'im."

| CHAPTER TWENTY-SIX

T HEY WERE BACK IN THE LONDON HOUSE, sitting around the big table in the dining room, less than half an hour later.

"Brathwaite..." Stone murmured. "I'm having a hard time believing it." He felt stunned, as if someone had recently set off a bomb behind him, and was having difficulty organizing his thoughts. Every time he thought they'd begun to get a handle on this situation, some new aspect popped up to complicate matters again.

"Believe it," Eddie said. "Unless somebody else was carryin' around 'is personal journal."

The journal in question lay in the middle of the table, and Stone, Eddie, and Ward were all staring at it like hungry cats. They'd only just arrived and sat down; Stone had insisted that the exploratory group remain in the ritual room for a while longer, watching with magical sight to verify there wasn't any arcane energy around the desiccated corpse before exiting. He wished he could have been down there—as much as he trusted his friends, he knew his own sensitivity to such things was higher—but had to be satisfied with their reports.

"Shall we 'ave a look, then?" Eddie asked, deceptively casual. "You want to do the honors, Stone?"

Stone *did* want to do the honors, more than just about anything, but this time he knew the best approach was to defer to greater expertise. "No, no—you two look. I'm betting whatever he wrote isn't in plain English, and even if it is I never got the hang of reading that old-fashioned writing. Let's put a preservation spell on it first, though."

"That, and examine it thoroughly for curses," Ward added.

"Curses?" Ian asked. "People put curses on books?"

"Not so much nowadays," Eddie said, nodding soberly. "But yeah, it was quite the thing back in those days. People didn't want anybody lookin' at their private stuff."

"How long is all that gonna take?" Jason asked. Even he was leaning forward in anticipation, clearly caught up in the excitement of discovery.

"Hour or so, to be safe," Stone said. "You lot didn't get much sleep last night—go take a nap or something and we'll meet back here then."

"What about you?" Verity asked.

"What about me?" He nodded toward the journal. "Do you honestly think I could sleep with *that* in the house? Off you all go—there's nothing you can do to help with this part, and it won't be exciting. Boring, scholarly stuff mostly. I promise we won't open it until we're all back together."

They grumbled a bit, especially Verity and Ian, but finally drifted off, leaving Eddie, Ward, and Stone alone in the dining room.

"You had another reason for getting rid of them, didn't you?" Eddie asked.

Stone shrugged, and didn't answer. "Come on, let's get on with this. I want to see what he had to say. I suppose it will be too much to ask that he's worked out why he was shut up down there in the first place."

❖

They reconvened in the dining room in an hour, with Verity, Jason, and Ian all showing up right on time.

"Did you find anything?" Verity asked, stifling a yawn.

"No curses," Stone said, returning the journal to the table. "Eddie put a preservation spell on it so we can page through without worrying about damaging it."

"Well, come on, then," she urged. "Let's see what he says."

Eddie pulled the book to him and opened it. Ward leaned in, holding up a light spell to provide brighter illumination. The first thing he did was riffle through the pages. "Not much written in 'ere," he said. "Maybe 'e'd recently started a fresh one. Stone, remember the one we found before, with the missin' pages?"

"Of course I do." He had a copy of it back at the Surrey house, and the original—or at least an original copy—resided in the London library. "Is this another copy?"

"No, definitely not."

"And you don't think these are the missing pages?"

Eddie shook his head in impatience, holding up a finger. "No. Just—'ang on a sec. This stuff is bloody 'ard to read." He returned to the beginning and studied the first few pages. "I'm sure this one came from a later date. 'E'd started a new journal, and 'adn't got much chance to make entries before 'e ended up—well, where 'e did."

"Why would they bury it with him?" Ian asked. "If they killed him, why would they leave a record?"

"Good question," Ward said. "Possibly they didn't know it was there—I *did* find it in what would have been a deep inner pocket of his clothes—or possibly they didn't care."

"Remember," Eddie added, "that whole place 'ad been sealed up right and proper—probably *re*-sealed, since it looks like that whatever they put in that room with all the protective enchantments came later, after the foundation sacrifice was completed and the 'ouse was already built. I doubt they expected any o' that stuff to be found. Just give us a few minutes to read, and we should be able to give you somethin', at least."

Stone fought to quell his impatience. The journal had been there for hundreds of years—a few more minutes wouldn't matter.

"Who was this Brathwaite guy anyway?" Jason asked. "It sounds like you already know who he is."

Stone didn't answer right away. Even now, he felt a deep reluctance to share the sordid bits of his family history with an audience—but he supposed they already knew the worst of it. When you've just discovered your ancestors had committed mass murder by imprisoning innocents in your basement and let them die of starvation to gain power, the rest paled in comparison. "He was an associate of my great-great...I'm not sure how many greats, actually—grandfather. Lived around the turn of the nineteenth century."

"He was a mage, then?" Ian asked.

"Yes." He sighed. "I haven't told you—not even you, Verity—the whole story of what I found out about my family last year. I found some old papers hidden away in one of the crypts in the mausoleum, and they hinted at some of what we've found here. I didn't know about the foundation sacrifice, obviously, but I did know my family had dabbled in human sacrifice back in those days. Ian, I would have told you, at least, eventually—you had a right to know. It's your family too. But as you might have guessed, it's not something I'm proud of."

Verity nodded, her eyes full of sympathy. "Yeah."

"Most of them belonged to an organization called Ordo Purpuratus. It was…sort of an old boys' club for powerful mages. My ancestors weren't the only ones who got up to this kind of thing—apparently it was more common than anyone wants to admit among the top echelon of upper-class mages back in the day. They'd do anything for more power, including commit murder."

"That organization isn't still around, is it?" Jason asked, frowning.

"Not that I'm aware of. And since I'm solidly in the demographic that they'd court for membership—wealthy, male, probably white British mages from strong bloodlines—I suspect I'd have at least heard rumors if it did. I think it died out when mages got a bit more…enlightened. The last references I could find to it ended around my grandfather's day."

"Wow," Ian said. "So that means it could have existed even as far as the twentieth century?"

"Quite likely, though probably not with anywhere near the level of power and influence they enjoyed in their prime."

"So this Brathwaite guy was in the group too?" Jason nodded toward Eddie and Ward, who had their heads together and were deeply buried in the journal's pages.

"Yes. The rumors Eddie unearthed before suggested he and my great-great-whatever grandfather were close associates, but they had a falling-out over something. He disappeared, and no one ever determined what the disagreement was about or what became of him."

"Looks like we know now," Verity said. "At least where he ended up, if not why."

"Do you think our ancestors killed him?" Ian asked. "Why would they do that?"

"Maybe he was going to rat them out," Jason said. "You know, tell somebody about all the bodies buried under your house."

"Do you think he was buried when the foundation sacrifice happened?" Verity asked. "Or later, when they sealed the chamber for the second time? I'm just wondering, if they fought, if it was over the sacrifices or whatever's in that room."

"Probably the room," Stone said. "I'm sure the house was constructed earlier than the early eighteen-hundreds, and Brathwaite was alive then. Even if that pedestal was there during the foundation sacrifices, before the house itself was built, they could have used magic to open it and seal the body inside." He wanted to urge Eddie and Ward to go faster, but he stopped himself. He knew them—they were reading as fast as they could, as anxious as he was to absorb whatever knowledge the journal could provide. Interrupting their concentration would only make the whole process go slower.

They didn't come up for air for another ten minutes, after flipping through several more pages and employing a large magnifying glass Eddie pulled from his pocket. The librarian let out a sigh and slumped back in his chair, swiping his hand through his thinning brown hair.

"I think we've got somethin' for you, mate," he said. "Though I'll be damned if I know what most of it means."

"Tell us," Stone urged, gripping the table.

"Well, for one thing, it looks like Brathwaite wasn't killed at the time of the sacrifice, but I guess we sort of knew that, unless the dates we knew were wrong. But 'ere's where things start to get interestin'. If you don't mind, I'm gonna paraphrase a bit. 'E got a bit flowery." He flipped a few more pages and began to read aloud.

> *"Tomorrow, at last, we will see the fiend dealt with.*
>
> *The preparations are complete, and utmost secrecy has been maintained. The chamber is prepared. We do not believe he has become aware of our plans, and he has no reason to suspect us. I find myself with a deep sense of exhilaration over what is to come, but I admit to fear as well. The fiend 'A' is not to be trifled with. If we do not exercise the greatest care, he will discover the trap we have laid and our lives—perhaps our souls—will be forfeit.*
>
> *"I remain vexed that they refuse to proceed with my own proposed plan, which would remove much of the doubt and uncertainty from our endeavor. Damn them for only now developing a conscience— as if they do not know they are already lost in the eyes of God for their past actions. For all their earthly advantage, they remain squeamish and weak in the face of true power. My methods are sound and well-practiced, and I could be of great assistance if only they would permit it. The fiend is strong in magic, but we could negate much of that advantage*

if only we were to gain the assistance of those which magic cannot harm.

"Damn their weakness!

"I will attempt to persuade them one final time before we begin. Though I would not reveal my thoughts to them, I am not confident our current course of action will prove successful. I grow ever more frustrated with their reluctance to do what is necessary. I believe that their connection to the fiend ultimately weakens their resolve to see the matter properly put to its end.

"That's the last entry," Ward said. "There are a few others before that—mostly about day-to-day activities. As I said, I think this journal was a new one, so he didn't have time to make many entries before he died."

Stone's mind spun. "So many questions..." he murmured. "What did he mean, 'the fiend "A"'? It sounds like that was what they put in that sealed room."

"Yeah," Verity said. "And it sounds like they—whoever *they* were—were really scared of it. Like they thought it was too powerful for them to be sure they could take it down. Do you think it was members of your family he was talking about, the ones he was doing the plan with?"

"Almost certainly," Stone said. "Whoever was the current master of the house, and possibly his son."

"But what is this 'fiend'?" Jason asked. "Some kind of monster?"

"Why would there be a monster running around in the house?" Verity glanced at the journal, then shot a questioning look at Eddie and Ward.

"I don't think we'll find that out from these pages," Eddie said. "It definitely sounds like 'e was tryin' to dance around the subject with this 'A' business, maybe because 'e didn't want to name whatever it was. True names have power, especially in something a bunch o' mages at their level were wettin' themselves over. 'E wouldn't've put it down in writing, 'specially since it looks like 'e never meant anyone else to read this journal."

"He might not even have known its true name," Ward said soberly. "But I think the Stones, at least, must have. If it was as powerful and dangerous as they imply, having its name would increase their confidence in their ability to imprison it."

"If it was in the house," Ian said, "maybe it wasn't a monster. Maybe it was…part of the family. You know, like the crazy uncle you keep locked up in the attic."

"Have to be a pretty tough crazy uncle," Verity said dubiously. "Like the crazy immortal vampire uncle or something."

"You lot are too hung up on vampires," Stone said. "But you might be on to something, otherwise."

"Honestly," Eddie said, "I'm more concerned about the other bit."

"What other bit?" Jason asked.

He pointed at the journal. "The part where Brathwaite talks about ''is plan,' the one the others didn't want to use because they were 'too squeamish.'"

"Why is that?" Stone got up and came around behind them, peering over their shoulders at the narrow, faded writing.

"That might have been what they had the disagreement over," Ward said. "The one that might have got him killed. He was in on the plan to imprison the 'fiend,' but he wanted to use a method involving 'the assistance of those which magic cannot harm.'"

"Yeah," Verity said. "And whatever it was, it was apparently so bad that even Doc's ancestors—guys who committed human sacrifices to get more power—didn't want to try. What could have been that bad?"

"You mentioned necromancy before," Jason said. "Are you sure that couldn't be it?"

"It's certainly bad enough to fit the parameters," Ward said. "But as we said before, there's literally no documented evidence that it existed. It's more of a...bogeyman used to frighten children."

Stone nodded. "I'm more inclined to think he might have wanted to do some sort of summoning ritual. Summoning was more common back then, but even in those days it was frowned upon because it was difficult to control the entities that came through. I'm wondering if Brathwaite thought they could summon up some magic-resistant beasties from another dimension and use them to subdue this 'fiend'. I could see how my ancestors would be reluctant to do that, especially if they didn't have faith in Brathwaite's abilities."

"Or even thought *he* might betray *them*," Ian added. "It sounds like none of these guys really trusted each other very much."

"But that still doesn't explain how Brathwaite might be doing all this, though," Stone said. "He's dead. You lot saw his body sealed up in that pedestal—assuming it *was* him at all, of course, but even if it wasn't, even mages aren't immortal. We live longer than mundanes, but not three hundred years. If he's not dead here, he's dead *somewhere*."

"Doc..." Verity ventured.

"Yes?"

"I'm just wondering...in Poppy's dream, she said she felt that hatred, and also felt like she was in that round room. That's what led us to Brathwaite in the first place. Is it possible...I know you said mages don't make echoes, but is it possible this time one did?"

Stone narrowed his eyes. He hadn't thought of that, and with good reason: as he'd told Verity, he'd never heard of a case where a mage, even a powerful one like William Desmond with definite reasons for wanting to stay behind, had left an echo.

But...it did fit.

"I...suppose it's possible," he said.

"If it *is* Brathwaite, could he have animated those skeletons and sent them after us, even as a ghost?" Jason asked.

Stone looked at Eddie and Ward.

Eddie shrugged. "Maybe so. Mage echoes are rare as 'ens' teeth, but I've read a few accounts of them from a long time back. They're said to retain a lot more of their mental capacities and free will than a standard mundane echo, which means it's possible they can still do magic. Who knows if it's true, though? If there are any around, they're not talkin'."

"Maybe we need to track this one down and talk to it," Jason said.

Stone got up and began pacing, pausing to look out the window. "Easier said than done. The sacrifices' echoes are probably bound to my house, but Brathwaite most likely isn't. And even if he is, do you think he'd talk to us? *I* wouldn't, if I were him. I'd be too busy trying to work out another scheme to get revenge on us. That's the thing about echoes—even hypothetical mage echoes. They still aren't fully-formed human…souls, as it were. I'll wager even if he retains more volition and your standard echo, he's still obsessed with whatever made him stay behind in the first place—revenge for what he perceives as a betrayal."

"If they murdered him, it might well have *been* a betrayal," Ward pointed out.

"Okay," Eddie said, closing the journal. "So let's look at what we've got 'ere, based on our current 'ypotheses. The echoes are still at the 'ouse and they're still angry, so they didn't pop into their skeletons and go on walkabout last night, and they weren't destroyed or sent on to the other side when the skeletons crumbled. We've also potentially got a *new* echo, which might or might not be Brathwaite, which is *definitely* angry, and which might or might not 'ave animated the skeletons and sent them after us."

"We've still got whatever was imprisoned inside that small room," Stone said. "And we haven't got a bloody idea about what it is, where it is, or if it even existed at all."

"That's true," Verity said. "If Brathwaite is behind the skeletons, and the echoes are possessing the house because they're pissed off at the Stones, that doesn't give any indication at all where the thing from the sealed room is involved in this, or even if it is at all."

"What, you think it just broke out of there and took off?" Jason asked.

Stone shrugged. "Possibly. I have to admit I hope it did, because we've got enough to be getting on with, without adding something possibly more powerful than the rest of this stuff combined that's *also* trying to kill us." He ran his hand through his hair with a sigh. "So what's our next course of action? We've got a lot of angles to pursue here."

"I think we should try to find out more about Brathwaite," Eddie said. "It's possible whatever the 'fiend' was in that sealed room, it's lying in wait so it can pounce on us when we're not expectin' it, but we still don't have any evidence it either exists or specifically wants to kill any of us. But if Brathwaite's echo *is* out there, it's certain 'e won't quit until 'e's got 'is revenge. We need to stop 'im."

"Do you think stopping him would stop the other echoes?" Jason asked.

"Honestly?" Ward shook his head. "No."

"But they were afraid of him," Ian said. "Maybe he's controlling them."

"Doubtful," Stone said. "Whether he and my ancestors got on or not, he was still a member of Ordo Purpuratus, the organization that thought nothing of sacrificing mundanes whenever they needed a bit of extra punch. Mundane echoes buried alive won't feel charitable toward him in any case, and I doubt he was powerful enough to control the lot of them against their will." He sighed. "But that doesn't leave us in a very good place. Where are we going to find Brathwaite? We can't do another séance—I don't want to put Poppy at risk again, even if she'd be willing."

"Might be able to 'elp you with that, mate," Eddie said thoughtfully. "At least for a start."

"How? Do you have any ideas where to find him?"

"Not necessarily. But I might be able to find where his 'ouse was."

"His house?" Verity asked, frowning. "What good will that do? If it's been two hundred years since he died, it must have changed hands dozens of times—if it even still exists at all."

But Stone smiled. "Oh, I'm sure it exists. Brathwaite was as wealthy as the rest of the Ordo, which means he likely had an estate somewhere. We Brits never tear down historical old buildings, unless they're crumbling around our ears. Sometimes not even then."

"So? You think it's still in his family?" Ian asked. "After this long?"

"Doesn't matter. Either way, it's entirely possible it's got some hidden areas the current residents know nothing about. Even if we can't find him there, we might find some clues to what he's been up to."

"And you think the people who live there will just let you poke around looking for those clues?"

"We'll have to see, won't we?" Stone turned to Eddie. "First things first, though. Do you think you can find the place?"

The librarian snorted. "Easy-peasy. Give me a few hours at the library with Arthur's 'elp, and we should 'ave somethin' for ya soon enough."

| CHAPTER TWENTY-SEVEN

B Y THE TIME EDDIE CALLED BACK, it was already dark. Stone woke from his doze when his phone buzzed in his pocket. "Yes?" he demanded. "Have you got anything?"

The librarian chuckled. "Oh ye of little faith. I 'ope you got some kip today, because I doubt I'll be able to stop you from runnin' off after this as soon as I give you the details."

Stone hadn't *intended* to sleep, which was why he was on the sofa in the sitting room instead of up in his bedroom like Ian, Verity, and Jason, but apparently he'd been more tired than he'd thought. He sat up, trying to work the knots out of his muscles. "So give me the details, Eddie. Don't keep me in suspense."

"It actually took a fair bit more diggin' than I thought to get through all the records. I 'ad to call in a few favors from mates to get access to some o' this stuff."

"Eddie…"

"Yeah, yeah. It took Ward and me hours to get this—you can wait a couple minutes. Anyway, as it turns out, Brathwaite's family *did* have an estate, in the Cotswolds. Big spread, apparently."

"Did?" Stone rubbed his chin. He needed a shave, and a nice long shower. "So they don't have it anymore? Or it doesn't exist anymore?"

"Oh, it exists. But it's not in the family. The Brathwaites didn't build it, as it turns out. Rumor 'as it that they—possibly with the assistance of other wealthy mage associates—drove the original family out if it sometime in the early sixteen-'undreds. That's just a rumor, mind you, but they did take it over for some reason. Possibly the original family couldn't afford to keep it any longer."

"All right...but you said it's not in Brathwaite's family anymore."

"No. I found references to a few family members—that's part of what I 'ad to ask some mates about. There's some bird in Basingstoke, an old lady in a care home in London, and some even older bloke in the U.S., but near's I can figure none of them are mages, and whatever wealth the Brathwaites might've 'ad back in the day is mostly gone now. I think the magical bloodline died out a long time ago—either that or they lost track of their magical 'eritage and never learned they 'ad the potential for the Talent. But that's neither 'ere nor there—you want details about the 'ouse."

"Yes. And while I'm still young, please," Stone said dryly.

"Oh, forgive me, Your Lordship." Eddie's grin came through in his mock-airy tone. "Ward and I slave all day over a load of dusty old books while you get your beauty sleep, and this is the thanks we get."

"Like I could have prised you away from those books with a crowbar and a block of Semtex."

"That's beside the point. Do you want the info, or not?"

"Please, Eddie."

"Surprised the 'ell out of me, it did, but as it turns out—the place is a school now."

Stone sat up straighter. "A school?"

"Yep. Place called Crofton Academy. 'Ave you 'eard of it?"

"Sounds vaguely familiar. Tell me."

"Posh place. Small, but expensive. Boys only. Been operatin' since the mid eighteen-'undreds."

"That's…fascinating information. But why did you expect I'd be excited about it? If it's been a school for that long, odds are good that even if Brathwaite *had* left anything there, it's long gone by now."

"Not necessarily. I 'aven't told you the interestin' part yet."

Stone sighed, wondering if this was how Jason and Verity felt when he drew out a good story for best effect. "Eddie…"

"Fine, fine. So I took the liberty of trackin' down a Crofton alum—bloke who left there about ten years ago. Pretended to be a reporter doin' research on the place for an article I'm writin'."

"What did he tell you?"

"I told 'im I was on a long deadline, puttin' together a 'Alloween piece on alleged 'auntings in old properties. Asked if 'e'd ever 'eard any rumors of spooky stuff goin' on at Crofton."

Stone struggled not to roll his eyes. "Eddie, *every* old public school has rumors like that. Bloody hell, Barrow was rumored to have anywhere from three to eight individual ghosts, at least four suspicious deaths, and a hanging."

"Yes, well…you'd be right, most likely, except for two things."

"And those are…?" Though he was growing tired of Eddie drawing the story out, he leaned forward in anticipation. His friend might be guilty of stretching his tales for maximum impact, but they were never dull. Unless he was talking about football, anyway.

"First one is, the main building at Crofton—the one that used to be the main house when it was Brathwaite's estate—has a ley line runnin' right through the middle of it."

"That's not surprising, is it? A lot of old properties owned by mages have those."

"Nope, not surprisin'. But when coupled with the fact that there aren't any rumors of strange things bein' found in the 'ouse, and one other interestin' bit of information, it gives me an idea of somethin' to check out."

"And what's this other interesting bit of information?"

"The previous owners of the 'ouse—the ones who 'ad it before Brathwaite, and who 'is family may or may not 'ave driven out—were Catholic."

The triumphant flourish in Eddie's tone suggested to Stone that he should have caught on to his friend's line of reasoning. But given that he'd barely darkened the door of a church except for weddings and funerals since he was a child, and his secular study of religion and the history surrounding it had ended during his undergraduate days at University, the answer eluded him. "Eddie, I slept on the couch, I've got a stiff neck, and I need a shower. Could you get to the point, please?"

"Aw, c'mon, Stone. Surely you must've heard of priest 'oles? Didn't they teach you nothin' in that 'igh-class education of yours?"

"Er—" Once again it seemed a bit familiar, but not enough to recall. "Sounds like something scandalous involving altar boys."

"You're a riot, mate."

Stone got up and began to pace. "All right, then—so what's a 'priest hole,' and why do you think it's relevant to whatever Brathwaite might have left behind?"

"That's more like it. And as a reward, I won't give you the full answer to that question, because it could take a good hour. It's fascinatin' stuff, it is, but I doubt you'll share my enthusiasm."

"Thank you. I appreciate that."

"Short version: surely you know that back during the reign of Elizabeth the First at the end o' the fifteen-'undreds, it was illegal to be Catholic in England?"

"Well, yes, of course. Even *I* couldn't have slept through *that* much of history class."

"Right. So wealthy Catholic families brought in priests to live with 'em, pretendin' they were distant cousins or teachers or whatever. But when even that got too dangerous, they built little concealed 'idey-'oles in their 'ouses. That way, when the Queen sent out priest-'unters to look for 'em, they could 'ide there until the 'eat blew over."

Now that Eddie explained, Stone did remember hearing something about such things during his days at Barrow. "And…you think there's one of these holes at Crofton Academy? Wouldn't someone have found it by now?"

"It makes sense there is, since the previous owners were Catholic. That might even be why they got run out— somebody, maybe even Brathwaite's family, found out and ratted 'em out. But in any case, the architects who built the priest 'oles knew their stuff." He chuckled. "The most famous of 'em, a bloke called Nicholas Owen, got canonized as the patron saint of illusionists. Go figure. Anyway, they're still occasionally findin' the 'oles to this day—and if Brathwaite's people found one when they took the 'ouse over, they might've used magic to make it even 'arder to locate. It would make a great place to 'ide secret stuff, wouldn't it?"

"I suppose it would," Stone conceded. "But that's still a bit of a reach. I can't very well break into the place and start poking about looking for hidden passages, can I?"

"Maybe you can. The school's closed for summer break, so there won't be many folks around. And I didn't tell you what Darvin Cooley told me."

"Who the hell is Darvin Cooley?"

Eddie made a dramatic sigh. "*Do* follow along, Stone. He's the bloke I talked to. The alum."

"You didn't tell me his name, you prat."

"I thought a genius like you'd be bright enough to infer it from context."

"Sod off, Eddie. So…" he continued more patiently, "what did Darvin Cooley tell you?"

"That a supply room in the west wing of the main build-in's rumored to be 'aunted."

"Haunted."

"Yep. It's locked most o' the time and they don't let any o' the kids in 'cept the prefects when they need to fetch somethin' from inside, but there's stories about how sometimes when somebody goes in there, they feel this sense of dread and…evil. Not my words—that's what Cooley said. He thinks it's bollocks, 'imself."

"And you don't?"

"I would've," Eddie admitted. "Except that we didn't know until now that Brathwaite might've been up to some pretty nasty stuff. If he left anythin' behind that was never found, that'd be a good place for it to be. It's possible there's psychic energy leakin' off it, and that's what the more sensitive o' those kids are pickin' up on."

Stone sighed. "You make a good case, I suppose. It's worth a look, at any rate."

"Not plannin' to take the whole crew up there for a spot o' B and E, though, are you?"

"Is that your diplomatic way of telling me you don't want to come along?"

Eddie chuckled. "I'm a librarian, mate, not a burglar, and I'm sure Ward will feel the same. But if you really want me to—"

"No, no, that's all right. I'll talk to the others."

"If you find anything, though, please bring it back and let us 'ave a butcher's at it. I'm dyin' o' curiosity 'ere, I 'ope you know."

"You can't die of curiosity, Eddie. If you could, you'd have been dead before I met you."

"Look who's talkin'."

"Yes, well…anyway, thank you for the information. I'm not sure whether I hope you're right or you're not, but I suppose we'll know before too long."

"Be careful, Stone." Eddie sounded more serious now.

"What, you don't think I can do this? Believe me, I've broken into far more dangerous places than some old school."

"It's not the school I'm worried about. It's whatever you might find 'idden there."

CHAPTER TWENTY-EIGHT

STONE GATHERED VERITY, Jason, and Ian in the sitting room for what he was sure would be an unpopular announcement. He started by explaining what Eddie had told him about Crofton Academy.

"So," Verity said when he finished, "you want us go up there, break in to some old school, and try to find this priest hole or whatever? You really think there's something there?"

"It sounds like there could be. Possibly not a priest hole, but the fact that more than one person has picked up so-called 'evil' feelings in that closet suggests there might be something to it. But here's the thing," he added, bracing for protest. "We can't all go."

"Why not?"

"Because we can't have six people breaking into a school," Jason said. "Even if their security's some old guy, a dog, and a burglar alarm they never turn on, *somebody's* gonna notice."

"Exactly," Stone said, surprised at the unexpected support. "It wouldn't be six—Eddie and Ward aren't coming—but it can't even be four."

"You're not planning to go alone, are you?" Verity asked.

"No. I was thinking I might take one of you with me, if you want to go. Absolutely optional, though. I doubt this will be dangerous, but it's definitely illegal."

To his surprise, Verity looked uncomfortable, and so did Jason.

"What?" He tilted his head. "Jason, I can see why you wouldn't want to go, and honestly you'd be my third choice, despite your expertise with mundane security systems. You have the most to lose if we're caught."

"It's not that," he said. "I called Gina back home while I was upstairs, and there's been a development on one of the cases I'm workin' on. I really should be home to handle it."

"And you, Verity?"

"Well—if Jase needs to go home, somebody needs to take him through the portal. And I got so caught up in all this that I forgot I was supposed to help Scuro out with a job tonight."

Stone wasn't surprised—this whole situation at the house had been so outside any of their experience that he himself had almost forgotten there was a real life going on away from its events. "It's fine," he said, waving them off. "Both of you go. I can handle this."

"*We* can handle this," Ian corrected. "I've got nowhere to be. I'll go with you. I'm the best one anyway—this mess is about my family too."

"You sure?" Verity still looked uncomfortable. "Because I hate to leave you guys in the middle of this."

"Not a problem," Stone said. "Come back when you can, if you want to. I'll call you with any new developments."

"Are you planning on doing it tonight?" Jason looked at his watch. "It's almost ten already. How far away is this place?"

"If we pop up to Caventhorne, it will take a couple of hours from there. And yes, best to get it over with as soon as possible."

They all exchanged uncomfortable glances, and finally Verity nodded. "Okay. We'll—well, at least *I'll*—come back as soon as I can."

Stone patted her arm. "Don't worry about it, Verity. It's not as if we need to solve this problem tomorrow. As long as Ian and I don't try to enter the house, everything should be relatively calm."

"Except for Brathwaite trying to kill you, and whatever this 'fiend' is, out running loose somewhere," Jason muttered.

"Yes, well, one problem at a time."

They took the portal to Caventhorne. Stone had called ahead, so Kerrick was there to meet them.

"It's good to see you, sir," he said. The estate steward's eyes widened when he spotted Ian. "And…this must be young Ian."

"Yes. Sorry—I'd hoped the introductions might be more formal, but we're in a bit of a hurry. Ian, this is Kerrick. He was my master's oldest friend, and now he sees to looking after the non-magical aspects of Caventhorne."

The two shook hands, checking each other out.

"I hear you've got a bit of trouble down at your Surrey house, Dr. Stone," Kerrick said. "Mr. Monkton didn't give me many details, but he and Mr. Ward have been popping in and out to check Mr. Desmond's library over the past day or so."

"Yes. Long story. I hope we'll get it sorted soon. I don't want it affecting the opening." Stone could hardly believe it—after all this time and so many unexpected delays, Caventhorne's magical resource center would finally have its formal gala opening in less than a month.

"Don't you worry, sir. Everything's going according to plan."

"Brilliant." He patted Kerrick's shoulder. "You go on with whatever you were doing. Ian and I will be taking the Mercedes. We'll be back later tonight, but probably not for long."

"Of course, sir. Good luck with whatever you're doing."

When Kerrick left, Ian looked around the ornate room. "This place is amazing. You don't own it too, do you?"

"No. Dear gods, no. I'm not sure what I'd have done if Desmond had left it to me. No, it's been a long-term project, in accordance with his will, to turn it into sort of a library-slash-resource center-slash-meeting facility for mages, and he left me in charge of facilitating it. I've mostly delegated it to Eddie, Ward, and Kerrick. There'll be a big gala do in a couple of weeks, if you're interested in attending."

Ian gave a dubious half-smile. "A bunch of stuffy old mages in tuxedos and evening gowns? I'll pass, I think. No offense."

Stone chuckled. "Quite all right. They're hardly your crowd. Hell, most of them are hardly *my* crowd. But do keep the place in mind—once you apprentice to someone, you'll find a large amount of useful reference material here. Including some that won't be available to the general public."

"Yeah, I'll do that." He followed Stone out of the room. "So how old is this place? As old as yours?"

"At least."

When Ian didn't reply, Stone turned back around. "Something on your mind?"

"I was just wondering—if it's that old, do you think there are any dark secrets buried under this one too?"

Stone tensed. He *hadn't* thought of that—not until Ian brought it up. "Damned good question. And to be honest, I'm not sure I want to know." It wouldn't have surprised him, though—Desmond's family was even wealthier and had reached back longer than Stone's, and at least some of his master's ancestors had almost certainly been part of Ordo Purpuratus. "We've got enough problems to be getting on with right now without trying to dig up more."

They retrieved the car, a black Mercedes sedan, from the garage and drove off.

"So it will take a couple hours to get to this place?" Ian asked.

"Yes. It's about eighty miles."

"That must have been quite a trip, back in horse and buggy days. You think there was a private portal there?"

"The portals weren't even discovered back then, so I doubt it. And even if they added one later, it's probably gone by now."

"Gone? What, they can disappear?"

"They can, if you don't keep them calibrated and tended every now and then. Especially the older ones, before they worked out better ways of stabilizing them. I suspect quite a number of the earliest hidden portals might have gone that way over the years. That's part of why Desmond left me the London place—Imogen didn't want it, and she couldn't exactly sell it. It's difficult to dismantle portals, and sometimes malfunctioning ones can be dangerous."

He hadn't even thought about Imogen since he'd returned to the Surrey house following the wedding reception and discovered the echoes. It seemed as if he'd been dealing with this problem for weeks, but he realized with shock that it had only been a couple of days. She'd still be on her honeymoon with Blakeley now, probably lying on a sunny beach somewhere in the south of France. He shook his head, trying to clear that thought from it before it took root. He couldn't afford to let himself get distracted now.

"Why didn't you two get married?" Ian asked.

Stone glanced over, surprised. His son was looking straight ahead, watching the road, his sharp profile so much like Stone's own. "What?"

"You and Imogen. I can see by the way you talk about her that you two are close. What happened? If you don't mind me asking, I mean. We've got some time to kill."

Stone didn't answer, not sure where to start—or if he wanted to.

Ian leaned back in his seat. "Aubrey and I talked a little back at the house, the night you went to the wedding. He didn't tell me much, just said it was something about you having magic and her not. Don't blame him for it—I kind of got it out of him."

"That was…the gist of it, yes." Stone continued to fix his gaze forward, telling himself it was because he had to watch the road. There was no other traffic, though; the Mercedes' powerful headlights picked out a narrow, winding lane bounded on both sides by waist-high hedgerows. "We were together for a few years, but hadn't ever formalized anything.

We weren't even properly engaged. I suppose I always just assumed we would be. That was my fault."

"Wasn't she used to the magical world, though? Didn't she grow up with her dad?"

"She didn't. Desmond and his wife divorced before I met him. I never knew why, and never asked."

"So his wife wasn't a mage too?"

"No. That always struck me as odd that Desmond, who was even more caught up in the magical world than I was, married a mundane. But it wasn't my business. Desmond was a very private man, and didn't take kindly to anyone poking their noses into his personal business." He gave a bitter chuckle. "Not even his prized apprentice. And come on, Ian—you can't be interested in the sordid details of my early life."

"Sure I am. You're my dad, and I barely know you. I've got friends in L.A. that I know better than I know my own father."

Stone shot him a quick glance. "Well, you've hardly been around, have you?"

"I thought you said that wasn't a problem."

"It isn't. I'm happy you're having a good time, off seeing the world. But popping in for half a day hardly lends itself to heartfelt talks. Which is fine by me," he added hastily, "since I've always been rubbish with them anyway." He tightened his grip on the wheel.

Ian fell silent, leaning against the window and watching the lights flash by, and Stone didn't push it. The truth was, he didn't want to talk about Imogen right now. Every time he tried to think about something normal like that, the images of the shambling skeletons and the ledger full of carefully notated sacrifice victims crowded them out. He couldn't shake the feeling that he didn't have a right to "normal" until he'd gotten this whole affair sorted out.

❖

It took them almost two hours to get to Crofton Academy, which was located a few miles outside Burford. Stone pulled the car off the road some distance down from the front gates, shut it off, and retrieved a bag from the back seat. "We walk from here. I can put a disregarding spell on the car, but if we drive right in through the front door and anyone's around, they'll notice."

Ian got out, slipping on his leather jacket against the evening's light chill. It was a clear night with only a few clouds. "I hope you know where this closet is. That place looks as big as yours. It would take us all night to search it."

Stone shifted to magical sight as they approached, easily spotting the clear, strong ley line running through the middle of the campus, and then pulled a folded sheet from his coat pocket. "Eddie described it. He didn't have a floorplan, but he got the directions from the man he spoke with. Those will have to do. They've added quite a number of new buildings to the campus since Crofton took it over, but it's the big one at the center we're after."

They didn't go in the front gates, even though they were open—that would have been too conspicuous if anyone had been watching. Instead, Stone led them off the road a short distance down. They crossed a field and paused behind another building.

The campus was spread over a considerable space, with numerous other darkened buildings dotting the area around the main manor house. Perimeter lights around several of the buildings provided illumination, but not much. Stone saw no indication of anyone around—if anyone was, it was probably a security guard or two making occasional rounds. If they were careful, they could get in and out quickly before anyone spotted them.

Using disregarding spells, they crept across the open field and around the rear of the main building. Stone was pleased to see a set of double French doors leading out to a courtyard area—probably a place for students to congregate during breaks.

"Do I remember you saying you were good at invisibility?" he asked Ian.

"Yeah. I can hold it for about five minutes if I have to."

"Can you hold it while doing another spell?"

"Yeah, if it's one I'm comfortable with."

"Brilliant." He pointed toward the doors, then upward. "I suspect those floodlights over the doors are motion-sensitive, and I'd rather not have them come on. Sneak over there and unlock the door, then go inside and leave it unlocked. I'll follow you."

Ian, looking like he was enjoying this adventure, faded from view. Stone shifted to magical sight, following his progress as he jogged over, slipped the catch on the doors, and opened one just enough to get inside. The floodlights didn't turn on.

In a moment, Stone had joined him. "Good job," he whispered. "We'll use the disregarding spell from now on."

There wasn't much light where they stood now, but the moonlight illuminated a large room full of several long tables. "Dining hall," Stone said, getting his bearings. He pointed left. "There's a hallway that way. We need to go past the main staircase and five doors down. The closet is a small door at the end, on the left side."

"At least it's on the main floor," Ian whispered. "That'll make things easier."

"Don't say things like that." Stone gave an arch smile. "The universe is always listening, and it *loves* making lies of that sort of statement. Come on."

Unexpected memories struck Stone as the two of them wended their way between the tables and out the other side of the dining room. He'd never been to this school, obviously, and hadn't been back to Barrow since the day he'd left at age fifteen to go study with William Desmond, but apparently old boarding school dining rooms had a few things in common. He took in the smells of old wood, furniture polish, and hundreds of years of institutional food with a sense of satisfaction. As much as he and the other boys had complained about the accommodations at Barrow, overall his early school memories had been good ones.

He glanced at Ian's tall, slim form moving ahead of him, and realized with some regret that if Jessamy Woodward had told him of his son's existence when he'd been born, it was possible the boy might have attended Barrow as well.

It was hard for Stone to say what he might have done. When he'd first found out about Ian, the idea that he might have tried to gain custody was a ludicrous one, but after getting to know his son, and especially after finding out the kind of tyrannical, ultra-religious grandparents and stepfather Ian had to contend with, he wondered. Not that it mattered at this point, of course: Ian was an adult now, and such things weren't relevant any longer. But as he crept through this unfamiliar-yet-familiar space, he couldn't help picturing what his son might have looked like a few years ago, dressed in the neat blue-and-gray Barrow uniform and gathering his gear to head off for another school year. He wondered if his own father had had similar thoughts.

Ian stopped as they exited the dining hall, jolting Stone from his nostalgic reminiscence. They stood in a wide hallway paneled in fine wood. Faded carpeting covered the floor, and sconces lining the wall provided enough illumination to see their path but little more. Occasional small tables stood along the walls, along with a tall, glass-fronted cabinet halfway down containing various trophies. Stone picked out a series of framed paintings along both sides between several doors, but couldn't make out their subjects. He wondered if any of them had been around since the days when the Brathwaite family had owned the place, and how much renovation the hall had required to make it suitable as a school.

Shifting to magical sight again, he took another look around. Aside from his own and Ian's auras, he saw nothing out of the ordinary. The general ambiance of the place was a combination of a long-term satisfaction, anticipation, and a hint of youthful excitement—just what he would have expected to find in an institution of learning populated by an ever-changing collection of boys ranging from seven to seventeen. He chuckled softly as he realized what else was probably floating around here, but fortunately raging hormones didn't show up to magical sight.

They continued down the hall, staying in the center to avoid running into any of the small tables or knocking anything off them. Ian pointed. "Is that it down there?" he whispered.

Stone risked a feeble light spell, blocking it with his body. Ahead on the left side, a door that looked exactly like all the others sported a small, tarnished bronze plaque. When he drew closer, the word *SUPPLIES* came into view.

Ian, who like Stone wore thin gloves, tried the knob. "Locked."

"Not surprising. Eddie said it would be. Watch the hall—this will only take a second."

The old-fashioned lock was laughably easy to pop. Stone wondered if they'd added it later, after some of the boys had reported the eerie feelings they'd experienced when retrieving copy paper or staples. Boarding school life often fell into stultifying routines, so anything that deviated from those routines would be catnip to a bunch of bored boys. Once the story got out that something weird was going on in the supply closet, the staff would have had constant trouble keeping curious explorers out if they hadn't locked it.

Stone shifted to magical sight again, but still nothing caught his attention. Inanimate objects didn't have auras, of course, but buildings—particularly ones as old as this one—had general feelings to them. This one continued to give off exactly the sort of impression he expected. If anything was here, it was well hidden.

He turned the knob and pushed the door slowly open. It didn't creak, which surprised him, and he chuckled. "Been watching too many horror films, I guess," he whispered to Ian, then pushed it the rest of the way open. The two of them hurried inside and Stone closed it behind them.

"Block the crack under the door, will you, in case they've got someone doing rounds. Then I'll switch on the light."

When Ian had slipped off his jacket and pressed it against the bottom of the door, Stone dropped his faint light spell and pulled the chain hanging from the ceiling.

Harsh light sprang up from a naked bulb, illuminating a ten-by-ten-foot space. Stone took a quick look around. Shelves lined three of the walls, sides and back, and each one was stacked with the sorts of supplies you might find in every school: reams of paper, boxes of clips, neat piles of old textbooks, and similar items. A box on one of the bottom shelves held a mishmash of what might have been lost-and-found or confiscated items. The floor was scarred wood, worn smooth by many feet.

"I don't see anything strange," Ian said, bending to pull a deep maroon blazer with a torn sleeve from the lost-and-found box. "Are you sure this is the right place?"

"Give me a moment." Stone shifted once again to magical sight, sharpening his focus. Right now, he wasn't looking for anything hidden, but simply trying to pick up any odd feelings or emanations that might be bleeding from the room. If a number of schoolboys had noticed something, a fully trained mage should have no trouble picking it up.

And he did pick it up, almost instantly: a strong sense of wrongness that sent an uncomfortable chill running through his body. A wave of nausea settled over him. "Bloody hell..." he murmured.

"Got something?"

"Yes. Do you feel it? Use mundane senses."

Ian paused a moment, turning around slowly in the center of the room. "I feel something. Can't quite put my finger on it, though, except that it's not good."

"Keep your eyes open—magical and mundane. I'm going to take a closer look around, and I don't want anything to jump us."

"Yeah, go ahead. I've got this."

Stone swallowed hard, trying to drive down the nausea. It wasn't strong, but it was definitely distracting, making it hard to focus. Whatever was in here wasn't just garden-variety magic. The more he concentrated, the more he got the sense that it was something that shouldn't *be*. What had Brathwaite been up to?

He closed his eyes, trying to get a better sense for a more specific location where the queasy feeling originated. It took a few moments, but eventually he turned toward the back part of the closet. "I think it's back here. Anything?"

"Not yet." Ian sounded tense.

Stone began pulling items off the back shelves, shifting them to the sides when he could or stacking them on the floor when he ran out of space. He ran his hands over the wall behind each of the shelves, reluctantly heightening his focus once again.

When he reached the lowest shelf, crouching to press his palms against the wall, he shuddered.

The wall felt warm.

Not just warm, but oddly *soft*, as if he were pressing not against wood, but rather the smooth hide of some disgusting otherworldly creature. He jerked his hands back.

"You okay?"

Stone swallowed again as another wave of nausea crested. "Fine. But I think I've found what I'm looking for."

"What is it?"

"Not sure yet. Keep watch."

Stone didn't want to touch that wall again. Whatever was down there wasn't simply malevolent, the way the chamber beneath his own house had been. It was more than that—something worse. Now that he'd noticed it, he wondered how anyone could *not* notice it. No wonder this place had gotten a reputation for being creepy. He was surprised that any boy with even a shred of magical potential hadn't either run screaming from the closet or lost his lunch all over the floor.

"Dad?" Ian's soft voice came from behind him.

"Yes?"

"I don't feel so well all of a sudden."

Stone turned back around. Ian leaned against the door, and his tanned face had taken on a decidedly green cast. Tiny beads of sweat dotted his forehead. "Yes," he said. "I don't either. There's some serious psychic nastiness around this place. Mental shields help, but mine aren't taking care of it completely. You can wait outside if you like."

"No…it's okay. But if you could hurry a little, that would be great." He levitated a small trash can closer to him and swallowed hard again. "Just in case."

Stone nodded and bent back to his task, forcing himself to reach out once more and touch the warm, yielding surface of the wall. It had to be an illusion, probably sustained by the ley line running through the building. With only one ley line, though, and this much time having passed since it was cast, it couldn't be much of an illusion. He should be able to punch through it easily, except for the distraction from the nausea. If only he could…

"Hang on…"

"What?" Ian sounded like he was speaking through gritted teeth now.

Stone shifted back to mundane senses. Immediately, most of the nausea abated. The creepy feeling still persisted, but that he could handle. "Shift back. It's affecting magical senses." He didn't look back this time, but instead got down on his stomach and used a bright light spell to peer at the wall beneath the lowest shelf.

Behind him, Ian let his breath out. "Yeah. That's better. What's going on?"

"Not sure. Something designed to affect mages, obviously. Bloody strong—it would have to be, to still persist after all these years. Why don't you wait outside, and keep an eye out for anyone who might be approaching? I'll yell if anything happens."

"I don't like leaving you alone in here."

"You won't do me any good if you're getting sick all over the floor. Leave the door open if you're worried. I hope this won't take too long."

Ian still looked reluctant, but opened the door and slipped outside. "It's better out here."

"I thought it might be. Now let me concentrate."

Still flat on his stomach, Stone continued shining the light around and feeling the wall. To mundane senses it felt like a normal wooden wall, but the problem was he couldn't see anything else—no hidden catch or other indication there might be another passage or chamber behind this one. If Eddie was right and it *was* a priest hole, there had to be a way in, but if Brathwaite's family had discovered it and repurposed it for something more magical, they'd have hidden the entrance more carefully.

Reluctantly, Stone shifted back to magical sight, taking a deep breath and holding it against the fresh rising nausea and focusing his concentration to see past the illusion.

As the feeling he was going to be sick any second grew, he feared he wouldn't spot it—or that it wasn't there at all. But then, in the corner of his eye, a tiny imperfection appeared. Without changing his perspective, he shot his hand out toward it before the illusion reasserted itself.

His triumph as his fingers closed around a small catch mechanism nearly submerged the nausea for a second or two. He flipped the catch and then pushed, feeling the lower part of the rear wall swing a couple inches inward. The shelves remained where they were.

"Got it," he called, scrambling up while still keeping his hand on the wall so it didn't swing back into place. From his new vantage point, he could see that the break in the top part of the moving wall section would have been hidden behind one of the shelves when it was in place, making it impossible to spot.

Ian hurried back in and closed the door behind him. "Open it. I want to get out of here."

Stone didn't waste any time on slow reveals this time. He pressed against the wall and pushed harder, leaning forward. "Check the shelves. At least one of them has to move—I'm guessing the lowest one."

Ian squatted next to him, cleared the items from the lowermost shelf, and tried to lift it. It came free readily. He pulled it out and leaned it against the wall. "I guess we crawl."

"Makes sense. If this did used to be a priest hole, they wouldn't have wanted a large entrance." He got back on his knees and held a light spell out, peering through. The nausea was rising again; he paused a moment to quell it with a meditation technique, but it was harder each time. "I'll go first. I'm with you—I want to get out of here too."

Conjuring a shield around him in case anything was waiting for him inside, he dropped down and belly-crawled through the opening. Once through, he got back to his knees and held the light spell up, examining the area.

He still didn't know if the space had originally been a priest hole—it was impossible to tell now—but it definitely wasn't very large. Barely five feet deep by four wide and five high, it had rough wooden walls and floor and smelled of mold, dust, and a hint of decay. Its rear wall contained several shelves haphazardly stacked with items, and in front of the shelves stood a locked metal strongbox, larger than the one they'd found in the alcove back at the Surrey house. Garish, hand-painted sigils and symbols lined the other two walls.

"Do you see anything?" Ian called.

"Yes. Give me a moment."

Stone swept his gaze over the shelves. He blinked a couple times as dizzy disorientation joined the nausea. He hated to risk magical sight, but he didn't have a choice: whatever was in here was obviously profoundly magical, and he needed to get a good read on it.

"Keep an eye on me," he muttered. "If I pass out, pull me out of here."

"I've got you. Be careful."

He took several deep breaths, reinforced both his shield and his mental barriers, and then shifted.

The entire place lit up with a miasma of horrific energy.

To his left and right, the sigils glowed a faint red, pulsing like the viscera of some massive creature. He glanced up, spotting more of the same sigils on the ceiling, and suddenly he felt as if the entire space were pressing in on him—almost as if the creature were trying to digest him. A sense of profound unease gripped him, and he almost pushed himself backward out of the space before he got control over it.

He took more deep breaths. His shields were holding so far; he couldn't be sure, but it almost seemed as if opening the hidden space had dissipated some of its energy. He wasn't sure if that was a good thing or a bad thing, but he did know he needed to get out of there soon. Before that, though, he needed to do something to disrupt the space's power. He couldn't leave something this malevolent in a school where it could affect innocent mundanes.

"Dad?"

Stone swallowed and pulled his bag around in front of him. "I'm all right. It's too small in here for both of us. Just—keep watch."

"Did you find anything?"

"Yes. Let me work."

Ian fell silent, and Stone continued his examination of the shelves in front of him. There were only two, and each included items that looked as if they'd been returned there hastily. He spotted several dusty candles and holders, a collection of grime-coated jars and bottles, some rolled scrolls, and a few books. Ritual materials, it looked like. This room was too small to do any rituals in, though, and the bare floor supported that hypothesis. Whatever they were, Brathwaite had probably done them in some other part of the house. This was likely just a concealed storage closet.

Stone scanned the area for obvious magical traps, and relaxed a bit when those he found appeared inert. That made sense—while it might have been possible with the ley line to sustain a tiny illusion for all these years and even for the vile sigils to hold on to some of their power, traps required more active energy. If they weren't reinforced periodically, they eventually faded.

He swiped his hand across his face, surprised when it came away damp. It was getting warm in here, and the nausea was growing again. He didn't have a lot of time for a full examination—he'd have to take the items with him and look at them later.

He opened his bag and pulled a few of his own ritual materials out, setting them aside. Then he grabbed the stoppered jars along with all of the books and scrolls, and stuffed them inside. "All right out there, Ian?"

"I still feel like I'm going to be sick any time now. Are you done soon?"

"Moving as fast as I can."

He blinked sweat from his eyes and dug his notebook from his pocket. He wished he'd thought to bring a camera with him, but he hadn't so there was no point in regretting it now. The sigils probably wouldn't photograph properly anyway. Instead, he made quick sketches of several of them from both side walls and the ceiling, then stowed the notebook away. "All right," he called. "I'm going to shove a strongbox out there. Grab it and move it out of the way."

He didn't touch the box, but used levitation to slide it across the floor and through the opening. As he did, he attempted to lift it. It was heavy, but not overly so. Working together, he and Ian could probably get it back to the car without too much trouble. He blinked again, bracing himself against another wave of dizziness. If he didn't get out of here soon, he thought he might pass out. The energy in the room was draining.

"Got it? Use magic to move it. You can—"

"Wait!"

Stone stiffened. Ian's voice sounded suddenly urgent. "What is it?"

"I heard something! Hold on."

Stone heard footsteps as Ian crossed the room, and then a moment later: "Somebody's coming!"

Damn.

He couldn't panic now. They could deal with this, but only if they kept their heads. "Send the strongbox back in here, and come in after it."

"Is there room?"

"I'm coming out."

He crawled back out, looking around. The door was closed now. In all likelihood, anyone coming around wouldn't bother to check inside the storeroom, but they couldn't take chances. "Go on," he urged Ian.

His son cast him a questioning look, but didn't hesitate. He used magic to shove the strongbox back through the hole, then crawled in after it.

As soon as he was in, Stone slipped the panel shut and levitated the shelf back into place, then listened at the door. All they'd have to do is wait for the footsteps to recede, and then—

A key rattled in the lock.

Bugger!

Heart pounding, Stone quickly used magic to move the objects on the floor back to the shelves, though they were nowhere near as organized as they had been. Then he pulled up his invisibility spell and levitated to the top of the closet, flattening himself against the ceiling. The nausea persisted; he swallowed hard, hoping he could keep control long enough not to be sick all over some security guard's head.

The door began to swing open, and only then did he realize Ian's jacket still blocked the crack and the light was still on. Concentrating harder than ever—even after all the power he got from Calanar, invisibility was still difficult for him—he wrenched Ian's jacket across the room and into the lost-and-found box, and flipped the light switch off a mere second before the door opened and a heavyset figure with a flashlight appeared in the space.

"Anyone in here?" he asked tentatively, shining the light around. When he didn't see anyone, he flipped the light switch on.

From his vantage point, Stone could see a balding head, a portly figure dressed in a blue shirt and work jacket, and a hairy hand holding a flashlight. He swallowed again, harder. *Get out...get out...*

The guard looked around suspiciously, his gaze falling on the haphazard items on the lower shelf. He clumped over to give them a closer look.

*Go...*Stone urged him. His stomach was doing flip-flops at this point, exacerbated by the energy he had to expend to keep the spells going. A drop of sweat dripped from his forehead and landed in the guard's thinning hair, and Stone froze.

The guard stopped, absentmindedly reaching up to swipe at his hair, and then looked up.

Stone gritted his teeth. Even in his current state he could hold the levitation spell for a long time, but the invisibility would drop any moment now. *Get out of here...*he projected at the man, shaking.

"Hm," the guard said to himself. "Weird. But whatever." He switched the flashlight back on, turned off the overhead light, and exited the storeroom, closing the door behind him. The lock rattled again.

Stone let his breath out, dropping the invisibility spell mere seconds before it failed. He lowered himself back to the floor and listened once more at the door. When he didn't hear anything for a solid minute, he hurried over to release Ian from the priest hole.

"What the hell—?" his son demanded, scrambling out.

"No time. We've got to get out of here in case he gets suspicious and decides to take another look. Take the box out and let me do what I can to take care of this room."

He didn't do a very good job—he would have liked to take at least an hour to make sure all the magic in the room had been neutralized—but by the time he and Ian carefully crept out of the storeroom with the strongbox levitating between them, he was reasonably certain the feeling of "haunting" the Crofton boys had experienced over the years would be a thing of the past. Some of them might find that disappointing, but it couldn't be helped.

| CHAPTER TWENTY-NINE

S TONE WANTED TO DIVE RIGHT IN to examining the items they'd found as soon as they returned to the London house, but he forced himself to wait until the next morning when he could call Eddie and Ward to join them.

The strongbox continued to give off unpleasant waves, but a quick trip to secure it in Desmond's warded vault at Caventhorne—the same one that had held the extradimensional ritual object his grandmother and her crew of mad druids had used in their powerful ritual—proved sufficient to block the waves from getting out. That meant the only reason for starting early was to assuage his own curiosity. He decided even that could do with a brief rest, especially since both he and Ian still felt dizzy and out of sorts by the time they returned.

He retired to bed, but didn't sleep well, haunted by nightmares featuring the throbbing sigils and the persistent feeling that they had something important to say and he was putting himself and his friends at risk because he couldn't read them. Finally, he dragged himself up at six a.m. and fixed an industrial-strength cup of coffee. He'd have preferred something stronger, but even he couldn't justify drinking this early.

He *did* justify calling Eddie, though. He stood in one of the sitting rooms, looking out over the gray, overcast day, and waited for his friend to pick up.

"Mmm?"

"Eddie. It's me."

"Me who?" Eddie's gravelly voice sounded like he wasn't fully awake yet.

"Stone."

"Nope," he said immediately. "Not Stone. Stone would know better than to be up at the bleedin' crack o' dawn. And 'e'd *definitely* know better than to wake me up then."

"All right, then. Sorry. I thought you might like to have a look at what we found up at Brathwaite's place, but if you can't be arsed to drag your sorry carcass out of bed…"

"Wait—you found something?"

Stone had to grin at how much more awake his friend suddenly sounded. "We did. Something nasty, I think."

"And you 'aven't looked at it yet?"

"I thought we'd save it for you and Ward."

"Come on, mate." Now suspicion laced Eddie's voice. "What's wrong with it?"

"Not it—us. Ian went up there with me, and we both felt fairly ghastly when we got back. Whatever Brathwaite was up to, it wasn't anything that should have been waiting out the centuries in a priest hole."

"Uh—wow. Yeah, give me an hour to call Ward and get over there." He paused. "You…didn't 'ave any trouble with Brathwaite, did you?"

"Don't think so. Why? Did you expect us to?"

"Who can say? If 'e really did leave an echo, it might not want you messin' with its stuff."

"Well, either you're wrong or he's taking a break, because all we encountered was the space itself—which was bad enough—and one wandering watchman we had to avoid. Enough talk, Eddie—get over here. I'm not waiting much longer to see what we've got."

Eddie and Ward arrived less than an hour later. Unlike Stone and Ian, both of whom looked rather disheveled even following showers, shaves, and fresh clothes, they appeared to have taken the time for a good night's sleep.

"Right, then—let's see it, mate," Eddie said without greeting.

Stone didn't take issue with his lack of manners—he'd been pacing the place for the last half-hour waiting for them to show, and didn't think he could have waited much longer.

He took them to the warded workroom on the second floor, then retrieved the box and placed it in the center of the table.

"Blimey, that thing feels nasty," Eddie said immediately, looking uncomfortable.

Ward nodded, examining it with the fuzzed look of magical sight. "Indeed it does. Did you get any indications of what Brathwaite might have been up to?"

Stone dropped his bag on the table and began removing the bottles, books, and rolled papers he'd taken from the room. "I couldn't take everything, but I grabbed all the books and papers, and a representative sample of the other stuff. There wasn't much there—it was a small space." He added his notebook to the stack, open to the first page of his notes. "No photos, but here are sketches of some of the things I found on the walls. I've never seen anything like them. Have either of you?"

"Let's 'ave a look before we open the box." Eddie pulled the notebook over, and a moment later the two researchers had scooted their chairs close together, heads bent to examine Stone's hasty scrawl, muttering to each other in voices too low for anyone else to hear.

Stone watched them fondly, glad to have them on his side. He was no slouch as a researcher, but even he didn't have the temperament for the kind of focused study his two friends lived for. During their University days he'd seen them disappear on more than one occasion into some secluded corner of the library, coming up only long enough to grab quick meals or a grudging couple hours of sleep until they'd gotten to the bottom of whatever problem they were examining. Both of them had made careers of it—Eddie taking over the curation of the London library, and Ward as a historical researcher.

It was nearly twenty minutes before either of them said anything, and when they finally looked up, both of them wore grim expressions.

Stone leaped from his chair. "Have you got something?"

"We do," Ward said, "but I'm not sure we believe it."

"Believe what?" Ian, who'd been lounging at the other end of the table, sat up straighter. "What did you find?"

"I think we should 'ave a look in the box first," Eddie said. When Stone started to protest, he raised his hand. "I'm not tryin' to stall, mate. I just want to be sure before we say anything."

"Have you checked it for traps or curses?" Ward asked.

Stone nodded. "Last night, before I tried to sleep. It looks like it might have had a couple at one point, but they've faded."

He circled around the table until he stood in front of the metal box, pausing to study it once again with magical sight. Nothing had changed: the uneasy miasma hovering around it still remained, but he couldn't see any indication of active magic. The lock holding it closed was complex for its time, but nothing compared to modern-day mechanical ones. Stone concentrated for a moment, took hold of the mechanism, and popped it free. Then, still using magic, he swung the lid open.

All four of the observers stared into the revealed space.

The first thing Stone noticed was more writing. Symbols and sigils resembling the ones he'd seen on the walls lined every one of the box's interior surfaces. Unlike the neatly ordered lines of the sealed room beneath the Surrey house, these were scrawled almost haphazardly, with a hand not altogether steady.

"Was that...some kind of skeleton?" Ian asked softly, leaning in for a closer look.

"Looks like it," Eddie said, no trace remaining of his usual humor. "Or a model of one—but it looks like the real thing."

It looked like the real thing to Stone, too. It lay on one side of the box on a bed of rotting fabric, a jumble of bones in the vague shape of a creature the size of a cat or small dog. A divider separated its section from the other side, which contained more books, along with sheaves of notes and diagrams.

"What kind of animal is it?" Ian asked. "A cat, maybe?"

"Hard to say," Ward said. "I wonder if you two might have disturbed it when you moved the box, or if it hadn't been intact before."

"That doesn't look like any cat I've ever seen," Eddie said, peering closer with a light spell around his hand.

"That doesn't look like any *animal* I've ever seen," Ward said.

Stone, meanwhile, was examining the other compartment. Using magic, he carefully lifted the small stack of dusty books and papers free and spread them on the table. "Those aren't magic tomes," he said. "They look more like notebooks or journals." He narrowed his eyes. "All right, you two—what are you keeping under your hats here?"

Without replying, Eddie picked up one of the notebooks and carefully flipped through it. "Preserved," he said idly, as Ward looked over his shoulder. At one point, he stopped flipping and merely stared down at one of the pages.

"Eddie—"

It wasn't Eddie who spoke next, but Ward. He indicated the items on the table, including the bizarre broken skeleton. "I wouldn't believe it if I didn't see it with my own eyes. And of course we've no way to know whether any of this is genuine, except that it appears you've seen a first-hand demonstration of it."

He picked up the book Eddie had been staring at and turned it around so it was facing Stone. "There's really no denying it, though. It seems James Brathwaite was a practitioner of the allegedly lost and universally reviled art of necromancy."

| CHAPTER THIRTY

S TONE'S FEET ACHED, which wasn't surprising. He'd
been trudging around London for the better part of the
day, to the point where he wasn't even sure he knew
where he was any longer.

He'd had to get out. He didn't explain or offer excuses for
it, but merely told Eddie, Ward, and Ian that he needed some
time to himself. Without a further word to any of them, he'd
left the London house, switched off his phone, and boarded
the first train that pulled into the High Street Kensington
Tube station. From there, he'd changed trains twice, ignoring
the crowds of chattering tourists and commuters and paying
no attention to where he was going. Eventually, after more
than an hour had passed, he'd left the Tube behind and set
off walking, changing directions when he felt like it and
watching his route only enough to avoid wandering into
traffic.

He found, though, that as much as he'd wanted to, he
couldn't keep his brain shut off forever. As he paused for a
brief rest on a bench in a sketchy neighborhood somewhere
on the east side, his thoughts returned, not for the first time
that day, to the time before he'd fled the house.

Necromancy.

He still didn't entirely believe it could be possible. It was one of the fundamental laws of magic: you couldn't raise the dead, just like there was no such thing as true teleportation, or time travel. The idea that James Brathwaite, a known associate of his own ancestors, had been dabbling in such a vile practice seemed absurd.

But yet...a lot of Stone's assumptions about magic had been challenged lately. Trevor Harrison and the other denizens of Calanar had proven to him that teleportation without a gateway *was* feasible. He'd thought it impossible—or at least highly unlikely—for a mage to leave an echo behind when he died, yet it seemed Brathwaite had done just that. The animated skeletal remains of the foundation sacrifices had been strong, supernaturally tough, and immune to direct magic, all rumored properties of necromantically-raised creatures. And if Brathwaite had somehow managed to do it *as* an echo, without any ritual materials, that suggested a level of power and control that placed even his echo among the top ranks of mages currently alive.

Eddie and Ward had all but confirmed it after they and Stone had flipped through the remainder of the notebooks, journals, and papers in the strongbox. The material in the jars hadn't been much help; aside from being dried out after nearly two hundred years, it was impossible to identify what it was without a lot more apparatus than they had on hand.

"This is nasty stuff, mate," Eddie had said, looking even more serious than he had before. "I'd need a lot more time to study these notes—which I'll be honest I'm not sure I even want to do—but from what I'm seein', there's enough 'ere for somebody with brains and motivation to replicate at least some o' the techniques. I'm not sure it's all 'ere, but I think there's enough that a trained mage could extrapolate the rest."

Stone had looked at Ward for confirmation, and his friend had nodded soberly.

"They should be destroyed," Ward said.

"They should," Eddie agreed. "And you know I don't say that lightly."

Stone knew that all too well. Books and research material were even more valuable to Eddie and Ward than they were to him, and the idea of destroying them would normally be anathema to any of them. He thought about what might happen if these books, these techniques, got into the wrong hands—someone like Elias Richter, perhaps…or even Stefan Kolinsky. He wasn't sure Kolinsky would have any interest in raising the dead, but after their recent conversations, he realized there was a lot he didn't know about his black mage associate.

He'd dropped back into a chair with a loud sigh. "That's got to be what his other journal meant—the bit about wanting to try something he knew would work. It appears we've finally found the limits of my ancestors' consciences, which I suppose should be comforting but isn't. They'll brick dozens of mundanes away alive to use their death energy for their own purposes, but they draw the line at raising them back up again." He snorted, his voice dripping with bitter sarcasm. "Brilliant, that is. Just brilliant. Give them all a bloody gold star."

"Dad—" Ian had begun. He'd remained mostly silent during Eddie and Ward's study of the material, even after they'd revealed what Brathwaite had been up to.

Stone waved him off. "No, Ian. No. I'm...I think I've hit my limit for the day. I need a break. I've got to get away from this, or I'll go mad." He leaped back out of the chair and used magic to gather the books, papers, and vials into a pile, which he picked up and dropped in the box. "I'll put this back in Desmond's vault for now."

"You're not planning to destroy it?" Eddie asked.

He shook his head. "Not yet. I don't want to make any sudden decisions, and until this whole bloody mess is sorted, we might need some of it."

Ward narrowed his eyes and frowned. "Stone, you're not thinking of—"

"No. No, of course not. You know me better than that, Ward, or at least I hope you do." Suddenly, Stone felt exhausted—not just physically, but mentally and emotionally as well. He simply had no more resources for dealing with the mounting collection of problems that kept piling up around him. "Listen—I'm done for a while. I've got to clear my head. You two—thanks for coming by. I appreciate all your help. I hope you won't think me rude, but...I need to be alone for a while."

"I get it, mate," Eddie said with sympathy. He too got up and patted Stone's arm. "I honestly don't know how you've dealt with all this so far without goin' off your bleedin' nut. Take some time, get the 'ell away from it for a while, and come back with a fresh perspective. We'll be around. And if you just want to go get a few pints—I'm up for that as well."

"As am I," Ward said. "You don't have to handle this alone, Stone."

No, I don't. Except it isn't your *ancestors that murdered dozens of people, or the ghosts of those people keeping you out*

R. L. KING

of your house, or some mad necromancer raising them against you because your ancestors betrayed him.

He smiled bitterly, his hands jammed in his pockets as he watched the traffic filtering by in the late-afternoon sunlight. Jason had once commented that he didn't get involved with *normal* problems. This one might be the prize-winner.

He pulled his phone from his pocket and switched it on long enough to check the list of voicemails. There were two from Ian, spread several hours apart, one from Eddie, and one from Verity. He switched the phone back off without listening to any of them, and didn't even feel guilty about it. He'd told them he wanted to be alone, and he *still* wanted to be alone.

No, he decided. What he wanted was a drink. Or more than one. Preferably in a place where nobody knew him.

He dragged himself off the bench and looked around, taking a true interest in his surroundings for the first time. He still wasn't sure exactly where he was, but it wasn't one of London's better areas. That was all right, though—good, in fact. People in seedy pubs knew how to leave each other the hell alone so they could get on with their drinking. If he caught a cab and went to the Dancing Dragon, it wouldn't be half an hour before somebody tried to join him. Eddie and Ward had probably already called there looking for him—in fact, they might be there now, waiting for him to show up.

As he walked, scanning the streets for a likely place, another thought flitted through his mind: *I could just go.* Give it all up. Catch a flight somewhere else and start a new life, far away from his family's entanglements. All his life he'd been proud to be a Stone, proud to be the sixth in an unbroken line of powerful mages. But back then, he hadn't known everything that meant—everything that had come before him and contributed to making him what he was.

Hell, he wasn't even limited to this dimension. He could go back to Calanar. Harrison would no doubt let him stay in New Argana, and he'd finally have the time to learn all the things he wanted to learn there: teleportation, dimensional travel, how to build mechano-magical constructs. And best of all, nobody from Earth could find him there. He could stay for months, get his head together, and only a few days would have passed back home. It was the best of both worlds.

Damn, it sounded tempting.

"No," he murmured, stuffing his hands back in his pockets. "You don't get to do that. This whole mess is your responsibility. It's *your* family, and you're stuck with them. Nobody else is going to clean up after them for you."

A man glanced at him oddly as they passed each other, and he fell silent as he realized he'd been speaking aloud. No doubt he sounded like a madman.

Was he becoming a madman?

He wondered if that was a question he could even answer for himself.

Up ahead, he spotted a small pub with a scarred black façade, no windows, and *The Night's Rest* spelled out in faded, peeling gold letters across the front. Below it, several neon beer signs flickered.

Good enough.

He pushed open the door and stepped inside, releasing a wave of warm beer aroma and dueling TV football matches into the street.

The place was already crowded, mostly with what looked like workmen stopping for a pint or two before heading home. Stone hadn't bothered with an illusion and knew he looked out of place in his long black coat, but he didn't care. If anybody chose to mess with him, they'd soon learn what a bad decision that was.

Nobody did. A few of them cast him looks—some curious, some suspicious—but no one approached him. He pressed his way up to the bar and ordered a Guinness.

The bartender, a beefy, balding man who looked like he should be fronting a punk band, looked him up and down. "'Aven't seen you 'round 'ere before, mate."

"No, and you probably won't again after tonight. Is that a problem?"

"No, no problem. You got moola, you're good."

Stone produced a fifty-pound note—no credit cards to identify him today—and slapped it on the graffiti-carved wooden bar. "Start a tab, and keep them coming. I plan to be here a while."

"You got it, mate."

He found a tiny table in the back corner, as far away from the several televisions blaring football games as he could manage. All around him, men laughed and shouted, cheering and clapping each other on the back when their team scored. He spotted a couple other lone men seated at the long bar, but most of the customers were in groups.

He could be in a group now, if he wanted to, at the Dragon. Eddie and Ward were always up for a pint, and you could almost always find some small collection of mages hanging around there to have a drink with. He realized he'd never even shared a drink at a pub with Ian. He'd have to fix that someday—but not now. First, he owed it to his son to sort this mess out. Ian hadn't asked for any of this.

It wasn't long before he'd lost track of the time. The pub's only windows were high, narrow, and caked with years' accumulation of dust and grime, so all he could tell when he glanced up was that at some point it had grown dark. He slumped at his small table, feeling more morose than tipsy, and watched the shifting crowd as some left and others took their place. This was most likely a local pub, judging by the occasional sideways glance he still got, but everybody left him alone. That was a good thing. He pulled out his phone again and consulted it; several more voicemail messages popped up, mostly from Eddie and Ian along with one more from Verity.

I should probably call them back.

Instead, he switched if off again, having to try three times before he hit the tiny button with his unsteady thumb. He didn't need to talk to any of them tonight.

More time passed, though he still didn't pay any attention to how much. He kept to himself, steadily downing pints while occasionally glancing at one of the TV. screens even though he didn't give a damn what was on it. At least nobody was trying to talk to him. That was good.

"Doc…"

Stone raised his head, surprised. The voice had sounded like Verity, but that was impossible. Verity was in California.

Two figures swirled into view: one small and slim, the other taller and dark-haired. Stone blinked until his vision cleared.

"Hi, Doc," Verity said softly. "Can we sit down?"

Regardless of whether she was actually there or merely a figment of his intoxicated imagination, he didn't want to see her, or anyone else. "What do you want?" he muttered. He wondered if it came out as clear as it sounded in his head, and doubted it. He tilted his head back a little more, and the taller figure resolved itself into Ian. "Go away, both of you."

"We were worried about you. You haven't been answering your phone." She grabbed an empty chair from another table and sat down across from him. After a moment, Ian did likewise.

"How did you even find me?" Stone glared down into his half-full drink. Maybe if he stopped looking at them, they'd fade back away into the ether and he could get on about his business.

Her warm hand covered his. "You know you can't hide from me. Ian called a little while ago. He said you'd disappeared, you weren't responding to voicemail, and you were pretty upset when you left. He was worried too."

"Sorry, Dad," Ian said. "I know you wanted some space, but it's almost eleven. You've been gone most of the day, and I don't know how to do the tracking ritual yet."

"What are you doing here?" Verity asked. "This...doesn't look like your usual place. Isn't the Dancing Dragon where you go to drink in London?"

"Should have been a clue, shouldn't it?" Stone heard the growl in his voice and part of him regretted it—*you shouldn't talk that way to Verity*—but the rest of him didn't care. "Ever think I might have wanted to get *away* from you lot for a while?"

She refused to take the bait. "Yeah. That's exactly what I thought when Ian called. But if you want to get away from us, maybe you shouldn't go off the grid for this long—especially when there's dangerous stuff after you. Would it have killed you to check your voicemail and maybe reply to somebody so we knew you were okay?"

She was right, even if he didn't want to acknowledge it. Maybe in the old days he could have gotten away with dropping off the face of the earth without informing anyone. Nobody would have cared, except maybe Aubrey. But now...things were different, however good or bad that might be.

"Brilliant," he said, with a swiping motion across the table that nearly knocked his drink over. "Bravo. You've found me. Good for you. Here I am. Now—leave me the hell alone, all right? I'm not fit company right now, and I just want to sit here and drink. Alone."

"Why?" Ian asked.

"Why? What do you mean, why?"

"Why do you want to drink by yourself until you pass out? Are you trying to forget about what happened today?"

"Ian told me about Brathwaite," Verity said. "About what you guys found in his stuff."

"Great. Fantastic."

"Hey." Verity gripped his hand again, but not gently this time. "Look at me, Doc. You're not getting away with this."

"You don't think so?" He snatched his hand back. "Listen, Verity—I didn't ask either of you to come here. I don't want you here. There's nothing you can do to help, so why don't you just go? I know I've got to deal with this whole gods-damned situation—but I don't have to do it tonight. Tonight, I'm trying to *forget* about it, and neither of you are making that any easier."

A speech that long might have been a mistake. He took another swallow of his drink and glared at them.

Neither of them moved. "Sorry," Verity said. "You don't always get what you want. Why don't you come back with us to the London place? You can get a good night's sleep. This is all going to look better in the morning."

Stone's bitter, barked laugh was so loud a couple of the guys at a nearby table glanced in their direction before returning to their pints. "You think so? You *honestly* think this whole flaming debacle is going to look better in the morning?"

When neither she nor Ian answered, he flung himself backward against his seat. "Let's think, shall we? I've got more than three dozen three-hundred-year-old echoes living in my house, dead set against anyone in the family ever stepping foot inside again. They want revenge—and bloody rightly so—for what my ancestors did to them, but I can't even honor their requests anymore because the remains I was supposed to bury have turned to dust. And who did that? A bloody *necromancer*, which isn't even supposed to be *possible*, who hates my family as much as the echoes do because they betrayed him too. Damn lot of upstanding citizens I come from, isn't it?"

Verity started to reply, but he held up a decisive, albeit shaky, hand. "Not done yet. Or have you forgotten that whatever broke out of that sealed room is still out there *too*, and gods know what the hell *it* wants." His voice rose in volume, but he did nothing to quiet it. "For all I know, it might be in this pub with us right now, or it might have nipped off to the south of fucking *France* to lounge on the beach with Imogen and old Blakely! How the hell am I supposed to do anything when I don't even know what's going *on*?"

Verity and Ian exchanged glances, and she murmured something to him that Stone couldn't make out. Normally he would have been curious, but tonight he didn't care. He just wanted them to go and leave him in peace—or whatever approximation of it he could manage.

"Look," Verity said softly. "I get it. This whole situation sucks. I honestly don't blame you for wanting to get away from it for a while. But this isn't the way to do it. Do you even know where you *are*?"

"No idea. Don't care. Except I *thought* I was somewhere I wouldn't have to deal with anyone I knew. Guess I was wrong about that." He waved toward the bartender for another drink. Normally he'd have had to go to the bar himself, but the punk-rock barman, perhaps sensing a kindred spirit, had taken pity on him an hour or so ago.

"I don't think you need anything else to drink, Dad," Ian said.

Stone snorted. "Here's *you* lecturing me on drinking? That's a laugh. Tell me, Ian: how many clubs would I have to pour you out of if I ever came looking for you—which I wouldn't do, since I, unlike you two, respect your desire to be left the hell *alone?*"

Ian didn't reply, but Verity did. Her eyes flashed as she glared at him. "Doc, enough. None of this is Ian's fault. Just come back with us, okay? You can sleep it off at the London house and we'll revisit this whole thing in the morning—or maybe the afternoon, because you're gonna feel like shit when you wake up tomorrow."

Stone stared down into his nearly-empty glass again. If he realized the bartender hadn't brought him another one, he didn't comment on it. Instead, he said suddenly, "Maybe I should just do what they want."

"What?"

"Do what who wants?" Ian asked.

"The echoes." He swirled the amber liquid in the bottom of the glass, then downed it decisively and smacked it back on the table. "That would solve this whole problem, wouldn't it?"

"What are you talking about?" Verity demanded.

"Wait," Ian said, leaning forward across the table. "Dad, do you mean you should—what—sacrifice yourself to get rid of them?"

"Why not? It's not like they're being unreasonable. It's unconscionable, what my family did to them. Unforgivable. Somebody's got to pay for it, and it can't be my misbegotten family because they've all got the bad grace to be dead. And since I don't believe in Hell, I figure they must have got away with it."

Verity sighed. "Doc, you're being ridiculous. You aren't killing yourself to get a bunch of ghosts out of your house. It's just a *house*. Maybe you can find, I don't know, an extra-strength exorcist somewhere. Or even if you can't do that and they won't leave, what's the worst that will happen? You sell the place to somebody else who isn't related to you and stay in the London house when you're in England. It's not a great solution, but it's better than dying."

"You're right. It's *not* a great solution." Stone jerked his head up. Somewhere in the back of his mind he heard the snarl in his voice, but that was what she and Ian got for coming after him when he so clearly hadn't wanted them to. "That place is *mine*. Even if my family were a load of vile bastards, it's still mine. It'll be Ian's someday. This is bigger than me, or Ian, or anybody. But someone's got to pay for what was done to those people. Why not me? I haven't exactly been a choirboy myself, have I?"

"Doc…Alastair…" Verity scooted her chair around the table until she was sitting next to him. At the next table, a couple of the burly workmen wolf-whistled, but shut up when she shot them a warning look. "This is the drinks talking. You don't know it now, but you'll see it tomorrow. I know it's easy to just sit here and feel sorry for yourself, but—"

He wrenched away from her. "I'm not feeling *sorry* for myself, Verity," he snapped. "If that's what you think this is, you don't know me as well as I thought you did. None of this is my fault. I know that. Of *course* I know it. I didn't kill those people. I didn't shut them up and wait for them to die so I could steal their power. But don't you see that doesn't *matter*? Whoever did it, it's done, and there's nothing I can do to change that. And Brathwaite's made it so I can't even do the right thing. I can't identify them. Their bones are dust, washed away with the rain now. I can't give them a proper burial. Even with all that hatred they've been festering with for hundreds of years, they managed to ask for a reasonable thing and I can't even do *that*."

"So the alternative is to kill yourself? That's just stupid, and you know it. Or you would, if you weren't drunk off your ass." Her voice took on a hard edge.

"Why the hell not?" He slapped his hand on the table and glared at her. "Look at me, Verity. All my life, I've enjoyed all the privileges of being a Stone. I grew up in wealth. I went to the best schools. I had respect. I could have had any material thing I wanted. I've got magic, and was trained by the finest bloody teacher in all of Britain. I never wanted for anything my entire life—and why? Because my ancestors murdered people for money and power. They didn't give a damn about who any of them were, what they wanted, who would miss them—all they were was *mundanes*." He bit out the word like it was the vilest insult. "Worthless, in other words." He met her gaze, and this time he wasn't glaring. "Don't you see, Verity? This is what I come from. This is what got me where I am today. What gives me the right to just…take it all? Maybe it's finally time for someone to stand up and say, 'I'll take responsibility for this.' At least I'll save Ian having to deal with it."

Verity stared at him in shock.

Beyond her, Ian began a slow, mocking clap. "Nice one, Dad."

Stone blinked. "What?"

"Very…I don't even know what to call it. You're planning to sacrifice yourself to make things better for *me*? You want to die to absolve the sins of your ancestors? Very Christ-like, but I didn't think you were into that kind of thing."

Stone, stunned into silence, could do nothing but sit there, gripping his glass. "Ian…you don't get it."

"What don't I get? Trust me, I've seen plenty of guys falling-down drunk, and I've heard them say some pretty damned stupid things. But this one's the best. I never thought I'd be saying that about *you*."

When Stone still didn't reply, he continued: "What about me? I'm a Stone. Maybe I should do it."

"No!" His answer came quick and sharp. Then, quieter: "No. That's not an option."

"Why not? Because you're you and I'm me?"

"Because it doesn't make sense. You've barely benefited from any of what happened."

"So?" Ian leaned forward, eyes narrowing. "They want a male Stone. That's all they specified. I'd work as well as you would."

"Uh—" Verity began.

"No, Verity, it makes sense."

"It does *not* make sense!" Stone yelled, slamming his fist down on the table so hard his glass jumped. Once again, several of the other customers glanced over at them. "Damn it, Ian, stop it. This is absurd."

"Yeah. It is. Finally got one right. This whole *thing* is absurd. Listen—I understand what you're feeling like right now. I've been there."

Stone snorted.

"You don't think so? Maybe I haven't had a bunch of ghosts living in my house, but that's not the only bad thing that can happen to somebody. Trust me, I could tell you stories you probably wouldn't even believe. There's been more than one time I've wanted to kill myself. Trust me—I thought it would solve everything. It would make the pain go away, and nobody would miss me. And you know what? I was an idiot. Just like you're being now."

Verity touched Stone's arm. "He's right," she said softly. "You think this looks like a real solution, but it's not. And you'll see that when you're not drunk." She put her arms around him and pressed her face into his shoulder. "Come on, Doc. Come back home with us. If you still feel this way in the morning after you've sobered up, we'll talk about it. But not now."

Stone didn't want to let go of his plan, even though he knew it wasn't a viable one. Even through the foggy haze of far too many drinks, he knew that—but some stubborn thing down deep in his core refused to admit it.

Finally, he sighed and shook his head, fingers still curled in a death grip around his empty glass. "Let's go home," he said. "You're right. I know you're right. But...I don't know what to do, Verity. I don't know how to deal with this. I don't know how much more I can cope with. I'm starting to think it's never going to end."

He dragged himself to his feet, swaying, barely noticing both of them taking positions on either side of him and gripping his arms. Whatever pleasant buzz he'd gotten from the first few drinks had long since departed, leaving behind a heavy, morose depression that settled over him like a weighted blanket.

"It's too bad you can't fool them somehow," Ian said.

"What?" Stone looked up from where he'd been staring at the grimy rug. He wasn't yet sure he wouldn't make the ugly pattern worse by throwing up on it.

"I said, it's too bad you can't fool them. You know—the echoes. Make them *think* one of us has done the sacrifice, long enough to get them to cross over."

Stone trudged along with them toward the door. His brain was having trouble putting together complex thoughts, so it took him a few seconds to make sense of Ian's words. "Even if we could, that wouldn't be right."

They got outside, and the cool bite of the evening air cleared his head, if only a bit. "Wouldn't be right..." he mumbled again.

"Why not?" Ian, with Verity's help, led him to a nearby bench, then pulled out his phone. "Look—whatever these echoes went through, it's not your fault. It's not fair of them to expect you to atone for something you never would have even considered doing. But we need to get rid of them, or you'll have to abandon the house. Is that what you want?"

"Of course I don't." Stone shook his head and swallowed hard. He hoped he wouldn't cap off the night by getting sick in a cab. "But it doesn't matter. We can't do that. Echoes are creatures of the astral. They can see life. We can't fool them into believing a living being is dead."

Verity had been silent up until that point, pressed against Stone on the bench to help keep him upright. Now, though, she tensed. "Wait a minute."

"What?" Stone and Ian both asked.

"Maybe we can..." she murmured. She wasn't looking at them, but watching the traffic go by in the street.

"What are you talking about, Verity?" Stone asked. Once again, he felt as if he might have lost track of the conversation.

She waved him off. "Just—don't worry about it for now. I need to check something, but first we have to get you back home where you can sleep this off."

"Verity—"

She leaned over and kissed his cheek. "First things first, Doc. Trust me. And anyway, there's no point talking now. You probably won't even remember this conversation in the morning."

| CHAPTER THIRTY-ONE

S TONE DIDN'T TURN UP DOWNSTAIRS at the London house until early the following evening. When he entered the sitting room he found Ian there, sprawled on the sofa in his stocking feet, a book open in front of him.

"Nice to see you alive," Ian said, swinging his legs around and closing the book. "I was starting to wonder."

Stone swiped a hand through his hair, still damp from the shower. "Why didn't anyone wake me up? Where's Verity?"

"She and Jason were here earlier. They went off somewhere—I don't know where. I figured I should stick around in case you needed anything. Feeling better?"

"Define *better*," he said sourly, throwing himself into a nearby chair.

"Well, at least you're speaking in coherent sentences now. That's a start. Are you hungry? We got pizza before, and there's some left in the fridge."

Stone swallowed hard at the thought of cold pizza shining with congealed grease. "Er—no. Maybe later."

"So, do you remember anything about last night?"

"It's all a bit of a blur," he admitted. "I remember you and Verity tracked me down at whatever pub I'd crawled into."

"Yeah. That place was a real dive. I couldn't imagine you in a place like that, but by the time we got there, you seemed to fit right in." He shoved the book aside. "So, are you still planning to sacrifice yourself to get rid of the echoes?"

"Bloody hell, did I say that?" Stone's stomach clenched. "I thought it was a bad dream. Guess I forgot to warn you, I've got three settings when I'm pissed, depending on the mood I started with: I either get silly, nasty, or maudlin. I think I can see which one you two got treated to last night."

"A little of the last two, actually. It's okay, though. Trust me, I've done some pretty embarrassing things after a few drinks. But yeah, you really did say it. So we're done with that now? You didn't mean it?"

He stared at his hands. "No. I didn't mean it. But I *did* mean the bit about running out of options. I don't think an exorcist is going to do the job. They might be able to get rid of some of the echoes, but I can't imagine they'll manage all of them. Even if they drive off all but a few, that's still several angry spirits chucking things around and shouting their heads off. Won't exactly lend itself to pleasant occupation of the house." He sighed. "I wish Brathwaite hadn't buggered up their remains. It would have been difficult to track down enough about them to identify them, but not impossible. But now…"

"Yeah."

"Plus, we've got to work out what to do about Brathwaite himself."

"Maybe not."

R. L. KING

"What do you mean?"

Ian shrugged. "We haven't heard anything from him since the skeletons. Maybe he shot his wad. If he's still around, maybe he's got better things to do with his time than try to kill you."

"Possibly. I wouldn't count on it, though, given how the rest of this mess has been going."

"Well, you said if mages make echoes, they're probably more self-aware, right? Not just single-focused on whatever made them stick around in the first place?"

"That's the theory."

"So maybe he's smart enough to realize it wasn't you who betrayed him. The other echoes are stuck on punishing the whole Stone family, but maybe Brathwaite sees there's not much point in that."

Stone slumped in the chair. "You might be right. But then why did he send the skeletons after us in the first place? That probably took a lot of energy. I'm more inclined to believe he's holed up somewhere, regaining his strength until he can try something else." He shuddered, thinking about what would happen if Brathwaite managed to raise the remains in the cemetery or mausoleum on his property. Fighting nameless skeletons was one thing, but what if the mad necromancer sent his own father's remains after him? Or Desmond's, at Caventhorne? He knew nothing about necromancy, so he had no idea what Brathwaite might be capable of.

"Anyway, have you heard anything from Eddie and Ward?"

"Not yet. We didn't turn your phone back on when we got you back here, so you should probably check your voicemail."

Stone pulled his phone from his pocket and switched it back on. Sure enough, there were several more voicemail messages to go with the ones he hadn't answered before, including three from Eddie. He punched the librarian's number.

"Evening, mate. Nice of you to finally get back to me."

Eddie didn't sound annoyed, which Stone supposed was encouraging. "Sorry about that. I was…a bit indisposed last night."

"Yeah, I 'eard. Pissed off your arse in some armpit pub in Hackney is what I 'eard, actually. Did you sort out whatever was eatin' you?"

"Not…sure yet. But Verity and Ian found me and talked a bit of sense into me. I suppose that's where you heard?"

"Yeah, Verity rang me after they tracked you down. Not that we was worried or nothin', you understand. Just wanted to make sure you didn't run off and do something monumentally stupid. You know, as you do sometimes."

"Sod off, Eddie."

"Anyway, you feelin' up to visitors? Ward's up at Caventhorne, but both of us want to get some more time with that stuff from Brathwaite if you're willin'."

"Sure, come on over. I think Verity and Jason will be back soon. I might even feel up to eating something by then."

"We'll bring takeaway from Baljeet's."

Stone's stomach did a little flip-flop at the thought of spicy curry. "Maybe something a bit…milder, if you don't mind."

| CHAPTER THIRTY-TWO

EDDIE AND WARD ARRIVED around seven, bearing bulging bags of Chinese food. Verity and Jason showed up as they and Ian were spreading out cartons on the dining room table.

Verity found Stone in the kitchen, where he was gathering cutlery and plates. She looked him up and down and gave him a quick hug. "You look a lot better. At least you don't smell like a brewery anymore, and you don't look like you're going to be sick any second."

He took her hand, forcing himself to look at her. "Listen—I wanted to thank you for last night. For…tracking me down and talking sense into me, even when I didn't want to hear it. I know I said some dreadful things to you, and I apologize."

"Eh, don't worry about it." She waved it off. "I can't really blame you for freaking out a little bit. You've had to deal with a lot of pretty horrible stuff lately. Even you have to crack every now and then. You okay now?"

"I'm not sure I'd say I'm 'okay,' but I'm better."

She grinned. "Well, you couldn't have gotten much worse."

They returned to the dining room, where the others had finished unloading the bags. Stone retrieved a few bottles of wine and beer, then settled into the chair at the table's head. "So," he said. "What have you lot been up to while I was sleeping off my bout of idiocy?"

"Research," Ward said. "And I think we might have a bit of good news for you."

"You've worked out how to get rid of the echoes?"

"Not *that* good," Eddie said with a snort. "No, but we might have a line on how to get rid of Brathwaite."

Stone stared at him. "You do?"

"Maybe. A theory, anyway. That's the best we're gonna be able to do, since there's blessed little material on echoes at all, less on mage echoes, and none on mage echoes who are also necromancers, since they're not even supposed to exist."

"Well, don't keep me in suspense. What have you got?"

"I wish we'd found this information before the other echoes' remains were destroyed," Ward said. "It might have been the answer to them as well."

"But it isn't now?" Verity asked.

"No," Eddie said, loading his plate. "The only thing we've found that might do the trick is to ritually destroy the body. That might—*might,* mind you—break the connection binding the spirit to this world."

Stone frowned. "That's all?" He couldn't believe there wasn't a catch. *Nothing* connected to this whole mess so far had been that easy. "What are you leaving out? Do we need to track down some rare and exotic ritual components? Do it on the night of a full moon? Find an old priest and a young priest?"

"None of that," Ward said. "It's a fairly simple ritual, actually. We could do it tonight."

Eddie lifted a bag from next to his chair. "I 'aven't been holdin' out an extra bag of egg rolls. We took the liberty of gatherin' what we'd need, figurin' you'd go for it for a shot at gettin' rid of the old bastard."

Stone toyed with his fried rice. Unlike the others, who were shoveling down food with abandon, he'd taken only a small portion. "Could be dangerous. Ian and I can't go down there with you. What if he tries to fight back?"

"'E 'asn't since the skeletons, 'as 'e?" Eddie seemed unconcerned. "What's 'e gonna do? 'E's run out o' bodies to send after us. Besides, 'e might not even be around anymore. I'm willin' to take the chance, if you give the word."

Stone considered, reluctant to answer. The last thing he wanted to do was put his friends in danger. "I don't know…"

"I'll go with them, Doc," Verity said. "I think between the three of us, we can handle him if he tries anything—at least long enough to get out of there." She patted his hand. "It's worth it if we can get rid of him. That'll make it easier for us to figure out what to do about the other echoes."

He remained silent, looking at each of them in turn. Eddie, Ward, and Verity looked determined, as did Ian, even though he couldn't be part of this any more than Stone could. Only Jason looked concerned, and Stone didn't blame him— as a mundane, he couldn't affect what happened. You couldn't whack an echo with a baseball bat.

"Fine," he said at last. "Try it, anyway. But only if you give me your word you'll get yourselves the hell out of there at the first sign of trouble. I don't want your deaths on my conscience. Do you agree?"

Eddie nodded instantly. "Of course, mate." He offered a cheeky grin. "I mean, I love ya and all that, but I ain't dyin' for ya."

"That's good—it saves me the trouble of coming up with something complimentary to say at your funeral."

Ward chuckled. "We can do it tonight if you like—in fact, I'd like to. Eddie and I would like to study those papers from Brathwaite's hidden cache if you're willing, and that will likely be both easier and less dangerous if we don't have his echo to worry about."

Stone shrugged. "Might as well get it over with, I guess. We'll head down after we're finished here."

When everyone had eaten their fill, Stone used magic to gather the plates. "Verity, could you help me in the kitchen for a moment?"

Perceptive as ever, Verity caught on immediately and leaped up. "Sure."

Stone had already stacked the dishes neatly in the sink when she arrived. "What's up?" she asked. "You're not having second thoughts about this, are you?"

"No, not at all. I know how Eddie and Ward work—if they say they're 'reasonably sure' of something, you can safely bet the mortgage on it. They've probably been off researching this whole mess all day."

"What, then?"

He leaned against the counter and studied her. "I remember something from last night, but it might just have been my brain having a go at me."

Her eyes narrowed. "What?"

"Ian had mentioned something about fooling the echoes into believing I'm dead. I said it wouldn't work and wouldn't be right anyway. And then some time later, when we were outside waiting for the cab, you said maybe we could do it, and that you had to check something. Did that really happen, or was it a figment of my drunken imagination?"

"Wow, you've got a pretty good memory even when you're sloshed. Yeah, I did say that."

"So…what did you have to check? And what did you find out?"

She frowned. "I'll tell you. I *do* have an idea, and I'll tell you about it later. Let's deal with one problem at a time, though. If this thing with Brathwaite goes wrong, it might change some things."

"Verity—"

"Come on, Doc," she said with a grin, leaning in to kiss his cheek. "I learned a lot of things from you when I was your apprentice, including a few you probably didn't want me to. Like not telling things until I'm ready. And I'm not ready yet. But I will, I promise. You need to concentrate on this right now, though."

Stone sighed. "Am I this annoying when I hold things back until I'm sure of them?"

"Every bit. A taste of your own medicine will do you good. C'mon—let's go back out before Jason starts thinking I'm doing you over that fancy range."

He glanced at it with a sly smile. "You know…"

She punched his arm. "I can't take you anywhere."

He didn't miss the tension in her aura, though, and he doubted she missed his, either.

| CHAPTER THIRTY-THREE

SEEING NO POINT in waiting any longer, the group adjourned through the portal to the Surrey house immediately after dinner.

"Hey," Verity said to Jason as they all stepped through into the tiny room beneath the mausoleum. "You're getting pretty good at this whole portal-travel thing. You didn't look even once like you were going to wet yourself."

He glared at her, but then shrugged. "It was a short trip, and I'm surrounded by five mages. I figure I'm probably pretty safe. But don't get any ideas about taking me on any world tours."

Stone glanced at Ian at the mention of "world tours." Watching his son follow the others out of the room and up through the sarcophagus, he wondered when the boy would tire of his hedonistic travels and return home. Ian certainly seemed to be enjoying magic, and between his quick mind and his prodigious potential, he had the makings of a fine practitioner—*if* he'd devote himself. Stone didn't want to admit it, even to himself, but he often feared Ian would choose to continue as he had, learning the Art in bits and pieces from various friends while gallivanting around the world. There was nothing wrong with that, *per se*—Stone didn't even mind supporting him, as long as he didn't develop embarrassingly expensive tastes—but there was no denying it would disappoint him, on several levels.

No time to worry about that now, though. If they didn't deal with this situation, he'd have a lot bigger issues to concern himself with than whether his adult son wanted to find a magic teacher. He followed the others out and pulled the cover back over the sarcophagus.

It was already dark, a clear, cool night with a half-moon that settled silvery light over the headstones in the small cemetery. Stone wondered if he'd ever feel peaceful here again as he always had before, or if every visit would bring memories of shambling skeletons and uneasy thoughts about whether the place's denizens might someday make a return appearance as well.

Verity noticed him hanging behind, and dropped back to join him. "You okay? You look like you've got something on your mind."

"Nothing specific. Just…hoping we can deal with this."

She slipped her arm around him. "We will. Eddie and Ward are good. They've got this."

"I know. And you're good too. Don't forget that."

"Oh, I won't." Her eyes twinkled in the moonlight. "Just trying to be humble."

"Around *me*?"

She laughed. "Gotta get *some* practice in. C'mon, let's catch up. The faster we do this, the faster it'll be over."

They reconvened in the garage, where most of what they'd spread out on the table remained. Eddie dropped the bag of ritual materials on top of it. "Okay," he said. "We'll go back down to the catacombs and put up a new circle around the altar, and then see what we can do."

"How are you planning to destroy the body?" Stone asked.

"Burning's the best way, I think," Ward said. "Since it's mostly still interred inside the altar, there shouldn't be any issue with the fire spreading."

"Yeah, and we can use magic to contain the smoke," Eddie added. "If we use a 'ot enough fire, it's essentially like cremation. Should be in and out in less than an hour."

"Be sure to check it first," Stone said. "Make sure there aren't any other journals or papers secreted away."

Eddie patted his arm. "We've got this, mate. Don't worry. Do you honestly think Arthur and I are gonna take any chances of destroyin' perfectly good research material?"

"Good point. All right—let's do this. But remember your promise. Get out of there at the first sign of danger. And stay in communication as long as you can."

"I want to go along," Jason said suddenly.

They all looked at him in surprise.

"Why?" Verity asked. "You can't really help, and I thought you hated it down there."

He picked up the baseball bat, which he'd left leaning against the table. "Just in case. Yeah, I know that guy probably isn't gonna get up and attack you, but if he does—" He raised the bat. "I got it covered."

The mages exchanged glances, but nobody could come up with a good reason for him not to accompany the group. "Right then," Eddie said, reclaiming the bag. "Let's do this."

❖

The process, after all their careful planning, research, and concern, turned out to be almost anticlimactic. Verity and the others returned an hour and a half later, dropping into chairs.

"Well, that was a lot less exciting than I expected it to be," she said.

"That's a good thing," Ward reminded her. "I could certainly do with a bit less excitement for a while."

The group hadn't found anything amiss in the catacombs. Brathwaite's body had been right where they'd left it, with no indication that anything or anyone had been moving around down there following the mass breakout. Ward had searched the body while Eddie and Verity altered the circle around the altar, and was disappointed to find no other papers or books hidden among Brathwaite's rotting clothes.

After that, it had been a simple matter of performing the ritual and burning the body with magical fire. The smoke hadn't even been an issue, because Eddie had discovered a hidden vent in the ritual room's ceiling, probably used by those performing the sacrificial rites. They had to take a few minutes to unstick and clear it, but once they had, the smoke had vented nicely upward and disappeared.

"So you didn't notice *anything*?" Stone demanded. "No...chills, unexplained winds, feelings of dread?"

Verity shook her head. "Nothing. The body just burned. Nobody screamed or threw things or tried anything else to prevent us from doing it." She shrugged. "That's what the ritual was supposed to do, after all—get rid of him. Are you surprised it worked?"

"Not surprised, but I would have expected a bit more...pushback."

"Maybe he was just ready to go," Ian said. "If your ghost was stuck on Earth for two hundred years because of somebody messing with you, maybe you'd be ready to move on too."

"Yeah," Jason said. "Except from what you've said about this guy, he's not going anywhere good."

"That's assuming you believe in Hell," Stone pointed out. "A lot of mages don't—they didn't even back when Brathwaite was alive."

"Well, in any case," Eddie said, "it looks like one problem might have been dealt with. That just leaves the rest of the echoes."

"Just," Ian said. "That's kind of a big 'just.'"

"Yes, well, I think this is enough for tonight." Stone stood and pulled on his coat. "For tonight, I think we should head back to London so you lot can get some sleep. Given that I slept most of the bloody day away I doubt I'll be doing that, but the rest of you look tired. I'm sure that ritual took something out of you."

Nobody argued, so they gathered the rest of their gear and trudged back toward the cemetery. Once back at the London house, they parted company, with Stone, Eddie, and Ward agreeing to call if they came up with anything new in their research.

"Thank you for everything," Stone told the two of them. "I couldn't have done this without you."

"Yeah, well, we're not done yet," Eddie said. "But at least we're on the right track."

When they were gone, Ian found Stone in the sitting room. "Hey, Dad, do you mind if I head out for tonight?"

"Head out where?"

"A couple of friends called earlier today. They're in Paris, and they want to go have some drinks and catch up. I told them I'd get back to them if things settled down."

Stone almost sighed, but caught himself. "Fine. Honestly, you don't need to be here for any of this, if you'd rather be off again."

"No, no, I'm not leaving you in the middle of this. But…" He shrugged. "I could stand a little time away from it if you're okay with it."

"Yes, all right. Go. I'll call you if anything comes up. Please stay close to a portal."

"You got it, Dad. Get some rest."

After he'd left, Stone stood by the window, gazing at the cars crawling by on the street below.

"Doc?"

He turned; Verity stood in the doorway, watching him with an odd expression. "Ah. Hello. I thought you went back to California with Jason."

"I did—he had some stuff he needed to take care of. But I came back." She drifted over to him, standing close but not touching. "He'll die before he admits it, but I think he's finally starting to see how convenient the portals can be."

Stone chuckled. "About time. At least he's not losing his lunch on the way out anymore."

"That's progress, I guess."

"I never told you an amusing story about him—well, it's amusing in retrospect. It wasn't at the time." He pulled the heavy drapes shut and headed back into the room, where he poured himself a drink. "Want one?"

"No, thanks. And are you sure *you* should have one?"

"Eh, it's just the one. If I can't hold my liquor that well, I'll have to turn in my Brit card." He sat on the couch and patted the spot next to him. When she'd settled in, he chuckled again. "The first time I went through the portal with him, very shortly after we'd met, we'd just had lunch at A Passage to India. As soon as he popped out in the portal room at the Surrey house, he proceeded to bring the whole thing up for a return engagement. At least he managed to find a bin to do it in, which was a blessing, I suppose."

She wrinkled her nose. "That's...gross, but not really very funny."

"No, that's not the amusing part. The thing is, we were quite occupied with other matters at the time, and we returned to California through the portal very shortly after that. I just had to retrieve a book I needed."

"Okay..."

"And it was quite some time before I used the portal again."

She twisted around to face him, wincing as she got it. "You mean you—"

"Let's just say it took several weeks and some fairly potent chemical cleaners to get the smell out of the portal room. And that's *after* I used a fire spell to incinerate the entire bin."

She stared at him, her eyes wide. "Uh—eww. Did you ever tell Jason?"

"No. I think he had quite a lot more on his mind at the time. He probably forgot all about it. So there's something you can use as ammunition against him if he ever annoys you. You have my permission."

She snuggled in closer, burying her head in the crook of his shoulder, and was silent for a while. Finally, she said, "Ian left, didn't he?"

"He did, yes. Off to Paris to meet up with some mates." He kept his voice neutral.

He shouldn't have bothered, though. "Are you okay with that?" she asked softly.

"Why wouldn't I be? He's an adult. He can do what he likes."

"That isn't what I asked."

He sighed and sipped his drink. "I know. But it doesn't matter whether I am or not, does it? I want him to be happy. He didn't ask to be dragged into this whole sordid affair. Let him have some fun."

"Is he coming back?"

"I told him I'd call if we needed him, and asked him to stay near a portal. I'm sure he'll return if he's needed." He remembered something. "Speaking of needed—are you finally going to tell me what you had on your mind last night?"

"Yeah." She looked serious. "That's actually why I came to find you."

He finished his drink and leaned back. "All right, then—out with it. How can we fool the echoes into believing I've sacrificed myself long enough to get them to cross over?"

"Well…when I went home with Jason before, I talked to Hezzie. I didn't tell her anything specific," she added hastily. "No details. But I asked her if there was some kind of potion that could simulate death."

That was something Stone hadn't considered—which wasn't odd given his lack of knowledge about alchemical techniques. "And is there?"

"Yeah. It can put the drinker in a kind of suspended animation, and temporarily separate their spirit from their body. It's sort of like astral travel, except instead of your body sleeping, it's...well...dead, for all intents and purposes."

"Bloody hell. I've never heard of anything like that."

"It's pretty rare, apparently. Hezzie doesn't know how to make it, but she thinks her teacher does. There isn't much call for it, because it can be risky if misused, especially by mundanes."

"Why mundanes?"

"Because they don't have any control over their spirit when it vacates the body. If something goes wrong, they can't get back in. It's like when somebody's clinically dead—you can only do it for a short time before you start risking things like brain damage."

She gazed off into the middle distance. "The only problem I can see about it is if you separate your spirit from your body, even though your body is technically 'dead,' the echoes will still see your spirit floating around, right?"

Stone sat up straight. "Maybe not. I haven't done much astral traveling—the tracking spell is a form of it, but a very minor one—but the few times I've tried it, I've never tried to use magic in the astral realm. I might be able to do a disregarding spell so they don't notice me, although I'm not sure it would matter if they did."

"Why not?"

"Well...that's the definition of death, isn't it? The spirit leaves the body? Remember, these echoes are three hundred years old, focused on vengeance against the Stones, and mundane. Even if they *knew* the nuances of how magic worked, they probably wouldn't care. We're fulfilling the condition of 'death' as far as they're concerned, so that should be enough to satisfy them." He gripped her shoulders. "Verity, you're brilliant. I knew this whole alchemy thing would pay off. Can you talk to Hezzie and see about getting some of this potion from her teacher? I'll pay whatever she asks, of course."

"I'll talk to her. But are you sure you want to do this? It still could be dangerous. And how do you know the echoes won't come back?"

"They won't. It's not a two-way door. If they're stuck here, it means there's some reason they can't cross over, but once they do, there's no going back. I'm certain of that." He sighed, remembering something. "But...that still leaves the biggest question: should I do it at all?"

"Why shouldn't you?"

"Because of what I said before. Those echoes have every right to be angry at my family. Look at what was done to them. Wouldn't I just be...perpetuating things by deceiving them?"

She took his hand, and her eyes were serious. "I don't think so. For one thing, yeah, your ancestors did terrible things to them. But *you* didn't. It's not right to expect you to pay for something you didn't do and never would have supported."

He looked down at their clasped hands, tensing.

"What?"

"Can I be so sure I wouldn't have?"

"What's that supposed to mean?"

"Come on, Verity." He pulled away and got up, pacing around the sitting room. "How can I be sure I *wouldn't* have done it? That if I'd been born into my family three hundred years ago when this sort of thing was just...*done* among many mages, who's to say I wouldn't have done it too? You can't deny I can get a bit full of myself, even these days. Arrogant. Stubborn. Prideful."

"Yeah. But you're not cruel. You've never been cruel."

He waved her off. "You don't get it, Verity. People are a product of their times—things that we consider horrific now, and rightly so, used to be accepted. Do you think many people who kept slaves thought they were doing wrong? We like to think we'd be better, but I'm not convinced many of us would be. Hell, look at what happened in Nazi Germany, and that was less than a hundred years ago. Look at our own century, where children are still indoctrinated from the time they're born to believe they're doing a noble thing by blowing themselves to bits."

She got up and came to him, taking both his hands and turning him to face her. "I see what you're saying, and it's definitely something to consider. There's no way to know whether you would have done those things—I don't think you would have, but there's no point in talking about it, since we'll never have the answer. The point I'm trying to make is that you wouldn't do them *now*. Look at yourself—drinking until you pass out to get away from even thinking about what happened. I know this has been eating at you ever since you found out about it. I know you want to make things right. But maybe the best way to do that is to help the echoes move on. Especially if there really *is* a Heaven. I know you don't believe there is, but I guess I still do."

He still didn't look at her.

She squeezed his hands. "I don't really see another option, unless you want to give up the house. I don't know—I guess you could try to track down their descendants and turn the house over to them, but that would take years to unsnarl and you *still* don't know if the echoes would leave. This way, you get the house back and the echoes get peace."

Pulling him into a gentle hug, she added, "There's no good solution, but this might be the best one we have. And once the echoes are gone, you and Eddie and Arthur could still use that journal to try to find out as much as you can about them. Maybe you can do something to help, if it would make you feel better."

Stone stood for a moment, then returned the hug. "Yes…I suppose you're right. Thank you, Verity."

"No problem. God knows you've helped *me* out with enough problems. Nice to be able to return the favor now and then." She pulled back. "So…do you want me to talk to Hezzie?"

"Yes. Please. If we're going through with this mad plan, I suppose it's best to get started as soon as possible."

CHAPTER THIRTY-FOUR

EDDIE AND WARD weren't in favor of Stone's new plan, at least initially.

"It's too dangerous, mate," Eddie said when they'd returned to the London house to discuss their next steps. "I've 'eard of these kinds of potions, and they're not foolproof. What if it separates your spirit from your body and you can't get back in? What if you stay out too long and your body dies?"

"Well, then, I suppose the echoes will really get what they want, won't they?"

"Stone..." Ward's expression was even graver than Eddie's. "There are a lot of variables here, and you can't correct for all of them. You're taking a risky chance."

Stone shrugged. "So I am. I think I owe these people *that* much, especially if there's a chance I can help them move on and find some peace. If I have to take a bit of a risk to make that happen, it's the least I can do, don't you think so?"

Verity had left, heading back to California to consult with Hezzie and see if she could convince her teacher to make the elixir for them. In the meantime, Stone had invited Eddie and Ward back over to examine Brathwaite's documents. He hadn't slept since the previous night; his mind was far too agitated to even consider it. He could sleep when this whole thing was over.

Ian still hadn't returned, and Stone hadn't called him. There wasn't any need for him to be here now, so at least *somebody* might as well be having some fun.

"There's one other bit of this you're not thinking about," Eddie said. He and Ward had Brathwaite's papers and journals spread out over the dining-room table, along with several reference texts they'd brought along with them.

"And what's that?"

"The echoes are confined to the 'ouse. Aside from Brathwaite's little walkabout with the skeletons, they 'aven't bothered you unless you enter it—but they won't *let* you enter. If you're to do this ritual properly, you'll need to do it inside the 'ouse. Preferably downstairs in the ritual room. 'Ow are you planning to do that?"

He was right—Stone *hadn't* thought of that. "Well…" he said slowly, "I've got an idea, but you won't like it."

"Try me."

"Our best guess is that it was Brathwaite trying to break through Poppy's barriers, right? And now that you've burned the body, we think he's gone. Do you think she'd be willing to return long enough to have a chat with the echoes and explain what we've got planned? Maybe they'll agree to let me in if they know they're getting what they wanted."

Eddie frowned. "I don't know, mate. That whole thing spooked 'er right and proper."

"Yes, but this time we'll be prepared. Between you, Ward, and Verity, you can make sure nobody gets near her. It wouldn't have to be complicated or take very long—just long enough for her to get them to agree to leave me alone so I can get inside to do the sacrifice. Then she can leave. There's no need for her to hang about for the rest of it—in fact, I'd rather she didn't."

When Eddie still looked dubious, he leaned across the table. "Will you at least ask her? I'll pay well—better than last time, for less work. If she won't go along with it, we'll have to find another solution, but please try."

"Stone, did anybody ever tell you that you're a stubborn bastard?"

"Only a couple times a week, these days. More often when I'm with you lot."

Eddie let out a loud sigh. "Fine. Fine. I can see there's no changin' your mind. I'll give 'er a ring. But don't be surprised if she laughs in my face and tells me to get stuffed."

Poppy didn't tell Eddie to get stuffed. He returned to the dining room fifteen minutes later, looking contemplative.

"Did she go for it?" Stone asked. He sat across from Ward, paging through one of Brathwaite's journals. The necromantic techniques were every bit as vile as he'd expected them to be, and he'd already decided to destroy the material once Eddie and Ward had had their fill of studying it. It was too dangerous even to lock up in his warded library or Desmond's sealed vault.

"Surprisingly, she did." Eddie resumed his seat at the other end of the table. "Didn't even take much convincin', which surprised me. I guess 'avin' a couple days to sleep it off gave 'er a new perspective. But she did take you up on your offer, so this is gonna cost you dear."

"That's fine. It's worth it if she can convince them."

"She says she's free tonight, so we can do it then if you want."

Stone had been planning to wait until Verity returned with the potion, since there was no point in holding the séance if she couldn't obtain it, but he found himself once again gripped with a compulsion to move this process along as much as he could. "Tonight's fine. I'll call Ian and ask him to return—we can't go inside, but maybe we can help from outside. The more protection she has, the better, just in case Brathwaite isn't really gone."

"Do you think he is?" Ward asked.

"Well, if he isn't, he's certainly been quiet. Let's hope so."

Ian, true to his word, had remained in Paris and thus near a portal. Stone thought he might have trouble convincing his son to return, but he agreed readily. He showed up at the London house later that afternoon.

Like Eddie and Ward, he didn't agree with the plan, though. "So you don't want to do a real sacrifice, but you're okay with a pretend sacrifice that might kill you anyway if things go wrong? That's crazy."

"Not even close to the craziest thing I've ever done," Stone said. "You'll learn that as you get to know me better."

Ian pondered, looking out the window, then turned back. "Let me do it, then."

"Out of the question." Stone's reply was immediate and firm.

"Why not? It's okay for you to take the risk but not me?"

"Yes. That's exactly right. Don't argue with me, Ian—I'm not changing my mind. I don't know why you might think you'd be a better choice in any case."

"Why not? It's my family too. I'm younger and—no offense—probably in better shape physically."

"I wouldn't be too sure of that, actually."

"Wouldn't be too sure of what?"

Stone glanced up to see Verity coming in. She had a leather bag slung over her shoulder.

"Perfect timing," he said. "Ian thinks he's in better physical shape than I am."

She tilted her head. "Depends on how you define it. But why does that matter?"

"Because he says he's better suited to do the sacrifice."

"I am," Ian said. "He's just too stubborn to admit it."

Verity snorted. "Guys are funny. Listen to you two, arguing over who gets to pretend to die. But trust me, Ian—I've known him longer than you have, and getting him to change his mind when he's set on something is like trying to divert a freight train. Don't waste your time."

"Did you get the potion?" Stone asked, trying to change the subject before things got out of hand.

Her expression sobered. "Yeah, I got it. Hezzie's teacher wanted to know what I wanted it for. She's...very strange, by the way. Like, strange enough to make *me* uncomfortable around her." She opened her bag and withdrew a tiny, clear glass vial, displaying it for Stone to see.

He took it, holding it up to the light to observe the oily liquid swirling inside. It was a deep red, and when it caught the late-afternoon sunlight, it seemed to have silver flecks wriggling around within it. "Did she need the blood I gave you?"

"Yeah. I destroyed what she didn't use, so you don't have to worry about it getting out."

"Do you trust her?"

"Hezzie does, and I trust Hezzie."

"What did you tell her about why you wanted it?"

"I was honest with her, as much as I could be. Told her a friend needed to fake his death to fool a few echoes that were bothering him. I didn't tell her how *many* echoes, though. And," she added, shifting her gaze to Ian, "it doesn't matter if you convince Doc to let you do it. You can't. The potion's made specifically for him. That's true for a lot of the more complicated alchemical preparations, as it turns out."

"So it won't work for me because I'm not him, even though we're related?"

"Nope. Well—it might do *something,* but almost certainly not what it's supposed to do. So you're off the hook."

Stone wasn't sure he caught a fleeting look of relief on Ian's face, but he wasn't sure he didn't, either.

| CHAPTER THIRTY-FIVE

POPPY WILLOUGHBY returned later that evening through the portal. This time, she didn't look as if she'd just stepped away from a club date, except for the blue Mohawk and bright purple satchel. Stone didn't miss the fact that both her expression and her aura revealed her apprehension.

"Are you sure you want to do this?" he asked her. "Believe me, I appreciate it, but I don't want you to do anything you're not comfortable with."

"Don't worry, luv. I wouldn't be here if I didn't think you lot could keep me safe. I'm not thrilled about it, mind you, but for what you offered—" She flashed a cheeky grin. "Part of your last payment got me a pair of sexy Louboutins I've had my eye on for months, and some o' this one's gonna buy me a matching bag." Patting his arm, she added, "You just make sure I make it out of here so I can enjoy them, and I'll be happy."

Instead of waiting in their makeshift garage command center while Eddie, Ward, and Verity headed up to the house with Poppy, Stone and Ian stationed themselves outside a window where they could observe the proceedings. They'd decided since this was a simpler séance, there was no point in taking the extra step to try convincing the echoes to allow the two of them inside. Either they'd agree to the sacrifice or they wouldn't. Unless something went catastrophically wrong, their position outside the window should allow Stone and Ian to assist in protecting Poppy if she needed it.

Ian leaned against the wall, peering in as the séance participants set up their table. They used the same circle Poppy had constructed last time; it had only taken her a few minutes to refresh it, and another few to rearrange the items on the table. "Do you think Brathwaite will bother them?"

"I hope not. If Eddie's right, burning his body released him and he's already moved on to…wherever he ended up."

"This is all pretty unreal." His sigh sounded in the darkness. "I mean, I've gotten my mind around magic fairly well in the last couple of years, but the stuff Trin taught me was straightforward. Powerful, but simple. But necromancy…that's a whole different level."

"For me as well. Remember, this is new to me too. I've been studying magic for longer than you've been alive, and no one even hinted that it might be possible." He watched as Eddie, Ward, Poppy, and Verity clasped hands around the table. "And let's hope it won't be much longer," he added. "I plan to destroy those materials as soon as Eddie and Ward and I finish looking them over."

"I thought mages didn't destroy stuff like that."

"Normally that's true. But in this case, I don't think it's wise to take any chance of someone getting hold of it." He pointed. "Looks like they're starting."

They hadn't bothered with a radio because of the interference, so Stone couldn't hear what the people around the table were saying. Poppy had her eyes closed and was speaking, probably reciting the invitation for the spirits to rejoin the group. He couldn't see Verity's or Ward's faces, but Eddie appeared calm. When Stone shifted to magical sight, their auras likewise looked watchful, tense, but mostly untroubled. He gripped the windowsill, barely breathing, his gaze locked on Poppy's face and ready to add his power to a shield at the first sign of agitation.

The sign never came. Poppy continued to speak calmly, her eyes closed and her head tilted forward slightly, for several minutes. Then everyone around the table pulled back and released their joined hands. The candles winked out, followed a second later by a light spell flaring around Verity's hand. The group got up from the table and headed back toward the front door.

Stone and Ian hurried to meet them. "How did it go?" Stone demanded. "Did they go for it? Did you have any trouble?"

"No trouble," Poppy said. "I almost feel guilty about taking such a big payment this time. Almost," she added with a grin.

"You didn't get any feeling that the other presence was there? The one from last time?"

"None," Eddie said. "Believe me, we were watchin'. If 'e was there, 'e was keepin' it quiet."

"I don't think he was," Verity said. "Last time, he seemed to agitate the other spirits just by being there. They were a lot calmer this time."

"I'm not sure 'calm' is the right word," Poppy said. "They're still pretty worked up. I could still feel how much they hate you, Alastair, and your whole family. But they perked up when I suggested you'd be willing to go through with the sacrifice."

They'd almost reached the garage by now. She waited until they were inside, then dropped to a near-whisper. "You...uh...*aren't* planning to really sacrifice yourself, are you?"

"No. But I don't want to let the echoes know that." He explained their plan, with Verity adding more information about the potion and its effect. "You know spirits better than any of us do, Poppy. Do you think it will work?"

She pondered. "It's a little underhanded, but I can see why you don't have much choice. Yeah, I think it'll work. Echoes are simple things, really. They can get violent if they're wound up about somethin', but it's not like they're givin' things careful consideration." She tilted her head, her smooth brow furrowing. "It's more like...they have a condition they need to fulfill, and if they do it, they move on. That's why you never see people who died peacefully in bed leavin' echoes. They don't have any conditions left before they go."

"So if they think Doc's dead, if his spirit leaves his body, they'll all go?" Verity asked. "That should be it?"

"Should be. They're mundanes, so it's not like they know about what magic can do—though even if they did, it probably wouldn't matter. They're not complex enough for that kind of thinkin'."

Stone nodded in satisfaction, pleased to have his hypothesis validated by an expert. "Brilliant. Thank you, Poppy, for everything."

"No problem, luv. Give me a ring when this is all over and we can all go have a drink."

"I'll do that. Let me walk you back to the portal."

The others remained behind in the garage while Stone accompanied Poppy back to the mausoleum. When they reached it and had climbed down the stairs to the portal room, the young medium paused. "Listen…Alastair…I didn't want to say it in front of everyone, but I'm not sure this plan of yours is the best idea."

"Why not? I thought you said the echoes wouldn't know the difference."

"They probably won't. But…any time you interact with the spirit realm as a living being—even a living spirit—it can be dangerous. Living people aren't supposed to be there."

A little shiver ran up Stone's spine. "What happens to them when they are?"

She shook her head, her cheerful face uncharacteristically serious. "There isn't a lot of data to go on, but I've heard stories of people…getting lost. Just wandering off and losing their way back to their bodies."

"Isn't there a…sort of cord joining the two together? Similar to what you have in a tracking ritual?"

"Normally, yes. But I've heard of this elixir you're plannin' to use. The whole point of it—the reason it feigns death so well—is that it obscures that cord to the point where it's nearly invisible. It would have to, or else the echoes would see it and know you weren't truly dead."

She gripped his arm. "All I'm sayin' is…be careful. Don't stay away long, and don't stray far away from your body. I'd hate to see your spirit wander off and never come back."

"Er…yes. I will. Thank you, Poppy."

Stone began to wonder if this had been a good idea after all.

| CHAPTER THIRTY-SIX

VERITY TOOK STONE'S HAND. "You okay? You don't have to go through with this, you know."

Stone looked around the circular chamber, which didn't look much different from the last time he'd seen it. "I think it's the only way to be sure," he said softly. "I trust you." The two of them stood off to the side, watching as Eddie, Ward, and Ian transformed the circle surrounding the burned-out altar where James Brathwaite's remains had lain. Normally, Ian wouldn't have been able to help, since he as yet had no training in ritual magic, but since this particular circle was only for show, that didn't matter. It gave him something to do, anyway, and he seemed grateful for the diversion.

"I'm not sure *I* trust me. What if Hezzie's teacher got something wrong with the formula? What if it doesn't work?"

"It will work. I know I'm taking a risk, but I think it's a reasonable one. And once it's over, the echoes will have peace. Believe it or not, I care more about that than I do about getting the house back. I don't know if I'll ever be able to fully come to terms with what my family did to these people."

They'd already walked the hallways, Verity a silent presence next to Stone as he examined the blasted remains of the bricked alcoves. As he suspected, no trace of the skeletal remains had been left behind, and no identifying information marked the insides of the small chambers.

"It's as if they've disappeared from the earth," he murmured, gazing into one of the last ones. "That shouldn't be. They need to be remembered."

"We'll do what we can, once they're gone. I'll help if I can, though I'm not sure what I can do."

He hadn't responded to that. What could he say? Aside from the incomplete records in the ledger, they had nothing to go on. He could donate the items they'd found in the chest to a museum and attempt to track the descendants of the more well-documented of the victims, but he might have to settle for that.

Stone didn't like settling for things.

He'd spent nearly half an hour examining every surface of the sealed chamber at the end of the wider hallway, but it likewise had sparked no flashes of insight. All he could do was agree with Eddie and Ward that the sigils and symbols lining the walls and ceiling had been put there for a protective purpose: to contain something and keep its magic suppressed. But as for what it was guarding, he had no idea. He hadn't spotted any names or identifying information during his own examination, and he knew Eddie and Ward were not only even more thorough than he was, but they'd had more time to look over the work. If anything had been there, they'd have found it.

That left only Brathwaite's journal, and the reference to the mysterious "A," also known as "the fiend." Who—or what—could they refer to?

Reluctantly he'd turned away from the chamber and headed back toward the circular ritual room. If the "sacrifice" ritual worked and the echoes departed, he'd have all the time he needed to do a careful study of all the data they had: the chamber, the journals and ledgers, and the rest of the catacombs. Reluctantly, he had to admit to himself that the destruction of the foundation sacrifices' remains did have one positive by-product: with no evidence that anyone had been killed here, he would no longer be required—by the law, anyway, if not by his conscience—to bring in the authorities. Technically he supposed he still should, but it was another decision he could put off for a while. One problem at a time.

"Have you got the knife?" he asked Verity.

"Yeah." She pulled it from her bag and withdrew it from its sheath. "I don't like hurting you, even a little."

"We have to make it look good. Some blood will help sell it." He examined the knife. It had a wicked-looking black blade around five inches long, with a leather-wrapped hilt slightly longer. She and Ian had popped over to Tolliver's earlier to pick it up, and she'd reported back to Stone with amusement that the saleswoman had been surprised at their request. "They don't get much call for mundane magical gear," she'd said. "She had to hunt around for it."

He took it from her, pressing the blade against the wall and watching it retract into the hilt until a point barely half an inch long poked out. "Just be careful where you stab me. Pick somewhere that won't do permanent damage, and go straight in and out."

"Don't worry. I'm planning to make a mark on your chest to be sure. And I'll heal it up as soon as you give the word." She reclaimed the knife and returned it to the sheath. "Are you sure the echoes can't see what we're doing?"

"They can't—or at least they won't understand it. That's why we needed Poppy to play medium so we could talk to them. They can't follow anything that's not directly related to them."

"What about Professor Benchley? He could understand you, right?"

"Only when he was possessing Raider, I think. Otherwise, it was more of a generalized thing. Don't worry—it will be fine." He glanced at the circle, where the others appeared to be finishing their work. "I'd better go get prepared. Looks like it's almost showtime."

Stone walked past Eddie, Ward, and Ian to the other side of the room. Despite his confident words to Verity, he still had misgivings about this plan. He didn't try to hide his aura, though, in case the echoes were more aware of their surroundings than he expected. As far as they were concerned, he was preparing to die, so some apprehension would be expected.

The knife had been his idea. Verity had assured him that the potion, which was thick and viscous, would function equally well if he drank it or if he was stabbed with a blade smeared with it. "It's potent stuff," she said, indicating the tiny bottle. "She said you don't need much to make it work. We'll have to be careful that none of the rest of us touches it."

She hadn't been in favor of the idea, of course, but he'd convinced her. "We have to make it look good—like a real sacrifice. Having me drink something from that little nothing bottle and keel over isn't very dramatic. Let's give them a show."

Now, though, as he stood with his hands against the wall, doubts began to creep in. Would the potion work as advertised? Would he be able to return to his body when the ritual was done and the echoes were gone? Would the fake ritual fool the echoes?

You were ready to do it for real before, he reminded himself. Sure, he was drunk off his ass at the time, but he'd been drunk often enough in his life to know that sometimes the deeper emotions that surfaced then weren't altogether wrong. These people—forty-one innocent men, women, and children—had died because of his family. The least he could do was take a fairly safe chance to help them move on from a prison every bit as bad as the tiny brick alcoves had been.

"Dad?"

Stone turned, pushing himself off the wall. Ian stood there, looking pensive. "Finished the circle?"

"Yeah. We're ready when you are."

Behind him, Eddie and Ward had moved off to a table where they'd arranged some books and papers, and Verity had joined them.

"Everything all right?" Stone examined the circle. The three of them had altered it with chalk and sand, creating a simple but impressive-looking protective working. Much of it was extraneous, done only for show, but even from where he stood Stone could pick out its basic structure.

"Yeah."

He tilted his head. "Ian, you might be able to fool me into believing that normally—your aura control is that good already. But you're not even trying now. What is it?"

Ian's gaze skated away, not meeting his. "I…I'm just not sure you should do this."

"Why not?"

He shrugged.

"Ian…"

"Okay, look." He took a deep breath. "We barely know each other. All these years I had no idea you existed. When Trin told me you *did* exist and you were a mage…that took a lot of getting used to. And when I finally met you…" He turned away and then back, his jaw tight. "Maybe it's not worth it, getting rid of these echoes, if it means you might die. Does it really matter, whether or not you have this house? Let them have it. It's not like you don't have other places to go."

"Ian—" Stone sighed, reaching out to grip his son's shoulder. "I'm not going to die. But I've got to do this. I know you don't understand. You know I'm your father, but you haven't been around long enough to know what it means to be part of this family."

"That doesn't mean you're responsible for what they did."

"That's true. But it does mean if I have a chance to make it right, I've got to take it." He patted Ian's arm and gave him what he hoped was an encouraging smile. "Off you go, now. I'd like a few moments alone before we do this. I'm not going to die. Verity's damned good—I know, because I trained her—and so are Eddie and Ward. They won't let anything happen to me."

Ian still didn't look convinced, but after one last long look he headed off to join the others.

Stone watched the slump of his shoulders with a twinge of regret. If he had any other ideas, he'd try them, but he didn't. "Okay," he called after a moment. "Let's do this."

They gathered around him as he approached the circle. Verity pulled him into a tight hug, burying her face in his chest. "It'll be fine," she whispered.

"I know." He stroked her back and kissed her. "You know I trust you. And don't worry if I'm gone a while—I want to make sure they've all left before I come back."

"Yeah."

He stepped back and slipped off his coat and his black T-shirt, shivering a little as the room's chill hit his bare skin. Verity took them, squeezing his hand.

"All right...here goes." He scanned his companions' faces, noting they all looked as grim as he was sure he did. Without giving himself more time to reconsider his decision, he levitated upward, crossed the circle, and settled on top of the altar. It still felt solid even after the others had opened it to reveal Brathwaite's body. The body, of course, was no longer there—except perhaps as ashes. Stone hadn't asked if they'd moved the ashes. He knelt there, waiting.

Eddie stepped forward, taking his position at the top of the circle, facing Stone. Verity, Ian, and Ward moved to the other three points.

Eddie began a chant in Latin. Stone had no trouble following the gist of it, and had to admit his friend had outdone himself making it sound authentic. The Latin words were a combination of a religious invocation and a magical ritual, asking God and the spirits to accept Stone's sacrifice to pay for his ancestors' crimes, so the innocent victims might have everlasting peace. He spoke in a strong, singsong cadence, his voice swelling to fill the room. Ward and Verity followed along in response, with Ian doing his best to do likewise.

Stone, shifting to magical sight, already noticed a growing sense of power beginning to rise in the room. It didn't feel like magical power, but rather more of a force pressing on the room from all sides. Were the echoes here? Were they watching?

The chant lasted for several minutes. Stone remained kneeling, trying to project penitence and a desire for atonement. He didn't make any effort not to shiver, figuring his discomfort might add to the verisimilitude of the whole thing.

"Alastair Stone, son of Orion Stone," Eddie called, spreading his arms wide. "Please state that you 'ave come 'ere to this place of your own free will."

"I have." Stone's confident words rang against the chamber's walls.

"You 'ave chosen to sacrifice your life—to spill your blood to atone for the sins of your ancestors, so that those they have wronged may 'ave peace."

"I have."

"You 'ave not been coerced in any way to make this sacrifice."

"I have not. It is my choice." Stone tilted his head back, addressing the unseen presences in the room. "Although I have no hand in what was done to all of you, I deeply regret it. I beg that, by my sacrifice, I absolve my descendants of any responsibility for your fate. I ask your forgiveness, and seek both to send you at last to your rest and to wipe my family's slate clean from this moment forward."

Would they buy it? *Should* they buy it? Was he even doing the right thing, trying to deceive them like this?

No going back now.

"Then it shall be so," Eddie intoned. "Lie down, please."

Stone lowered himself down until he lay on his back atop the altar. It was ice cold against his skin, shooting a stronger, full-body shiver through him. Eddie and Ward had removed the manacles during their preparation, since it wouldn't be necessary to restrain him. He stared up at the ceiling, noting the tiny, previously hidden vent. It was a clever design, probably leading to a concealed passage that vented into one of the house's existing chimneys. Idly, he wondered how many other secrets this house hid within its walls, and whether he'd have the chance to try finding them.

"Are you prepared?" Eddie asked.

He studied the faces of his companions. Eddie and Ward looked solemn, Verity nervous but resolute, and Ian pale.

"I am."

"Verity, if you would be so kind…"

Verity stepped into the circle. Stone couldn't see her feet, but the way she moved made it obvious she was taking care not to obscure the lines. From her bag, she removed a small jar of black liquid and unscrewed the lid. She looked down at him, unsmiling and focused. "Are you sure?"

"Do it."

As Eddie, Ward, and Ian continued a soft chant, Verity dipped her finger into the jar and began tracing patterns on Stone's chest.

He felt his skin flutter beneath her finger, but fought to lie still as she went about her work. She met his gaze again as she traced the last of the pattern, finishing with a dot on the left side, just below his magical tattoo. Then she drew another pattern on his forehead, put the lid back on the jar, and set it aside. "He is prepared," she announced.

"Good," Eddie said. Once again he spread his arms wide, looking like a preacher giving a heartfelt sermon. "Prepare the sacrificial weapon with the ritual poison."

Verity drew the knife from her bag along with the little vial of elixir. With care, she held the blade up and tipped the vial, dripping a single drop on its tip. Stone watched her, noting the thick, viscous stuff didn't trickle down, but instead remained on the blade, coating it. She flipped the knife over and did the same thing on the other side. When she finished, the end of the black blade shone with the oily substance. She capped the vial and put it back in her bag.

"It is prepared."

"Good." Eddie lowered his hands, looking around the room. "Alastair Stone, this is your last chance to change your mind. For the final time: do you choose, of your own free will and without coercion or duress, to make this sacrifice, to spill your blood and give your life to clear the stain from your family's name?"

Stone swallowed. This was it. If he'd made the wrong choice, this was when he'd find out.

"I do so choose," he said firmly. He lay back on the table, tensing.

"Then let it be done," Eddie said, and nodded to Verity.

She raised the knife. Tears glimmered in the corners of her eyes, and her hand gripping the knife shook. "Let it be done," she repeated.

She brought her arm down, stabbing the knife into Stone's chest at the point where she'd made the dot.

Stone kept his eyes open, and it was one of the hardest things he'd ever done not to flinch away. The blade pierced his skin with a bright, stinging pain, but he barely noticed it along with the trickle of blood running down his side and pooling beneath him. What he *did* notice was another sensation—not pain, but rather a feeling of *diminishing,* as if a psychic whirlwind had gathered his soul and was pulling it free of his body. It was a profoundly disturbing feeling, its sense of wrongness far worse than the slight pain of the physical wound.

Suddenly, a deep sense of panic gripped him. *This was wrong. I never should have agreed to it. I've got to—*

Around him, the physical world began to fade. The faces of his companions swirled, their bodies becoming gray and indistinct. As his essence—his soul, if you believed that sort of thing—lifted free of his body, a dark, foggy haze engulfed him. He looked around for any sign of the echoes clustering near him, but saw nothing but the darkness.

Had something gone wrong?

Panic rising higher, he tried to reverse direction, to plunge his astral body back into his physical one. This had been a mistake. They'd have to try something else. He couldn't—

And then, a sudden wrenching.

Something gripped his essence and pulled, a strong, inexorable force yanking him free of his body. He struggled, flinging himself back and forth like a wild animal caught in a trap, but the grip didn't fade.

The last thing he consciously remembered before the dark fog enfolded him was deep laughter—the same laughter he'd heard at the end of the séance—and the feeling of something strong and determined brushing past him on its way toward his unmoving, unconscious body.

CHAPTER THIRTY-SEVEN

THE FOG DIDN'T CLEAR, not entirely. It still floated all around Stone, obscuring the view above him, below him, and off in the distance.

Nearer, though, the world settled into hazy focus.

He looked around, confused. Where was he? Where was this place? Why couldn't he return to his body?

Slowly, the haze drifted away, revealing a large room.

It wasn't a room, though—not in the physical sense. It was more correctly the abstract concept of "roomness"—walls, floor, ceiling all made of the suggestion of wood. On either side and in front of him rose several levels of tiered seating, each row behind its own waist-high panel. When he spun to look behind him, he saw they were there too. Surrounding him. The room, or whatever it was, did not appear to have an exit.

"Where am I?" he called. His voice didn't echo, but fell flat almost as it did when he tried to speak in the Overworld. *Was* he in the Overworld? The fog was similar, but he'd never seen anything like this when traversing the tunnels. "Is anyone here?"

Slowly, a series of figures swirled into view.

Like the wooden room, they weren't substantial. They flickered and twisted, almost as if they weren't fully there at all. They had no weight to them, no sense of physicality.

They did have faces, though.

Suddenly, with a certainty he didn't question, Stone knew exactly how many of them there were.

Forty-one.

If he'd had breath, it would have caught in his throat.

He looked down at himself. Unlike the other figures, he *did* look substantial. He was naked, his body traced with the hint of a silvery glow. A trickle of blood ran down his chest, and his magical tattoo glowed faintly in the dead air, but he no longer felt the chill of the ritual room, nor the slight pain of the stab wound.

All around the room, the figures were watching him. All of them wore the same expression: stern, cold, unyielding. Each was dressed in the suggestion of old-fashioned clothes, and even though Stone couldn't get a good look at any of them, he didn't need to. Even the vague, shifting hints gave him what he needed to know: some of the clothes were threadbare and ragged, while others were fine and well-tailored.

"*Deceiver,*" boomed a voice.

"No…" he whispered. He put his hands to his ears, but it didn't help. All around him, other voices repeated the word: *Deceiver.* It seemed to be coming not from the room, but inside his head.

This had not gone at all as he had expected.

Desperately, he tried to find the thin cord that would lead him back to his body. The elixir should have rendered it invisible to the echoes, but he should still be able to see it if he looked carefully. If he could follow it back to his body, he could—

"*Deceiver,*" the deep, unseen voice intoned again, and this time several more picked up the refrain as well.

Stone looked around, trying to pierce the strange, foggy room's walls. The others—Verity, Eddie, Ward, and Ian—were out there somewhere. If he could reach them, he could find his body even without the cord. Surely they must have realized something had gone wrong, and were even now working from their end to bring him back.

The indistinct figures were all glaring at him, their burning hatred beating at his astral body with as much force as if they had been throwing physical knives at him. Pain buffeted him, driving him to his knees.

"*Deceiver!*"

"*Murderer!*"

"*Betrayer!*"

"*He must pay!*"

"*No!*" Stone shouted. "No…" His body jerked and shuddered as the power of their hate continued to slam into him. He braced himself against it, trying to fight it with the power of his mind—the only power that mattered here.

It didn't work, and he knew why.

Because they were right.

He *had* sought to deceive them. Despite his precautions they'd caught on to his game, and now they wanted to punish him for it. He felt the ghostly trickles of more blood running down his body, but when he looked down at his chest he saw nothing save the original wound from Verity's knife.

"No…" he said again, struggling to rise. "Please. Listen to me. You're right—I did try to deceive you. But only because I had no other choice. I want to help you. I *tried* to help you. Please—just listen to me, I beg you. Let me help you."

He did his best to project genuine sincerity, apology, shame for what his family had done. In the astral realm, intent, emotion, and mental power were the only things that mattered. It was no surprise that his body was naked, mirroring the state of his mind. There were no lies, no deception, no places to hide.

Their cold gazes continued slamming into him, opening fresh but unseen wounds. Here, the expression "glaring daggers" took on literal meaning. "Please…" he begged. "Let me help you. Listen to me. Or—"

A sudden thought struck him.

He jerked his head up. "No. Don't listen to me. Let me listen to *you.*" He pulled himself up straighter, facing them without flinching. "Tell me your stories. Show me what you've endured. Help me remember you."

For a moment, he thought his words wouldn't do any good. Their hatred, steeping against his family for three hundred years in one of the most magically potent locations in the world, would be too strong for mere words to overcome—and if it turned out to be so, he didn't blame them. He couldn't. Unless his friends could figure out how to bring him home, he'd have to accept his fate. He'd known the risk existed when he tried this mad plan.

But…slowly, some of the slicing pain receded. Stone didn't look at their faces, but he sensed dissention in the echoes' formerly solid wall of hate. Now the voices murmured and whispered to each other rather than booming in his head. He couldn't make out their words, but he sensed discussion.

"You wish to see?" the male voice asked. It still sounded hard and cold, but it also carried disbelief.

Stone lifted his head again, realizing that, for the moment, at least, the blades piercing him had ceased. "Yes," he said. "I want to see. I've *got* to see. Please—show me. Let me share your pain."

More murmuring. Stone still sensed their hatred, their judgment, but it didn't seem quite as monolithic as before.

Then, so quickly he had no chance to prepare himself, to brace against the onslaught, images and sensations began to flood him. Although on some rational level he knew they came fast, bombarding him from all sides as each of the echoes struggled to make its own voice heard, for him it was as if time had slowed, giving him a front-row seat to each and every one of their stories.

He was a child, a starving, sickly orphan living on the streets of St. Giles, picking through scraps and begging for his next meal, dazzled by the well-dressed stranger offering to show him another world where he'd never want for anything again...

He was a woman, a prostitute, desperate to feed her three hungry children in any way she could. Perhaps the handsome, wealthy man might fancy her, so she could make her children's miserable lives a bit better...

He was a teenage boy, running from a tyrannical father, seeking only honest work so he could gather enough money to leave England. The promise of a job was a godsend, taking him far away from the man who sought to kill him...

He was a wealthy businessman, owner of a firm that imported exotic items from the Orient, facing ruin. The stranger who approached him about an alliance showed impressive cre-

R. L. KING

dentials. Perhaps there might be a way free of his crushing debt after all...

He was a workman, who made his living by the strength of his muscles and the sweat of his brow. Work was sparse lately, but after he heard of a grand mansion being constructed, he could barely believe his good fortune when he was chosen...

He was a traveler, a young man far from home, seeking only to see what the world had to offer...

He was a runaway child...

He was a barmaid from a disreputable tavern...

He was a skilled carpenter who was caught speaking against his employer...

He was a stonemason...

He was a tramp, living in squalor in an abandoned building in Liverpool...

Stone barely realized he was on his knees again, bent over with his hands pressed against a floor that looked like fog and felt like scarred wood. The images kept coming, crowding their way into his head until he was sure he couldn't endure any more of them.

And then, suddenly, they changed.

He was no longer any individual person. The faces flowed together like water—the child, the grizzled old man, the prostitute with her garish makeup, the powdered and privileged businessman all blended into a single entity, a single representation of all the people his family had destroyed.

And then he was in darkness.

As he watched with a terror he knew wasn't his, an unseen hand set a final brick into place, blocking the last of the faint light from the outside—his last lifeline to the world of the living. As the tiny hole disappeared, he heard a pair of voices, jovial and laughing, and then even those faded.

He tried to stand, but couldn't. His hands hung above his head, his wrists shackled in cold steel manacles, and when he tried to rise to his full height his head hit the ceiling before he got close. But when he attempted to sit, he realized the chains held him too high to do it. He could only kneel, barely, pressing his back against the wall. Already his body ached from the uncomfortable position, even though deep in his mind he knew the pain wasn't his own.

Time moved again, in a strange, folded way that was more a function of thought than actual chronological progression. Hunger crept in, making his belly rumble, then ache, then spike sharp pains. His mouth grew first dry, then parched as thirst increased. All around him, he heard the screams of his fellow prisoners, faint and muffled through the tiny chamber's stone walls, as they begged for someone— anyone—to release them from this horrific ordeal.

Begging to die.

He grew weak. Eventually, he no longer even had the strength to hold himself in a kneeling position, so he sagged in the manacles, no longer caring that they dug bloody furrows into his wrists and pulled his arms from their sockets.

The smell was terrible: sweat, and fear, and filth.

The air around him was getting bad. He couldn't draw a decent breath.

The screams from the other prisoners grew quieter and eventually stopped.

Was he alone? Was he the last one to die?

"No…" he whispered, bowing his head. "I'm sorry…I'm sorry…"

Around him, the fog rose and engulfed the scene.

CHAPTER THIRTY-EIGHT

FROM THE INSTANT she plunged the trick knife into Stone's chest, Verity regretted her decision to be part of this charade.

She yanked it backward, a thrill of cold dread fluttering up her spine as blood welled around the wound, meandering down to collect in a small pool beneath his side. With a spasmodic jerk, she flung the knife, its spring-loaded blade now back to its full length, aside. It clattered on the stone floor and rolled away.

"Now what?" she whispered.

"Now, we wait," Eddie said grimly. "It's all up to Stone now."

Verity looked down at Stone's face; his eyes were closed, and he didn't appear to be in pain. In fact, he showed no expression at all, his features slack as if he were not merely sleeping, but in a coma.

Or dead.

When she shifted to magical sight, she instantly saw that his normally blazing, purple-and-gold aura no longer surrounded him. Her own emerald green one was still there, as were Ian's silver and purple, Eddie's orange, and Ward's dark purple. But Stone's body was as inert as a rock, or a car, or

422 |

any other non-living object. The spark that had made him Alastair Stone was gone. For all intents and purposes, he was no longer alive.

"How long can he stay like that now?" Ian's characteristic self-assurance had deserted him; he sounded worried. "I can't see his aura. How can he still be alive?"

"The…potion has suspended most of his body's functions," Verity said. She spoke in dull tones, parroting the words Hezzie's strange teacher had told her when she'd delivered the little vial. "We've got…a few minutes before we need to worry. Ten, maybe. I wouldn't want to let it go much past that."

"What happens if it does?" Ian's gray eyes, shadowed with concern, shifted between his father lying on the altar and Verity. "Is there something we can do to get him back?"

She bowed her head. "No. His spirit is out there. He'll have to find his way back to his body on his own. I can't pull him back." She glanced at Eddie and Ward, hoping they might contradict her, providing some solution from their greater experience.

"That's right," Eddie said. He leaned forward, his palms flat against the altar's surface. "But don't worry, you two. Stone's strong, and 'e knows his stuff. If 'e can't convince those echoes to clear out, 'e'll follow the cord back to 'is body and try somethin' else. We just have to trust 'im."

None of them moved. Eddie, Ward, and Ian remained at their points on the circle, but Verity didn't return to hers, choosing instead to stay next to Stone. She put a hand on his shoulder, comforted that he still felt warm. More than anything—except for him to open his eyes and announce their ploy had succeeded—she wanted to heal the small wound she'd made on his chest. The bright red blood welling up against his pale skin served as a constant reminder that *she* had been the one to put him into this state. If he didn't wake up again, it would be her fault. But she couldn't even do that—not yet.

The time crawled by, and around the circle their impatience and concern grew. Ten minutes was usually a short period, passing by without notice dozens of times during a normal day, but now every second seemed to drag out to several times its length. Verity kept glancing at her watch, thinking surely two minutes had passed, or three, or five, only to discover it had been barely thirty seconds since the last time she'd looked.

Under her hand, Stone's shoulder grew colder. The warmth was still there—even if he were truly dead it wouldn't fade in such a short time—but the chilly altar beneath him was already bleeding out his body's heat. She wanted to throw herself across him, to take him in her arms and give him her own warmth. But once again, she didn't do that. All she could do was remain where she was, shifting her gaze between Stone's face, her friends, and her watch.

As they inevitably do, no matter how slowly, the minutes passed. Five. Seven. Nine.

Stone's body remained motionless, his expression still.

Verity's heart pounded harder, her shoulders tightening, a warm flush of dread forming in the pit of her stomach and creeping through her body. She leaned in closer, watching his face, pleading with God, or the universe, or whoever would listen for a faint twitch of his eyes behind his closed lids, a shift of his jaw, a shallow breath. Anything to show her he was still alive.

Nothing.

"It's been too long," she said, casting a desperate glance at Eddie and Ward. "He should be back by now."

"We have to do something," Ian pleaded. "Something's wrong. Can we—I don't know—slap him? Pinch him? Go after him somehow?"

Eddie shook his head. "Pain won't work. And going after 'im would require a ritual that would take longer than we 'ave."

"This isn't good," Ward said, "but it's not bad yet either. It hasn't even been ten minutes, and that's only a guideline anyway."

"But he's dying," Ian protested. "Look—he's not moving at all. He'll get brain damage if he doesn't come back soon."

"No, 'e won't," Eddie assured him. "It might look like 'is body's shut down, but it 'asn't. Not the way you understand. It's more like in one o' those science fiction stories where they ship people off on spaceships that take twenty years to reach their destination."

"Suspended animation," Ward said.

"But you said he can't stay that way too long."

"No." Eddie looked as concerned as the rest of them. "I'm not sayin' this is good. 'E *should* be back by now. But it's not—"

"Wait!" Verity yelled. "I think I saw him move!"

Immediately, everyone whirled, fixing their attention on Stone's still body.

For several more seconds nothing happened. He lay as quiet as before, his eyes closed, his chest unmoving, his hands flat against the altar's cold surface.

"Doc, come on," Verity pleaded, gripping his shoulder again. "You can do it…come on…Come back to us. You—"

Stone jerked, lurching under her hand and drawing a sharp, hitching breath.

"Doc!" She didn't even care that she was yelling.

Eddie, Ward, and Ian crowded around, taking hold of Stone as he struggled upright, coughing.

"It's all right, mate. We've got you." Eddie took his other shoulder, helping him to a sitting position.

Stone's face contorted in an expression that could have been pain, or merely discomfort from lying so long on the chilled surface. He hunched over, shivering, still coughing, his eyes still closed. His skin remained pale, beads of sweat standing out on his face and torso.

"Doc…Alastair…are you all right? Did you do it? Are they gone?" Unwilling to leave his side, Verity used magic to bring Stone's shirt and coat to her. "Here…put these on. You're freezing. But let me heal that wound first."

Stone raised his head, and at last opened his eyes. He blinked a few times, swallowed, and looked around as if he didn't recognize where he was. "What…?" he whispered.

"Here, hold him still so I can heal that," Verity ordered the others. The wound wasn't severe, and it took her only a few seconds to work. When she finished, no sign of it remained, except for the blood that had dried on his chest and side. "Doc, talk to us. Are you okay? Did you fool the echoes into thinking you were dead? Are they gone?"

"I—" He seemed to be having trouble locking in on their faces. He looked down at the shirt and coat Verity had offered him as if he'd never seen them before.

"Give 'im some space, you lot," Eddie said. "'E needs a bit of time to recover from that."

"Here, let me help you," Verity said, ignoring Eddie, trying to stuff one of Stone's arms through the T-shirt's sleeve. "You're freezing. You've got to warm up."

"Let's get him out of this place," Ian said. "If the echoes are gone, we don't need to be down here anymore. He needs a hot drink or something."

Stone didn't protest as Verity continued trying to dress him as if he were a small child, but he didn't help, either. It was a lot harder with a grown man than it would have been with a toddler. Finally, she managed to pull the shirt over his head. "I…can't…" he began.

"It's okay. It's okay," Verity assured him. "Whatever happened, it's over now. You're back. You're safe." She tried to encourage him to swing his legs around. "Can you stand? Let's get you out of here. We can get you something to eat, or a drink, or you can go to your room and sleep. It's up to you. Just tell us what you want."

"Are the echoes gone, mate?" Eddie asked. "Did our trick work?"

Stone didn't reply, but Ian looked around the room. "They must be. He's back, and they're not attacking us. They must have gone for it."

"Thank the gods for that, anyway," Ward said.

"Can you tell us anything?" Verity asked Stone. "Doc, talk to us." As Eddie and Ward held him up, she tried slipping his arms into his coat. She didn't like the way he was still shivering, but even more disturbing was his continued disorientation. That shouldn't have lasted. The elixir should have done its job and its power dissipated, so it shouldn't be affecting him any longer. He looked as if he had no idea where he was or what he was doing there.

"I...feel ill," he said. His voice sounded odd—slower and deeper than his normal tones.

"Not surprised," Eddie said. "Let's get you back upstairs, and—"

Stone's wandering gaze fell on Eddie first, then Ward, then finally settled on Verity. "Yes..." he said slowly. "I...wish to be alone. To...sleep. Let us...go."

From behind them, Ian frowned. "He's acting strange. Is that normal after something like this?"

Verity took Stone's hand. In truth, she was concerned as well. Hezzie's teacher had said nothing about ongoing confusion. In fact, she'd assured Verity that the mixture would do its job and leave his system quickly.

A thought struck her, almost as if it weren't her own: *Look at his aura.*

Surreptitiously she shifted to magical sight, hoping she might spot some obvious strangeness in Stone's aura that would give her a clue about what was going on and how to fix it.

It took all of her willpower not to gasp.

Stone's normal, brilliant violet-and-gold aura was gone—but not as it had been before, when he'd been unconscious.

Instead, it had been replaced. Where the purple and gold had been before, a nimbus of darker purple, so dark it was almost black, surrounded his body. It flickered at its edges, shooting tiny disturbances upward and away. It almost looked like an otherworldly flame had taken him over.

Forcing herself to remain calm, she let go of Stone's hand and dropped back behind him. "I'll—catch up," she said. "I just have to pick up a couple things we left behind."

Eddie shot her a questioning look.

She jerked her head toward Stone, then shook it.

It took him a second to catch on, but then he shifted to magical sight as well. His eyes widened. He exchanged glances with Verity again, an unspoken communication passing between them.

As they both moved up to take places at Stone's side, though, Ian suddenly stopped. "Guys—something's wrong with Dad's aura," he said, frowning. "He—"

Before any of them could react, Stone whirled around. He barely looked like their friend anymore. His eyes burned with an unfamiliar madness, his face set into a grinning rictus.

He swept his hands out, flinging all four of them backward and slamming them into the walls.

CHAPTER THIRTY-NINE

STONE LAY ON THE FLOOR of the wooden chamber, drawn up into a fetal ball, his arms wrapped around his knees. Slowly, realizing he was no longer manacled, he opened his eyes and lifted his head.

He was back in the wooden room again.

Shaking, he pulled himself first to a seated position, then upright. He feared he might be too weak to do it, but the weakness from his imprisonment—*their* imprisonment—had faded, along with the hunger, the thirst, and the pain. He looked around.

He was still surrounded by the tiered levels full of faces. They all leaned forward, their hands gripping the dividers, watching him. Their gazes were as hard as ever, their eyes ad flinty and unyielding—but something had changed.

It took him a moment to realize what it was, but when he did, a faint hope fluttered in his chest.

While the figures certainly didn't look at all friendly or welcoming, some of the hatred was gone. The daggers no longer pierced his skin.

He dropped back to his knees, sweeping his gaze across as many of them as he could see without turning around. "I'm sorry," he said, and was surprised his voice sounded strong, with just a hint of a shake. "I'm so sorry. I see it now—I see what they did to you. If I could change it, I would. You've got to believe me."

A rumble of murmuring voices again, and then a gravelly male voice spoke alone: "*Someone must pay.*"

"I know…I know…" He looked around, trying to spot the speaker among the implacable faces, but he couldn't. "But killing me won't bring you back. It won't erase your pain, or what you suffered. Don't you see that? It's not just that I don't want to die—of course I don't. No one does. But it won't do any good even if I do. Look at me—look in my mind, or my heart, or wherever you look—and tell me you believe I would have done any of those things to you."

He stood again, spreading his arms wide, dropping his defenses, opening himself to their judgment both physically and mentally. "If you *do* believe it, then do what you must. I won't object. I won't fight you. If that's what it takes to make this right, then I'll do it. But make sure it *will*—that you're not just letting yourself succumb to your desire for vengeance. That makes you no better than they were, you know."

He braced himself, fully expecting more knives to pierce his unprotected skin and mind.

If that was what it took, then so be it.

Nothing happened.

He raised his head again, hesitantly.

The figures were still there, still watching him, but they hadn't moved.

"*Someone must pay,*" the voice said again. But this time the tone was subtly different—not accusatory, but merely stating a fact.

"Who must pay?" Stone looked around, still trying to spot the speaker so he could address him directly. Still, he had no success. The faces around him remained as still as statues. "If not me, then who? Not my son. He shares even less guilt in all of this than I do."

"*We must be remembered*," said another voice—a woman this time.

"*There must be payment*," said a different man.

Stone bowed his head. "I can't remember you—not all of you. I wish I could. Look at me and tell me you don't believe I wish I could. It's been too long. I've got the records, but they're incomplete. I'll do the best I can, I promise, but I won't be able to commemorate all of you. And I can't bury you as I'd intended because Brathwaite destroyed your remains."

"*Foul magic*," a man intoned.

"*The work of Satan*," a woman said.

"*He must be punished, for what he has done to us.*"

"Yes—I agree with you that it's foul magic. I want to punish him. But I can't. He's gone. We destroyed him—sent him on."

"*No.*" This time, several voices spoke at once, from all around him.

"No?" What did they mean? Stone looked around again. "I don't understand."

"*He has not passed on. He remains.*"

"He...remains? You mean Brathwaite? He's still here?"

"*He remains.*"

"But we destroyed his body."

"*He destroyed* our *bodies.*"

Even in spirit form, a chill passed through Stone as he caught on to their implication.

Oh, bloody hell, no…

They were right. Brathwaite had destroyed the sacrifices' remains—not directly, perhaps, but he might as well have by directing them to a place where the light of sunrise would turn them to dust.

And yet the echoes still lingered, as potent as ever.

Mundane echoes hadn't been scattered by destroying their physical bodies.

James Brathwaite hadn't been a mundane. In life, he had been a powerful and resourceful mage—one with access to long-forgotten, forbidden techniques.

No…

"You're saying…he's still here?"

"*He is here. He is close,*" said a man.

"*Very close to you.*" The last voice was a child's, and had a hint of a giggle.

And in a sudden flash, Stone got it.

All at once, a single thought rose and submerged everything else: at that moment, the echoes, the crimes committed against them, the hazy room no longer mattered to him.

He had left his body unprotected.

Vacant.

When Verity's elixir had cast his spirit into the astral realm, his physical form remained on the material plane, an empty shell. He hadn't thought anything of it at the time, since even if mundane echoes could possess mages' bodies, the protective circle would have prevented them from doing so.

But if destroying Brathwaite's body *hadn't* sent his spirit on—

The echoes watched him, expressionless, as he cast about for the silvery cord that connected his spirit to his physical body. "I've got to go back," he told them, and heard the desperate edge to his voice. "Please—I'll return. We'll work this out, I promise. But now I've got to go."

He didn't wait for their answer. As soon as he identified the cord, faint and barely visible against the shifting fog, he took hold of it, gripping it in his fists like the lifeline it was. "We'll talk again!" he called to them, and tightened his grip as he prepared to follow the cord back to his body. It should be a simple matter of merging the two together, at which point he would awaken.

For a moment, his astral body flowed along the cord just as he'd expected it to. The hazy fog began to lift, and he caught a distorted glimpse of the circular room, the altar in the center of the circle, and the brighter glows of his friends' auras. The cord snaked down and disappeared into his still, prone form lying atop the altar.

Just another moment—

His astral form slammed hard into his body…

…and stopped, bouncing off as surely as if he had attempted to run into a solid wall. In his reeling mind, he heard mocking laughter.

Staggering backward, he nearly fell over. He looked wildly around him.

The echoes were back. The wooden-walled room with its tiered platforms was back. But this time, they seemed even less substantial than before. Voices swirled around each other, around his head.

"Punish the foul one for what he has done to us…"

"Remember us…"

"Aid those who come after…"

"Will you do these things, son of Stone? Will you give your word?"

Stone had no idea at this point if he could ever even get back to his body, but that didn't matter. "Yes. Yes," he called. "I will. I'll do my best, I promise you. I'm sorry."

Around him, the room grew hazier.

One by one, the faces, their gazes still locked on him as he stood surrounded by them, began to fade.

The men, the women, the children—the innocent souls his family had committed a monstrous act against—shimmered from view. Some went quickly, others more slowly, but they all went. Stone stood where he was, turning slowly in place, watching the astral fog swallow them. Shaking, he clenched his fists and bowed his head as a profound sense of completeness settled over him. He felt as if all around him, something was being cleansed.

At last, only one remained: large eyes regarded him out of the streaked, dirty face of a child. *"Don't let us be forgotten…"* it whispered, and then it, too was, gone, leaving Stone standing alone and naked in a foggy chamber devoid of any substance.

"I won't…" he growled. "I promise—I won't."

But before he could keep that promise, he'd have to kick James Brathwaite's squatting arse out of his body.

And that wasn't going to be easy.

CHAPTER FORTY

"SUCH POWER!" Stone said with an unwholesome smile, backing up, a shield shimmering around him. "Ah, yes. This will do nicely. Fitting, too."

He surveyed the fallen figures around them as they struggled to rise. "It's unfortunate that you saw through my ruse so quickly, but no matter. It changes nothing. If you are wise, you will remain where you are and make no attempt to impede my exit." The voice was Stone's, but yet it wasn't. Everything about it that made it uniquely Stone—his accent, his manner of speech, his cadence—had changed. While the accent was still British, the tones were deeper, more precise, and far colder.

"What the hell—?" Ian demanded, scrambling to his feet. "Dad—?"

"That's not your dad, Ian," Verity said grimly.

"What?"

"Oh, bloody hell," Eddie said. He was slower to rise, and bent to give Ward a hand up. "No."

"What's going on?" Ian's gaze shifted between his friends and Stone, his confusion obvious.

Instead of Ian, Eddie addressed Stone. "James Brathwaite, I presume?"

"*What?*" Verity didn't know where to look. Like Ian, she shifted between Eddie and Ward, who stood next to each other with similar expressions of shock, and Stone, who looked smug and possibly mad behind his glowing shield. "Eddie, what—"

"He played us," Eddie said. He didn't move forward, but his whole body tensed as if he was preparing to. "The bastard played us for bloody *fools.*"

"Brathwaite? I thought he was gone."

Stone chuckled. "Not gone, woman. Merely concealed. Waiting. I am nothing if not patient. When I heard Stone's foolish plan to placate those pathetic wretches, I saw my chance."

"Your chance for what?" Ian looked as if he was ready to attack Stone, but he held back for the moment.

"To take over your father's body," Ward said, glaring at Stone. "With his spirit absent, his body became an empty vessel."

"What?" Ian's voice rose with his anger. "And you let him *do* it, knowing that could happen?"

"We *didn't* know," Eddie said. "Mundane auras can't possess mages' bodies. Remember, we thought we'd sent Brathwaite on when we burned 'is body."

Stone chuckled. "Thank you for that as well, fools. You thought you had rid yourself of me, but in truth all you did was exactly as I had hoped—you released my spirit from its confinement to this accursed house." He took a step backward toward the exit, his steady, mad gaze never leaving the four of them. "And now, I will take my leave of you. In gratitude for the opportunity you have given me, I won't kill you where you stand—*if* you make no attempt to follow me."

"That's not happening," Ian said. "You're not taking off with my father's body. Get the hell out of it *now.*"

"He's right," Verity said, raising her hands to summon crackling lighting around them. "You're not going anywhere."

Stone laughed. "So you intend to destroy Stone's body, then? Even if you succeed in driving me out—no simple feat, I must add—his lost spirit will have no vessel to return to."

"Oh, God…" She realized he was right. It would take strong magic to punch through his shield—strong enough that they could risk doing serious injury to Stone if they managed it. Was Brathwaite somehow making use of Stone's own magic, or channeling his own through his borrowed body? "Eddie—Arthur—what do we do?"

"Yes, what do you do?" Stone's voice was mocking now, a singsong parody of Verity's. His gaze fell on her, crawling up and down her body in an uncomfortably lascivious way. "I must say, Stone is a lucky man, to have such a fine, nubile young wench at his command. Perhaps I should remain here for a while and sample a taste of your charms as well. It has been far too long since I've experienced the pleasures of the flesh." His expression turned contemptuous. "Though I know not why he allows you to go about in such unseemly garments."

"*Wench?*" Verity's entire body clenched, and lightning flickered around her hands.

"*Allows?*"

"Verity—" Eddie warned. "Don't."

"This guy's an asshole, Eddie, and he's not getting away with Doc's body."

"Listen to the man, wench," Stone advised. "The lot of you together could scarce touch me. You would be wise to slink back into your holes and let me depart without issue."

"We can't let him go!" Ian said. "If he gets away we might never find him. And what will happen to Dad's spirit if it doesn't have a body to return to?"

"It will die," Ward said grimly. "Spirits of the living can't remain in the astral realm forever. If he can't return soon, the anchoring cord will fade, and his spirit will linger there until it dissipates."

Stone smiled. "Indeed it will—and a good riddance to the accursed spawn of my betrayers."

Verity got a sudden, desperate idea. The man seemed to like the sound of his own voice, and obviously didn't doubt his own ability to deal with them if they attacked him— perhaps if they kept him talking, Eddie and Ward would have time to come up with something.

"What do you mean, your betrayers?" she asked. "Is that what happened? Did you have something planned with Doc's ancestors, and they betrayed you?"

Stone had been backing toward the door, but at her words he stopped. "Indeed they did, wench."

"Is it because they wouldn't agree to your plan to use necromancy?"

His eyes widened in surprise. "Truly, perhaps there is more to you than a mere foolish woman. How do you know of these things?"

Eddie caught on to Verity's plan. "We found your journals. Stone's ancestors were tryin' to deal with somethin' powerful and dangerous, and you thought you had the answer."

"I *did* have the answer!" The madness bloomed in Stone's eyes again, and the others flinched back. "My companions—I *thought* they were my companions—were weak. They made as if to follow my suggestion, but at the last moment they turned on me like the curs I should have known them to be."

"How did they do that?" Ward asked.

"They incapacitated me as I worked my preparations!" Stone began stalking back and forth, but he neither moved away from the door, dropped his shield, nor took his gaze off the others. "They conspired together, Cyrus and his damnable fellows, to take advantage of me when I was at the most vulnerable stage of my ritual."

"And they sacrificed you to gain your power," Eddie said. "They rejected your dark ways for their own, which were almost as dark."

Stone snorted. "They were not virtuous men, as much as they might have liked the dull-witted masses to believe they were. My methods, at least, did not require murder. The dead are dead—their souls have moved on to their rest. I merely sought to use the strength of their bodies to contain the fiend long enough to seal it away."

"Who was this 'fiend'?" Verity asked. "We found the sealed chamber—is that where he is? Who is 'A'?"

"Ah, yes." He chuckled, but it wasn't a pleasant sound. "After all they have done, their efforts ultimately proved for nought. The fiend is loose in the world again, and if you should encounter him, you might wish I had given you a clean death here."

"But who *is* 'e?" Eddie asked. "Is 'e a monster? A man? A powerful mage?"

Stone's chuckle rose to a cackling laugh. "You are all such fools, and know so little. Is he a monster? Most certainly. A man? He plays at being a man, but I know better. He is a foul creature, best consigned to the pits of Hell."

Verity glanced at Eddie, but she could see from his face that he hadn't come up with anything, and neither had Ward. "Where will you go if you leave here?"

A slow, unpleasant smile spread across Stone's face, making him nearly unrecognizable as their friend. "You know, wench, you do make a good point." He spread his hands. "I have a fine, new body now—far more hale and strong and fair than my old carcass—and with it, a new face." He raised his hand, first rubbing it over Stone's jaw, then pointing toward the ceiling. "Perhaps I cannot return to my own home, but this one will suit me nicely, I think. The only flaw in my plan is that all of you remain to reveal my duplicity. Let us see if I might remedy that."

Perhaps because she knew Stone so intimately, Verity saw the slight change in his expression first. "Down!" she yelled.

She barely got the word out before Stone whipped both hands around and unleashed a sheet of pure magical energy at her and the others.

CHAPTER FORTY-ONE

STONE HAD NEVER FELT so truly, profoundly alone.

No sign of the echoes, the room, or the partition remained. He stood in the center of the hazy space, surrounded by the indistinct shapes of the circular ritual room, the altar in its center, and the glowing remains of the circle.

Do not *panic,* he ordered himself. *If you lose your mind, you'll never get back.*

If he tried hard, focusing with all his effort, he could barely make out the glowing figures of his friends. They were still in the ritual room, staring down at his unmoving body, their auras alight with unease and concern.

They don't know.

How could *they know? They think Brathwaite's gone. How would they suspect?*

He tried again to follow the cord back to his body, mustering all the strength he could manage, but it did no good. Unlike his friends, James Brathwaite knew exactly what was going on, and he had no intention of relinquishing his freshly-gained new body to its original owner.

Hell, he'd probably planned this all along. He probably remained quiet to let us believe we'd sent him on, waiting for an opportunity just like this one.

Damn you, Brathwaite—you're not *getting my body!*

He pounded again and again, but he might as well have been a small child battering a brick wall. As long as Brathwaite was in there, as long as he was focused on shutting Stone out, there was little he could do.

Like Brathwaite himself, he'd have to wait until the current occupant was distracted, then make another attempt. But unless Brathwaite deserted his body—highly unlikely—it would be much more difficult even then.

He stepped back, forcing himself to think. He couldn't simply flail away like a madman—that would only deplete his strength, and strength wasn't infinite here, even for a spirit as powerful as his. Brathwaite had somehow figured out how to access magical power even as a spirit, but Stone had no idea how he'd done it. Given time he might, but he didn't have that.

He did have one thing working in his favor: a body maintained a natural affinity for its own spirit, even when the two were separated. Just as a physical body or even a construct wanted to remain in its own dimensional space, a living spirit retained a connection to its body. That was why even mundanes were difficult to possess, except by powerful spirits, and why mages were nearly impossible.

The only exception, and the reason Stone couldn't help feeling foolish even though he knew he had no cause to, was if the mage's spirit vacated the body voluntarily. Doing that created an empty vessel, and magic, just like nature, abhorred a vacuum. That was the reason mages almost always cast elaborate protective rituals when traveling the astral realms, and why most of them didn't even have the courage to do it. Stone had taken a dangerous chance, but not a foolhardy one:

normally, the protections around the house and the more minimal ones from the simple circle would have kept out any opportunistic spirits. But Brathwaite's presence complicated things.

Stone growled, the sound echoing around the chamber. He did have that one thing in his favor—but he also had something equally potent working against him.

Time.

It was another reason why astral travel wasn't common among mages: the spirit wasn't meant to leave the body for lengthy periods. Normally, the separation of the spirit from its body only occurred at the time of death, and while mages and other mystics had long ago figured out how to perform the technique, none of them had ever discovered a way to prevent the silvery cord connecting the two from steadily degrading. How much time passed before it severed and stranded the mage's spirit in the astral realm varied from mage to mage based on a combination of innate magical strength and willpower, but even the most powerful mages couldn't remain separated from their bodies for more than a few hours.

Even staying away that long usually resulted in exhaustion upon returning, and if the spirit tarried in the astral realm long enough for the cord to fade completely, the connection severed and the spirit was left to roam, untethered, until it finally dissipated. No one knew where most such spirits ended up—whether they passed on to whatever afterlife awaited them, became one with the Universe, or merely faded away. Some of them (like Brathwaite, apparently) figured out a way to continue existing on the astral, but that was exceedingly rare.

Meanwhile, the body left behind, if not occupied by an-other spirit almost immediately after the cord severed, would simply slip into a coma and die. Spirits couldn't occupy dead bodies—or at least that was the prevailing belief in magical circles. Brathwaite and his necromancy might cast doubt on that.

Stone glanced down at the cord leading to his own body. He could see it more clearly now that the fog had dissipat-ed—that must mean the elixir's power had likewise faded. It remained strong now, but that was no cause for celebration: another spirit already occupying his body would increase the cord's degradation rate. Eventually, the vessel would accept the new occupant as the rightful one—and that wouldn't take long.

Gods damn you, Brathwaite, you—

His body on the altar moved.

Bloody hell, he's waking up.

He watched in increased consternation as his body sat up. His friends immediately clustered around him, Verity taking him in her arms and pulling him close. Their auras lit up with relief.

No, Verity—don't touch him! Leave her alone, you bastard.

He tried to bull his way in again, but Brathwaite was still on guard. He wondered if the slow, unwholesome smile spreading across his features was due to Brathwaite's proxim-ity to Verity or his knowledge that his body's original owner was trying to repossess his property.

Damn.

Why don't they realize it's not me? Can't they tell?

He tried a different approach. Instead of trying to fight his way back to his body, he focused all his energy on trying to reach his friends. Verity and Ian were particularly sensitive to astral energy, as indicated by their skill at aura reading. *Look at my aura, you two! Can't you see it's different?*

They would figure it out in time—of course they would, as soon as they looked at his aura. But would it be too late? Already, the cord had faded noticeably since he'd looked last, and the more it faded, the less he'd be able to affect the physical world.

Verity! Ian! Look at him!

Brathwaite was speaking now, feigning illness, providing little assistance as Verity attempted to help him into his T-shirt and coat. As Stone continued trying to project his thoughts to her, to figure out a way to affect the physical world, she encouraged Brathwaite in his body to sit up.

Verity! I'm here! That's not me! Please, you've got to see before it's too late. Look at his aura!

He struggled to get a clearer view, to make out her expression.

Finally, after what seemed like an eternity, she tensed, settling her gaze on "Stone." Her aura flared in shock as finally she used magical sight and saw the truth.

Yes! Now get away from him. Don't let him know you've seen! If she caught on, if she could incapacitate him before he realized she knew what was happening, Stone would have an easier time shoving him out and reclaiming his body. *Just be careful...*

But then alarm flared around Ian's aura too, and he spoke.

No, no, no...

R. L. KING

"Stone's" head jerked up. He whirled around, making a sweeping gesture that sent all four of the others reeling backward into the walls.

No! Don't let him leave. You can't let him leave—

He couldn't hear his friends' words—they came through to him as muddy, indistinct tones—but he couldn't miss their agitation. They struggled back to their feet, shouting at Brathwaite. He spoke back to them, calmly, confidently, backing toward the door.

Don't let him go!

But then, Verity said something and he stopped. After a moment, he replied, and seemed to be settling in for a brief conversation before departing.

Yes, that's it. Keep him talking. Keep him here.

Once more, he renewed his efforts to force his way back into his body while his friends kept the spirit distracted, but once again the effort proved futile. Brathwaite obviously had some serious power to command, though Stone still had no idea where it was coming from. Had he been patiently planning, preparing all those years when he'd been trapped in the underground catacombs? Had his spirit gone mad down there, or had he been mad all along? Stone didn't know, and right now he didn't care. All that mattered was figuring out a way to kick Brathwaite out before it was too late.

Keep him talking, Verity...

And then, with sudden swiftness, something changed. Brathwaite's pulsing aura flared, going from calm to rage in an instant. As Stone watched, unable to do anything but look on in shocked horror, he spun and unleashed a brutal magical attack at the others.

CHAPTER FORTY-TWO

VERITY'S WARNING might have saved all their lives, but it didn't fully protect them.

She yelped in terror and pain as Brathwaite's sheet of magical energy blew her backward along with the others. This time, the blow slammed her into the altar and tumbled her over it, where she came to a rolling stop halfway across the room. Her shield had borne most of the brunt of the attack, but her head reeled with psychic feedback as she struggled to get it back up.

"Don't let him get away!" she yelled, though it came out more like a loud croak. She scrambled up, taking cover behind the altar, and looked around.

Eddie lay against the far wall in an unmoving heap.

Ward had apparently hit back-first and slid down; he now slumped in a seated position, blinking in confusion.

Ian was already up, his shield flaring bright and strong around him. He waved a hand and the heavy wooden door slammed shut. "Verity! I'll hold the door! Do something!"

Verity didn't know what to do. She darted her gaze around the room, trying to find something, anything, to hit him with. She knew her own magical attack wasn't strong enough to pierce Brathwaite's shield, and even if it was, she

R. L. KING

was terrified of doing serious injury to Stone's body. Attacking him at all filled her with fear and uncertainty—how could she throw spells at a man she loved more than almost anyone else in the world? She'd have to do something indirect, but—

Brathwaite stood sideways, keeping most of his attention on the room while trying to yank the door open. So far, Ian's magical grip was holding.

"Verity!" Ian yelled. "I can't do this forever!"

Ward staggered up, his dark complexion gray with fatigue. He pointed both hands at Brathwaite and loosed a concussion beam, driving Stone's body back against the wall near the door.

The shield absorbed it all, and Brathwaite laughed. "Is that all you've got? Pathetic! This will take little effort, then!"

He pointed one hand at Ward and threw him backward. The researcher hit the wall with a crushing *thunk* and slid down again. A second later, one of the standing lamps went out, bathing that side of the room in shadows. The cord snaked around Ward's neck and began to constrict.

"No!" Eddie screamed, pulling himself up. "Arthur!" He launched himself across the room in a kind of staggering leap and fell to his knees next to Ward, clawing at the tightening cord.

"Verity!" Ian cried. The heavy wooden door was rattling in its frame. His cry changed to a shriek of pain as green flames erupted upward within his shield. His barrier vanished and he stumbled backward, dropping to his knees.

Verity's thoughts tumbled and spun. She had to do something, but what? If she didn't do something soon, Brathwaite would kill all of them and take over Stone's identity. Nobody would know the difference—and if anyone found out, he'd kill them too. But she had no weapons, no way to attack Brathwaite directly, and even if she did, she couldn't risk killing Stone's body. She couldn't—

But wait!

She *did* have a weapon!

Her gaze fell on the tiny, dark form of the trick knife she'd flung into the wall after she'd used it on Stone. If she could get it without Brathwaite noticing—

But it was no weapon. Even if she stabbed him with it, it would only sink in about half an inch—hardly far enough to do sufficient damage to take him down, even if she sliced him with it.

She spotted her bag, which lay next to her behind the altar where she'd dropped it at the beginning of the ritual.

And then she remembered what was inside.

On the other side of the room, Ian had gotten his shield back up and was once again attempting to hold the door shut. His body shook and his face shone with sweat; it was obvious he wouldn't last long at it as Brathwaite's spells continued to buffet him.

She spun around, still on her knees behind the altar, and met Eddie's gaze. The librarian had succeeded in pulling the constricting cord from a sputtering Ward's neck, and both were dragging themselves up. She caught Eddie's eye and, under cover of the altar, pointed at Brathwaite. Then she spread her fingers in a dramatic "explosion" gesture.

Eddie was either humoring her or he got it, because he nodded instantly and muttered something to Ward. The next second, both of them aimed showy blasts at Brathwaite, then ducked forward to take cover behind the end of the altar.

As Verity hoped, their diversion worked, drawing Brathwaite's attention—and his ire. He moved away from the door, circling around the altar toward them.

Verity, moving fast, raised a hand toward the wall. The knife streaked into her grasp, and she quickly fumbled in her bag for the tiny vial of elixir. Around the altar, she heard Eddie and Ward scrambling to the other side, trying to keep it between them and Brathwaite.

Ian flung another blast at Brathwaite and then dived away, barely avoiding an answering volley of flame that scorched both the wall and the door.

Verity's fingers fumbled as she struggled to open the vial. It slipped from her hands and fell to the floor, but fortunately it was made of strong stuff and the liquid was viscous enough that it didn't spill. Moving fast, she snatched it and shook it over the knife blade. There was no time to be careful.

Under cover of the yells and blasts of the spells flying around, she poked her head around the altar. "Hit him all at once," she breathed, talking fast. "Take that shield down." She raised the knife to show them what she intended.

The altar exploded in a hail of flying shrapnel, flinging Verity, Eddie, and Ward in three different directions.

Ian yelled an inarticulate curse and dived toward Brathwaite, throwing double-barreled blasts from both hands.

Verity rolled to her feet, thanking the gods she'd managed to hang on to the knife. "Now, guys!" she cried. "Do it!" She hoped the altar's explosion hadn't taken them out—they weren't combatants, after all. If they were out of the fight, it was over.

They weren't out of the fight. With twin yells like a pair of football players surging down the field, they both pointed their hands at Brathwaite's shield and let fly with pure magical energy.

Verity leaped up, keeping the knife hidden, and ran forward. She'd only get one chance at this, and if she failed they were all dead.

Doc, I hope you're out there...

Brathwaite screamed, as much in shock as in pain, as their combined onslaught slammed into his shield, turning it first pink, then red. It lit up with color, so bright Verity had to flinch away from it, but she kept going. She couldn't stop now.

The shield winked out, and Stone's body staggered backward, his hand going to his head as the psychic feedback hit him.

Now!

Verity sprang forward, gripping the knife with all her strength, aiming for Stone's center mass. *You can't hurt him with this,* she told herself, hoping desperately she was right.

Until the last second, she thought it was going to work. She barreled into him, throwing her arm around him to hold him close as she drove the knife downward. Brathwaite was still disoriented. All she'd have to do was—

"No, wench!" he screamed, his burning gaze turning back on her. He gestured and she felt her grip wrenched free of him so hard it send spikes of pain searing through her shoulder, and then she was flying. The last thing she saw before she hit the wall and blacked out was the knife clattering to the floor, still shining with the oily elixir, and Stone's familiar-but-not-familiar face lit with a mad, enraged grin.

CHAPTER FORTY-THREE

I T WAS GETTING EASIER to watch them now, as all around the room their auras flared with their emotions.

Stone's own body was the easiest of all for him to track, so he stayed close to it. There wasn't anything he could do to stop Brathwaite from attacking his friends—not from here—but he watched with pride as Verity, Eddie, and Ward recovered from the magical blast and scrambled behind cover, while Ian rushed to block the door with magic so Brathwaite couldn't escape.

They made quite a team—even Eddie and Ward, who fancied themselves "boffins" and avoided combat whenever possible. He'd always known they could step up when they needed to. He'd have a great time ribbing them about it at the Dragon later—if he made it back.

But none of that would matter if they couldn't take Brathwaite down. They didn't have time on their side—he didn't know how much power the necromancer could call upon, or more precisely how much of *his* power the man could access. Because mage echoes were so rare, little literature was available in the magical world covering what happened when one possessed another mage's body following an astral jaunt. Stone didn't think Brathwaite could access the Calanarian energy, which meant he'd have to be drawing on his own black-magic abilities, but clearly those were formidable on their own. The X-factor was Stone's body and how much power it could add. Was a skilled mage occupying a highly trained body the magical equivalent of an expert driver piloting a Ferrari, or was it all Brathwaite?

The light on the far side went out, and the cord attacked Ward, snaking around his neck.

No! Get away from him! For the first time, it occurred to Stone that Brathwaite might kill one of them—or all of them. Clearly, the man had given up the idea of trying to escape and changed his focus to getting rid of them. It made sense: he couldn't leave witnesses behind if he planned to usurp Stone's identity.

The others were up to something—he could see it in their auras now. Eddie had helped extricate Ward from the constricting cord, while Ian continued struggling to keep the door shut. Where was Verity?

He spotted her green aura a moment later, crouched behind the altar with it between her and Brathwaite. She held up her hand as if summoning something to her, then appeared to be fumbling with something else on the floor. It was hard for him to tell what it was—everything that wasn't alive or magically active appeared as hazy gray forms in the astral realm.

She pulled something free and then hunched over whatever she held in her hand, her aura showing her deep concentration as magic flew all around her.

What was she doing? There wasn't anything in her bag that would help her with this—

—or was there?

He smiled as he caught on to what she was up to.

Oh, Verity, you're good. You're very good.

He focused hard on sending her his encouragement, his approval, and then moved back to Brathwaite. He still couldn't interfere with the man directly, but if Verity's wild plan was to have any chance to succeed, he'd have to be ready. He'd only get a single shot at it.

Brathwaite pointed his hand, and the altar exploded.

All around Stone came the pained shouts of his friends. *Oh, gods, no, did he—*

—but no, Verity was still there, scrambling back to her feet—and in her hand she still held something that now glowed with faint but powerful magical energy.

She yelled something, and then Eddie, Ward, and Ian all focused magical blasts at Brathwaite.

As his shield flared and he was forced to divert more power to keeping it up, Verity launched herself across the room toward him, concealing the knife behind her body.

Stone moved in closer, until he was next to Brathwaite, separated only by the shield.

Be ready...move fast...only one shot...

The shield flashed bright and died, sending Brathwaite reeling backward into the wall, psychic feedback wracking him.

Now, Verity!

She reached him, still moving fast, and raised the knife.

So close—only inches away! Her aura flared with bright determination as she arced the tiny blade toward his now-unprotected body—

—and then yelped as he caught her movement at the last second, shrieking something and waving his hand.

Screaming, she flew away from him and slammed into the wall, dropping to lay unmoving on the floor. Her aura dimmed. The knife fell away, its point still glowing.

NO!

Stone's rage grew until he thought his astral body would explode trying to contain it. He acted without conscious thought, all rational considerations driven away by the bright-red haze of boiling hatred at Brathwaite.

If he *had* thought about it, he probably wouldn't have thought what he did next to be possible.

But he didn't think.

With Brathwaite still distracted by the others' continued onslaught and Verity's failed attack, Stone moved fast.

Get out of my body, you bastard!

This time when he attempted to enter his body, he encountered resistance—but this time it wasn't a solid wall.

This time, it felt as if he were trying to push himself through a barrier of wet concrete. Resistance, yes—but not total blockage. His astral form pressed into his physical body slowly, so slowly—but it did press in. It did move forward.

The effort required was immense. Time slowed for him as he barely made progress—but it *was* progress.

It was the rage. He knew it. That was what was giving him the strength to do this. He couldn't let it fade, or he was lost.

He forced himself to picture Verity's prone form, not knowing if she lived or died. He pictured Brathwaite's leering expression, and thought about what the man might try to do to Verity if he didn't stop this madness. He didn't think he had any more rage, but there it was, bubbling up from some deep wellspring he didn't even know he possessed. It encompassed not only what had happened here, now, but all his pent-up hatred of his horrific ancestors the atrocities they'd committed upon countless innocent people, all in service to their hunger for more power.

At that moment, James Brathwaite became the face of all that hatred.

Stone kept pushing, head down, his astral strength driving him forward. He would push forever if he had to. He couldn't give up now.

He couldn't.

He—

Suddenly, the wet-concrete sensation gave way. He staggered forward into a bright red haze of shifting lights and disorienting sensations—but at the center of all of it, he saw an even brighter core, glowing with as much rage and determination as he knew his own was.

Almost as much.

Like a mad dog that had finally spotted its quarry, he leaped forward, reaching out to wrap his hands around the core.

Get. OUT!

He heard his voice, a crazed scream in his mind, as he clawed at the bright core. It came apart in his hands, flying to pieces, darting around with mad confusion. It tried to flow around him, its desperation growing, but he gathered his energy and forced outward. It felt like trying to fight a swarm of bees.

Stone knew he couldn't keep this up forever. Even rage fades to exhaustion eventually, and if he let his die, Brathwaite's spirit would kick him back out and he'd be lost. He gathered his energy and his rage and his frustration into one last blast, and lashed out with it, detonating it like a bomb. At that point, he didn't care if it destroyed his own body along with Brathwaite's essence. If he couldn't have his body back, Brathwaite wasn't going to have it either—one way or another.

Brathwaite's scream rose. He tried to resist, but even his powerful spirit couldn't fight back against Stone's determination.

But then the scream turned to a high, mad, triumphant laugh. Brathwaite raised his arms and shrieked something to the skies—

—and then he was gone.

Stone's spirit slammed into place, his head and body suddenly lighting up with a pain and exhaustion he hadn't felt when Brathwaite's spirit was in charge.

He staggered backward as all around him sounds battered him. He struggled to make sense of them: screams, yells…

Rumbling?

A last surge of adrenaline lit him up as finally the crazy sensory inputs came together and made sense.

A head-sized chunk of the ceiling tore loose and crashed to the floor, barely three feet away from him. The rumbling from above grew louder. It sounded like he stood at ground zero in a tunnel with an onrushing train bearing down on him.

Across the room, Ian was shouting, running toward the fallen Verity.

More pieces of ceiling fell, and one of the stone support columns began to crack.

Oh, bloody hell, he's brought the whole place down!

| CHAPTER FORTY-FOUR

D ESPITE HIS EXHAUSTION, pain, and disorientation, Stone acted instantly.

"It's coming down!" he screamed. "Get out, all of you! Now!"

He was closer to Verity, so he reached her before Ian did. He bent and snatched her up, his pounding adrenaline running so strong he barely noticed her weight. Then he spun, taking in the rest of the room.

Eddie and Ward stood on the far side, across from the door, looking stunned. Ian was nearer the exit. Between them, another support column began to tremble. More chunks fell from the ceiling, clattering and crashing, breaking the stone floor into a mosaic of cracks.

"Go!" Stone yelled again, and this time he was joined by Ian. He exchanged a quick, desperate glance with his son, and an unspoken communication passed between them. As one, they reached out with magical power.

Stone grabbed Eddie, who was closer to him, and Ian grabbed Ward. Together, they yanked the two men across the room just as another section of the ceiling came down and obliterated the space where they had stood. Ian flung the door open.

More chunks landed behind them. The ceiling was buckling now, its center section dropping noticeably.

"Go! Go! Go!" Ian shoved Ward out through the door into the hallway, and Stone did the same with Eddie. He tightened his grip on Verity and followed them, slamming the door shut behind them. It was an absurd gesture, he knew, but he did it anyway. Behind the door, more crashes—louder now. The whole place was rumbling.

Dear gods—has he brought down the whole house?

By the time they reached the other end of the tunnel and burst through the opening into the initial antechamber, Eddie and Ward had recovered their wits enough to move under their own power.

"Stone?" Eddie panted. He was breathing hard, with streaks of drying blood running down his forehead and streaking his jacket. "Is that you, mate?"

"It's me. I'm back. We've got to get out of here. Now."

Another rumble, followed by a massive crash and an earthquake tremor, punctuated his words.

"Bloody hell!" Ward yelled. "What did he *do*?"

Stone didn't answer.

Already, Ian had levitated up through the floor. "Send Verity up," he called.

Stone did, as the thundering roar around them grew even louder. Ian grabbed her and pulled her backward. As soon as she was clear, he shoved Eddie and Ward. "Get up there! Now!"

They didn't waste time. Both of them shot upward through the floor, disappearing over the edge out of the range of Stone's light spell.

"Dad!" Ian's face appeared at the edge. "Come on!"

A chunk of rock the size of a refrigerator landed behind Stone, nearly knocking him off his feet. As he staggered, he felt a strong telekinetic grip grab him, and then he was lifting off.

As soon as his feet hit the floor outside the hole, he cast a quick glance around the room. So far it seemed to be standing, but the rumbling was almost as strong here. The floor rattled beneath him. "Come on—we've got to get outside."

He bent to pick up Verity, but she was already stirring. "What—?" she said, confused, blinking and raising a hand to rub her forehead.

"Got to go." Stone hauled her up and dragged her toward the room's exit. "Brathwaite's brought the place down around our ears."

"What?" She didn't protest further, but allowed herself to be shepherded along with Stone on one side and Ian on the other. Ahead of them, Eddie and Ward left the room and headed down the hall.

Once again, Stone slammed the door shut behind them, and once again, more rumbles sounded. *Not the whole house,* he begged. *Not after all this...*

A few moments later they reached the nearest exit door. They poured outside and dashed out onto the grounds, not slowing until they'd put fifty feet between themselves and the building.

Stone skidded to a stop first, whirling to look back.

Even from here, in the dark and the light rain, he could see the far end of the east wing still shaking and rumbling, as if a tiny earthquake had gripped it. As he and the others continued to watch, panting and aghast, the structure began to sink. Pieces fell off, crashing all around. Windows shattered with loud pops. A section of the roof caved in and smashed down into the house.

Stone didn't even blink. He stood, still and shocked, watching part of his ancestral home crumble and collapse. He barely felt Verity's warm hand slip into his and grip tight.

"Bloody 'ell," Eddie breathed when it seemed to be over.

Stone could only nod. He didn't trust himself to speak yet.

It hadn't taken the whole house, at least—not even close. He supposed that was something to be grateful about. They were alive. Aubrey was safe, and the garage with his flat was untouched. Most of the house—even most of the east wing—still stood.

Not the best possible outcome, but certainly not the worst.

"Well…" he said, contemplatively, ignoring the rain pattering down and soaking his hair as he continued to survey the ruin. "I've been saying for years that I wanted to have the east wing renovated. I suppose I haven't got a choice now, do I?"

Verity's arm snaked around him, and she rested her head against his shoulder. "Way to look on the bright side, Doc. I'm proud of you."

| CHAPTER FORTY-FIVE

One week later

T HE CROWD AT THE DANCING DRAGON was brisk, but Stone's group had no trouble commandeering a large table in the back room. All it had taken was a quick call to Gus, the proprietor, to secure a *Reserved* sign waiting for them when they arrived. Stone supposed there were some advantages to three of their number having been loyal customers for over twenty years.

They hadn't all seen each other since the night of "the recent unpleasantness," as Stone referred to it. After they'd all gotten their fill of staring at the house and its crumbling east wing, they'd filed around to the front long enough to verify that Stone and Ian could once again enter the place without objection from the flock of vengeful echoes. Nobody had asked him questions—they could all see he was in no mood to answer them, and the answers could wait.

When they took stock, they discovered that despite being tossed around by Brathwaite's powerful magic, none of them had sustained serious injuries. Verity healed what she could, but it was obvious she was tired too. Then, after they all shared a drink in the great room, they trooped off to the portal to the London house, where they went their separate ways—Eddie and Ward to their homes, and Verity and Ian up to their rooms—after promising to meet up again when everyone was feeling better.

Stone studied them as they came in tonight. Ian was already there, relaxed after a couple of pints. Eddie and Ward arrived soon after, Ward in his usual professorial tweeds and Eddie in a West Ham home shirt. They had Poppy Willoughby with them, lighting the place up with her electric-blue moto jacket and matching Mohawk. All three of them looked relaxed and completely over their recent ordeals.

"Hey, Stone," Eddie called. "You're lookin' a bit less like death warmed over. You manage to get some kip, or did the ghosts turn up again?" He pulled out Poppy's chair for her and then settled in across the table. Ward took the spot on Poppy's other side.

"No ghosts. It's been quiet."

"Aubrey come home?"

"I rang him a few days ago and he turned up right away. I think he was waiting to hear from me."

"And—?"

"He was…a bit taken aback," Stone admitted.

"Bloody gobsmacked, in other words," Eddie said in a chuckling aside to Ward, who gave a sage nod.

"Well, yes, that too." Stone glanced past them to spot Verity and Jason coming in. She'd gone back to California a couple hours ago to collect her brother and bring him through the portal so he could join the celebration.

Eddie waited until Verity and Jason were seated and had drinks and appetizers before speaking again. "So—" he said, more seriously, "any sign of you-know-who?"

Stone chuckled. "He's not bloody Voldemort, Eddie. You can say his name."

"You've got no sense of whimsy, mate. But it's a real question. Any sign of 'im?"

"No." He stared down into his drink, remembering how close Brathwaite had come to killing Verity—and him. "I don't remember the events clearly, there at the end, but I do remember I was seriously furious when I went after him. I think I might have ripped him to shreds."

"Well, good riddance if you did." Eddie raised his glass. Everyone else did likewise, clinking them together. "So what're you gonna do now?"

Stone shrugged. "Get my house back in order, I suppose. There's still a lot of cleanup to be done, not even taking the east wing project into account. Aubrey's already on that part—he's rung a few contractors for quotes. I trust him to handle that end of it. I'll just write the checks."

"Those will likely be some big checks," Ward said. "I'm glad I'm not in your shoes, Stone."

"Ain't all beer an' skittles, bein' lord o' the manor, is it?" Eddie said haughtily, but he couldn't hold the expression and his face split in a cheeky grin.

Verity looked troubled. "Are you sure you're not going to run into problems with that, Doc?"

"What kind of problems?" Stone asked.

"Well...the whole underground catacomb complex got buried when that part of the house came down, right?"

"Unfortunately, yes. It's a good thing most of the complex extended out past the walls, or we'd be looking at a lot worse damage."

"But…what if they find something while they're digging?"

"Find what?" Stone caught a passing server's attention and motioned for another round of appetizers.

"She's right," Jason said. "What if they find part of the circle, or those alcoves, or the secret room?"

"What if they do? It's one thing that worked in our favor, I suppose—the fact that the skeletons left the catacombs and took most of their manacles with them, I mean. The worst the workmen might find are a few bits of wall or floor with some sigils carved on them. But remember, they're on private property, and I'm under no obligation to share anything with the world. And besides, with what I expect to be paying them, they'd damned well better keep their curiosity to themselves and their noses out of my affairs."

He'd gone back earlier in the week with Ian to look the place over in daylight, and it hadn't been quite as bad as he'd feared. The collapse of the underground chamber had left a sunken area in the cleared land east of the house, but only the end section of the house itself had crumbled, leaving a gaping open hole. Stone had put up some supplemental emergency wards to ensure nobody could gain entry without permission, but aside from that it would be a simple—well, relatively simple, anyway—matter of reconstructing that end of the house. It would take time, sure, but it wasn't insurmountable. Between himself, Ian, and Aubrey, they'd already made decent inroads into clearing out the scattered glass and other damage inside the main house. It had taken Stone quite some time before he stopped looking over his shoulder, expecting to get beaned by a falling timber or run through with an antique sword.

He looked at his drink again, then at Ward and Eddie. "Any progress on tracking down the people in the journal?"

"Not yet, mate." Eddie looked apologetic. "We've been workin' on it in our spare time, but with the Caventhorne opening in less than a month we've been 'avin' to make up a lot o' lost time."

"Don't worry," Ward added. "I'm confident we can track at least some information about most of the entries."

Stone nodded without looking up. He still didn't know how he'd keep the promise he'd made to the echoes, but he'd figure something out. It had been less than a week—even a bunch of vengeful echoes couldn't expect him to work miracles in that short a period. If nothing else, he supposed he could always sell the coins, jewelry, and artifacts they'd found in the strongbox and create a fund, supplemented by a significant amount of money from his personal accounts, to aid any descendants of the sacrifice victims he could track down. He felt a bit guilty about it—the items truly belonged in a museum—but trying to explain where they'd come from and what they were doing in his possession would be more problematic than he cared to take on. At least this way the families would be taken care of. Once he had as many names as Ward and Eddie could get him, then he'd work on the "remember us" part.

"Anyway," he said, raising his head to study his group of friends around the table, "I want you all to know how much I appreciate your help. I couldn't have done it without you—without all of you. I know I'm rubbish at asking for help—"

"No, really?" Eddie drawled. "Never knew that."

"Sod off. I am, and it's one of those things I suppose I should work on. This has gone a long way to convincing me of that. I just...want to thank you all."

He raised his glass, and once again they all clinked.

"Hey," Ian said, "I just found out my dad is some kind of British bigwig who lives in a house the size of a museum. No way I'm letting anything get in the way of that."

Verity laughed. "You'll realize pretty soon that it's not as fun as it sounds. Especially when he won't run the heat in the middle of winter."

"*Et tu,* apprentice?" Stone drained his pint and stood. "Speaking of heat, I'll be back—it's bloody stuffy in here. Just need a bit of air."

He left the group chattering away happily, nodding to Gus on his way out, and moved a bit down the street to put some distance between himself and the crowd of smokers loitering just outside the door. The cool bite of the evening air was a welcome change from the Dragon's close, beer-scented ambiance.

"You okay?"

He turned to see Verity drifting up to him, her hands jammed in the pockets of her leather jacket. "Ah. Yes. That wasn't code for anything—I literally did need some air." He didn't mind that she'd followed him, though. He never minded.

She chuckled. "Want some company? Eddie's already started telling football stories, and I'm afraid he might be turning Jason into a fan."

"I'm surprised he waited this long. And of course. I always enjoy your company."

She stood next to him, pressing her shoulder into his, and stared out over the traffic and pedestrians meandering by. Together, they remained silent for several minutes, each content to merely be where they were.

"Do you think he's really gone?" she asked suddenly.

"What?"

"Brathwaite. Do you think he's really gone?"

He thought about it. He hadn't been lying before: he truly *didn't* remember much detail from the end of his struggle to boot Brathwaite out of his body, but he did remember feeling the kind of fury that led to madness if allowed to rage unchecked. He certainly could have ripped the other mage's spirit to shreds without a second thought, and not regretted it in the slightest.

"I...don't know," he said at last. "I think so. I'm fairly sure I took care of him—either destroyed him or sent him on."

"But you don't know for sure?"

Again, he pondered. "I suppose I don't. But if he *is* still knocking about in the astral realm, I hope he knows having another go at me or my friends won't be a wise choice. If he's got any sense, he'll go about his business far away from us."

"Yeah...I hope so." She put her arm around him, sticking her hand in his coat pocket. "We should go back, though, if for no other reason than to rescue Jason from Eddie's stories. And then later tonight, I'll take Jason back home, check on Raider, and...come back, if you want me to."

He pulled her close, still watching the traffic, thinking about all the things he could have lost if he hadn't managed to get rid of Brathwaite. What she was promising was definitely at the top of the list. "I absolutely want you to. I was hoping you'd suggest that. Come on. You're right—inflicting Eddie's football stories on Jason has got to constitute cruel and unusual punishment."

| EPILOGUE ONE

Three weeks later

"**A**ND IN CLOSING, before I set you all loose to explore what we've put together here—and visit the bar, if you're so inclined—I'd like to extend a special thanks to three men without whom this whole mad plan wouldn't have come together. I'm sure William Desmond would have been proud of what they've accomplished. Ladies and gentlemen: Mr. Eddie Monkton and Mr. Arthur Ward, who've taken charge of the magical end of the Caventhorne project, and Mr. Theodore Kerrick, who's continuing his stewardship of the house itself and the day-to-day operations here. Gentlemen, please come up and take a well-deserved bow."

Stone stood at the raised podium that had been constructed in Caventhorne's great room, surveying the crowd gathered around. He'd kept his speech short; these people weren't here to listen to him bang on, and he could see from their anticipatory auras that they were eager to explore the newly opened rooms and displays.

Eddie, Ward, and Kerrick mounted the steps to stand next to Stone amid a swell of applause. Their eyes shone with pride; they obviously appreciated the recognition, though all three of them looked as if they'd prefer it to be a bit less public. Like the rest of those in attendance, they were dressed in formal evening wear—Eddie fidgeted as if he'd prefer to tear off his jacket and tie and toss them in a corner somewhere, while Ward appeared calmly comfortable. Kerrick, as always, projected quiet dignity, with just a hint of decorous merriment twinkling in his eyes.

"Take a bow, gentlemen," Stone said. "You've earned it."

All three of them did so, making quick bows as once again the applause rose. Then Eddie strode over and threw an effusive arm around Stone's shoulders. "And let's not forget this bloke right 'ere," he announced. "'E's had a lot to be gettin' on with over this last year, but e's been devoted to makin' Mr. Desmond's wishes into a reality. Let's 'ear it for Alastair Stone."

"Eddie…" Stone growled, as the crowd began clapping and cheering again.

"Sauce for the goose, mate," Eddie said with a grin.

"Thank you," Stone called to the group. "But this night is for you. Please—enjoy yourselves. Look around, see what the place has to offer. Starting next week, Caventhorne's facilities will be available to the magical community for research, study, and group meetings. Please contact Kerrick for scheduling. Thank you all for coming."

He hurried off the podium before Eddie could get any other ideas.

Verity met him at the foot of the steps. "Nice speech." She leaned in closer and lowered her voice. "And *damn,* you look hot in that tux. You know I've got plans for you later tonight, right?"

"I was hoping you might." He gave her a sly side-eye. "Just make sure you *wait* until later tonight, please."

"Damn. I was gonna rip your clothes off and ravish you on top of the grand piano."

"Well…I suppose it would give the old gaffers something to gossip about. But perhaps a bit of decorum might be in order." He looked her up and down, admiring her elegant gown of black silk. "You look stunning as always. I've been so busy with all the preparations I didn't get a chance to get a proper look at you. I don't think I've seen you in that one before."

"It's new. I went shopping with Poppy a couple days ago. She knows all the good shops in London, and she was pretty eager to spend some of that money you gave her."

"Brilliant." He steered her toward the bar, where he picked up a drink. "Well, that's it for my official duties tonight, aside from answering questions. Let's enjoy the party. I think we've earned it, don't you?"

"Oh, definitely."

Stone looked around at the crowd. He recognized many of them, at least by sight. Walter Yarborough stood by a window, drink in hand, gut straining the buttons of his old-fashioned tuxedo, and massive mustache waggling as he tried to chat up an attractive woman who was making a game effort to be polite. His young apprentice, as usual, lounged by the bar attempting to do the same thing with even less success. Lavinia Bromley perched on the edge of a brocaded sofa, deep in conversation with a small group of middle-aged women. On the far side of the room, Ian, resplendent and elegant in his designer evening clothes, leaned in close to a handsome young man with dark auburn hair.

"I'm glad he decided to come," Verity said, following Stone's gaze.

"So am I."

"Are you hoping it might mean he's ready to settle down and start studying?"

"Oh, I doubt that will happen yet. He's already talking about a trip to India with some of his mates next month." He shrugged and sipped his drink. "He'll do it when he's ready. There's no point in my trying to hurry him along." He took Verity's arm and deftly steered her away from the bar when he noticed Yarborough's lecherous apprentice taking an interest in her. "Too bad Jason decided to give this a pass, though."

"Yeah, well…he said he wouldn't be comfortable as the only mundane in the middle of a bunch of mages. I get it." She grinned. "Besides, I'm pretty sure he has a date. So there's that."

Stone nodded. "That's him keeping his priorities straight, then. Good for him."

For the first time in quite a while, he felt content. The renovation of Caventhorne had been more than a year in the making, taking far longer than any of them had expected, but now everything seemed to be coming together. The soft chamber music and gourmet refreshments aside, this place would soon be a venue for serious study, and hopefully a magnet for magical practitioners from all over the world. Even tonight, he'd already spotted guests dressed in the formal styles of Japan, Africa, and the Middle East. They'd extended invitations far and wide, and even if, as expected, the majority of the guests were from the UK, Europe, and the United States, there were enough representing other parts of the world to prove gratifying. William Desmond's influence obviously had considerable reach.

He and Verity circulated through the crowd for the next half-hour, chatting with various individuals and small groups. Normally Stone hated small talk, but with the more gregarious Verity on his arm, he soon found himself enjoying the feeling of not being responsible for anything. He let her lead the way, introducing her to those he knew and conversing amiably with those he didn't.

Eventually, after they'd made the rounds of the great room, she excused herself to refresh her makeup. "Go ahead," she said, smiling and giving him a little push. "I know you want to go talk shop with Eddie and Arthur. I'll just mingle around on my own and get to know people, or go see what Ian's up to. It's all good."

He took her up on her offer, but only part of it. In truth, though he did want to chat with Eddie and Ward, he didn't want to do it right now. There was somewhere he wanted to be, and he wanted to do it alone.

Glancing around to make sure nobody was paying attention to him, he drifted down a hallway past a few open rooms containing shelves of books, conference tables, whiteboards, and other amenities. At the end of the hall was a closed door. He opened it, slipped inside, and flipped a switch. Dim, soothing light bathed the space from multiple sconces along the walls.

This room was not ready for public consumption yet, but Stone nonetheless felt drawn to it. It wasn't surprising, since its inclusion had been his idea.

He stepped forward, his footsteps making no sound on the plush carpeting, until he stood in front of a small display:

a pair of shining glass cases on either side of a large rectangular block of highly polished black marble.

Sipping his drink and swallowing hard, he started at the leftmost glass case, gazing at the few items inside, arranged on black velvet: a jewel-hilted dagger in an ornate scabbard, a collection of gold coins, and an intricate cameo with the face of a beautiful, unknown woman.

In the opposite case, more items were similarly arranged: several gold rings with colorful gemstones, and two golden necklaces with jeweled pendants. All of them glimmered under the cases' subtly hidden light.

Stone bowed his head, suddenly feeling a heavy weight settling on his shoulders. His sense of contentment from before vanished, but that was fine. That was why he was here, after all. This wasn't meant to be a place of contentment.

He moved to the marble block, which had been carved so its top face was at an angle facing the viewer, and studied the names inscribed there.

Some of the spaces were still blank. When the project was finished, the surface would include forty-one names, but right now scarcely half of them had been finished. Stone extended a silent hand and laid it flat against the surface. "We'll find you," he said softly. "I'll see that you're remembered. I promise."

He wasn't sure how long he'd been standing there before he sensed another presence in the room.

He spun, and it took a lot of willpower not to raise his magical shield as he did it. He hadn't locked the door, so it wasn't entirely impossible that one of the guests had wandered in here by accident.

But he hadn't heard the door open.

A man stood just inside, watching him with a calm, serene expression.

"Er—may I help you with something?"

"Thank you, no." The man's voice was deep, melodic, and had the faintest hint of an unidentifiable, vaguely British accent.

Stone took a step toward the man, studying him in the dim light. Tall, slim, and broad-shouldered, he appeared to be in his middle to late forties, exuding the easy confidence of a man in the prime of his life. He had medium-brown hair with a hint of silver at the temples, a handsome face with high cheekbones, heavy brows, and a thin, patrician nose, and dark, glittering eyes. He too wore an exquisitely tailored tuxedo as if he were well-accustomed to it. He appeared to be examining Stone with an equal level of interest.

"I'm sorry, but this part of the house isn't open to the public yet," Stone said. "Could I direct you somewhere else?"

"No. Thank you. Forgive me for intruding, but I wished to speak with you in private."

Stone narrowed his eyes, shifting to magical sight. At first, he thought the stranger had a dual-toned aura—deep red close to his body with a brilliant gold around the edge—but as he looked more carefully he spotted a third color, a narrow band of pulsing purple. He tensed, realizing that, aside from this other man, no one else knew where he was. The house was so heavily shielded and warded that it would be difficult to track him even if someone missed him. And the man stood between him and the door.

"You...wished to speak with me? Why? I don't believe we've ever met, Mr.—"

"Dunstan. Edmund Dunstan. And no, I am certain we have not met." Dunstan took another step forward. He still looked relaxed, perhaps even a trifle amused at Stone's discomfort. He didn't offer his hand.

Stone didn't, either. He searched his mind for the name, trying to recall where he might have heard of Edmund Dunstan. If the man's aura was any indication, he was likely a powerful mage—but then again, Stone had been seeing more tri-colored auras than ever before since he'd returned from Calanar. Perhaps they were more common than he'd been led to believe.

"I'm afraid you have me at a disadvantage, Mr. Dunstan. Did you receive an invitation to our event tonight? I don't remember seeing your name on the guest list."

Dunstan offered a thin-lipped smile. "No. I hope you will excuse my intrusion nonetheless. This is an impressive place you have here. I would like to have met your Mr. Desmond."

Hmm. So Dunstan wasn't an old friend or colleague of Desmond's. That would have been Stone's first guess. Despite the fact that the man still looked relatively young, you couldn't always tell a mage's age from his or her physical appearance. He could be older than he looked.

"Indeed," he said, glancing past Dunstan to the door. "What did you wish to talk about? I haven't got a lot of time at the moment, but—"

"Oh, I assure you, I won't take much of your time, Dr. Stone. In truth, I mostly wanted to meet you. I've heard a great deal about you, and I wanted to see for myself how much of it was true."

"You've heard about me? Where?"

Dunstan shrugged. "Ah, here and there. It wasn't difficult to discover." He offered another thin smile that didn't reach his eyes. "I am not surprised you have heard little of me. I've been…away for quite some time."

"Away?" Stone tensed, his mind immediately going to James Brathwaite. Had the necromancer survived and sought out another body to steal? But that seemed unlikely—Verity had told him that when Braithwaite's spirit had possessed his own body, his normal aura had changed to a dark purple. Even if she hadn't spotted a third color, she couldn't have missed a second, nor could she have mistaken this man's clear, deep red for purple.

"Yes. I have been…sequestered for many years, out of communication with the world as a whole."

"I see." Stone glanced at the door again. Something about this man was making him uncomfortable, but he couldn't identify what it was. Oddly, too, something about him seemed eerily familiar, as if they might have met at some point.

He didn't have time for this at the moment, though. His friends would miss him if he didn't show up soon, and likely someone would come looking for him. "Well," he said at last, "it was a pleasure to meet you, Mr. Dunstan. I'm afraid I must ask you to excuse me now, but perhaps we can talk some other time. I'm not difficult to reach."

It was an obvious hint, but Dunstan either didn't pick it up or, more likely, ignored it. "Indeed," he said unhurriedly. "I would like that very much. I have some…propositions I would like to share with you. I think you might discover you and I have…a few things in common."

"You're very cryptic, Mr. Dunstan. That's all right, though—as I said, I haven't got time for a discussion right now. But I do hope you'll reveal more of these propositions at some later date." Once again, he moved toward the door.

This time, Dunstan stepped aside and allowed Stone to open it. He made a courtly little bow. "Of course. I will look forward to it." Before stepping through and out into the hall, Dunstan glanced back toward the memorial. "I applaud your efforts to memorialize those who were forgotten, and I hope the renovations to your home don't prove too arduous."

Stone froze. "How did you know about that?"

Dunstan raised an eyebrow. "I know many things, Dr. Stone." He exited the room and closed the door behind him. "Good evening."

Stone stared at the closed door in confusion. Who *was* this man? How did he know so much about him? Stone prided himself on knowing most of the Western world's powerful mages, by reputation if not personally. He'd never heard of Edmund Dunstan; it was as if the man had appeared spontaneously in the world from somewhere else.

Maybe he did, said his little interior voice.

Without giving himself time to ponder, he flung open the door and hurried out into the hall, intending to catch Dunstan before he lost himself in the crowd or left the party. He half expected the man to have vanished completely, with no sign of his passage remaining.

But no, Dunstan was still there.

He had stopped and now stood, facing away from Stone, only a short distance away. His stiff, tense posture shared nothing with his previous confident grace.

For a moment, Stone couldn't see what might have caused the change. Then he looked past Dunstan, farther down the hall toward the great room.

Another figure stood there.

A familiar figure: Tall, dark-haired, powerfully built, clad in meticulous but old-fashioned black evening clothes.

Stefan?

Stone stopped where he was, his gaze shifting between the two. He couldn't see Dunstan's face, but Stefan Kolinsky's looked every bit as tense, his dark eyes locked on the new-comer. Stone could easily picture Dunstan's attention similarly focused.

Kolinsky appeared not to have noticed anything else around him, so firmly was he fixed on Dunstan. Stone had never seen such a cold expression on his old friend's face. It wasn't rage, or even anger, but yet it gave the impression of both.

"Er—" Stone began, stepping forward. He wasn't sure he should have. He got the strong sense that if he strayed into the space between these two men, he might be vaporized where he stood.

Instead, he drew up next to Dunstan and tried, as any good host, to defuse the situation. "Stefan, what a pleasure. I had no idea you were coming tonight. I was sure you'd want to arrange a private visit later on." They had, of course, sent Kolinsky an invitation to the opening gala, but never in a thousand years did Stone think the reclusive, antisocial black mage would accept it.

Kolinsky's gaze flicked to Stone for a fraction of a second, then it was locked back on Dunstan again. "Alastair."

Stone looked between them again. Now that he was closer, he could see he was right: Dunstan was regarding Kolinsky with the same cold, leashed tension.

"Er—" he began again. "Do you two know each other?"

Neither replied to him. Instead, they continued sizing each other up. Despite their unmoving stances, Stone wouldn't have been at all surprised if the two of them leaped at each other like a pair of predators in a contested territory.

They didn't do that, though. They continued to hold each other's gazes for several more seconds, and then Dunstan's shoulders relaxed and he smiled. "Such a surprise. One never knows whom one might encounter unexpectedly." He bowed to Kolinsky—unlike the one he'd made to Stone, this one was clearly mocking—and swept past him.

"Good night, Dr. Stone. I will be in touch." And then he was gone, around the corner that led to the great room.

Kolinsky did not turn to watch him go, but neither did he relax his tense posture. His attention remained fixed down the hall, on the spot where Dunstan had stood.

Stone took a deep breath. Part of him wanted to follow Dunstan to see where he'd gone, but another part was grateful the man had departed and hoped he'd leave Caventhorne completely. Finally, he approached Kolinsky. "Stefan? Are you all right?"

The black mage blinked, and then his intense, obsidian-chip gaze settled on Stone. "Good evening, Alastair."

"It's—er—good to see you. I didn't expect you'd come, but I'm glad you're here. May I interest you in a drink? I can't give you a personal tour tonight, but I'm sure we can…" He let it trail off, suddenly uncomfortable as he recalled he hadn't seen Kolinsky since the night the black mage came to his home. He'd thought about visiting the shop a few times in the weeks since then, but always found excuses not to.

"No. Thank you. I won't be staying long tonight."

Stone looked past him again, toward where Dunstan had disappeared, and went for it. "Stefan—what the *hell* was that about? Do you know him?"

Kolinsky didn't look at him, nor did he answer.

"Stefan? Do you know Edmund Dunstan?"

"Is that what he is calling himself?" The black mage's eyebrow rose. "Amusing."

"That's not his real name, then." Stone narrowed his eyes, his own annoyance growing. Few things wound him up faster than knowing there was a puzzle out there, but the people who knew the answers to it were willfully keeping them from him.

"No. That is not his real name."

"So—who is he? Where did he come from? How do you know him?" He let out a loud sigh. "I haven't got time for this tonight, Stefan, but you've got to tell me. I'm sure we can work out some sort of understanding—assuming he's not got some connection to…the other bit you refuse to tell me anything else about."

Kolinsky pondered that. "Not directly, no." He glanced at the door Stone had just exited. "What do you know of him? How did you encounter him? I heard him say he would 'be in touch.' Have you entered into some sort of agreement with him?"

Stone gave a bitter chuckle. "I know bugger-all about him, and that doesn't make me happy. He just…turned up while I was alone in that room, looking at one of the displays that's not ready for public viewing yet. How do *you* know him?"

"I knew him…a long time ago. I have not seen him in many years. I thought perhaps he had died."

"A long time ago." Stone shook his head in frustration. "Stefan, with you that could mean anything from ten years to a hundred—or more. I know you've got your little secrets, but I'm not in the mood for it tonight. I've got things I need to do. But if there's something about this Dunstan I should know—especially if he's potentially dangerous—please tell me. After what I've been through recently, I've had my fill of enemies from the past popping up."

"Indeed?"

There it was—old Stefan's curiosity was every bit as strong as Stone's own, and he wasn't much better at hiding it. "Yes. It's a long story, and not one I fancy relating right now. But if you tell me about Dunstan, I promise I will later, and I'm sure you'll consider it worth your time."

Kolinsky studied the door to the memorial room, deep in thought. At last, he sighed. "Let me…think about it. I must do a bit of research first."

"*This* again?" Stone growled. "Stefan—"

Kolinsky held up a hand. "No, Alastair. It is not the same thing. Not…precisely, though the two are tangentially related. I merely want to ensure that what I tell you is true and correct, rather than relying on my speculation. I will tell you two things now, though, free of obligation."

"Yes?"

"First, Dunstan is perhaps closer to you than you might expect, and you should keep that in mind that if you wish to seek more information about him on your own. Consider, especially, how he has chosen to identify himself to you."

"What the hell does *that* mean?"

"Second," Kolinsky continued as if he hadn't spoken, "it sounds as if he might wish to enter into some sort of arrangement with you. I strongly advise against doing so, should he propose such a thing."

Stone swallowed, trying to drive down his growing frustration. "I can see why you aren't charging me anything for those, Stefan. Could you *get* any more bloody vague?"

"Forgive me. It is the best I can offer at the moment. His appearance caught me off my guard, which as you know is not an easy thing to do." His posture relaxed more, and he inclined his head. "I think for now it is best for me to go. I trust your offer of a private tour is still available at some later date?"

"Er—yes, of course. Just—get in touch with me and we'll work something out. But Stefan—"

"Excellent. Thank you. Good night, Alastair. And congratulations on your endeavor here. I predict it will prove to be a success."

Before Stone could reply, he turned and headed back up the hall toward the great room.

This time, Stone didn't hurry after him. He paused a moment, thoughts in turmoil, and then strode in the same direction. When he rounded the corner, he was not at all surprised to see no sign of Kolinsky—or of Dunstan, but he hadn't expected that either.

Eddie spotted him from across the room and hurried over. "Where've you been, mate? Been lookin' all over for you. I've got a couple of folks all the way from Nigeria who want to meet you."

"Er…Yes, of course. Eddie…"

"Yeah?" The librarian frowned. "You okay?"

"I'm…not sure. Did you happen to see a man come through here—tall, brown hair, middle forties? You probably wouldn't have recognized him, but you'd definitely have noticed him. He was the sort you don't miss."

"I—don't think so. When?"

"Just a few moments ago. He'd have to have come through the great room, from the hallway over there."

"Uh…no, definitely not, then. I was right over in that area chattin' with Mr. Eze and Ms. Okafor. I kinda thought you might've wandered off to the memorial room, but I didn't want to follow you there."

"So…he didn't come out of that hallway?"

"Nobody came out of there, far as I saw. Except you."

Stone narrowed his eyes. "No one else? So you didn't see a tall, dark-haired man in an old-fashioned suit either? A different one, less than a couple of minutes ago?"

Eddie gave him a sideways, suspicious look. "Stone, are you sure you 'aven't been 'ittin' the bar a bit too 'ard? I told you—I didn't see anybody but you."

"Okay. Okay." He rubbed his face. He'd been feeling so good tonight, too—as if things had finally begun to settle. "Eddie, have you ever heard of a man named Edmund Dunstan?"

"Nope. Should I 'ave?"

"I don't know. I hadn't. That's the man I was talking about. He knew who I was, but I'd never heard of him. It's probably not his real name."

R. L. KING

"Well, 'e wasn't on the guest list, at least not under that name. What did 'e want?"

"I don't know that yet, either. He didn't say, in so many words. My friend—the other man you didn't see—suggested I should consider what he's chosen to call himself. I don't know what he meant by that."

"Hmm." Eddie stroked his chin thoughtfully. "Well, I don't know about Edmund, but if you're considerin' names, 'Dunstan' is kind of a funny one to be comin' to you with."

"Why is that?"

"It's from the Middle English. Means 'dark stone.' Maybe 'e was 'avin' a joke on you."

Stone tensed. "He…didn't seem the joking type."

"I don't know what to tell you, then, mate. I'll look into it for you at the library on Monday if you want, but right now you really should come with me to meet Mr. Eze and Ms. Okafor."

"Yes, of course."

Stone had trouble keeping his mind on his host's duties for the remainder of the evening, but he doubted any of the guests caught on. He circulated around, chatting with various people until late into the night. Though he always kept an eye out for Dunstan and Kolinsky, he saw no sign of either of them. By the time the last guest had thanked them and said his goodbyes shortly after one a.m., Stone was exhausted from his vigilance, and no closer to solving the enigma of Edmund Dunstan.

Perhaps it *was* a coincidence. It wasn't a common name, but it wasn't uncommon, either.

Verity drifted over, the remains of a drink in her hand. "You look preoccupied. Everything okay?"

"I'm...not sure yet. I've got some things on my mind. Where's Ian?"

She gave him a sly smile. "I saw him and that red-haired guy he was talking to slip off together an hour or so ago. I wouldn't expect him home tonight." She took his hand. "Speaking of home—you want to head there? You still look hot in that tux, and I've still got plans for you."

"Yes—let's do that. Kerrick tells me he and the staff have the cleanup well in hand, so there's no reason for us to hang about."

He'd already said his good nights to Eddie and Ward, so he and Verity took the portal back to the Surrey house.

They could have stayed in London, but over the past few weeks Stone had felt an even closer connection to his ancestral manor. By now, much of the superficial damage had been cleaned up and repaired, the broken windows replaced, and new chandeliers re-hung in the great room. The only major work that remained was the reconstruction in the east wing, which was proceeding, albeit slowly.

As soon as they got to the house and closed the door, Verity reached out to tweak Stone's tie, pulling it loose and tossing it aside. Then she leaned in to kiss him, drawing him close. "Mmm...I've been waiting all night to do that."

"So have I," he admitted. For the moment, as they hurried upstairs to his suite, all thoughts of Edmund Dunstan and the strange scene back at Caventhorne departed his mind in favor of more immediate considerations.

Afterward, though, as he lay next to Verity listening to her soft breathing, his mind once again returned to the puzzle. Their words swirled around—Dunstan's, Kolinsky's, and Eddie's—refusing to make sense. Why would Dunstan choose that name as a pseudonym? Was he trying to tell Stone something with it? Where had he been "away," and "sequestered"? What had caused the obvious antipathy between him and Kolinsky? He felt as if the answer danced just out of reach, nebulous and maddening.

Then, suddenly, Kolinsky's words came back to him:

I knew him…a long time ago. I have not seen him in many years. I thought perhaps he had died.

He is perhaps closer to you than you might expect.

The name "Edmund" seemed familiar, but where had he heard it before? It was Eddie's full name too, but that couldn't be right. Aside from the fact that Eddie never used it, it had to be somewhere in connection with him or his family…

He sat up, so abruptly that he flung Verity's arm off his chest.

Bloody hell, no. It can't be.

"Mmm?" Verity murmured, trying to snuggle back into his warm side.

"Shh…" he whispered back, bending to kiss her forehead. "Go back to sleep. I'll be back soon. I want to check something."

"Check…what?" She still wasn't fully awake.

"I'll be back," he said again.

"Mmmm…" She was asleep before his feet hit the floor.

His heart pounded hard as he jogged across the grounds toward the cemetery. Dew from the tall grass soaked the legs of his jeans, but he barely noticed.

This was absurd.

It wasn't possible.

His brain was spinning so hard, trying to solve this puzzle by any means necessary, that it was now giving him solutions so ridiculous they were almost embarrassing.

But...what if it wasn't?

On his way to the cemetery he took a detour, stopping at the garage. The place had been restored now, all three doors replaced. He carefully unlocked one and shoved it up, hoping the slight sound wouldn't wake Aubrey.

No such luck, as usual. The caretaker's aged beagle, Mullins, barked as soon as the door began to lift, and a moment later Stone heard the creak of Aubrey's upstairs door opening.

"Who's there?" a familiar, suspicious voice called. "I'm armed, so—"

Stone sighed. "It's me, Aubrey. You can put the gun away." He stepped free of the garage and around to the foot of the stairway where he was visible in the light.

"Sir?" Aubrey immediately lowered the shotgun. He wore pajamas, slippers, and robe, and now sounded confused rather than suspicious. "It's three in the morning. Is something wrong? The house—"

"No, no. The house is fine. We've been here for a couple of hours now, back from Caventhorne."

"Well...then, sir, why are you out here at this time of the night? Is there something I can help you with?"

"I—" Stone paused. Should he share this absurd delusion with the caretaker? If he was wrong, he'd look like an idiot.

But if I'm right...

"I—er—was looking for a crowbar."

"Why on earth do you need a crowbar at three in the morning, sir?"

"I might not. But if I do, I don't want to come back to get it. Go on back to bed, Aubrey. I'm fine. I've just—got to do this. It can't wait until morning."

Aubrey paused on the stairs, obviously debating. "Please wait just a moment, sir," he said at last. He hurried back inside and returned a few minutes later. He no longer carried the shotgun, but wore work trousers and had stuffed his feet into heavy boots.

"Aubrey—"

"Please, sir. If you're planning to use a crowbar on something, you—er—might need some assistance. No offense intended."

Stone had to chuckle. "Fair enough, and none taken. But I want you to keep quiet about what we're doing. Especially if it turns out I'm wrong."

"Of course, sir." His answer came immediately.

Good old Aubrey's loyalty was one of the enduring constants in Stone's life, and he rarely treated it with the gratitude it was due. "Thank you, Aubrey. Bring two—it will be faster."

Crowbars in hand and Stone holding up a light spell, they tramped across the grounds to the cemetery. Aubrey followed in silence with a lamp until they stood in front of the door to the mausoleum, then cast Stone a questioning look when he used magic to open it.

Stone didn't respond. Once again, his heart pounded harder as he stepped inside. He held up the light spell higher to get his bearings, then headed to one of the lower sealed vaults along the wall and crouched to read the inscription on it.

Aldwyn Aristide Edmund Stone
1762-1851

"I was right…" he murmured.

"Sir?" Aubrey moved the lamp in closer.

"Aldwyn Aristide Edmund Stone. My great-great-great grandfather."

"What…about him, sir?"

In answer, Stone gripped his crowbar. "Come on, Aubrey—let's get this cover off."

"Sir—" Still Aubrey didn't move. "Are you expecting to find more papers hidden here?"

"No. Come on. Let's do this. I'll tell you after we know for sure." Without waiting for a reply, he bent and jammed the crowbar into the space between the crypt wall and the cover.

Aubrey, clearly sensing he wouldn't get anywhere with his mercurial employer until he'd gotten what he wanted, bent to help, and before long they had pried the cover off the crypt.

Stone used magic to set it aside, then held the light spell up again.

Inside, as he'd expected, was what had once been an elaborately carved wooden casket, rotted now after over a hundred and fifty years but still intact enough to conceal the remains inside.

"What…are you looking for, sir?" Aubrey stood back now, holding the lamp, and rubbed his head.

"Stand back."

"What are you going to do?"

"Stand back," he repeated. At this point, he had no time or desire for explanations or delays. His heart thundered with anticipation. As soon as Aubrey stepped away, he used magic to carefully draw the casket free of the alcove and lower it to the floor. Even with his careful handling, some of the old wood splintered and fell away.

He swallowed hard, half-afraid of what he might see, and raised his hand. The top of the casket lifted off and settled next to the bottom.

Stone and Aubrey both stared into what was revealed.

"It's...empty, sir," Aubrey whispered.

Stone nodded. "Yes."

"You...you expected that, didn't you?"

"I did. I'd hoped I was wrong, but—" He gestured at it, moving the light in closer. The casket's elaborate, white silk interior was yellowed and rotted with age, but he saw no stains indicating a body had decomposed there. "I don't think anyone was ever in here at all."

Silence hung in the air for several seconds, broken only by the slight squeak of Aubrey shuffling back and forth in his boots. "Why...did you expect it?"

Stone pointed at the plaque on the wall next to the now-opened alcove. "Because I think I met him tonight."

Aubrey gasped. "My God, sir! What—"

"And not only did I meet him, but I'm fairly sure now that he was the '*A*' mentioned in Brathwaite's journal. The 'fiend' that was sealed in the hidden room in the catacombs."

| EPILOGUE TWO

Basingstoke, England

MIRIAM PADGETT, forty-four, had never thought she had much to live for, honestly.

Her life, such as it was, was about as ordinary as it could possibly be: she resided in a tiny flat in a tiny building in a part of town that nobody ever went to unless they had some obligation to visit someone and they couldn't worm their way out of it. She worked at a dress shop, where she spent most of her days doing alterations and repairs in the back room because the proprietress didn't think she had enough personality to wait on the customers. On Saturdays she took the train into London to visit her aged mother, who lived in a rather shabby nursing home in Brixton. Every week she expected to get the call that her mother had passed peacefully away, but every week the old lady stubbornly persisted in hanging on. Miriam didn't mind. Even though she and her mother didn't get on all that well, the trips to London were nonetheless the highlight of her otherwise drab week.

Sometimes, if she was feeling particularly cheerful, she might stop for a dish of ice cream before heading home, or spend a couple hours at the cinema.

She hadn't done either of those in a while, though, because she hadn't felt cheerful in a while. Lately, in fact, she'd been entertaining herself as much with thoughts of sticking her head in the oven or turning the gas on and letting herself drift peacefully away as she did with *The Great British Bake-Off* and *Strictly Come Dancing*. It wasn't as if anyone would miss her. She wasn't even sure her mother would.

The truth of the matter was, whether she wanted to admit it to herself or not, she didn't feel there was much point in remaining alive. When she considered what her life might be like in ten years, she couldn't come up with much that would be different from now. She'd still work at the shop, cook meals in her tiny kitchen (she was good at cooking, but didn't have the space or the resources to do the thing properly), go to sleep each night in her single bed with its patchwork comforter, and then get up and do it again the next day. The only difference might be that her mother might be dead by then, but judging by the old lady's stubbornness so far, that hardly seemed something she could take for granted. Given that her mother's continued existence had been the primary reason Miriam had failed to implement one of her suicide plans thus far (the other reason was fear), she supposed it was a good thing Mum hadn't shuffled off this mortal coil quite yet.

The worst of it all—and once again, she would die of embarrassment before she'd ever admit it—was that she was fairly sure there would never be any romance in her life. She was a practical woman, and she knew she didn't have the face, the body, or the temperament for romance, but that didn't mean she'd have turned it away if it had presented itself at her doorstep. She never told anyone about the little flutters she got while watching the handsome young men on *Hollyoaks*, because she was sure the other women at the dress shop, not to mention her mother, would merely laugh at her. She almost wished she fancied women, figuring she might have an easier time of it if she did.

In any case, she was quite surprised when a man started appearing in her dreams.

At first she thought nothing of it. Her usual dreams of men were usually more erotic in nature, involving being swept off her feet and ravished in a field of windblown flowers by the likes of Tom Hiddleston or Benedict Cumberbatch, but in this case both the man and the subject matter were at the same time stranger and more…ordinary.

For one thing, the man talked to her.

A lot.

Most of the men in her previous dreams had other things than conversation on their minds.

In the beginning she barely remembered the exchanges, but as time went on they reinforced themselves to the point where she could recall them clearly when she awoke in the morning. The man, who told her his name was James, spoke of their connection, of power, of how unfortunate it was that she was wasting her life. Didn't she want something better? Didn't she want to be strong, make the rules, interact with people on her terms instead of slinking along life's sidelines like a mouse? Didn't she want to get back at those who'd wronged her? Didn't she want to be special, rather than a frumpy, forgotten middle-aged spinster living in a backwater flat?

Slowly, she realized she *did* want those things.

She wanted them more than anything, in fact.

After that, the conversations changed. She could have them, he told her, but only if she followed his instructions to the letter. That was very important. She could have her dream only if she did as he directed.

That Saturday, for the first time in four years, she did go into London but didn't visit her mother. Instead, she followed James's directions to a tatty little magic shop in the West End. She didn't even think it odd when he instructed her to walk through the wall. It almost seemed as if he was controlling her actions at that point, but that was all right. She was following his directions, and he hadn't steered her wrong yet. She rattled off a series of items to the saleswoman in the much more interesting shop behind the wall, departed soon after with a bulging bag, and two hours after that she was back in her tiny flat in Basingstoke, firing up her stove.

She could sense James's approval as she put her long-dormant cooking skills to work, combining the strange ingredients according to his recipe and heating them in a metal pan. When he asked her to add some of her own blood to the mixture, she didn't hesitate. At last, near midnight, she'd distilled the solution down to less than an ounce of viscous red liquid with silvery flecks. She held it up to the light, staring at it, marveling at its beauty. *She* had made this.

Now drink it, he told her. *Drink it, and you will have everything you desire.*

Miriam Padgett didn't ask questions. She tilted the little bottle up and felt the warm, oily liquid crawling down her throat, already thinking about how nice it would be to get back at some of those people who had mocked her, or pitied her, or disregarded her.

Her last conscious thought as something wrenched at her from deep within, tearing her soul away from her body and casting it off into the ether like so much unwanted detritus, was one of surprise.

❖

James Brathwaite deeply regretted what he'd been forced to do.

It wasn't because he'd used his spiritual and magical abilities to enter the mind of an innocent woman, leading her on with promises of power and admiration until she agreed to brew the potion that would rip her spirit from her body so he could replace it with his own.

No, he'd intended to do that all along. What he regretted was that his only viable choice was a mere woman—and a pathetic one at that.

He could have tried for someone else, he supposed, but after nearly two hundred years' imprisonment within the altar back at Stone's house, he wanted to get on with his plans. Being driven from Stone's body had weakened his spiritual form, to the point where trying to possess another body—a body with magical potential—would require not mere permission from the occupant, but an actual vacant vessel. And the only way he had a chance of contacting someone on the material plane and guiding their actions was to choose someone directly related to him, even if distantly.

There weren't many to choose from—apparently the Brathwaites had been unsuccessful in building a large family, and most of those he tracked down hadn't an ounce of magical potential.

He'd begun to grow desperate when he'd finally found Miriam. Although she wasn't anything impressive, she did possess latent magical ability—probably due to some long-forgotten alliance between the Brathwaites and another clan that passed the Talent down the female line. By that point, James Brathwaite knew he didn't have time to be picky: once he'd been released from his prison, his spirit had begun to degrade. The fiasco with the Stone heir had only hastened the process, and if he didn't secure a body soon, he wouldn't have the power left to do it.

In other words, beggars couldn't be choosers, and now his magnificent intellect was occupying the frumpy, unpleasant body of a weak and unremarkable woman.

If he'd had any sense of humor, he might have thought it ironic.

In any case, it was what he had to work with, so he had to make the best of it. At least in this new world, females had more freedom and rights than they had in his day—by the gods, they were treated for the most part as equal to men! He found the whole concept distasteful, but given that he was now stuck inside one of them, it was also useful.

Having a body—even a wretched one such as this— meant he could continue his work. He would have to be patient, as many things needed to be done before he could begin in earnest, but patience was a quality he had always possessed in abundance.

He'd taken the biggest step. Now, everything else would be much easier.

Now, late one Saturday night several weeks later (he had not gone to London to visit Miriam Padgett's aging mother today or any of the previous Saturdays, and even after he learned how to use a telephone he didn't return her calls), he sat in the kitchen of his tiny apartment, writing notes in a journal he'd found in one of Miriam's drawers. It had flowers winding up and down its pages, but he didn't care.

He'd cleared the table in front of him and taken most of the day to draw a small, complicated magical circle on its surface. Now, he lit the black candles carefully placed around it, sat back in the chair, and began a familiar ritual incantation. He didn't need the books and other materials he'd hidden back at the family's old house, the ones now in the Stone heir's possession and thus likely destroyed—he'd memorized the incantation long ago.

As power swelled around him and the orange candle flames turned to a brilliant blood red, he carefully lifted a tiny form from a nearby shoebox. The shaggy gray rat hung limply in his hand, its tail and head drooping, its filmed eyes open and staring at nothing. He hadn't had much trouble finding it in a nearby alley today, and a quick spell had ended its life before it could scurry away.

He stroked it with a long, gnarled finger. "Be patient, little one," he murmured. He placed the rat's body in the center of the circle, wrapping its tail around it almost lovingly, and then began the incantation again.

It took fifteen minutes of intense focus before anything happened. The candles' red flames continued to dance, casting weird shadows over the furry body. It almost looked as if it might be moving.

James Brathwaite smiled a smile no one who knew Miriam Padgett would have recognized—certainly not her employer at the dress shop, or her old mother—as in the center of the circle the rat writhed and twisted as if in pain.

Then, slowly, it climbed back to its feet and looked up at Brathwaite, its oil-drop eyes milky. Its nose twitched, and its tiny paws scratched at the table.

"There we are," Brathwaite said in Miriam's voice. "Well done, my little friend. And now, after far too long's delay, I can finally take up my great work again."

The rat, unsteady and strange in the flickering candle-light, did not reply.

Alastair Stone will return in

Book 19 of the Alastair Stone Chronicles

Coming in Fall 2019

If you enjoyed this book, please consider leaving a review at Amazon, Goodreads, or your favorite book retailer. Reviews mean a lot to independent authors, and help us stay visible so we can keep bringing you more stories. Thanks!

If you'd like to get more information about upcoming Stone Chronicles books, contests, and other goodies, you can join the Alastair Stone mailing list at **alastairstonechronicles.com**. You'll get two free e-novellas, *Turn to Stone* and *Shadows and Stone!*

ABOUT THE AUTHOR

R. L. King is an award-winning author and game freelancer for Catalyst Game Labs, publisher of the popular roleplaying game *Shadowrun*. She has contributed fiction and game material to numerous sourcebooks, as well as one full-length adventure, "On the Run," included as part of the 2012 Origins-Award-winning "Runners' Toolkit." Her first novel in the *Shadowrun* universe, *Borrowed Time*, was published in Spring 2015, and her second will be published in 2019.

When not doing her best to make life difficult for her characters, King enjoys hanging out with her very understanding spouse and her small herd of cats, watching way too much *Doctor Who*, and attending conventions when she can. She is an Active member of the Horror Writers' Association and the Science Fiction and Fantasy Writers of America, and a member of the International Association of Media Tie-In Writers. You can find her at *rlkingwriting.com* and *magespacepress.com*, on Facebook at www.facebook.com/AlastairStoneChronicles, and on Twitter at *@Dragonwriter11*.

Made in the USA
Monee, IL
05 August 2023

40489847R00298